Bloodprint

Also by Kitty Sewell

Ice Trap

Bloodprint

A Novel of Psychological Suspense

Kitty Sewell

**Doubleday Large Print
Home Library Edition**

A Touchstone Book
Published by Simon & Schuster
New York London Toronto Sydney

This Large Print Edition, prepared especially for Double-day Large Print Home Library, contains the complete, unabridged text of the original Publisher's Edition.

Touchstone
A Division of Simon & Schuster, Inc.
1230 Avenue of the Americas
New York, NY 10020

TOUCHSTONE and colophon are registered trademarks of Simon & Schuster, Inc.

Manufactured in the United States of America

ISBN-978-1-60751-568-5

**This Large Print Book carries the
Seal of Approval of N.A.V.H.**

Go to the ant, thou sluggard; consider her ways, and be wise

PROVERBS 6:6

Bloodprint

Prologue

Angelina was her name. She was born to Cuba, and like most originating from that beleaguered island, she was spirited and temperamental. Cuban women are known for the way they move. Young or old, they have that bodily confidence, that liquid sensuality, no doubt a legacy of their African ancestry. Angelina was no exception. She was awesome in her movements—in fact, quite breathtaking to behold.

Yet she was different from other hurricanes. She possessed an internal fury that made her devious and unpredictable. By stealth she gathered her centrifugal force from an abnormal chain of weather systems, and even the most sophisticated instruments devised by man failed to detect the scale of her strength—even less predict where she was heading. Angelina, searching for a suitable landfall, scanned the islands beneath her with the undefined eye that made her so dangerous, and thus Cuba was the first place to suffer her ferocity.

As it happened, some people in Havana believed that an old woman triggered Angelina. The woman was a Santera, a priestess of the ancient Afro-Cuban religion, and in Havana, where the practice of Santeria flourishes undeterred, she was well known for her spells. Over three decades earlier, her daughter had abandoned her, stolen her sacrificial knife and a much valued crucifix, and escaped one night on a raft bound for Florida. The Santera had never got over the defection, and as she grew older she became ever more obsessed with vengeance.

In the poor Havana neighborhood where she lived, she had long declared to her neighbors that she was concocting the bitch of all storms, making offerings of blood to the Orishas, the Yoruba gods, asking them to let wild winds wreak havoc on the state of Florida and duly humble her daughter.

The Santera had a fatal stroke on the night Angelina's first treacherous wisps of cloud started swirling above the ocean, so she never knew the devastation the looming hurricane unleashed—not on her daughter, who had long since left the United States, but on her daughter's daughter.

Perhaps it was merely superstition, coupled with the old woman's timely death, but in Havana her name became forever linked with the terrible Angelina.

On another island, at the southernmost tip of the United States and only ninety miles from Havana, people were busily preparing for Angelina. Most residents—"Conchs" as they called themselves—were not unduly concerned. Tropical cyclones were a common feature of their lives and the island was not in Angelina's direct path. The landfall was forecast farther north, somewhere between Miami and Fort Lauderdale.

Still, the winds could be fierce, and among the gingerbread-trimmed houses, old Cuban cigar rollers' cottages, and shacks tucked away beyond the dead ends of secret alleys, Conchs were closing window shutters, filling water bottles from rainwater cisterns, and taking in garden furniture.

On Houseboat Row, the residents had a routine for these summer storms. Houseboat owners were more vulnerable than their earthbound neighbors, but conversely they were, by their nature, also a more devil-may-care sort of people. Futhermore, it was Sunday morning. With a mug of coffee or a bottle of beer to hand, they were idly tying down a few possessions, roping potted plants, lounge chairs, and bicycles to the railings. The edge of the storm was to touch Key West midafternoon, so there was no need to hurry. The more cautious live-aboard residents, like the elderly and those with children, were packing picnic hampers to go and see out the choppy weather in friends' houses on terra firma.

Madeleine was in bed with Forrest, as they were every Sunday till well past midday, making love, eating, listening to music, and reading the papers, though not always in that order. It was her favorite time of the week. Forrest was an inveterate doer and sometimes it was difficult to pin him down and make him relax. Despite his philosophical attitude to life, he had an ingrained work ethic that she constantly strived, and sometimes successfully managed, to counteract. Once his mind relaxed and his pent-up body let go, he was the most languidly sexy and funny and talkative slob on earth, looking as if he never got his lazy ass out of bed.

Madeleine was propped up by pillows with her sketch pad on her knees, sketching him lying on his stomach across the bed in the act of searching his dictionary for a word they'd argued about.

"*Resipiscent*," he read out, triumphantly. "*Adjective. Having returned to a saner state of mind. From Latin: to recover one's senses.*"

"Stay still, sport." Madeleine's piece of charcoal moved rapidly across the paper. Outside there was some kind of commotion. Judy Montoya screamed at her kids, as she always did, and Fred next door shouted something to her. Running foot-steps clattered along the boardwalk and died away.

"Let's send for more coffee," Forrest slurred. "Where the hell is the bar staff when you need them?"

"I gave them the day off."

Their rusty old barge was a hand-me-down from Forrest's maternal grandmother, and the only bar staff ever to set foot on it had been Granny herself, who used to serve drinks at the Turtle Kraals.

"Oh hell. I'll make the coffee," he said, jumping up and wrapping a towel round his hips. "How about a glass of champagne with a squeeze of orange juice? And straw-berries. I saw some in the fridge."

"On principle, yes, please." She tried to grab him by the wrist, fearing he'd get di-verted and start washing the deck or tak-ing the laundry off the line.

"I'll be back, honey. I swear!"

She listened, her hearing attuned to his movements. The barge was bobbing on the waves, water sloshing loudly round the bow. A gust blew a plastic bag horizontally past the porthole. Her watch said twelve-thirty. She got up and stuck her face into the concave glass. Marian and Greg Possle were running along the boardwalk, carrying bundles. They seemed in a hurry, despite being normally so laid-back; their respective ponytails whipped about them in the gathering wind. Over the noise she heard Forrest moving things around on the deck. *Come back to bed, you renegade,* she thought, and went back herself. *I want you.*

Ten minutes later he returned, empty-handed. His expression was focused and he went straight to his shorts and drew them on. She raised herself on an elbow.

"Aw, now what? Where's my champagne?"

"Better get dressed, honey."

"Why? What's going on?"

"There's not a soul around. Seems everybody's left."

She smiled, patting the bed beside her. "So we're all by our lonesome."

"Better tie a few things up, Madeleine. There's a wind afoot."

"No kidding," she said, but didn't move.

"Turn on the radio, see how it's comin'."

"Another half an hour won't make a difference."

He shook his head and she thought she'd lost him, but he hesitated when she wantonly drew apart her dressing gown and opened her arms to him. "Come here and kiss me before you run away."

He kissed her at length, then murmured, "All right, you shameless hussy, but regretfully this cannot take too long."

His soft, fair hair trailed across her breasts as he moved against her. He had a way of looking at her when they made love, his gaze never leaving hers, hypnotizing her and shutting out all else. A sudden swell made the barge roll from side to side, and laughing, they rolled with it, but holding back, neither of them willing to finish what they'd begun. No matter the years they'd been together, making love had always been like that between them, a sense of losing the grip on space and time, lulled into a place in which there was no desire to let go. A climax was an ending, a separation, and as such it was best avoided.

Another deep swell made Forrest frown. His eyes left hers for a moment and he became still, listening intently. He drew away and got up. She stayed in that faraway place, trusting he had some variation in mind, but he slapped her flank and said, "Hey, come on! This is crazy. You've got five minutes' respite, honey. No more."

From the bed she watched him work through the starboard window. *That's a mighty fine angle,* she thought with a chuckle, and grabbed her sketch pad. She was quick, but he was quicker. Her charcoal merely traced the outline of a flexed arm, an extended thigh, or his upper torso, under which muscles worked in apparent isolation from one another.

Five minutes were long up and she knew she should be doing her share, packing an emergency bag, putting stuff away, tying the handles of the kitchen cupboards together, strapping a belt around the fridge. She had a list of "things to do in preparation for a hurricane" somewhere, but she knew it by heart, more or less, having been through a dozen or more tropical storms. Every Conch had been there. But her eyes were on Forrest or the piece of charcoal in her hand. She never stopped paying attention to the play of his anatomy. He'd been a shrimper since he was sixteen and for the next two decades had done little else but work with his hands and his body.

He had an intellect, to be sure, but was indifferent to its application, apart from the odd obsession he developed with things like astronomy, or botany, or learning Spanish. He'd come to share her fascination with myrmecology and they'd been on a few amazing expeditions to look at rare species of ants in exotic places—finances allowing, which was not all that often.

Suddenly it darkened. She looked up from her sketch and saw her view was blocked. Forrest was starting to put up the sheets of marine ply he'd cut to fit the windows. She was mildly surprised he thought it necessary. The whirr of his power drill cut the air, and she realized how quiet it was outside. The quiet before the storm.

Reluctantly, she got up and started to get organized. A gust made the barge shudder; a few minutes later, another. She ran through the gallery, out on the fishing platform.

"Forrest," she called, "perhaps we should be on land?"

There were twelve windows, and he'd done only half. Behind him the sky was a black mass, thick and menacing. Cars had disappeared from Roosevelt Boulevard. Even the birds had gone.

"Yes, we should," he said as he heaved another board into place. "Everybody else seems to have thought the same. You ready?"

She bit her lip. "Almost."

Forrest stopped and scanned the neighboring barges, all boarded, tied, and anchored, braced for the worst. "What's the forecast?"

"I haven't turned the radio on."

He looked up at the strange cloud formation and frowned. "Christ! I think we've got some real weather coming." There was a sudden urgency in his voice. "Come on, honey, let's get going."

There was a rumbling in the air.

"Why don't you leave the windows?"

He looked up again, scanning the skies, his long hair torn by the wind. "No, better get the boards up. This might be a bad one after all."

She was spurred into action, frantically running around with a bag full of spider clips, hooking them over doors and furniture, taking down loose objects and flinging them on the floor, while trying to get to a weather update. The radio crackled and at first she could not find a signal. As she tuned in to another station, the news came through loud and clear: ". . . *immediate evacuations from the lower Keys. Despite satellite imagery, sophisticated radar, and surveillance planes, specialists at the National Hurricane Center contend that because the system lacks strong steering currents and has an undefined eye, this could not have been predicted. Hurricane Angelina has swerved off track and is now upon Key West. Shelters are being . . .*"

She stopped listening and ran toward the door to warn Forrest.

Then the noise.

It didn't appear to come from out at sea, but overland, like a huge, angry machine. Madeleine could just hear Forrest on the upper deck, his drill still working on the boards. Perhaps the drilling made him deaf to the noise; she ran up the stairs, shouting as she went, but it was useless. The roaring grew, and through the upper gallery window she saw the palm trees along the boulevard bent like bows with their fronds pulled seaward like streamers in a fan. When she tried to open the door she found it stuck fast by the force of the gale. All at once the whole barge vibrated as if preparing to explode. Then it stopped dead. An eerie lull followed, and she flung open a window to the stern.

"Forrest," she called, trying not to let panic infect her voice.

"I'm here." His head popped up before her.

"Shit, Forrest, you won't believe this! It's a full-blown hit. Angelina has veered off course and is coming straight for us. I've just heard it on the radio. It's happening . . . right now!" She reached for his hand through the window. "I'm scared," she whispered. "Let's get the hell out of here."

Forrest didn't answer; he was looking up into the sky. He knew weather like no other person; it was something his father had taught him. He could read the clouds and sense the pressure in his temples. It had saved him more than once on the open seas, but this time he'd been distracted: he'd been in bed, looking at her.

"Hold my hand," he said, turning to her. "Here it comes."

The storm had merely been catching its breath and now screeched dementedly.

The next moment the barge was flung sideways. As it rolled, furniture and objects shot across the floor. The television fell off its stand and smashed against her ankle. At the sound of a crack inside her leg, she cried out, but strangely felt no pain. Forrest held on to her hand, and with the other he gripped the sill. Again it stopped.

"You're very beautiful when you're scared."

"Get inside. You'll get blown away."

"Hold on," he said, turning his head into the wind. "Jesus! . . . *Hold on tight.*" The next burst tore his hand out of hers as he was snatched away from her. She called his name as she too lost her balance, realizing as she fell that her ankle was fractured.

The rain came in flat, solid sheets of water, bursting through the window and pouring under the door. The window banged shut and the glass shattered. She got herself up with difficulty and screamed in panic, "Forrest? Forrest, are you all right?" She could not even hear her own voice above the thundering sounds.

She hopped across the moving floor on one foot, grabbing at solid surfaces, searching from one window to another for a glimpse of his sun-bleached hair, but all she saw was debris flying through the air, fences, signs, trees, huge panes of metal that could slice a body in half. A whole pitched roof rolled like tumbleweed down Roosevelt. The noise of the barges crashing into one another was loud, scraping and whining, metallic echoes that wailed over the roaring wind.

She could not keep upright and as she fell she screamed and screamed his name. She was trapped and he was outside somewhere on the slippery deck, in the eye wall of the hurricane. As she tried to imagine where he might be, she knew he couldn't possibly be on deck. No matter how strong, how powerful, and fit, Forrest would not have been able to hold on in that sudden and violent onslaught: he'd be helpless against the power of the storm. Fighting the certainty that came from somewhere inside her, she rationalized that if he was in the water, he could perhaps swim away from the moving, crashing barges, but as she scanned the surroundings through the bottom panel of the door, she saw how wild the sea was.

From the boulevard rose another wall of water, the storm surge pushing itself clear across the land toward her. Farther out, huge waves rolled and shifted relentlessly, like a moving mountain range.

Suddenly she caught sight of him. He was flailing against the choppy surface, carried up one enormous wave then disappearing behind another. Being a strong swimmer, he would last awhile, but the thought did nothing to comfort her. Against the motion of the barge she tried to keep her eyes on her husband as he fought the sea he had always mastered and that had, till now, sustained him so well. Quickly he was carried away, soon only a speck in the distance, surfacing and vanishing on the rolling swell, surfacing and vanishing, until she saw him no more.

A howl tore from her throat. At the same time there was a prolonged screeching noise, like metal ripping. The cabin seemed to be coming apart. She prepared for the walls to split open and welcomed the destruction of the home she'd so loved. She would perish quickly. Though grief-stricken and trembling with pain, she got on her hands and knees and looked through the broken window. She wanted to watch death coming for her, but all she saw was the devastation across the pier.

Three or four houseboats were already splintered heaps of planks and metal, and the terrible noise she could hear was the Possles' barge upending like a cardboard box and one side of it ripping off. Sheets of siding whirled out to sea in slow motion, and one hit the door where she knelt, knocking her down in a shower of flying glass. A window exploded, then another. Madeleine curled up on the floor, waiting for her turn; the sooner the better, now that Forrest was gone—she would not fight it.

The barge moved in a roller coaster motion, intermittently crashing into the pier. Paper and debris whipped around the cabin. She saw one of her drawings flying through the air and caught a fleeting glimpse of a sketch she'd just made of the man she'd loved. Covering her face with her hands, she thought of her husband and lover, the truest friend she'd ever had. She had killed him. Her greed, her laziness, her selfish passion for him had delayed them. He was dying in that wild, dark sea because of her. She was to blame.

No matter who was to blame, she was as good as dead herself. She waited for the inevitable so she could be delivered. If they met again in some place beyond, perhaps he would forgive her; he had never blamed her for anything, not even for the child they'd lost.

As the hurricane ripped and raged around her, her mind became still. Suddenly she felt him, that sense she possessed that had so often scared her. His rasping breath was against her cheek and she could hear his fluttering heartbeat. He was still afloat in the water, fighting for his life. Little by little, his breath began to fade, slowing until she could feel it no more. At last his heart stopped beating. She willed her own heart to stop, but it would not. With cool objectivity she reckoned that drowning was more pleasant than being crushed. The sea had entered and swirled around her. She turned her head and breathed in, attempting to fill her lungs with water. At long last, her vision blackened and she slipped away.

Chapter One

City of Bath

Madeleine Karleigh Frank, humanistic psychotherapist, artist of modest note, expert
on rare species of south Florida leaf-cutter
ants, was behind locked doors in a prison.
Not as a convict but as an OPV, official
prison visitor, that noble cause by which
lonely prisoners get friendly visits from
equally lonely do-gooders with a dodgy
conscience.

That's me wrapped up, she thought
with a wry smile. Her conscience had
never been clear, and after eight years of

widowhood, her friends had branded her a loner.

"What are you smiling at?" asked Edmund Furie, the subject of her do-gooding. "You're miles away, my beauty. You're not getting bored with me, are you?"

Her hand was resting on the edge of the hatch and he reached up to touch it.

"Bored? Never," she said, shaking her head. "All sorts of things, but never bored." She pulled her hand away. She cared about this prisoner but didn't really want to be touched by him, considering the deeds his hands had done, and anyway, it was against the rules.

"All sorts of things?"

She laughed. "Stupid of me, thinking I could get away with that comment. All right, then: I'm fascinated, disturbed, amused, surprised . . . what else?" She scratched her head theatrically.

"Fulfilling your need for a charitable cause?"

Her laugh froze. It seemed Edmund could read her all too well. His lips drew back. A smile did not sit naturally on his features; besides, one's attention was drawn inexorably toward his teeth. They were most unusual, so plentiful and crowded in his lower jaw they'd distributed themselves into two rows, rather like sharks' teeth. Surely, in this day and age, some dentist would have offered to pull some of them and line the rest up properly with the use of a brace. Many a time she'd been tempted to offer to investigate such treatment, but it was, after all, something he could do for himself should he be bothered.

"You don't have to answer that, my dear. Why don't you tell me about your day?" he said.

"Edmund, *no*. We always end up talking about me."

"Oh, go on. I love hearing about your work. What sort of human conundrums did you grapple with today?"

"I can't think of a single one that would interest you," she said. "And you know it's not ethical for me to blabber about my patients."

She rested her weight on the other foot. It was hard on her back having to stand for up to an hour, talking to the prisoner through the hatch of his cell door. In the beginning, over a year ago now, she'd asked, first the chaplain, then the governor himself, to let her see Edmund inside his cell, or even sit on a chair in the open doorway, or in the corridor. Mr. Thompson had looked at her in amazement; she obviously did not realize how dangerous and unpredictable Edmund was.

Edmund snapped his fingers in front of her face. "Hello . . . You can confide in me, Madeleine, you know that. I would never, ever compromise you in any way. Remember that now. I might be a murderer, but I would never let a friend down, and you are my friend, aren't you?"

They looked at each other for a moment in silence. They knew each other quite well by now. Or, it seemed, he knew *her* very well. Almost too well.

"Yes, Edmund, I'm your friend." She meant it, despite the horror she felt about his crimes. She would think about this on the way home. The long drive always gave her space to question things like the sincerity, or at least the trade-off, of her friendship with a psychopathic assassin.

Edmund's face loomed closer, framed by the hatch, his eyes swiveling, trying to take more of her in. She reminded herself that psychopaths do not really fall in love with people, though of course they might think they do. He was fixated with her, but she had no particular worry on that score. That penetrating stare of his was not of a sexual nature. He told her once that he was through with that side of life, and she believed him. The ministrations of his mother had given him a loathing of his own penis, and anyhow, "It didn't work very well." He was a prematurely old fifty-two; had never been married, had no children, no siblings or relatives that he knew of.

"Look," he said, "talk of the devil . . . Another friend of yours." He bent down for a second, then brought his hand up to the hatch. A small yellow ant was running across his wrist. "I've seen quite a few of these buggers in my cell."

"Possibly the most hunted creature in the civilized world," said Madeleine with a smile. "It's a *Monomorium pharaonis,* or Pharaoh ant. They thrive in institutions, probably because it's nice and warm and there are big kitchens. These guys know what's good for them. Smart as could be."

"This little fellow wishes to say . . ."

Edmund brought his hand to his mouth and mimicked a squeaky voice. "Happy Birthday, ant woman."

Madeleine was taken aback. "How did *you* know?"

"You must have told me."

"No, I never tell patients . . ." She stopped. "I didn't mean . . ."

Edmund looked fiercely at her. "So we are not really friends."

He slapped his wrist, making Madeleine jump back. The blatant aggression in his gesture made her remember that taking life meant nothing to him. They stood in silence for a while. Edmund shook his head, perhaps regretting squashing the ant. It was not in his interests to alienate her; she was the only person ever to visit him.

"What the hell. I'll settle for being your patient. It's better than being a charitable cause," he said.

"Oh, come on, Edmund. You're neither." She knew there was really no point in trying to deny or take back what she'd said, though it had been a genuine slipup.

He looked at the floor, pensively; the wicked twinkle in his eye was gone. The craggy lines in his face contrasted incongruously with the smooth, chalk white dome of his skull, which shone like a peeled egg under the harsh strip lighting. If he let his hair grow (if indeed he had any hair) it would undoubtedly be white, judging by the snow white eyebrows and lashes. He was as close to an albino as she'd ever seen, at least in Britain, where they were rare. She'd asked him once about his coloring, and he'd told her that as a punishment for wetting his bed, his mother had made him drink a bleach solution and it had made him all white. (Was that really possible?) He'd had a horrific upbringing and a rough life, so no wonder he looked so ruined.

Remembering that particular conversation about his mother, some eight months previously, softened her. Hidden inside that podgy, bleached man was a little boy who'd suffered terribly. There was no doubt his mother had applied some cruel and unusual punishments, and to cope with them he'd developed an early obsessive-compulsive disorder that was as crippling as it was necessary for his emotional survival. Madeleine's punctual visits had become his mainstay, and his ritualistic preparations for her arrival took all day.

Edmund broke into her train of thoughts. "OK, now we've broached the subject— why the hell *do* you do it? Why are you wasting your precious time 'befriending' me, especially in view of the fact that you see dozens of screwed-up people every week? Why do you put yourself through this, the drive and all?"

Madeleine paused, knowing he was giving her an opening to put right her blunder. There was a long answer to this question, involving too much of her history, but there was a short one too.

"I'm not sure why I started," she said. "But now I do it because I genuinely look forward to our meetings. I only work part-time and get paid lots of money, so in comparison, this feels more real." She looked him in the eye. "Besides, I've got a nice life, rich in variety and choices. It does me good to see how the other half lives." She raised an eyebrow. "As you can see, my motives are purely selfish."

"Purely selfish. Yes, I like that. Modern culture is pervaded by a taboo on selfishness. I'd say it's the most powerful and legitimate drive in man, and by following this elemental drive he also does the most for the common good."

"My God. One of these days I'll ask you to explain that to me," Madeleine exclaimed, knowing she never would. It was too closely connected to his justification of his crimes: the common good—ridding the world of scum.

He placed his hands on either side of the hatch and leaned into the hole between them, fixing her with his pale gray eyes. "You and I have an unusual human relationship where we can be more than honest with each other. We can't get involved except through this little hole in the door, so anything goes . . . Isn't that right?"

"Not really, Edmund." *Where was this leading?* "We've defined our boundaries. I've told you mine, at any rate."

"Will you take a piece of personal advice?"

She gave him a stern look. "I have a feeling you're about to offer it whether I want it or not."

"Get rid of that boyfriend of yours." He paused, searching her face with sharp eyes. "Whatever you say, you don't look happy."

She blinked. "I'm perfectly happy," she said coolly. "I don't need advice on my love life."

"I think you do," he countered, smiling a little. "You might have all those fancy qualifications and diplomas hanging on your wall, but as you know, I'm a bit of a psychologist myself. I understand quite a lot more about you than you think, and I can tell there is a problem. I see it in your face."

"He suits me just fine," Madeleine said edgily.

Edmund shook his head dismissively. "Listen now. If you can't get rid of him . . . that is, if he won't go . . . I can teach you a few things."

Madeleine looked away. *Bet you can,* she thought. *Something to do with vats of quicklime, or big lumps of concrete.*

"My sweet Madeleine." His voice became soft, hushed, like a caress. "Don't look so worried. I'm only trying to help. You and I must look out for each other. I know you feel as out of place in your own skin as I do."

"Oh, come on. You assume it because I'm American." She let slip a nervous laugh. "I don't feel at all out of place."

Yes I do.

Edmund leaned toward her menacingly. "Madeleine, *get rid of him*." He smacked the sides of the hatch hard with both hands, hard enough to make her glance down the corridor to see if the guard was at hand.

"I'm not hearing this, Edmund," she cautioned. "You're out of order. Read some interesting book and tell me about it next week, will you?"

"I bet Gordon is messing around."

"No, he isn't," she snapped. She couldn't remember having mentioned his name. Most unwise.

"How do you know he isn't?"

"Stop it."

"A man is a man, my beauty. You should keep him on a tighter leash. If you keep him at all, which you should not."

Edmund often pulled some stunt like this just as it was time to go. It was the frustration of losing her every week, the only person who seemed to care about him. And as he had somehow found out it was her birthday (how had he?), he correctly surmised that she'd end the day in the arms of some man—another man. She could understand his distress.

She heard a door clang, and out of the corner of her eye she saw Don Milligan making signs at her. It was six o'clock.

"Our time's up," she said, giving him a hurried wave. "You keep well now, buddy. I'll see you next week."

"Happy Birthday," he said quietly. His fist appeared in the hatch and instinctively she drew back. But no, there was something concealed in his hand. On a whim, she reached up and he passed a small object to her. Too late she remembered that accepting anything from a prisoner was a "terminal" offense. *What the hell am I doing?* she wondered as she moved away from his cell, and in that moment of bewilderment, she turned away from the closed-circuit TV camera and slipped the object into her jacket pocket.

It started raining heavily as she drove the hour and fifteen minutes from H.M. Prison Rookwood toward Bath. Though it was mid-March there were no signs of spring. The forecast for the weekend was more of the same, possibly combined with a frost. Even so, she had to fight for space with week-enders on the M4, then got stuck behind a horsebox on the A46.

The A46 ran along the side of the east-ern slope of a steep, narrow valley. Down there, encircled by the river Avon and wooded hills, lay the ancient city of Bath. Underneath it, invisible, lay another city, built two thousand years earlier by inter-lopers from the Roman Empire.

The rain had let up, and in the falling dusk she caught sight of the city, the mighty Abbey at its center already illumi-nated by bluish floodlights that gave it the appearance of a vast fortress made of ice. A myriad of other church spires dotted the panorama, and honey-colored ter-raced houses followed the contours of the surrounding hills. The Roman army arrived here forty-three years after the birth of Christ, already inspired by the stories of this Druid stronghold. They might have stood atop this very valley, looking over the circular basin where trees grew excep-tionally tall, and clouds of steam drifted up into the air, and where, at its center, bub-bling up from the rust red rock, were the hot springs, guarded by Sulis, the mysterious goddess of the Druids.

Coming from the New World, Madeleine loved this aspect of Bath, its dark and ancient history. (Was it a coincidence that she was sleeping with an archaeologist, a man obsessed with its past?) As far back as seven thousand years, when Stone Age hunters discovered the valley, water, boiling up from the bowels of the earth, had drawn men to it. *But not me,* she reminded herself with unease; *it was not the waters that drew me back.*

She drove on, dismissing from her thoughts of the painful reason for her return to Bath, and turning her eyes away from the rolling Somerset landscape, she focused on the bumper of the horsebox in front of her.

Sometime later she was startled out of a reverie by her phone ringing inside her handbag. She had already reached the city and turned off on London Road, now practically at a standstill in a traffic jam. She didn't answer the call, having broken too many laws for one afternoon. The thought made her slip her fingers into her pocket to feel the object Edmund had given her. It was small and egg-shaped, but weighed heavily in her hand.

She crossed the river between the Doric tollhouses on Cleveland Bridge, passed under the railway arches, and was soon at her house, on the south curve of the city. It was part of a row of squat eighteenth-century cottages built for the stonemasons who had worked and dragged the Bath stone down from its quarries up on the hill.

She parked in the lane behind the row and sat for a moment in the car. Her phone beeped a message. Hopefully not Gordon, canceling their date. He did this a bit too often for her liking. She fished the phone out and put it to her ear.

"Sylvia here. Ten minutes to five. Howard Barnes canceled his appointment on Monday morning. Again! But if you're imagining a lie-in with your sexy archaeologist, I'm sorry to disappoint. A Miss Rachel Locklear walked in just a few minutes ago, wanting to see a woman therapist. So I exercised my initiative and gave her the slot. I know, I know, there are people on your waiting

list, but it was too late to start phoning around. I just hope she shows up . . . she wasn't your regular posh professional type, if you know what I mean. Well, Happy Birthday again, and have a good weekend."

Madeleine smiled to herself. Where would she be without her receptionist's famous initiative? Hardly having a lie-in with the elusive Gordon!

Gordon Reddon was, at thirty-six, almost seven years younger than Madeleine. Worse, or better—Madeleine couldn't quite decide which—he seemed several years younger than his age, both in appearance and in attitude. She tried not to feel flattered or, God forbid, *grateful*, but she was just a little bit pleased with herself.

An hour after she'd come home, and had showered off the cloying prison smell and changed into a simple black dress, coupled with sensible woolly tights and knee-high boots, he rang the doorbell. She let her eyes slide over him as he stood, framed by the yellow glow of the streetlight. He was one inch shorter than she was, but she didn't mind that. For a man of

his "down-to-earth" profession he was conspicuously vain about his appearance. His
gym-honed physique was encased in
black jeans and a fitted shirt in the palest
possible dusky pink, with expensive-
looking belt and shoes. Over it all was
draped a black capelike rain garment.

"Happy Birthday," he said, smiling, and
whipped a small bouquet of yellow roses
from behind his back. "You *did* tell me."

"Yes, well . . . I'm not one of those older
women who hates birthdays. Every year is
a triumph of endurance and survival. Why
not celebrate?" She planted a peck on his
designer-stubbled cheek, and let him into
the house.

"You look delectable." Gordon laughed
and put his arm around her waist. "I can't
believe you're getting older and older than
me."

It was just a little more than she'd bar-
gained for. She moved away from his arm
and led the way into the living room.
"Where are you taking me?"

He grinned. "Anywhere you want to go.
Give us a beer, love."

With a slight frown she made her way to
the kitchen, while Gordon approached the

large painting leaning against the living room wall. It was the last in her Cave Series. Madeleine had brought it down from her attic studio in order to sit on the sofa and mull over its strengths and weaknesses. With fair quantities of alcohol she could unleash that part of her brain responsible for evaluating these self-indulgent works of art.

"What's my favorite myrmecologist painting now?" Gordon called to her.

She smiled, visualizing him tilting his head this way and that in an attempt to make sense of the ants' feverish entrance into, and exit from, an apparently vast black cave. Knowing he wasn't really interested in contemporary art, she couldn't fault him. He always showed willing, ready to listen with genuine interest to her drawn-out explanations should she care to offer them. The one and only subject of her paintings, ants, had intrigued him from the start.

"As you can see," she called from the kitchen, "it's simply workers on their way to and from work. An ant rush hour."

"Are these giant monster ants, or is their pad just a tiny crack in a pavement made to look cavernous?"

"Which would you feel more comfortable with?"

"For God's sake," he groaned, laughing. "Am I having my head examined? I bet this has something to do with some complex about the size of my penis."

Madeleine finally located a liter bottle of lager in the vegetable crisper. She'd drunk half of it the other day, but hell, it had the cap screwed on tight. With a slight Schadenfreude, the kind of "will-I-get-away-with-this" trepidation you get from having an unsuspecting guest sleeping in some previous guest's sheets, she poured the flat liquid into a tall glass and brought it to him.

"I didn't hear you," she said and placed the glass on the table before him. "What about the size of your penis?"

"You bitch," he growled and tried to grab her arm. "Come here and you can examine it."

She slithered from his grasp and sat in the chair opposite him. Gordon's eyes twinkled seductively. She laughed, wondering if she was laughing with him or at him. Even after sleeping with this man for almost eighteen months, she couldn't quite, not one hundred percent, take him seriously. The term "boy toy" came to her mind more frequently than seemed healthy. Was that really fair to him?

She watched as his hand went to the glass. He picked it up and looked appreciatively at the rich golden fluid, brought it to his lips and pursed them for a second as he drew it into his mouth. Another second passed, then he roared in disgust. Gordon fancied himself a purist among beer drinkers and she'd deliberately outraged him. Always willing for a little self-analysis, she asked herself: Now where was the satisfaction in that?

Despite the freezing rain, they left the house on foot and walked along the canal, following the black, still water toward its source. On the bank where it joined the river, a majestic weeping willow dangled its branches into the water. Gordon stopped her under its canopy, as he'd done so many times before, and kissed her passionately.

"Creature of habit," she whispered against his cheek, but regretted teasing him when she saw his mouth turn down.

Gordon was impulsive enough and had a wry sense of humor, though not when he himself was the butt of a joke.

"So much for romance," he retorted, grabbing her by the arm and marching her across the iron footbridge that straddled the river and through the stone arches beyond which the city unfolded.

She chose the new fish restaurant next to Poultney Bridge. The old building leaned perilously toward the river and appeared even more top-heavy because of the throng in the restaurant upstairs. They got the last table. It was far from intimate; they were placed on the crossroads between the gents' toilet and the kitchen. Once they were seated it seemed too late to change their minds. Gordon was assertive about food and settings but the evening had already taken on a slapdash feel. It wasn't helped by the fact that he glanced at his watch more than once.

"You in a hurry?" she asked, trying to sound lighthearted.

His eyes narrowed. "Of course not."

They looked away from each other.

"What have you been up to?" she asked after a pause.

He turned, a little too abruptly. "What do you mean?"

She shrugged. "The question hardly needs explaining, Gordon. I haven't seen you for nine days."

His face relaxed into a rueful smile. "I'm mainly in the lab at the moment," he said. "Looking at the stuff we got out of the Southgate dig. You know me, I prefer being out there on my hands and knees in a pit. Like this time last year."

She nodded, remembering his excitement at finding a cobbler's shop, a large selection of two-thousand-year-old Roman shoes, together with the tools of shoemaking and other leather clothing, preserved in a waterlogged pit, dug into the impermeable blue Lias clay right in the middle of the city. He'd written a brilliant paper on Roman footwear and been invited to the States for a series of lectures.

Gordon tried to catch the waiter's eye, while complaining about the general boredom of archaeological "homework" and specifically about some bits of a Roman floor mosaic he believed had disappeared into a janitor's pocket, while Madeleine's attention was drawn to the image of a forty-three-year-old woman in the large mirror behind him. *Forty-three!* Like most women, she was more than familiar with her own appearance, but this was different. Furtively observing herself in action, she saw how much of a foreigner she really was. It showed in the way she talked, laughed, gesticulated, and, quite disconcertingly, in that constant languid movement of her shoulders (did she do this with patients?). Though half of her was British, her other half was astonishingly Hispanic. She noted how much more golden her skin color was than that of the pale diners around her. Brought up in the unrelenting sun of Key West, Madeleine was blessed with a natural year-round tan; but in addition, her mother was Cuban, and though no one would ever guess it, her great-great-great-grandmother had been a Yoruba slave, brought from blackest Africa to Cuba by the Spaniards to work the sugar plantations. Yet Madeleine was her father's child too: she was tall and slim and unadorned, having nothing of her mother's petite stature, sexy Latin curves, and sizzling temperament.

Giving her appearance a last glance,

she decided that it had "impostor" written all over it: her easy smile, the way she moved, the occasional flick of the head to toss a black curl away from her face, seemingly quite at ease with herself, while actually, Edmund Furie had been right, she felt out of place.

She turned back to Gordon just as his mobile phone rang shrilly in his jacket pocket. He could have ignored it but instead he turned away, speaking in hushed tones to the intruder. Madeleine tried to overlook the interruption but when the phone call ended could not resist commenting on his rudeness and constant availability on the phone.

"This is the point where a drink would be really good," she added quietly.

"Yes, but not here."

Gordon stood up and started for the door, and Madeleine had to scramble for her bag, jacket, and umbrella to catch up. A haughty waiter looked on.

"Sorry," Madeleine said to him. "We're going to miss our tram."

"Madam," said the man with a frown, "Bath has no trams."

"And this place, sir, has no service," she grumbled as she brushed past him.

Under Poultney Bridge the waters of the Avon River murmured quietly. Gordon was slightly ahead of her, advancing on the restaurants on Argyle Street, his hands shoved deep into his pockets, his cape slung carelessly over his shoulders. She was already familiar with his habit of keeping her behind him when he was annoyed. The faster she walked to catch up, the faster he would go too. It was one of those things Gordon did that she could never properly confront.

Lengthening her stride, she reached out for his hand and said, "Hey, come on. Let's not spoil the evening. You're grumpy because you're hungry, that's all. Why don't we just go back to my house? Best bar in town, and there *is* food. I stocked up at Safeway for the weekend."

He slowed a little, squeezing her hand forgivingly. "Safeway is rubbish. I shop at Marks."

"OK, your place then," she said, forcing him to stop and face her.

For an instant a look passed over his face.

"Marks is off." He shrugged disarmingly. "I guess it's *your* place."

She peered at him ... She always trusted her instincts; they were sharp, fine-tuned to the most subtle messages. "Oh hell, forget food. Let's go to your place for a change."

He glanced at his watch again. "My sheets need changing and ..."

She looked at him for a long moment. "Why am I suddenly thinking that there's someone else between those sheets?"

Another shifty look flashed over his face, but a second later his shoulders relaxed. "Come on, Madeleine, we never did make any promises. That's not what our relation-ship is about, right?"

She stared at him, speechless.

"I never gave it a thought," she said fi-nally. *Not until this afternoon. Thank you, Edmund.* She couldn't believe she was so naïve. With all the gritty observations about the dynamics of their partnership, she had never really raised the question of fidelity. He was a stickler for protection even though she kept reassuring him that they could dispense with the inconvenience. According to Emma Williams, her gynecologist, the risk of pregnancy was now practically nonexistent. She'd desperately hoped to get pregnant during the fourteen years of her marriage, but it had not happened. Still, Gordon meticulously rolled on his condoms. Of course he did. He wasn't worried about an unwanted pregnancy, it was all those sexually transmitted diseases he was in danger of catching from other women. How very responsible of him to protect her. And how very stupid of her not to put that simple two and two together.

"Madeleine, you can't be angry," he said, taking her by the shoulders and looking into her eyes. "Listen, we're good together. There is no reason that can't continue. Quite apart from being exotic and lovely, you're the most sane, grown-up, and independent woman I know. That's what turns me on about you. Come on. Be sensible."

"I've got to think about this one."

Gordon's grip on her shoulders tightened. He shook her slightly. "Don't think so bloody much. Just go with what feels good."

"Is she at your place right now?"

"Who cares? This is about you and me."

"Is she?"

"I'm with *you*, aren't I?"

"Just say yes or no."

"Well, yes. But she's not expecting me anytime soon."

"I think I've got a problem with the idea of some other woman waiting for you in your bed as we speak," she said. "Quite a big problem, in fact."

"Oh, come on. What do you care about some little piece of fluff? Right now I'm exactly where I want to be. With *you*."

Well-dressed people under large umbrellas pushed past them as they stood apart, facing each other on the pavement. Madeleine refused to move even though rain was dripping from her hair. Her feminist hackles had risen. *Fluff!* At the same time she felt a small grain of smugness. Fluff she was *not*. But how many others? And why? Because what she had to offer was not enough, or because he was an incurable womanizer? Either way, he should have made it clear that he was not into exclusivity. As the shock began to subside, indignation set in. Some girl was in his bed right now, waiting her turn. If that was so, the reverse was bound to be true. He'd no doubt come to *her* bed straight after making love to someone else. The image of it made her sick with anger.

A taxi drove past, too close to the curb, splashing them both.

"Shit," Gordon exclaimed angrily, leaping away. "Well, where are we going to eat? I'm wet and starving."

Madeleine opened her umbrella. "I'm not prudish, nor am I that proud, but I don't want to be party to this, if you pardon the pun."

Gordon's handsome face looked more somber than she could ever remember. He grabbed her by the arm and pulled her into a doorway. "I wish you wouldn't feel like that. Listen, Madeleine, I'm very careful . . . they don't mean anything to me, but *you do*."

She shook off the grasp he had on her arm and laughed sarcastically. "I mean something, do I?"

He moved to bar her exit. "Hear me out . . ."

"I've never asked for commitment," she exclaimed, pushing him away. "I've made no demands on you, but couldn't you just *do* us one at a time?"

They stared at each other. Gordon shook his head.

"You can't change who I am. The fact that you've never tried has been so refreshing. Don't start now. Please."

"All right," she said with an angry shrug. "I won't try." She waited a few seconds, but as he had nothing more to add, she said, "Bye, Gordon," and darted out into the downpour, making her way back toward the bridge.

"Madeleine, come back," he called after her. Part of her hoped he'd come after her, grab her, tell her he couldn't live without her. She heard his footsteps recede and looked over her shoulder. The dark cape flapped wildly behind him as he marched off in the opposite direction.

An hour later, Madeleine sat on her living room sofa with a large glass of rum in her hands. *This is a great birthday,* she thought, *absolutely wonderful.* The phone remained silent. Rosaria, her mother, suffered from a chronic psychosis and could not be expected to remember. Her father, Neville, was too famous and important and selfish. Her few friends were not privy to her birth date—but that was her own fault. Her colleague, John, and receptionist, Sylvia, had known, and had taken her for an extended lunch in a fabulous restaurant. She reached over the coffee table and picked up the card they'd given her.

"How many psychotherapists does it take to change a lightbulb?" she read out loud. She knew the answer, of course, but chuckling ruefully, she opened the card and read it again. *"Only one—but the lightbulb has got to really want to change.* All love, John and Sylvia."

All love! Madeleine gritted her teeth against a swell of grief. She'd not cried for over seven years, not since Forrest died, and she wasn't going to now. All the tears of a lifetime had been used up, as if the hurricane had washed any capacity for feeling out of her, leaving her empty and dry. After years of self-punishing celibacy, Gordon had come into her life. She didn't think she loved Gordon, but she liked him very much. Or perhaps she liked *herself* very much around him. Now she felt he'd used her somehow; he'd broken some unspoken rule of hers. That was the problem: they hailed from different planets and played by different rules, having so much fun in the process that they'd never stopped to compare notes. He'd rescued her and made her feel like a woman again, so perhaps she'd used him too.

Coming back to Bath had not worked, after all. She was alone all over again. Beyond lighting up her mother's life, what did she have to show for it? Precious few friendships, four years of psychotherapy training and three years of practice, a pile of sinister ant paintings. And Edmund.

Edmund! She jumped up and went into the hall. The jacket hung over a chair and she reached into the pocket for his birthday present. In her hand it had felt like a small egg and looked like one too. It was made of some kind of stone, green with gray flecks, smooth, polished to a high shine. An egg— how nice! She shook her head in consternation, wondering about the symbolic content of the gift.

About to drop it into a bowl for useless objects, she felt a movement. She held the egg to her ear and shook it. It was hollow; there was definitely something inside.

She peered closely at the oval stone, turning it slowly in her hand, scrutinizing its surface. There it was: a seam, fine as the sharp edge of a razor blade. Determined to get to the object inside, she took the paper knife from the hall table, and returning to the living room sofa, worked at the seam until she managed to prise the egg apart.

Inside was a brooch. It was a twisted rope or cord made out of a dull gray metal, pewter perhaps, shaped into a teardrop . . . or was it a noose? She drew back in shock. Most of his victims he'd strangled with his bare hands, but on those who had been large or muscular he'd used a rope. Perhaps she was jumping to conclusions. Yes, of course she was. She was his only friend and he wouldn't want to frighten her. Didn't a rope also symbolize togetherness, commitment? In art, it symbolized passion, whereas in some cultures it referred to submission and enslavement.

She turned the brooch around in her hands. It was far from beautiful, but then Madeleine was not into bling or glitter. The more she looked at it, the more its austerity appealed to her. *Commitment,* she decided, warily choosing the least sinister explanation. He was in jail for several life-times. He was asking her to be his friend forever (till he died or she died). At least she hoped that's what he meant.

Love is not to be scoffed at, she thought drunkenly as she pinned Edmund's gift onto her dress. *There is not that much love around.*

Madeleine drained her glass and went to kneel in front of her myrmecarium. Her ants ran relentlessly from box to box, through the passages and cylinder, disciplined and methodical in their work, never lazy, never stopping, always searching, but the differ-ence was they knew exactly where they were running to . . . and what they were searching for.

Chapter Two

So what are you searching for, young Madeleine?" Forrest said, a finger tracing the line of her nose, moving over the curve of her lips and chin and down her throat.

They were lying close together, swinging in a hammock tied between two gumbo-limbo trees in the garden of a Bahamian-style mansion he was house-sitting on Telegraph Lane.

"A so-far-undiscovered species of leaf-cutter ant," she said, trying not to smile.

"You rude little devil," he said, tickling

her bare stomach. "I mean in life. I mean long-term, you know, stuff like love, travel, or something spiritual. Didn't you say your mom is a Cuban Santera?"

What she really wanted to say was: You. *I've been searching for* you. *But she was too proud. This new business of falling in love was too overwhelming. She had to hold on to her sanity or she might scare him and he'd run a mile.*

"Yeah, all those things," she said nonchalantly. "Love, travel, spiritual stuff. I'm born to a hurricane, under the goddess Oya. She'll protect me and see that I don't make an absolute ass of myself . . . specially where you are concerned."

"You're a little witch, you know . . ." He put his hand on her waist. "Come here."

She smiled. She was there already. She could hardly get any closer. She'd been wanting this for three long weeks, from the very moment they crashed into each other's bicycle on the corner of Fleming and Love Lane. Even the location had been providential. The collision had been her fault, but he immediately took the blame. She'd had a scrape on her bare shoulder. Digging into a well-used backpack, he'd produced a bottle of water and a clean napkin (from Randy's Steak House—she had it still) and proceeded to clean the wound. It had taken a long time and when he'd finally finished seeing to her minor injuries, he'd insisted on buying her coffee and then wheeling her bike back to her house.

"Wow, this is your place?" He'd said, looking up at the rambling clapboard residence with its majestic two-hundred-year-old banyan tree. "So your dad is our famous Hemingway of the canvas?"

Lying in his arms now gave her a bittersweet feeling. Soon she would be there no more. Papa Neville, the famous Hemingway of the canvas, and Mama had been arguing for months. Papa wanted to move back to London. He said he felt he'd exhausted what Key West could do for him, at least as an artist. Mama, on the other hand, had never lived anywhere else than Key West and her homeland of Cuba. She'd been to London twice with Papa and had been scared out of her wits. There was no beauty there, she said, no flowers or palm trees, no fragrances or warm winds, and above all, no ocean to listen to or sunsets to contemplate. Gray skies pressed down on those millions of people and made them ill. To appease her, Papa said they would live in Bath, a beautiful and ancient city, which had springs of hot water and was surrounded by green, wooded hills. Madeleine had been quite intrigued by the idea—until she met Forrest.

He raised himself on his elbow and looked down at her. His toffee-colored eyes practically pierced her and she shuddered involuntarily. Her whole body was ablaze.

"I told my old man to get another partner," he said slowly, "at least for a year or two, because I've decided to go traveling. I've always wanted to go to India and Nepal, see the Himalayas. Before I settle down, you know what I mean? I'm going to be a Key West shrimper for a hundred years, so if I don't see a bit of the world now, when will I?"

She stared at him. So he was leaving too. She felt hurt, already grieving for him.

"Oh well," she sighed, trying to sound blasé, "I'm off to England with my folks. My dad is famous over there too. He needs to sell his paintings in London, where he's gonna get lots of money for them. This place is too small for him."

Forrest stared back at her. Her face crumpled a little. She regretted the way she'd said it.

"I know we haven't known each other long, but I was going to ask if you'd like to come traveling with me," he said.

Oh God. What a bigmouthed bumbling idiot she was. A million feelings swirled inside her chest. He wanted to be with her, go away with her. He kept looking at her with those brown eyes, waiting for an answer. She reached up and put her fingers into his blond curls and brought his face down to hers. They kissed—not for the first time— and it was different. He tasted of salt like the seas he worked, and he smelled of warm sand.

He'd been shrimping with his dad for

three years and his hands were rough and calloused. He was careful not to snag her clothing. She had a beaded cropped T-shirt and a tiny tie-around cotton skirt. He wore nothing but a pair of shorts. One by one, the clothes dropped into the sea of ferns beneath the hammock. Above them a canopy of lime trees was laced together by vines, shading them from the sun. Cascades of Spanish moss hung from the branches and practically touched their naked bodies where they lay. As he kissed her breasts she looked up and thought, Why go anywhere? No place on earth could be as beautiful as this.

After a long while he raised himself up to look at her. "Is this all right with you, what we are doing?" he asked, his brown torso now glistening with moisture, the outline of his tousled hair edged in silver.

What could she say? Oh, yes—that she loved him and would go to the ends of the earth with him, making love in every bed along the way.

"Are you on the pill or anything?"

"Yeah," she said.

He looked at her again, more searchingly. "So it's OK?"

She nodded. She'd been told by friends that the first time was not all that great, not to expect anything. She didn't want him to see her grit her teeth or wince with pain. When, finally, she felt as if she could not bear waiting another moment, she guided him to her and he entered her slowly. The tearing flash of pain lasted only a moment and she knew she would take pleasure in the memory of it. Her friends had been so wrong. The first time had a magic she knew would never be repeated, a rite of passage into some vast unknown part of her. She held on to him, hoping to draw it out, but there was no need. His lovemaking seemed like a chain linked to itself . . . beginnings with no end. He had a deliberate, unhurried way about him, so different from boys her own age who'd sometimes lunged at her, hoping for a grope. But Forrest was a man, all of nineteen. She was so green, but he would teach her.

It had darkened a little by the time they finally fell apart. A cool breeze on her wet body felt delicious, and she was thirsty.

"What time is it?" she asked, laughing.

He rolled over and searched in his shorts beneath him for his watch.

"Nine twenty-eight," he said.

"Shit!" She sat up, upsetting the hammock and tipping onto her ass in the ferns.

He peered at her sprawled beneath him and grinned. "Well, that was a dignified ending to a mind-blowing pursuit."

She hardly heard him. Papa Neville was open-minded but he was a beast if she was late for dinner . . . and that had been nearly two hours ago. She crawled around, searching for her panties in the foliage. "I've got to go home," she said, not looking at him.

"Oh no. Stay, Madeleine. Don't go yet. Let's make the most of this place. The owners are back tomorrow." He gestured *toward the wraparound veranda with elaborately carved beams and enormous rattan sofas. "I make the best conch fritters on the island. And the best* mojito. *And*

I've got a joint, Colombian, smooth as could be."

He tried to grab her and pull her back. "You can't possibly deny yourself a dip in the pool?"

She hid her face, embarrassed, as she pulled away and got dressed.

"You never answered my question," he said. "Will you come?"

She stopped, her back to him.

"Will you come traveling?" he repeated. "I've got money saved up. We'll have to rough it a bit." He laughed. "We can even go looking for ants all over the place. You could discover unknown species along the way." He tried to reach for her hand from where he lay. "Mysterious Madeleine. Ant woman of my dreams, come with me."

His words touched her deeply but the sense of hopelessness was stronger. She turned to face him. "I want to. More than anything else in the world. I'll talk to my dad, but to be honest, I doubt he'll let me."

Forrest stood up. Apart from his rough hands and scarred forearms, he looked like a god in his nakedness.

"You could decide that for yourself, you know."

She lowered her eyes. She could not put it off any longer. "You're gonna hate me when I tell you this." She paused. "I'm only fifteen," she said. "I'm sorry."

The seconds passed. When he took a step toward her she thought he was going to hit her. But he touched her chin, as if to check if she was for real, then sank back into the hammock. "Fifteen," he wailed. "What have I done? You're a kid . . . a baby."

"I'm really sorry."

"Why did you lie? Why?"

"You know why," she shot back defiantly. "You wouldn't have looked at me."

His head sunk into his hands. "You're tall for your age, but I should have known you weren't eighteen. You don't really look it." He turned his sharp eyes on her. "You've just made me into a criminal, Madeleine. You're underage."

What could she say? She hadn't really thought of it that way.

"I'll be sixteen in eight months," she said dejectedly.

Forrest stood up and pulled on his shorts. He held her head between his hands, his eyes blazing with anger. "That was incredibly irresponsible of you, but then I guess I'm an idiot for believing you. Go away, Madeleine. I've got to get working on the job of falling out of love with you. Christ! If only we hadn't done what we just did." They looked at each other for a long moment. He pressed his lips to hers, hard, too hard. There was pain in his eyes when he let her go and he beat his chest with his fist. "You already got me here, you little witch."

He turned and walked quickly into the house, and Madeleine, crying, slipped through the garden gate into a future without Forrest.

Madeleine's best friend and psychotherapy colleague, John, passed her in the narrow corridor.

"I'm late," he blurted, panting heavily. "I had a puncture."

"It happens to the best, Johnny," Madeleine reassured him, reaching out to touch him on the arm.

"Don't humor me. I have a hangover and now I've got Mrs. Nettle." He made as if to bang his head against the wall. "I can't cope."

"Monday morning is a drag," she commiserated.

As she hurried toward her consulting room, he called after her, "We've not had our 'peer supervision.' It's overdue."

"Perhaps next week?"

"No, Madeleine. You know what the ethical handbook says: Therapists who practice without supervision shall be strung up and horsewhipped. So we're having it tonight, after work, over a pint."

She watched him grapple with his door handle, juggling briefcase, lunch box, and a stack of mail. His glasses were askew, his reddish hair on end, and his posterior quite a bit more ample than it had been. The mechanics of everyday life seemed too unwieldy for the dear man, and she ran to pick up the bits of mail he dropped, handing them to him and closing his door behind him.

"Monday morning is a drag," Madeleine repeated grimly to her own room and drew back the curtains. Especially after a shit birthday, dumping one's lover, a Saturday night drowning her sorrows with Patricia, her running buddy, and Jane, a local gallery owner, followed by a head-busting hangover on Sunday.

She filled a coffee cup from the watercooler and poured water onto her potted plants. The sun showed up the film of dust that covered every surface and she almost regretted forbidding Sylvia from entering with her duster. She pulled out a couple of tissues from the box beside the patient's chair, and, wetting them from the cooler, smeared the dust over the surfaces. Lifting the telephone to clean underneath it, she hesitated momentarily. She could phone Gordon and demand a more in-depth discussion about the matter of his multiple sexual partners. No, he was the one who did the fooling around; if he had something to say he could damned well phone her.

Suddenly the sound of a shrill woman's voice traveled through the walls between her room and John's. Mrs. Nettle was at it again, raging about one thing or another. Madeleine had told John more than once in their mutual supervision sessions that Nora

Nettle was a candidate for psychiatric treatment, not psychotherapy, but he'd chosen to persevere. Good old John, a caring and skillful therapist, but he was almost too soft for the job. They'd met at the Bath Institute while in psychotherapy training. Madeleine had just arrived in Britain, not long after Forrest's death, and they had been drawn to each other from the start. Hailing from Key West was an excellent reference with any sophisticated gay man. It had seemed they were destined to set up shop together in town. The practice had worked superbly for three years because, in her mind, there could be no better colleague, partner, and friend than she had in John.

Her phone rang. That had to be her new patient, the walk-in from Friday. She picked up the phone. "Thanks, Sylvia. Send her in."

"Ah, no, wait," Sylvia said in a hushed voice. "She's just coming through the door, but your mother's on the phone."

"My *mother*?" Mama very rarely phoned her, and had only once called her at work. "All right. Beam her down."

"Mama, *que pasa?*" she said, concerned. "Are you OK?"

Rosaria's strong Cuban accent had a peculiarly staccato and breathless sound over the phone. "Go home, *mi hija*, go home and lock the doors."

Madeleine wondered whether to enter into a demanding discussion or just say yes, she would go home. She didn't like to have her equilibrium upset before seeing a patient. "All right, Mama, I will, if you think it best."

"Pedrote spoke to me in the night, telling me to throw the cowrie shells for a message."

"Oh, yes?"

"I did, and the message was clear. Today is a dangerous day for you, *mi hija*. You hear what I am saying? A stranger . . . a stranger is wanting to come into your life that will . . ." Her voice trailed off, and then there was an abrupt click. It sounded as if someone had taken the phone from her hand and hung up. Mama had no doubt walked into the nurses' station and helped herself.

Madeleine stood still for a moment with the phone in her hand. How lucid Mama sounded. That was good, wasn't it? She shrugged off her unease and pressed the button for reception, telling Sylvia to send in the patient.

She did a quick once-over of the room. Tissues in place—a must for all sessions, especially the first—chairs in position, notes put away. She brushed away the straying curls from her face and applied a quick stroke of lip gloss.

The patient knocked.

"Hello, you must be Rachel Locklear," Madeleine said after opening the door. She shook the woman's hand. Her grip— the very first clue to a patient's attitude, background, and personality—was limp and hasty. A person who didn't habitually shake hands. A class thing perhaps, certainly upbringing. "I'm Madeleine Frank."

"I know."

"Please have a seat." Madeleine motioned to the patient's chair opposite hers.

Madeleine sat herself down and waited, preferring to give the patient space to begin the session without rushing in with questions or trying to put her at ease. The woman was somewhere in her early to mid-thirties, slightly hard looking, with a severe expression and shifty eyes. There were faint scars from teenage acne, and the telling outline of a once-broken nose, but underneath all that and despite her somewhat unfriendly demeanor, she was strangely attractive, almost beautiful. Her face was unusual, heart-shaped and fine-boned, her head perched on a long, graceful neck. Her hair came halfway down her back, abundant and of a dark, rich auburn color. Most remarkable were her eyes, a striking light hazel, deeply slanted and narrow, which gave her a sly, catlike expression. She was too thin; her long legs were encased in tight black leather jeans, ending in scuffed cowboy boots.

"I don't really want to be here," she said after an excruciatingly long minute, her tone defensive, "and you don't half charge for this lark."

"Yes, therapy is expensive," Madeleine said, her tone neutral. "And you're here despite not really wanting to be. How's that?"

She glanced at the ceiling. "Well, a social worker I know insisted I try this out."

Madeleine decided not to comment, but Rachel Locklear looked her defiantly in the eye, clearly expecting Madeleine to challenge her about being there under duress.

In the background Nora Nettle was wailing, and Madeleine cursed to herself.

"She said I'm a nutter and should see a shrink to have my head examined."

Yeah, sure, a social worker would tell you such a thing, Madeleine thought, remaining attentive but not challenging this absurdity.

After another moment of silence, Rachel said, "I guess I can afford it now. My father died recently and left me twenty-eight thousand quid. And his house."

"I'm sorry about your father," Madeleine said, then reminded herself that perhaps the patient was not sorry.

Rachel Locklear looked vacant. "Are you?"

Again, a long pause. Rachel was a smoker, that was obvious. That flicker of the eye toward her bag, her hands moving uncomfortably on her lap.

"Well, why don't you tell me how you feel about losing your father?" Madeleine said as the pause became downright tedious.

"I'm not here to talk about him," Rachel retorted sharply.

OK, we'll leave him out, Madeleine

thought, checking her mounting exasperation . . . *Give her time, she'll deliver.*

"I guess it's more about my ex-partner, the father of my son. He's really bad for me, and for Sasha." Rachel moved forward now, perching on the edge of her chair, perhaps remembering that this "lark" was costing her money.

"We lived in London for years, but I've finished with him, and when Dad died and left me the house, I moved back here . . . but I'm like, addicted to him. That's what I read in a book, can't remember the name of it now. No matter how much I decide to stay away from him, the minute he shows up, I'm in bed with him. It's pathetic." She shrugged angrily as if this state of affairs was anybody's fault but her own.

"What's attractive about him?"

Rachel sat back and crossed one long leg over the other. Her boot bounced nervously up and down. "He's very good looking, if that's what you mean. He's a Russian Ukrainian—tall, dark, and handsome." She grinned for the first time, showing strong straight teeth, slightly tobacco stained.

"Anything else that's attractive?"

"Fuck no! He's violent, unpredictable,

untrustworthy, mean with money, cruel, thinks women are shit."

"Right!" said Madeleine, slightly taken aback. "Delightful character in other words."

Rachel studied Madeleine with cool objectivity.

"He fought in Afghanistan when he was quite young. From what he's told me, he and his mates did some very nasty things to people, so perhaps the way he turned out is not surprising."

Madeleine tried to picture this. She remembered reading something about the ruthlessness of the Russian soldiers in that poor war-torn country.

"He wants Sasha," Rachel continued. "He thinks that if a couple splits up, a son should be with his father. Sasha is only seven and I'm scared shitless he's going to be kidnapped and taken to the Ukraine, or Poland, or Hungary. His father has got contacts and relatives everywhere. It's the business he and his brother are in. The point being, he'll make sure I won't find my boy ever again. Knowing his lifestyle, he'd probably just dump Sasha with some aunt in a remote village somewhere."

Madeleine almost winced at the tone of apathy with which this bombshell was delivered.

"Which is the greater reason you keep him in your life? The irresistible sexual attraction you were telling me about, or the fact that he's got a noose around your neck?"

Rachel reflected for a moment. "Both. Where sex is concerned, I'm one of those fucked-up women who gets off on violence. I mean, I must be. He's beaten me up lots of times and the next minute we're thrashing about in bed with the windows steamed up. I've had . . . quite a few men in my life, but no one does it for me like him. Afterward I'm like totally sick at myself."

Madeleine did her best to disguise how much this statement intrigued her, not so much for its content but because it was the very first thing that Rachel had said that seemed at all genuine. She even looked sick. Apparently to distract herself and retain her composure, Rachel spread her hands on her lap and looked at them. She had practical hands with long fingers, short nails, no polish. After a moment she leaned back and raked her fingers through her abundant hair, exposing scarred, disfig- ured earlobes. She caught Madeleine look- ing at them and quickly dropped her hair to cover her ears.

Staring out the window, perhaps to avoid Madeleine's silent scrutiny, she continued, "He doesn't know about my dad dying and me getting the house . . . and the money. He's never lived outside London and doesn't know Bath. I managed to keep the whole thing secret until the probate was sorted and Sasha and I could beat it back here."

A long moment passed in silence. Ra- chel's eyes sometimes focused intensely on Madeleine, then she would look away, almost angrily.

"Aren't you going to ask me anything?" she blurted at last.

"If you like, but I prefer hearing what you'd like to share with me."

"Share!" Rachel snorted. "We're talk- ing, not *sharing*."

The woman is right, Madeleine thought. *It's a ridiculous expression.*

"And forget about *feelings* and all that other bullshit," Rachel went on. "I want to know what I should *do*."

Madeleine suppressed a smile. She would certainly have to watch her clichés with this lady. "OK, Rachel. Here is a question. How would you like to see yourself in, say, a year's time?"

Again Rachel glared at her, then looked down at her hands, almost as if embarrassed. "Well . . . this situation now, you know, with the house and the money . . . it could be, perhaps, a new beginning for me and Sasha. I've come to a point where I'm really trying to clean up my act. I'd like to think I could give my boy some sort of normal upbringing now that we've actually got a home of our own." She raised her head and looked directly at Madeleine. "So in a year's time, I'd be sitting in my nice house, having peeled the red velvet wallpaper off the walls and assembled my new IKEA furniture, waiting for my clean and tidy son to come home from school, swinging his satchel, and we'd both break into song. Including the dog!"

"That sounds like a perfectly healthy ambition."

It was the wrong thing to say.

"*Healthy!* Quit patronizing me. I'm already going out of my fucking mind. I don't know how to live a 'normal' life. What I want to know is: what can you do for me?"

She looked so furious that Madeleine was momentarily stumped for words. She was used to rage, it was a common feature of transference, but rarely in a first session. This was quite extraordinary, and no doubt interesting. "I guess I can take on board your anger, for a start."

"Oh, forget that shit," Rachel shot back. "What I need is some way to deal with this guy, the father of my son." She sat back and took a deep breath. "Look, I'm sorry. I get like this when I can't smoke. And I'm on edge about my situation. I know my ex is going to come around soon enough. He's never been to Bath, to my knowledge, but when he decides to find us, he will . . . and I'd like to be prepared for it. Not give in to him like I always do. At the same time I'm terrified he'll take Sasha and run. That's what he says he'll do if we're not available to him, by which he means, us living in London, preferably with him."

Madeleine nodded, gradually realizing the enormity of the threat to this woman and her son. However good her skills, she was not used to patients in such a bewildering and frightening situation. Rachel must have sensed it.

"Do you think there is any point in me coming to *you* with this?" she said, her voice softer now. "Can you really help me?"

"I don't know yet," Madeleine admitted. "There are two issues here: your response to this man and the feelings of powerlessness in the face of this response, and the real physical threat of your son being kidnapped. One we can work on, but the other seems to be a police matter. Have you talked to anyone about the blackmail?"

"Are you serious?" Rachel said disdainfully. "I can imagine what sort of world you live in, but believe me, with people like him you don't go to the police."

"Has he got a name?"

Again that scornful look. "Why?"

"Can we call him *something*?"

"All right, if we must. How about Rudolf? As in Rudolf Nureyev, the dancer. Everyone says he looks exactly like him, but taller, heavier, none of that pansy stuff. He's all man."

"All man?" Madeleine raised an eyebrow.

Rachel said nothing, just gave her a surly stare.

Madeleine felt out of her depth. She wasn't sure which way to go, and her patient didn't offer to lead. "Could you give me a bit of background?" she said, partly to buy time. "Like how long have you been with Rudolf?"

"Rudolf? Oh, let's call a spade a fucking shovel. His name is Anton."

"Right, how long have you been with Anton?"

Rachel calculated quickly, using her fingers. "About ten years, off and on." She paused for a moment, then looked up at Madeleine. "Where are you from, anyway? What's that accent you got?"

"American," Madeleine said reluctantly.

"American?" Rachel frowned. "What made you come to Bath?"

"Circumstances," Madeleine said vaguely. "I'm half British."

"Ah." Rachel nodded. "Half British . . . which half?"

"Rachel!" Madeleine broke into a smile. "Who cares? We're talking about you."

Again that angry frown. "What else do you need to know?"

Madeleine leaned forward and looked earnestly at her patient. "Listen. In case you're wondering, therapy is entirely confidential. You were telling me about your relationship with Anton, and his threat to take Sasha away from you, and the fact that you feel you cannot involve the police. To me, at least, it sounds very frightening."

"Does it?"

Madeleine refrained from shaking her head in despair. "Would you like to tell me how it feels for *you*?"

"Can't I smoke?"

"In here? I'm afraid not."

"Just a couple of puffs . . . leaning out your window?"

"No. The window only opens an inch."

Rachel's jaws were working angrily, her hands moving on her lap as though grasping for the cigarette she could not have. Madeleine was almost impressed; this was true addiction, or was it a way of avoiding talking about her fear? Perhaps she was not ready for that.

"How old are you, Rachel?"

"Why do you need to know?"

Madeleine shrugged. "I'm interested."

"Of course. Silly me! You get paid for being interested. I'm thirty-three."

The session went on like this, sparring, almost bickering at times. Much as Madeleine tried to get a grasp on what this woman was about, why she was there at all, she slid away or countered any reasonable question with a defensive or sarcastic retort. It seemed as if she was challenging Madeleine to throw her out of the consulting room.

Soon enough, they'd used up the time, and bar a little background information, it seemed they'd got nowhere. Madeleine informed her they had five minutes left of the session. When Rachel did not offer anything else, Madeleine spoke.

"Referring back to a question you asked earlier: do I think I can help you? If you want to continue therapy, we need to look at what is achievable. We can't change Anton, or his threats, but we can certainly explore the reasons you keep going back to him, knowing how destructive this is for you. We can look at what this addiction is all about, and despite what you said, I'd like to explore what *really* stops you from going to the police. They should be able to advise you, at least. And who knows? A restraining order might make him take notice."

"No way." Rachel shook her head.

Madeleine was sure this was the last she'd see of Rachel Locklear. Her expectations of therapy had very obviously not been met, and she would not be back. There seemed no point in saying anything more. But Rachel surprised her.

"Same time next week?" she asked without looking up.

"Yes . . . that'd be fine."

"I'll try and be more civil," she continued, sounding genuinely desperate. "What else am I going to do? My parents are dead and I don't know anyone in Bath, no one that I can talk to. Actually, I don't trust people. I never have." She looked up, peering angrily at Madeleine. "But don't bring the police up again. That's not an option. I want to sort myself out because of Sasha, that's all. I don't want him ending up like . . . his father, or like me for that matter. I want my son to have a normal, happy life. That's the only thing that matters to me. Nothing else is important. Can you understand that?"

Madeleine felt a sudden crushing sadness and could not immediately respond. Rachel's statement had scored her very heart. If only *she* had felt like this, how different her life could have been. Then she felt a rush of compassion for this woman, and admiration for her wish to persevere. Psychotherapy was the luxury of privileged people, and rarely did Madeleine see anyone like Rachel—except perhaps in prison. If there had been time, she would have challenged her motivation, tried to get her to admit to her *own* need to let go of Anton, acknowledge that this was not only about her son, that *she* mattered too. But for now her little boy was the main incentive. Without it, Rachel Locklear would surely not be here.

Madeleine took out her diary and they agreed on another session in a week's time. Rachel shook her hand quite firmly, as if hanging on to a shred of hope that this woman, this therapist, would help her save her little boy from a life of brutality.

After the relentless rain and unusual cold of the weekend, this was the first day with a vague feeling of spring about it.

John and Madeleine ended up in the Horse and Cart, an out-of-the-way pub on the river near Saltford. The garden was overgrown and had not been cleaned up for the season, but the setting sun was spreading a pale orange warmth over the countryside. They decided to have a first drink in the open air, though the pine benches were damp, moss grew on the tables, and there were faded crisp packets and dog shit around the edges of the lawn.

"Here," she said to John as he returned from the bar with two pints of bitter. "Have half of this." She split a newspaper in two and they each sat on a piece, trying to get comfortable on the rickety bench. A family of four had unfortunately also opted for the outdoors. The children's strident voices and shrill demands cut the gentleness of the evening. A Frisbee shaved the top of Madeleine's shoulder. She turned and frowned at the culprit, a girl of about seven, and got a mocking glare in return.

"Where was I?" she said, taking up the account of Rachel she'd started in the car.

"You were wondering about her sexual obsession," John said.

"I guess I don't understand how a woman can go back time and time again to a man who is abusive and exploits her."

John chuckled. "You've obviously never had one yourself despite your lively background."

She frowned. "A man who exploits me?"

"No, darling, a sexual obsession."

"Hey," she exclaimed, "sure I have."

"Do tell me about it sometime," John said and smiled. She realized suddenly how seldom she talked about Forrest. She couldn't blame John for occasionally forgetting she'd been married.

In a characteristic gesture, he put his forefinger on the bridge of his spectacles and shoved them back against his face. He'd gained weight since falling for Angus Rowlands, an older man with chronic back pain, whose main love seemed to be food and cooking. The flesh on John's abdomen strained at the buttons of his shirt.

"It sounds as if the lady is genuinely worried that her son will be kidnapped," he reflected, "and she's looking for a way out of a dangerous and dysfunctional relationship. It would seem a pretty healthy reason to seek therapy."

"In my view it's a police matter," Madeleine insisted. "This guy is an Afghan War veteran. I read somewhere they became totally brutalized in Afghanistan and came out of there like ready-made gangsters, baying for blood and money. Surely she would want to speak to someone . . ."

"Yeah, you."

"I mean the authorities. He's an illegal alien. She could probably have him deported."

John poured his pint down his gullet. "She's scared."

"There is something a bit contradictory in this need to keep her son safe while denying *herself* protection," Madeleine insisted.

"Of course. Which is perhaps why the social worker sent her along."

"Oh, there is no social worker, I'm sure of it. If she was seriously worried about the kidnap threat, why isn't she going to the police, at least for advice? Wouldn't any mother?"

"Fear is a powerful emotion, and the people she's dealing with are dangerous."

"Yes, I suppose so." Madeleine rested her chin on her hands. "But—and here I have no personal experience either—isn't it true that the maternal drive, the need to protect one's offspring, is the most powerful urge of all, in practically all species?"

Her heart suddenly skipped and a familiar wrenching in her gut reminded her that what she had just said was a lie. She took a sip of her pint.

John was saying something.

"Sorry, what was that?"

"You're the one who's all over the place." He laughed. "I said: After the urge to procreate. Maybe that's why she's still subconsciously wanting to fuck him, the Russian. The nesting instinct."

"What?"

"Oh, for Christ's sake, concentrate," John insisted. "The urge to procreate is stronger than the maternal drive."

Looking at John's soft, kind face, she wondered why she had never told him the truth. When she came back from Key West, grief-stricken and disorientated, and decided to embark on psychotherapy training (which her father, Neville, in a gesture of largesse, had agreed to fund), meeting John had saved her. His best friend had just died of AIDS and they immediately gravitated toward each other. For many months they leaned on each other, sharing their wretchedness. After seven years of intense friendship and hundreds of hours of reciprocal counseling, of laying themselves bare, pouring out their frustrations, sorrows, and angst to each other, she'd never told him the most fundamental thing about herself, the event that had shaped her adulthood. Maybe because she refused to believe she was living a lie, and that underneath her well-polished life, her strong sense of self, her emotional equilibrium, she was steeped in shame.

"You're not listening to me," John said, slightly miffed. "Can we move on to Mrs. Nettle?"

"Do you mind if we don't?" Madeleine said. "You know my thoughts on her, or should I say, on you. It's an unhealthy, codependent patient-therapist relationship, and besides, she's mad. You shouldn't waste your time, and her money, when what she needs is a shrink with a prescription pad."

"Wow," John said, frowning. "You're full of good counsel."

"I'm sorry," Madeleine sighed, "but we've been over her so many times."

Out of the corner of her eye she saw a flash of baby blue, followed by a familiar rumbling noise. Perhaps it was just her instinct, but as she peered across a low privet hedge into the car park, she already knew it was Gordon on his old Triumph Thunderbird. Behind him, perched on the pillion seat, was a tiny passenger. She should have known better than to have brought John here; it was Gordon who had introduced her to the Horse and Cart.

John followed her gaze. "That's a venerable old motorcycle. Hey! Isn't that your toy boy archaeologist?"

"Please don't stare," Madeleine said and turned away. "He's not mine anymore."

"Really, since when?"

"Three days."

"My God, why have we been sitting here and . . . Why didn't you tell me? What was the—"

"Don't look or he might come over."

"He won't," John said. "He's with a woman—no, not a woman, a girl. His daughter perhaps?"

"He hasn't got a daughter."

Curiosity got the better of her and she turned. Gordon was helping a petite raven-haired creature out of her helmet. She shrugged off a leather jacket, revealing low-slung hipsters, a cropped top, and acres of bare skin in between.

John sniggered. "Don't worry, they'll go inside. With that tight little midriff on display she'd be far too cold to drink out here."

"That's nice," Madeleine snapped. "Rub it in. With your paunchy geriatric boyfriend, you can talk." She stopped, mortified. "Oh God, John, that was evil. I am sorry."

At that moment, Gordon's familiar voice barked out her name. He had left the girlfriend standing and was coming toward them. John frowned and put his arm protectively around Madeleine. When Gordon saw them in this intimate attitude, he stopped. An angry scowl twisted his face.

He indicated John with a toss of his chin. "Did you have *him* do it?"

Madeleine was flummoxed. "Do what?"

John glared at the intruder. "What are you talking about, man?"

Gordon pointed a finger in Madeleine's direction. "That was grotesque, Maddy. I didn't think you had it in you." He turned and strode back to the girl standing by the bike.

"*Maddy?* Is that what he calls you? Presumptuous git!" John said scornfully and kissed her on the forehead. "What the hell was he on about?"

Madeleine stared at the retreating back of her ex-lover. She had no idea.

Chapter Three

Rachel pulled her jacket tightly around her, wishing she'd worn her sheepskin coat. The queue for the cash point was painfully slow. When it was finally her turn, she was all fingers and thumbs. She jammed in her card the wrong way around and momentarily forgot her secret code. Despite her age she'd never before had her own cash card, or any of the other trappings of sophistication, apart from a mobile phone. She didn't know how to use a computer and had never sent an e-mail in her life. The world around her had speeded up, and she was still treading water in some state of back and beyond. Even Sasha came out with things she knew nothing about.

The screen was smeared with some sticky substance, but she glimpsed her balance as it flashed and was gone. There was a hell of a lot of money in there. Dad always said he was putting a little bit aside for Sasha's education, but with his paltry old-age pension, and the way cash burned holes in his pockets . . . Was it possible he had been into something shady? A shiver of disquiet went through her. Was this something that could bounce back, someone he owed money to coming knocking on her door, or someone he'd ripped off? Rachel shook her head as she pressed the keys. No, not Dad. He was a simple soul, not sharp enough to do anything that'd get him into trouble. He must have had a run of luck on the horses. That had to be it. Her old man had thought Sasha was the smartest kid on earth and should go to university, and if she never touched the money, perhaps Sasha would be able to. But look, she *was* touching it . . . Money rolled away like the tide, smooth and easy. It poured out of one's hands, taking things with it. Then the loss of it dried things up, including essentials such as milk, not to mention wine, whiskey, and the flow of life's lubricants generally. Yet money, or the lack of it, was not the problem. She knew her life would never be right until she could cure herself of Anton. Much as she wanted to protect Sasha from harm, money in itself was no security. Real danger could not be bought off.

A low hum, and the notes were coughed up. She took her gloves off in order to count them. The day was cold, unusually cold for spring. Her nails looked transparent, like ice. Her fingers were too long and the blood reluctant. Smoking does that. Fucks with your circulation.

The homeless girl selling the *Big Issue* was standing right there, strategically beside the cash point. Rachel tried to avoid looking at her, but it was difficult. A couple of weeks ago they'd ended up in conversation, and ever since, the girl had nodded at her and smiled. It'd been one of those days when Rachel had not talked to another adult for ages. Not really talked. The girl told Rachel her parents gave her a lot of flack and she'd run away from home, but that she was old enough to look after herself. Rachel had wondered whether to tell her she'd done exactly the same, run away to London as a teenager, and how ill-omened that move had turned out to be. Before she'd formulated her tale of caution, the girl had commented on her sheepskin coat and said she thought she'd seen it in the window of the Oxfam shop. She obviously didn't know it wasn't the thing to say. Besides, she'd been wrong. Anton had given it to her. It'd been expensive, once upon a time. They'd ended up talking for a good five minutes, which is quite long, considering. She'd told Rachel she often slept rough. Well, that was one thing she'd never done herself, though she'd come pretty close.

"Hi again." The girl smiled at her. *"Big Issue?"*

"Got it already," she said, her voice gruffer than she meant it to be, her eyes level with the girl's hands holding the magazine out for her inspection. The girl had black woollen fingerless gloves on. Her nails were dirty. Something about the nails was so pathetic that Rachel halted her stride.

"Actually, perhaps I haven't."

"I don't mind," the girl said and laughed knowingly, pulling a fresh copy from a stack under her arm.

There it goes, Rachel thought as money changed hands. Two down, ninety-eight to go. And only one minute had passed. At this rate, by the time she got to the psychotherapy clinic, a twenty-minute walk, the money could be as good as gone. "How many've you got left?"

The girl lifted her elbow and looked under her arm. "About ten."

"Get out of the cold, huh?" Rachel studied her face for a second. "How old are you?"

"Eighteen." The girl's eyes changed a little, drawing back. "Old enough."

She looked younger, and probably was, with her bobble hat and smooth pink cheeks. She lived on the street, but she was selling something for which most people showed a grudging respect.

"Do you like kids?"

"Sure," said the girl. "Why?"

Rachel hesitated. "I've got a little boy. You know, like, I was thinking babysitting. I'm . . . getting a job. Perhaps the odd evening."

The girl shrugged. "You know where to find me."

Rachel smirked. Eighteen and cynicism already set in concrete. "Yeah," she said, pointing her finger at the girl's chest in mock menace, "I know where to find you. What's your name?"

"Charlene."

Rachel walked away, regretting her impulse. Now it would be really awkward to ignore the girl. Besides, what bloody job?

She had twenty minutes to kill and ambled through the center of Bath. Despite the cold snap, tourists crowded the Abbey Yard. Even the outdoor cafés were full. The red double-decker tour buses circled the town continually; she'd even begun to recognize the voices of the guides. Dottie, her mum, used to enjoy listening to all those languages that people spoke, and she'd been proud as punch when the city became a World Heritage Site. As far back as Rachel could remember, every Sunday her mum would take her by the hand and they would wander down the hill and sit in Buskers' Square, next to the Abbey, eating ice cream and listening to one busker after another play guitar and sing Dylan songs.

As a child she'd been fascinated by the stone angels climbing up the Abbey. They clung to their ladders, scarred and mutilated by centuries of weather, and out of the corner of her eye she sometimes saw them dart up a rung or two. Then Mum would make her trudge back up the steep slope, feeling as if they'd had a proper Sunday outing, concert and all, for the price of a cheap cone of Devon vanilla ice cream. Sometimes Dad came along and they'd have a drink and steak-and-kidney pie in the pub. The pub was still there, the Volunteer Rifleman's Arms, tucked into the warren of passages next to the Abbey. The buskers, too, were still there, but they hadn't improved; they seemed older than they used to be, rougher.

She crossed the square and passed through a small court dominated by a giant plane tree. The Crystal Tavern was invitingly placed there, beckoning her to fortify herself with a quick half of lager and a fag, but you couldn't smoke in pubs anymore. And this they called civilization!

She turned her back on it and entered North Parade Passage, a narrow walkway flanked by historic buildings. Small, chic cafés crowded the ground level, none of which she had the courage (or the appearance) to patronize. The psychotherapy clinic was above one of these, up a flight of rickety stairs. The clinic was nothing but a run-down flat, made to look posh by a lot of plants and low lighting. Still, it was undoubtedly in the trendiest part of town.

The reception was a small room with four armchairs and the hippie-dippy receptionist, Sylvia, at her little desk. She offered Rachel a cup of tea to warm her up. It was a nice gesture, which she accepted gratefully, but Rachel didn't trust her. She had *tough love* practically tattooed on her forehead; the sort that needed to take care of everyone, and she couldn't stop nattering. Rachel sat down and cupped the mug to get the warmth from it, trying to avoid catching her eye. There was no one else in the waiting room and she didn't want to chat. Her thoughts went to the session ahead, the third in so many weeks. It was not going the way she had planned. She was losing control over the direction of things—at the same time getting far too comfortable with Madeleine's little tricks to make her talk. But was this getting her anywhere? Was this really what she wanted?

Predictably, the receptionist lasted no more than half a minute. "Goodness," she exclaimed. "Your hands are blue."

"Bad circulation," Rachel mumbled.

"You should try ginkgo biloba. It's incredible."

"Huh?"

"A South American herb. Absolutely dynamite."

"Nah . . . give me a fag anyday." Rachel put the mug on top of the magazines on the table. "As a matter of fact, I'm popping out for one now."

Sylvia's phone pinged and she put her hand up. "Forget the fag, Miss Locklear," she said, "Madeleine is ready for you."

"Don't *Miss* me, for God's sake!"

"I beg your pardon?"

Madeleine no longer shook Rachel's hand when she arrived. There was no telling if this was some sort of strategy. Rachel didn't offer either, though there'd been something vaguely comforting about being touched by a woman who is supposed to care for you (in exchange for money).

They sat down. In the drawn-out silence, Rachel studied her therapist. Madeleine was wearing a black pencil skirt and an ethnic-type cotton sweater in striking tones of cream, chocolate, and coffee, so rich one was tempted to eat it off her with a spoon. Despite this easy elegance, somehow she'd seem more at home in scruffy jeans and an old shirt. Her unplucked eyebrows and unruly black curls made her look undomesticated, as if she belonged in some forest, not cooped up in an office. Yes, there was definitely something untamed, feral almost, about her. Perhaps it was the way she moved, taut and languid all at once. Skin smooth as a baby's bottom with a gorgeous toffee-colored tan. Her eyes were dark, intense, as though she could see right through you, and she had obscenely long eyelashes.

"What's going on?" Madeleine said.

"Why?"

"The way you're looking at me."

"So what?" Rachel snapped. "How old are you?"

Madeleine pointed at her chest. "Me?"

Rachel looked theatrically around the room. "Yeah, you."

"Why? Is it important?"

Rachel cast about for an answer. "I'm wondering how big a generation gap there might be. I'd put you at about thirty-nine, forty."

"No," said Madeleine. "There is all of ten years between us."

"Really? Oh well!"

Madeleine smiled. "If you were after a reason for me not to understand you, I don't think there is enough of a gap."

"My mum was quite old when she had me."

Madeleine said nothing, no doubt waiting for her to talk about Dottie. She'd put subtle pressure on her in the last session, wanting to know about her mother. There was not much to know, and Rachel had told her: Her mum had died when she was twelve. Dottie had been a lovely mum. Old-fashioned, gentle, but anxious and overprotective.

"Tell me more about her," Madeleine prompted.

"We *did* her last week. Let's not waste my money on a subject that has nothing to do with why I'm here."

"Fine," Madeleine said with a faint hint of exasperation. She settled pointedly back into her chair. "What would you like to talk about today?"

"Can I remind you that I'm here for a reason?" Rachel said angrily. "Anton. Curing myself of that arsehole, and getting my life together."

"So you keep telling me." Madeleine suddenly sat forward and fixed her with a penetrating stare. "But I don't believe you. It doesn't ring true."

Not true! She felt an equal measure of anger and panic rising in her chest. What else was she going to dredge up to keep the session going? Perhaps now was the time to test how much her therapist could really stomach.

"All right, all right! I guess I should tell you something about me and Anton. It's not pretty . . . you won't be impressed."

"Try me."

"Brace yourself." Rachel drew breath. She could not remember the date, but she remembered the day she first met him. It was a Wednesday. She was working in London's East End, at Hungry Harry's . . .

She looked over at Irene, who was mopping the floor, wishing she didn't look quite so butch. Her hair was a short-back-and-sides kind of job, nice color though, blond, and blue eyes like an angel. Her body was a bit on the stocky side; she trained in a gym sometimes, and the muscles on her shoulders strained the checkered shirt she was wearing.

Three days after Rachel got the job, when she was making cheese rolls, Irene had approached her from behind and put her arms around her. She'd grabbed Rachel's wrist and said, "Here, sweetie, this is how you do it." With the other hand she lined up the rolls along the counter and guided the butter knife in Rachel's hand right over the whole row of them. Rachel hadn't minded; it had seemed like a friendly, almost motherly gesture. But when Irene let go of her wrist and measured her waist with her hands, she'd known something was up, but she was so starved for affection, even then she'd not minded.

They'd gone out drinking and had a great time. Afterward they went to Irene's flat, lit candles, and drank red wine. Irene had her own studio apartment in a big gray block, very different from the squat where Rachel was living. Irene paid rent, and she had the place to herself.

Once in bed, Rachel had not known what to do, but all the things Irene did felt nice. It was different from a man, velvety, fluid, beginning and end sort of flowed into each other. No roughness or sweat or hard edges. The time after that, she'd had her first orgasm. It was sweet, the only word to describe it, but had none of the fireworks she'd been led to expect. Rachel didn't think of herself as a lesbian, but hell, if a woman could make her feel so nice, so safe, she would try it for a while. She was young, she needed to test things, experience life. What was wrong with that?

She'd known Irene for five weeks, but in those short weeks things had turned right around. For reasons Irene did not want to discuss, she lost her flat. Something to do with a sub-subrental. She had nowhere to go so she'd moved into the squat. The room became a bit claustrophobic and behind Irene's back her squat mates, Dave and Lynne, had teased Rachel mercilessly. "Didn't know you was into women. A lezzie! Never would have guessed it."

Irene was unstacking the chairs now, looking aggravated.

"That bloody Martin, what planet is he on? He's supposed to mop and unstack last thing before he leaves, not leave it to us."

Rachel was putting cling film around tuna and cucumber sandwiches when the first customer walked through the door. At the counter he gave a cursory glance at the display unit.

"Do you have Continental breakfast?"

Rachel looked up. "What's that?"

The man smiled. He was tall and dark haired, over thirty for sure, and wore a fancy beige suit, a black shirt with a black tie, stylish, not like the customers they usually had. "Where I come from a cup of espresso, orange juice made directly from the fruit, croissant, butter and jam." He had a strong accent of some sort, but sounded so well spoken and confident.

Rachel smiled back. "We can do you regular coffee, juice from a carton, toast, brown if you like. Margarine and jam is on me."

The man threw back his head and laughed. He had the most gorgeous laugh.

"Sound terrible, but if you make it, I eat it," he said without once taking his green eyes off her. His gaze shone with a mixture of malice and humor, eyes slightly hooded but extremely seductive. She felt a sudden rush through her lower body, all the way down to her knees. God, he was good-looking. Even though he came from somewhere else. Perhaps he was Italian or Swiss or something. Somewhere sophisticated and exotic.

"Coming up," she said briskly, trying to hide the impact he'd made. She wished she weren't wearing this ghastly uniform, but she'd washed her hair that morning and put on some makeup. Fuck, she was supposed to be a lezzie now, what was she doing? "That'll be one ninety-nine."

He gave her a five-pound note. "Keep the change," he said, so she did.

Customers were supposed to take their stuff to the tables on the trays provided, but this man just turned and went to sit down. He wanted to be served, obviously. All right, with a tip like that, why not? It's wasn't as if they were exactly busy. Irene gave her a look when she took him the coffee and the juice. Ten minutes later, when she was about to take him the toast, Irene waylaid her.

"Let the bastard come and get it himself," she hissed. It wasn't the first time Irene had tried to tell her what to do.

"What are you? My boss?" she snapped back.

The man heard them, she was sure of it, but he didn't say anything when she came over. He did later, when he was about to leave. Irene was in the loo.

"When you finish?"

"Finish what?" she said, pretending not to understand.

"This evening?"

"Oh, this is the early shift. I don't work twenty-four hours a day."

He smiled that smile again. "Don't be clever now, little lady. You know what I'm saying about."

She glanced toward the loos. "You want to take me out? Is that why you're asking?"

He didn't answer, just gazed at her with his intense green eyes.

"Don't you think it's a reasonable question?" she said. "What do you want?"

"You are a terrible little person, I see that."

"I'm terrible?" It sounded funny with his accent, and she laughed. "It takes one to know one, and don't call me little. I'm five foot eight and a half."

"I take you for a coffee."

"I'm off at three so you can take me for a coffee if you want."

Straightaway he looked more businesslike, as if he'd done the deal and didn't have to sell himself anymore. "I'll wait in a taxi over the road."

She was disappointed by the abrupt turnaround, and . . . massively uneasy. How was she going to get around Irene? Why did she want to do this anyway? She felt safe with Irene. Hadn't she decided she was in love with her?

On that dreary Wednesday as the minutes and hours ticked by, her unease changed, mutated. She was sliding away from the safety of Irene.

It was about risk, wasn't it? She'd always been big on risk. Except in her case it was usually destructive, not the other way around. She'd had a games teacher when she was fourteen, a nice young woman who'd seemed to like her. She'd always been on about taking risks, getting ahead and above, not getting stuck. Rachel was sure that the stuckness had been a reference to her parents. "You're a very smart girl, Rachel," she kept saying. "You could really go places, and don't be too shy about trading on your looks, we women have to use all we've got to get where we want to be." Yeah, she'd traded on her looks all right. No problem there, but the risks . . . those she'd got all wrong.

She sensed that going out with this guy was going to be dangerous. She'd only exchanged a few words with him, yet the whole day she'd been feeling quivery inside with both fear and excitement. It was the risk, the sense of hidden menace that was pulling at her. He reeked of ruthlessness, sex, and money. I can handle it, she told herself. Fuck lesbianism; she didn't need all that softness and mothering, she just needed a man who could bring out the real woman in her. She needed a challenge.

In the end, the showdown with Irene had not been very nice. Irene had cried and begged her not to go. Rachel hadn't known it then, but she would never go back to the squat or to Hungry Harry's and she would never see Irene again.

"Where do you want to go?" he said after she hopped into the cab.

"Somewhere nice for a change." She already suspected how the day was going to end and she might as well get something decent out of it.

He'd changed out of the suit and was wearing black drainpipe jeans and a black leather jacket that looked slick and dripping with money. His dark hair was shining with some wet-looking substance. Altogether there was an oily quality to him. His hair was short at the sides but grew in waves over his forehead and neck, and, of course, there had to be a gold chain somewhere (she didn't see it until he took his clothes off).

"What's your name?" she asked.

"Anton," he said distractedly, looking out the window. He seemed miles away and didn't ask for hers.

They took the cab into town. He moved his thigh casually against hers, then gripped her hand as if he already owned her, but he wasn't exactly big on conversation.

"You want to see a film?" he asked to her surprise. It seemed a clean, healthy thing to do on a first date.

"I'd love to."

"Let's have a drink first," he said.

It was drizzling now and the cab let them off by a hotel in the West End, just off Shaftesbury Avenue. They went inside. She'd never set foot in a place like it, but she wasn't complaining. It was a palace, not for the likes of her, obviously. In the bar, a young waiter who thought highly of himself came to the table for their order. She asked for a rum and Coke, Anton for mineral water.

She got out her pouch of tobacco and Rizzlas, and started the process of rolling a cigarette.

"Oh, don't do that. Is so ugly," Anton said, grimacing as if she'd got out a dead slug. He signaled to the waiter and asked for a packet of Camels. In a flash, the waiter was back with the cigarettes on a silver tray, already opened and three cigarettes half sticking out. He produced a lighter and lit her cigarette. A moment later he brought the drinks and put a bowl of giant cashews on the table. Free cashews! That said something about the place. Anton took the bowl and offered it to her. She shook her head. She loved cashews, but she was too nervous.

"That's a girl," he said. "I don't want you eating." She wasn't sure what he meant, whether she wasn't thin enough or he wanted her hungry for some other reason. He was obviously interested in her appearance because almost immediately he began to pass judgment on her clothes: her jeans were cheap looking, her top had seen too many washes, her jacket was ugly and dated. Her hair, too, could use trimming and lightening, and the ring in her eyebrow had to go.

"How would you have me decked out?" she asked, more amused than offended.

"Stay with me and I take you shopping," he said smugly. "I'd love to dress you up." He looked her over and chuckled. "You sure have the right stuff. Good raw material there. You could be stunning."

She laughed too. "Flattery will get you somewhere."

"I know," he said. "I look forward to it."

So less than an hour into the date, without really having meant to, she'd signed on the dotted line. They had another drink, and Anton soon pointed out they didn't have to bother with the film.

"Where do we go?" she asked clumsily when he led her by the elbow out of the hotel. He didn't answer, so she chose, willingly, to abandon herself to whatever awaited. She almost relished her dread of the unknown, the thought of her body consumed in ways she couldn't yet fathom, ways merely hinted at by the iron grip on her arm.

They got into a cab. Though it was still broad daylight, and before the car had even pulled out into the street, his hand was up her back, under her jumper, unsnapping her bra. But that was all he did, just that, to let her know that her clothes were coming off her, soon. She couldn't remember ever feeling so turned on by a man or a woman. Or was it fear that turned her on?

It was not a long ride, but she didn't pay attention to where they were going. The burning tension within her made everything outside seem like a dull, slow film in black and white. The

cab pulled up in front of a nice-looking apartment block. It was tall and modern with real balconies. Anton slipped the driver a tenner, perhaps to impress her. She wanted to impress him too, show him that she was up for anything. The drinks made her brave. In the lift already she was on her knees.

"Rachel." Madeleine was leaning forward, giving her hand a soft tap. "You were going to tell me something," she said gently. "I really want to hear it."

Rachel pulled herself up. "Yeah, right. OK. I'd left Bath and was in London, as I told you, trying to make a living off this and that, waitressing mainly, and was dossing with friends in a squat. Then I met Anton, and the attraction was, like, instant. So when he told me to go and live with him, I did. He was in some big business and had loads of money. I was totally crazy about him. After about three or four months, he split up with some partners. He ran into money problems, don't ask me why, and got really edgy and mean. He seemed to change overnight. His brother, Uri, advised him to make use of my assets, so he told me I had to go on the game. I should have guessed it was coming, but still . . . I was gutted and tried to refuse, but he wouldn't take no for an answer.

"So, from being this rich guy's woman, I was suddenly a hooker. Nothing high class either, mainly the motor trade. Still, I was quite in demand. He was happy for a while and kept promising it would only be for another week . . . month, but it wasn't. Then he got in with some different people and other girls came from somewhere, the Ukraine mostly. I had to, like, share him, but I was the only one actually living with him. Some fucking privilege! I made tons of money for him, his personal gold mine. But I never got used to it. I didn't have the stomach for it."

Rachel paused. Madeleine was obviously trying hard to look impassive, but her eyes gave her away. She'd probably never met a hooker in her life.

"I was doing a lot of drugs, Valium mainly, and then I stopped eating. Finally I had some sort of nervous collapse. No amount of threats or punches would get me out of bed, so he had no choice but to give me a break. I got away from London and went to stay with my dad here in Bath for about a year. Anton seemed to lose interest in me. He had plenty of other girls to choose from. But . . .' She looked down, embarrassed. "I got bored in Bath and was drawn back to London. Anton got wind of me being there. He set about trying to get me back, saying I was the only woman he loved and that he couldn't live without me. He wanted to settle permanently in London, apply to be 'legal' and have a normal life, maybe get married, have children, all that crap. He made all these promises, and I believed him. He still had this kind of sexual power over me; much as I despised him, I couldn't resist him. So I went back to him, and we had Sasha. Things looked OK for a couple of years. He was away a lot, which made it easier, but then he fell out with some partner in Budapest, some heavy that—"

She stopped suddenly and peered at Madeleine. "Do you write notes about this?"

"Only for myself. I won't if you'd rather I didn't."

Rachel shook her head. "The details don't matter. Anton had to go into hiding for a few months. We moved to another flat and he was short of money. He wanted me back on the game, pleaded with me, threatened me, beat me, and for a while I gave in, but in the end I took Sasha and ran back to my dad's."

Rachel went quiet, looking at her restless hands.

"And then?" Madeleine prompted her after a while.

"This sounds so fucking pathetic," Rachel exclaimed angrily. "Sasha kept asking about his father so I took him to London for a visit. Anton was meek as a lamb. He showered us with presents and stuff. Like an idiot I believed all the usual promises and I agreed to try again, but guys like him never change, do they? They don't know the meaning of the word. The last time I left him was a year ago now. I found a flat for me and Sasha in another part of London, but Anton refused to let go. He'd be gone for weeks, months even, but then he'd come back, partly for Sasha and partly for me. He's just as addicted to me as I am to him. Sometimes I'm sick enough to be flattered." She smirked. "What a pair, eh?"

"How long were you . . . on the game?" Madeleine said.

Rachel chuckled at her discomfort. "Long enough, but I'll tell you. Doing men in cars and back alleys is enough to put a woman off sex for life, but there you go, I can still get really hot about Anton. And that's despite hating his guts . . . because I *really* do hate him."

"If you could, what would you like to say or do to Anton?"

"I'd like to see him in jail, that's what. Preferably gang-raped nightly by queues of muscle-bound inmates with a special interest in pain."

"Aha," Madeleine said, quite obviously unnerved by this image.

"Ask me another question," Rachel said impatiently. Exercising her revenge fantasies was just the sort of therapy she might enjoy.

"It sounds as if you have enough on Anton to do just that, put him in jail, if that was what you really wanted."

"That's not a question."

Madeleine peered at her through half-closed eyes. "So you don't really want that."

"Listen, I think you don't know what the hell you're talking about here," Rachel said sharply. "You don't take on someone like him. You think being in jail would stop him? His brother, Uri, would come looking for me. Uri's big on family solidarity, and he's far more ruthless and brutal than Anton."

Madeleine looked shocked. "I take your word for it."

They were quiet for a moment.

"I know what you're thinking," Rachel blurted out. "Society should be protected from people like us. You think you side with the underdog, right? But really you're convinced that society should be saved not from just gangsters and pimps, but *whores* as well."

Was there an imperceptible narrowing of Madeleine's eyebrows? God, the woman was cool. What would it take to expose her real feelings? Rachel read her face carefully, but could see no disgust or disapproval, no pulling back. Madeleine had passed the test—in a fashion. As Rachel stared defiantly at her, Madeleine now seemed to be struggling not to smile.

"So you think you've got me figured out?" she said. "I thought I was the therapist here."

"Well, fucking sort me out, then."

"I'd love to, but I don't need to sort you out. I'm watching you do it all by yourself."

"What good news!" Rachel snarled. "How am I sorting myself out?"

"You're venting your anger. And some of it you're taking out quite effectively *on me*."

"Well . . . yeah." She sat back and folded her arms. "And how the hell is that going to help me?"

"Your call," Madeleine countered infuriatingly.

Rachel turned away. Even if Madeleine never found out the real reason for her antagonism, she was right. True anger was different from belligerence, hostility, rudeness . . . even violence. If she was angry enough she wouldn't put up with the shit she'd suffered. Of course not. But she didn't answer. She wasn't here to be "analyzed," yet Madeleine was nibbling away at her defenses. She'd not meant to tell her so much, but how could she continue coming to therapy if she didn't offer something?

Rachel touched her earlobe, the symbol of her oppression. It was cloven like a devil's hoof, both of them were. She could have them fixed, a doctor had offered to do it once, but she'd rejected the offer. She'd wanted Anton to see them, look at them, but she'd soon realized it gave him pleasure, not pain or remorse. They were evidence of his ownership. The earrings had been a present from a besotted punter, and Anton thought ripping them out would teach her a lesson she'd not forget in a hurry. He'd certainly never asked her to have them fixed. He was *sick* . . . and she was *sick*. Being here, talking to this woman, was sick.

Madeleine's voice broke through her thoughts. "Since you brought it up . . . is that how you think of yourself? As a whore?"

"Once a whore, always a whore," Rachel said darkly.

"Explain that to me."

Rachel peered at her and smiled. "Am I your first whore?"

Madeleine hesitated, then nodded affirmatively.

They fell silent. Madeleine was no doubt waiting for her to go on with her story, offer herself up, explain her whoredom. Rachel got up from her chair and went to the window, looking down into the narrow passage. Between the buildings opposite was a small courtyard with wrought iron tables. She could see the waiter bringing someone a pot of tea and a hunk of cake. A woman was laughing, tossing her designer hair. The place was bustling. A row of pots containing tiny birch trees divided the café from the passage. Small gusts of wind made the branches quiver. She knew they were birches because her dad had planted one in the garden. He'd called it a trailing birch. With the years it had grown a canopy under which you could hide. It was still there, but gnarled and old and shapeless.

With her back to Madeleine she spoke about her childhood hideaway, she described it in fine detail. The tumbling, delicate heart-shaped leaves and the way they fluttered in the wind, making a rustling sound, the pure white of the bark that came off in horizontal strips. She'd liked curling them around her finger and the crackling noise it made when she peeled them off the trunk, until her dad told her that a tree could not live without its bark.

Madeleine was quite until she had finished.

"How beautifully you described that,"

she said after a moment, her voice soft. "It's the first real thing you've told me about your childhood."

"Is it?"

"If you'd like to tell me, I'm really keen to hear more about Rachel the little girl."

Rachel gave a huge synthetic laugh and went back to sit in her chair. She knew how phony she sounded and Madeleine was no fool. Christ, one couldn't get away with anything around her.

Madeleine cocked her head. "What's so funny about Rachel the little girl?"

"There never was one, that's what."

"Oh, come on. I don't buy that."

"Of course you don't."

Madeleine shrugged. "You know best, I guess. You burst from your mother's womb a fully formed and thoroughly pissed-off woman. Right?"

Rachel couldn't help laughing at the image of this spitting, cursing she-devil exploding out of her mother. Madeleine laughed too. But she was smart, and cunning. She led her straight back to the place Rachel did not intend to go.

"You're denying that you were a child once."

"Of course I was a fucking child. How is talking about my childhood going to cure me of Anton, or protect me from him? I wasn't harshly potty-trained, if that's what you're trying to get at. For the record, Mum and Dad were lovely people. My mum's death was a big-time blow, but my problem is *now*, not back then. If you must know, much as I hate Anton, I miss him. *That's* my problem. The longer he takes to find me, the more scared I get, yet I'm aching to have him."

She peered at Madeleine, trying to gauge her stamina for that sort of honesty. Madeleine simply nodded, a dark curl of hair falling forward over her face. Rachel felt a sudden inexplicable softness toward her, and an urge to flick the lock out of her face.

Madeleine must have sensed this change in her, because her voice faltered a little. "A case of 'better the devil you know'?"

"Well . . . I'm like, walking on hot coals. I'm waiting for him . . . both dreading him finding me and wanting him at the same time."

Madeleine sat forward, nodding encouragingly. "Dreading and wanting?" she said, tilting her head to one side. "How does that work?"

Rachel looked at Madeleine's well-shaped knees and the way her long hands grasped them when she got interested. "It's easier to open my arms—and legs—to him."

"The soft option?"

"Christ," Rachel burst out. "Soft option! You've got no idea. He is quite capable of inflicting a lot of pain." She searched for an example of Anton's capacity for violence, feeling that sinking fear he inspired in her. Like the time she'd been robbed by a punter. It was years ago now, before Sasha was born, but it still made her weak at the knees when she thought about the aftermath. Being robbed had been frightening and degrading enough (as she had already *delivered*), but returning home empty-handed, to be thrown around the living room like a rag doll by a drug-fueled Anton, her jaw broken, her hair half pulled out, then subjected to . . . No, why should she tell genteel Madeleine that story? "Look, I've got a little boy to protect."

"So you'd be protecting Sasha by letting Anton have his way with you?"

Rachel knew she was in a corner. What could she say? She could just get up and leave. She could take her bag and go, but Madeleine broke through her train of thought. "I remember you said he'd never hurt Sasha."

Rachel raised her brow in mock disbelief. "I can't believe you said that. A child has eyes, ears . . . and feelings. It's not like a dog, you know. If you don't know that, you can't possibly have any children of your own."

Madeleine looked at her without responding. It was plain that she knew that Rachel had turned the argument around and was dodging the real issue: that she herself was putting her child at risk.

"You don't, do you?" Rachel demanded.

Madeleine uncrossed and recrossed her legs. "Come on, Rachel. This is *not* about *me*, it's about you," she said, not meeting her gaze.

Rachel stared at her. She had hit a nerve. The therapist had a crack in her cool armor.

"Now, hold on," she said, fixing Madeleine with a probing gaze. "I'm paying for this session. I can ask you questions if I want to."

"Sure, but my job is to prevent you from sidetracking. The answer to your question is no, I don't have any children."

"Why not?"

Madeleine looked up, not at her but at some point beyond her head. "I think you want to talk about me so you can avoid talking about yourself."

"Ha! That sounds like a sentence you've pulled out of a manual."

Madeleine smiled. "Perhaps I have, and there you go again. You very cleverly steered us away from talking about being a prostitute just a moment ago. And then you did the same by talking about your childhood, and then the issue of why you cannot let go of a man who is violent, unpredictable, and cruel."

"So why don't you have any children?"

Madeleine avoided her gaze and shifted uneasily in her chair.

"Go, on," Rachel insisted. "Give me an honest answer. You prefer a career, right? Or you can't have them? Maybe you plain don't *like* children? Or there is no guy around to give them to you? Or, perhaps"—

she lifted an eyebrow—"you're not into men?"

Madeleine turned back to face her. She was shaking her head and swallowing repeatedly. To Rachel's horror, her eyes seemed shiny with tears, liquid, close to spilling over. Rachel cursed herself. Shit! She didn't need this. Madeleine opened her mouth to speak but no sound came out. She coughed and tried again.

"I don't think it's appropriate to talk about this."

"Yeah, you're right. I'm sorry," Rachel said, bending down and picking up her bag. "Can we just stop here? I'm gagging for a smoke."

Chapter Four

I take it that didn't go very well," Sylvia commented when Madeleine came out into the empty waiting room.

"What do you mean?"

"Your patient left after only thirty-nine minutes."

"Well, I'm glad you're keeping close track," Madeleine said, feeling irked by Sylvia's habitually unsolicited observations. Much as Sylvia tried to be discreet, there was within her an archetypal earth mother she was unable to suppress. In addition to offering patients vegan snacks and advice on health matters, Madeleine had caught her counseling them, using an astrological chart she kept under her in-tray. Madeleine had put a stop to it, but she suspected it was really the all-knowing Sylvia people came to see.

"And she looked annoyed," Sylvia added.

Madeleine cringed. What a blundering way to conclude a session. She shouldn't have let Rachel press her for personal in-formation. And that tearful display! Rachel didn't offer any tears *herself*, dammit, she was not in the crying game. No wonder she couldn't wait to get the hell out. Mad-eleine had attempted—rather clumsily—to stop Rachel leaving, but she'd claimed she couldn't stand another moment without a smoke. Expensive cigarette, but it was up to her; it was her money. And though Rachel had quickly gone through the mo-tions and agreed to their next appointment, Madeleine feared that, this time, she wouldn't come back. There was something in Rachel's background, something she both needed and wanted to deal with but would not allow herself to. Possibly her mother's death from cancer, perhaps some earlier event. Much as she was motivated to protect her son, therapy was bringing them too close to the core of the matter, and Rachel surely knew that she could not forever keep the lid on her emotions. She would have to bring her vulnerable, damaged self nearer to the surface for both of them to examine. It takes strength and will to undertake that journey, and having to pay for it often feels like adding insult to injury.

Madeleine retrieved her car from the parking lot on Pierrepont Street and paid the extortionate fee to the grumpy fellow that ran it. She avoided the rush hour traffic by following her own route out of town, taking narrow streets flanked by tall bath-stone town houses and crossing out-of-the-way squares of imposing Palladian villas where through traffic was frowned on but not expressly banned. Soon she was driving steeply uphill on a country road. The air cleared as the urban bustle receded. She lowered the window and breathed in. Where else in the world could you leave the heart of a city and a minute later see overgrown meadows covered with spring flowers and fields grazed by cows and sheep?

As she came nearer to her destination, Madeleine's grip on the steering wheel tightened. Though she loved and honored her mother, her twice-weekly visits could be volatile, and taxing. Madeleine knew she was not to blame, but it was on her conscience that her mother would end her days in this cold, wet land, not in beautiful, lush Key West or in her beloved Cuba. Rosaria, grieving for her past, often held Madeleine personally responsible for her captivity in hell, conveniently forgetting that it had been her husband who had insisted they move back to England, his homeland.

Madeleine drove through the arch that framed the avenue up to the house. Setton Hall was an imposing Tudor mansion now converted into a prison of sorts, a lavish lunatic asylum for the wealthy. It had been the seat of the duke of Setton, who drank and snorted his way through his money, then sold out to an entrepreneur who'd made a fortune out of luxury nursing homes. This guy had made a deal with

Neville, acquiring enough of his paintings to allow Neville's crazy ex-wife to live out her days in superlative comfort. Thus Neville was rid of her and his bad conscience at the same time.

Tall cypresses lined the avenue, and the grounds beyond were well cared for, three acres of undulating lawn dotted with majestic Lebanese cedars. Madeleine parked her Merc in the visitors' car park. The motorcar was another legacy of her father, a gas-guzzling hand-me-down but a real collector's item. She moderated her environmental culpability by using it as little as possible, and rationalizing that someone else would be driving it if she wasn't. Even so, it was modest compared to some of the other cars in the car park.

She signed in at reception and pinned the required name tag on her jacket, then made her way to the second floor. Rosaria was in the living room together with some of the other residents, watching a noisy reality program. It always gave Madeleine a shock to see this scene: a group of vacant-looking people with dead eyes, silent and immobile but for the various repetitive movements caused by medication or the sheer tedium of their lives. Rosaria stood out among them. She sat erect in her armchair, her thin wrists covered in gold bracelets. Amulets and talismans acquired over a lifetime hung from them and a heavy gold wedding band sat loosely on her finger. She was wearing black slacks and an elaborately embroidered Guatemalan blouse; on her slender feet were a pair of high-heeled silver sandals.

Though worn down by her illness, at sixty-five Rosaria was still a strikingly beautiful woman. Her waist-length black hair was gathered in a braid that curled dramatically around her head. Her eyebrows were black and thick, so abundant they almost met in the middle. It was her exotic "Frieda Kahlo look" that had enchanted Neville all those years ago. He'd met the famous Kahlo once in Mexico when she was already ill and dying, but he'd nevertheless, like so many men before him, found the painter's exotic sensuality totally mesmerizing. However, Rosaria, mysterious though she was, was no fellow artist but a refugee from Havana, a part-time barmaid in Key West and a practitioner of Santeria, the old Afro-Cuban religion practiced widely in Cuba. She'd claimed to be able to foretell the future and would cast spells on people for a dollar. Neville had been a young up-and-coming artist and had come to Key West to bask in the bohemian atmosphere, when he'd seen her sitting in a wooden booth on Duval Street. She was barely out of her teens but had a strong sense of her own exotic allure. Calling to him across the street, she'd offered to throw the cowrie shells and read his fortune. Her evident talent had captured his imagination and he still talked about the spell she'd cast on his heart. But now that Neville was a famous painter, married to a solid Englishwoman, he had no time for his crazy Santera of an ex-wife.

"How are you, Mama?" Madeleine said, kneeling to embrace her. She kissed the ancient silver crucifix hanging from her mother's neck, out of respect for her parentage. Having belonged to a long line of Cuban Santeras, it was rubbed thin by over a century of constant wear. Then she kissed the tiny glass flask hanging from the same chain. It contained a gray powder, ostensibly the ground-up hip bone of her Yoruba great-great-great-grandmother. One day soon, Rosaria kept saying, both would be hanging around Madeleine's neck, and then, only then, would she be imbued with power (from the flask) and protected from evil (by the crucifix).

"Ah, there you are!" Rosaria sighed, as if Madeleine were merely returning from a visit to the loo. "Have you got my rum?"

"Yes, Mama," she said. "Have you missed me?"

"I watch you always with my inner eye, Magdalena. I know where you are."

A vision of Gordon's imaginative love-making flashed through Madeleine's mind. Though her mother's illness had all but destroyed her mystic sensitivity, the thought of Mama watching her was disturbing.

Physically there was nothing wrong with Rosaria, but her mental frailty was compounded by the bodily manifestations of the antipsychotic drugs she'd been on for so many years. She could have spells of rocking back and forth in her chair, and her hands often flapped uncontrollably, but now she poured her indomitable will into one trembling finger and pointed it at her.

"Have you seen my husband, Magdalena? How is he?"

Madeleine groaned inwardly. Rosaria had not mentioned Neville for at least a month, perhaps two. In vain she kept hoping her mother would eventually accept that he was long gone, or just forget him.

"Neville is not your husband anymore. He's married to Elizabeth."

"You know what, Magdalena? I can tell you that his false marriage to that woman is almost over."

"I don't think so, Mama. They've been quite happily married for twenty years."

Rosaria's fists clenched. "I know how long it's been," she shrieked, "but I'm telling you it's almost over."

Madeleine looked around the room, wondering if her mother's escalating voice disturbed the other residents, interrupting their television viewing. Half of them were asleep, or at least had their eyes closed. Mrs. Campion was watching but was stone deaf. An unfamiliar-looking man seemed intent on the screen, his eyebrows knitted together in obvious disapproval.

Madeleine, seeking to distract Rosaria,

leaned close to her ear. "You've got a new resident?"

"Don't look at him," Rosaria whispered.

"I think he's quite handsome. Aren't you always telling me how decrepit the men here are?"

"Pshhht," Rosaria hissed. "Pedrote tells me his guts are black."

Mama's only connection with her past was the voice of Pedrote, who she was convinced spoke to her, all the way from Cuba, through a small receiving device that had been secretly embedded in her brain. Rosaria's own mother had been an infamous Santera in Havana, but Rosaria had turned to Pedrote, who'd become her mentor and lover. He had been the most powerful Babalawo, a high priest of Santeria, in her Havana neighborhood, and he'd taught her all sorts of dark skills.

"Pedrote might be jealous, have you thought of that?" Madeleine teased her. "You could use a new man in your life, eh?"

"No, I'm waiting for my husband. He is almost free of that woman."

"All right, Mama." Madeleine tucked a

few of Rosaria's straying hairs back under the braid. Rosaria was so proud of her hair and, as her hairdresser came only once a week, insisted on sleeping sitting up in an armchair that Madeleine had bought for her. It had been a struggle with the nurses, but they'd finally made this concession to her vanity.

"So tell me what you've been up to."

"In this prison? Nothing much. A young man in the guise of a doctor has forced me, twice now, to sit with him in a room. He's been trying to prise the *knowledge* from me. He interrogated me for a whole hour this morning."

Madeleine looked at her mother, wondering if someone was taking an interest in her condition and attempting some form of therapy. Perhaps some young geriatrician or psychiatrist with a special interest in paranoid schizophrenia. Rosaria would make an interesting subject, because despite the psychosis and the drugs, she was occasionally very lucid and had an uncanny insight into people, even ones she'd never met before. She could also, despite her strong Hispanic accent, be astonishingly articulate. In contrast to the other residents, who were mainly demented through age, she could be as sharp as the blade of a dagger. Her stare had a daggerlike quality too. Perhaps it was part of the insanity, an ability to reach through anybody's skin with those penetrating dark eyes. Rosaria had always been a strange woman and if Madeleine, at sixteen, had understood that her mother was slowly tipping over the edge, that her magic was transmuting into madness, things might have turned out so differently. Certainly she would not have made that fateful decision . . .

"Well, that's good, isn't it, Mama? The doctor obviously wants to help you. You should take advantage of it. Why don't you tell him all the things that worry you? I'm sure he'd be interested to hear about your life. People are usually fascinated by stories about Cuba and your hair-raising escape from Havana."

There was a sudden rattle of china and she looked up. A young care assistant called Beatrice was maneuvering a tea trolley through the door. Madeleine jumped up to help her, taking the filled teacups from her and placing them on tables in front of the dormant residents.

She put an empty cup on her mother's side table and furtively rummaged in her bag for the small bottle of rum. It wasn't a great idea to mix alcohol with medication, but what the hell, having a tipple was a small pleasure in Rosaria's dreary life. She was pouring a good measure into the cup when Rosaria suddenly grabbed her wrist in a tight grasp, making the cup tip and the rum spill onto the carpet.

"*What is that,* Magdalena?" she cried. "What is that dirty thing on your blouse?"

The cramplike panic of her mother's grip made Madeleine look down at her chest, wondering if some insect was crawling on her. But it was Edmund's brooch her mother was staring at.

Madeleine laughed uneasily. Was the thing so encumbered with evil vibes? "Take it easy, Mama. It's just a brooch. It's not dirty, it's made of pewter." She prised her mother's hand from her wrist and patted it gently to soothe her, but Rosaria's eyes were wide with horror.

"Take it off, Magdalena," she shrieked. "It's not a brooch. Take the thing off. The person who possessed it has *mal de ojo*, the evil eye. It's foul. Wearing it, and so close to your heart . . . It will make you sick."

"Calm down," Madeleine whispered. "Don't yell. The matron will come and tell us off." She quickly unclipped the brooch, dropping it surreptitiously into her bag. "Look, it's gone. Forget it now. Hush now, calm down."

Rosaria was shaking and her hands flapped wildly. "Whoever gave you the object, *hijita mia*, you must never look him in the eye. Promise me that. Never look at him. He will make you ill. He could kill you with *mal de ojo.* Never forget how sensitive you are, Magdalena. You must always be on your guard."

Madeleine stiffened at the memory. *My God,* she thought, *what if she is right?*

She pedaled as fast as she could down Fleming, despite the tropical heat. She crossed Duval, where people, tourists and locals, scurried in both directions as if on an ant trail. The man with the squawking parrot on his head rumbled past on his big pink-and-purple Harley. She turned left on Elizabeth Street and passed Mario's Café. Cuban men were

tossing back their cafesitos and smoking home-rolled cigars in the shadow
of a sprawling jacaranda. A radio tuned
to Havana crackled with a muted rumba.
Her eyes scanned the men, then she
waved at one of them, José Manuel, the
only one on the rum already. He was a
distant relative of Mama's, one-legged
on account of his raft capsizing while
fleeing Cuba. A shark bit his leg bad,
but he was luckier than his buddies,
who'd all been eaten alive. He'd been
found by a shrimper, clinging to the
roots of mangroves in the swamp of
some tiny key. His leg rotted and the
doctors cut it off. José Manuel was on
his second life and celebrated all day,
every day. He always told her to call him
Uncle, pinched her bum (since she'd
grown boobs), and insisted they speak
in Spanish.

The humid air stuck to her like a
drenching mist—and it was still only
May. Even so, she loved this time of the
year, when the thunderstorms would
soon begin and vegetation exploded so
you could all but see it grow with the
naked eye. Tourists would abandon the

town; the thinned-out sunset crowd on Mallory Square became dispirited, less interested in the jugglers and more drunk; and ticky-tacky Duval Street would be like a ghost town but for the few diehards who drank Cuba libres and icy beer under the thatched roofs of cheap bars. Sloppy Joe's and Captain Tony's Saloon would still carry on as usual, having their legacies to maintain. But what could be better than that lazy, quiet torpor settling over the island?

She took a right on Eaton and there in the distance was the vast crown of the banyan tree, a landmark in the whole of the town . . . in her very own garden. A hen with its flock of six little chicks crossed the road and she swerved around them. There was an obstruction ahead, and a man waved a red lollipop at her to slow down. They were digging up the drains again. She pulled into Cherry Lane, behind the fancy Bahamian-style houses where poor black people lived in shacks.

The road was full of potholes and loose gravel and she had to get off and push the bike. That was why she saw the old man she'd been told to avoid, sitting on the lean-to porch of his hovel. The shack had a rusted tin roof and windows and doors curtained in fabric that had long ago lost its pattern to the sun. He was Jamaican, black as coal and with no teeth. Mama had told her never to look him in the eye. He had mal de ojo, *and could make kids real sick. "Those Jamaica people make Yoodoo," Mama said. "They don't use the power to make people better or give love potions or nothing like that." (Mama wouldn't give herbs or spells to make someone sick, not unless the customer really insisted and paid extra.)*

The old man saw her coming and got up out of his rocking chair. He leaned over the railing to catch her eye. She didn't want to and she didn't mean to, but her eye was drawn, she couldn't help herself. As she passed, she looked him full in the face. He smiled his toothless smile. Nah, she thought, what bullshit. He is harmless.

That night she was violently sick. She vomited black fluid that stank of shit. There seemed to be no end to it. Nobody knew what the matter was, not even the doctor from New Orleans who drank with Papa. He wanted to call an ambulance, but when Madeleine confessed her encounter with the old man to her mother, Rosaria refused. She told Papa and the doctor it was a sickness that could not be cured in a hospital, and while they argued hotly about this Mama had already sent for a curandera, *a big black woman by the name of Esperanza. The* curandera *was there in a moment, bringing jars and baskets of* hierbas. *These she burned, wafting the acrid smoke over Madeleine while brushing her naked body with bundles of fresh herbs and bathing her with Florida water. Just as suddenly as her vomiting had begun, it subsided.*

Not long after that, she heard that the old man with mal de ojo *had died. People whispered about his death, which had been painful. Even so, she never went down that lane again.*

Outside Setton Hall the sun was sinking behind the woods. Soon the residents would be collected one by one, given their medication, and tucked safely away in their luxurious rooms for ten hours of dreamless oblivion. Most of them seemed asleep already. The sound of people screeching on the mindless television program sounded eerie in the otherwise muted and dismal atmosphere. Madeleine watched it for a while but when she turned back to Rosaria to comment on the stupidity of the participants who subjected themselves to these pointless humiliations, she had sunk into her chest and was fast asleep. Her upset over the brooch had exhausted her utterly. Her mouth worked rhythmically, moving her dentures round and round. Madeleine studied her face and was weighed down by an overwhelming sadness. Her beautiful mother, so crushed, so helpless . . . how she wished she could have kept her at home. But Rosaria could not be left unattended, not even for an hour. She was quite capable of setting something alight or "sacrificing" the neighbor's cat. And there was nowhere else for her to go, no other child, relative, or friend who could share the burden of her care, and Neville, having happily secured her incarceration, stayed as far away as possible. He was smart enough and selfish enough to say she was no longer his responsibility. Wasn't Madeleine the psychotherapist, he argued, the perfect person to be in charge of the barmy old witch?

Madeleine mopped at the spilt rum on the carpet with a wad of tissues. Rosaria was still sleeping soundly, and finally she decided she might as well leave. She stroked her mother's hand and kissed her forehead but there was no response, even her mouth had finally gone slack and fallen open. Just as she turned to tiptoe away, Rosaria's hand reached out to stop her.

"What, Mama?"

"You didn't listen to what I told you on the telephone. You didn't go home and lock the doors. So now you will have death on your conscience, Magdalena."

Madeleine paused and looked at her mother. Her voice, though quiet, had been unmistakably clear and articulate. Yet her eyes were still closed as if in sleep.

"You are not going to die," Madeleine said soothingly. "Not for a long time. You're still young."

"A rotting body!" Rosaria stammered. *"Fire!"*

"What, Mama?" Madeleine shook her lightly by the arm. "Come on, wake up."

Rosaria's hands started to quiver and her voice faltered. She stuttered, making a great effort to speak. "Magdalena, everything you know is about to change. You will have to leave me. Run away . . . so far . . . as far as you can."

Madeleine bent down on one knee and hugged her mother to her. "I will never leave you. Never! Don't worry." But Rosaria didn't hear her. She seemed fast asleep, almost comatose. Madeleine felt suddenly cold.

"I'll be back very soon, Mama," she mumbled as she got up and hurried away.

There was no one at the nurses' station and she almost ran down the corridor. She ignored the elevator, and her steps echoed on the marble circular staircase. On the ground floor she spotted Mrs. Ollenbach, the inscrutable manager, speaking to Dr. Jenkins, a retired GP who acted as official all-round doctor on the premises. He was a Colonel Sanders look-alike, full head of white hair, goatee, and an impressive mustache. Seeing them there, Madeleine slowed her dash for the door. It was quite difficult to get an appointment with the formidable duo, and an impromptu audience was a rarity.

"Mrs. Ollenbach, Dr. Jenkins," she called out, a bit too loudly. "Hold on a minute. Just a quick one."

"Oh look, here's our Madeleine," Dr. Jenkins said, his fatherly voice smooth as lard. "Lovely to see you." He took her arm and walked her out of the receptionist's earshot. "Isn't it wonderful about Mrs. Frank? She's in good form, isn't she?"

Madeleine frowned. "Really? You think so?"

"Oh, absolutely. So good, in fact, I think we can dispense with the last few sessions of ECT. I just want to alert you to some curious side effects—"

Madeleine cut him off. "ECT? My mother has had electroconvulsive therapy?"

Dr. Jenkins looked at her. "I thought you knew."

Mrs. Ollenbach was just behind them. "I couldn't get hold of you, Ms. Frank," she said, her tone defensive. "So I called your father. Mr. Frank authorized the treatment."

"I don't believe this!" Madeleine turned to her angrily. "You can always get hold of me at my clinic, and I'm here twice a week. Phoning my father should be a last resort, you know that. Why should my mother need ECT? She's on enough medication to flatten a horse."

Dr. Jenkins put up his hand defensively. It was bandaged and cradled in a metal brace. "It's a perfectly valid treatment for depression in the elderly, Madeleine," he said indignantly. "As her doctor, it was my opinion that your mother would benefit, and the psychiatrist agreed."

"I believe these days it's very much a last resort, Dr. Jenkins," Madeleine murmured, trying to tone down her disapproval. "My mother is not elderly and she is not a danger to herself or others. She is eating and speaking. Besides"—she turned to Mrs. Ollenbach—"she tells me you've got some doctor talking to her."

There was a pause.

"Oh well, him." Mrs. Ollenbach laughed awkwardly. "I meant to tell you. One of our visiting geriatricians was intrigued by your mother's background, so he contacted Dr. Alvarez . . . ah, in London. He's not a med-

ical doctor as such. His field is psychoan-
alytic anthropology. His subject is . . .
er . . . tribal cults, bizarre religions, and
that sort of thing. He and Mrs. Frank have
had a few nice little chats. He speaks your
mother's native language . . ."

"You mean Spanish, don't you?" Madeleine asked frostily.

A look passed between the duo.

Madeleine turned to Dr. Jenkins. "You
started to tell me that the shock treatment
has had side effects. What did you mean
exactly?"

The doctor put on his benign Colonel
Sanders smile. A bucket of fried drum-
sticks could have materialized in his arms.
"Oh, how should I explain it? Well, the depression has lifted, at least." He nudged
his partner-in-crime with his elbow. "She
really is onto us, isn't she, Mildred? The
other day she told me I would break my
little finger, and by God, she was right." He
laughed ebulliently, waving his bandaged
hand. "An hour later I got the damned thing
caught in the car door."

Mrs. Ollenbach looked embarrassed.
Madeleine stared at Dr. Jenkins, shaking
her head.

"You will discontinue the ECT treatment as of now. Really, Dr. Jenkins, I don't believe it's right for my mother."

"Mrs. Frank wants a subscription," Mrs. Ollenbach piped up hurriedly, "to some Cuban magazine. I've spotted it on the Internet."

"Anything she wants, Mrs. Ollenbach. Charge it to my father."

Madeleine took her leave, returned her badge, signed out, and hurried through the door. Making her way to the car park, she shivered in the cool breeze. Electroconvulsive therapy! Poor Mama. No wonder she seemed strange. At least it appeared she'd not remembered it. Such a cataclysmic jolt to the delicate tissues of her brain probably caused a wipeout of short-term memory. Yet, what had Colonel Sanders said?

She stopped, distractedly scanning the car park for her Merc. Now where had she read about this? Oh yes, in the library, an article in *Parapsychology Today.* Something about "higher sense perception" following electrical stimulation of the brain. What if the treatment had triggered something dormant in her mother's mind? Her reaction to the brooch . . . her conviction about the new resident . . . Dr. Jenkins's finger. What about the other strange things she'd said? Fire? *A rotting body?*

She backed out of her slot and drove down the avenue, noting that her hand trembled slightly on the steering wheel.

Chapter Five

It was a cool mid-April Saturday and Madeleine got out of bed feeling strangely claustrophobic within her four walls. She wandered downstairs, took the trouble to rig up her coffeemaker, then waited impatiently for the process to come to a gurgling halt.

Back in bed with her mug, conspicuously alone, she grudgingly asked herself: *Do I miss Gordon?* How long was it now, three weeks . . . four? She'd not seen or heard from him since his strange outburst in the garden of the Horse and Cart. Once or twice she'd been on the verge of phoning to ask him why dumping him was such a "grotesque" misdemeanor, especially under the circumstances. She kept asking herself whether she'd been justified in being so irked by his faults, his all-too-easy charm, his unreliability. So he had a number of irritating quirks and habits—didn't some of his good points balance these up? He'd been a wonderful, unselfish lover; he took an interest in her opinions, listened to her, made her laugh. His work was a continual source of fascination to her, and he, in turn, was intrigued by her ant paintings. Well, if she wanted him back, she'd have to deal with being the token "older woman" in Gordon's harem of nubile girls.

No way, forget that!

She told herself the cause of her jitteriness was not a case of sexual frustration, just an appalling lack of exercise. Either way, the former could be cured by the latter. She got up and looked out the window to check the weather. There was a dark cloud cover but no rain, so there were no excuses. The streets seemed empty of traffic and it was unusually quiet.

She picked up the phone and dialed Patricia's number. "Not possible," her husband explained. "Patricia is in the shower and definitely won't be able to come for a run. In-laws coming for lunch."

Still at the window, undecided, she spotted a fox running nonchalantly along the pavement on the other side of the road. In the last few weeks she'd heard their eerie mating calls in the night. The animal continued toward the piece of scrubland some fifty meters up the road. It was a small slice of nature surrounded by houses, and a perfect place for the wily animal to set up home. Suddenly the fox stopped dead and darted back. Madeleine's eyes followed its intended path and saw what had scared it off.

A man was standing fifteen meters up the hill, leaning against the stone façade of a cottage that she knew belonged to a reclusive elderly couple who rarely had visitors. She did not recognize him, but noticed he was looking at her house. Standing back and observing him for a minute or two, she was convinced that his gaze was fixed squarely on her front door. Who the hell was he, and why was he looking at her door? She wondered if there was something of interest on it, like some vandal having nailed a dead rat to it, or sprayed "Yankee, go home" in blood-colored paint.

Well, perhaps he was just a nutter who liked doors; it probably had nothing to do with her. She put on a tracksuit and running shoes and left the house. When the strange fellow saw her emerge, he straightened, threw a half-smoked cigarette in the gutter, and just stood there for a moment as if waiting for something to happen. He was somewhere in his late thirties or early forties, had dark hair and high cheekbones, Eastern European looking.

She closed the door and shook it pointedly, as if to test the lock, and started walking toward the canal. After a few seconds she turned around and saw the door gazer walking speedily in the opposite direction. So he had not been waiting for her to leave so he could ransack her home. *Oh hell, forget it,* she thought, and broke into a slow jog. Within a minute she was on the towpath.

The river Avon is navigable from its mouth all the way to the center of the city of Bath. From that point, a canal connects with the river. This ancient man-made waterway provides a link and through route for canal boats from Bristol in the west all the way to London in the east. In times gone past, shire horses walked the towpath right across the country, pulling barges filled with coal and other goods, but the canal had long since lost the function for which it had been constructed and now existed merely for leisure and for its beauty.

Madeleine often took a small detour to work along the towpath, and was more than familiar with the canal's complex series of locks and pumping stations. In the seven years she'd lived in Bath, she had watched the locks being filled and emptied by boaters hundreds of times. It was much like watching paint dry, a painfully slow process, yet sitting on a bench observing the narrow boats rise up or descend into the emptying lock was a meditative activity that soothed the often dark swirlings of her mind.

The early morning mist was still hovering above the ground and the grass was wet with dew. Tall poplars, oaks, ash, and weeping willows created a green canopy over the water. Madeleine struggled along in a halfhearted jog. The towpath was deserted, save for a man with two wet Labradors who strode past in the opposite direction. The dogs zigzagged purposefully along the path, their noses tracing some important scent.

She ticked off the locks as she went: Wash House Lock, followed by Abbey View Lock, then in quick succession Poultney Lock and Bath Top Lock. She'd told herself she would turn around here, but then felt revived by that reassuring second wind and decided to continue on to Bathampton, a village another half hour away. It had been weeks since she'd had some proper exercise, and it felt good to run.

On the way back her leg started to hurt, and she slowed to a walk. The fracture she'd sustained in the hurricane had healed well, but it was as if her broken bone chose to echo her broken heart. Within its cells it retained the memory of Angelina, and by an intermittent dull ache replayed her loss again and again.

Closer to home she passed a spot where her mother had once knelt in the mud, pleading with her. She should have guessed, even at that tender age, that Rosaria was teetering on the edge of madness.

A fine rain was falling over Bath, and the clouds were black and heavy. Her hideous English school shoes were squelching in the mud. Except for the woman following her, the towpath was deserted.

"Quit chasing me," she shouted over her shoulder to her mother, bitterly regretting having blurted out the truth to her over breakfast.

Rosaria caught up with her and grabbed her by the arm, forcing her to stop. "Look at me, Magdalena. Who is the boy?"

"A guy from home. A shrimper."

"A shrimper, from Key West? Why have you waited this long to tell me, child?" She shook Madeleine by the arm. "Do I know this man? What's his name?"

"Forrest . . . No, you never met him. I didn't know him for long. Go home now, Mama. You're going to get wet and I'm late for school."

"No, we must talk now."

Madeleine wrenched herself free from her mother's grip and backed away, almost slipping in the decomposing sludge of dead leaves. The towpath was very narrow in places and the canal looked murky and cold. Mama had a way of clinging to her with a sticky, needy insistence Madeleine had come to dread, especially in these last months since they'd moved to England. Poor Mama, she seemed so lost, so anxious, she'd grown so dependent on Madeleine. And now this.

"Please don't tell Papa." Madeleine *grasped a strand of her mother's long black hair and let it slide through her fingers. "Look, I was madly in love with the guy, and I've just . . . well . . . buried my head in the sand. But when I woke up this morning it just hit me. It's plain* locura, *isn't it, Mama? Madness."*

"Yes, but—"

"You can do something, can't you?" Madeleine pleaded. "Didn't Esperanza give something to those women back home?"

Rosaria tossed her hair over her

shoulders, her dark eyes flashing. "I know of no such thing." The collar of her gray coat chafed against her throat. Rosaria had never worn a coat in her life, and it looked alien on her. Her dark sultry beauty and colorful clothes were incongruous in this place where people were pale and stylish and spoke with clipped, snobbish accents.

"Well, if you can't, I'm going to see a doctor about it. I've talked to the nurse at school. I'm only fifteen, I'm not ready to have a baby. And the shrimper has gone off to India, so I can't even tell him. Anyway, he was so mad at me because I lied about my age, I doubt he'd wanna know."

She turned away and started walking again, with Rosaria in pursuit. They passed a lock and then another. Narrow boats were moored along the way and it appeared that people lived on them all year round. Bicycles, piles of firewood, and potted plants crowded the roofs, and smoke rose from the chimneys. She loved this route to school for that very reason; it reminded her of Houseboat Row in Key West and people living on the water. But there was no sea in Bath and she missed the smell and sound of it.

Rosaria tried again to stop her, grabbing her hand.

"If you have to follow me, at least don't stop," Madeleine exclaimed, shaking her off.

A young man, fishing from a bend in the canal, heard her. Mortified, she turned away and strode off along the path. For the first time in her life she was embarrassed by her mother. She'd noticed that people in Bath were uncomfortable with Mama's foreignness, and Madeleine had pleaded with her not to divulge that she was a Santera. It was one thing to practice in Key West, where there were loads of Cubans who shared the beliefs, but here in England people would think you were crazy. Even Papa had changed his tune. There was a time when he claimed he owed his fame to the ritual sacrifice of a goat (it made people laugh nervously, and he liked that), but now he didn't want his wife throwing the cowrie shells, and had even forbidden her to teach Madeleine any more "nonsense." Poor Mama. Papa seemed too busy to bother with her, now when she most needed him. He was always in London, "seeing his agent" (yeah, really?) or visiting galleries that might sell his work. Madeleine was secretly determined to go back home, back to Key West, and she'd try and convince her mother to come home too. The two of them didn't belong in this place and they never would.

She hurried along, with Rosaria following closely behind her.

"You listen to me, hijita," Rosaria implored, "killing a fetus is a sin. It's murder."

Without breaking her stride Madeleine pressed her hands to her ears, her fists bunched hard inside her mittens. "Stop it. I'm not listening."

"You can't just choose like that, between life and death."

Madeleine stopped abruptly and turned to face her mother. "Only last year you helped one of your Havana friends. You took her to Esperanza for an abortion. I overheard you."

"That was a different matter," Rosaria

said, her face dark with indignation. "You are too young to understand."

"Oh yes, I do understand. You're a hypocrite. Do you know what that word means, Mama?"

Rosaria stared at her, then sank to her knees.

"Cut it out. Don't be crazy." Madeleine took a step forward, then glanced around, but in the icy morning rain the towpath was deserted.

"C'mon, Mama, get up. I'm sorry. I didn't mean it. I know you were just helping people."

"It's our baby, Magdalena," Mama wailed. "We can't kill our baby."

It was too much. Madeleine tore away from her and ran, her satchel bouncing hard against her thigh, her coat flapping. Before the last bend in the canal, guilt made her stop and turn back. Her mother was still kneeling in the mud on the bank, her long black hair spread around her like a cloak, hands clasped and head tilted back. That haunting image of her anguished and grief-stricken mother imprinted itself on her mind's

eye, and Madeleine knew her fate was sealed.

A sudden downpour drenched her, but the temperature was mild and her body was still burning fuel from the run. She slowed for a moment to keep alongside a mother duck with half a dozen newly hatched ducklings. They were just tiny balls of yellow fluff, but they nipped along in the water at an astonishing speed. She passed a swan she recognized by the black spot at the back his neck. Closer to Bath, narrow boats lined the canal side, some of them in a state of abandon, others housing eccentrics who chose to live there year-round, and the odd family having an early boating holiday. The traffic had started up by the time she approached her house. Nothing seemed untoward, the strange man was nowhere to be seen, and her house had not been ransacked.

Wednesday was her painting day, a welcome midweek break from needy, troubled people. Between her mother, Edmund Furie, her patients, and few friends, she needed time and discipline to keep up her artistic legacy. She'd been a full-time painter in her younger years, and she suspected that someday in the future she would be again.

Yet the peculiar restlessness that had seized her in the last week made it hard to focus. She fiddled about, tinkering with insignificant tasks in the house. It was already two o'clock and she'd not actually got down to any painting. She was finally on her way up to her attic studio when the phone rang. She hesitated but decided to answer.

"Madeleine Frank here," she said wearily.

"Hi, Madeleine. Rob Reese at Rookwood. Sorry to bother you at home. I tried you at the clinic, but your secretary said you paint on Wednesdays."

"That is so, Rob," she replied. "I'm just a part-time therapist."

"What are you painting? Your house?"

"Ants."

There was a pause. "You're painting ants? How?"

"Never mind." Madeleine laughed. "What's up, Rob?"

Rob was the governor's new secretary.

He was a dream compared to the mean, humorless woman he'd replaced.

"Just wanted to tell you in good time, so you can plan something else for your Friday. Edmund is in the sick bay and I doubt he'll be out by then."

"Why? What's wrong with him?"

"He's been taken ill. They're not quite sure what's wrong, but it's genuine. Bad case of diarrhea and vomiting. On a drip. Very twitchy and agitated too . . . you know what I mean. They're having to keep him sedated."

"Oh no! Poor guy," Madeleine said with feeling, remembering how quick they always were to drug Rosaria when she got agitated.

"Poor *guy*?" Rob quipped. "Give some thought to the nurses."

She laughed, embarrassed. "Yes, you're right. But if you get a chance, tell him I said to get better soon, and I'll be there next week."

"Sure." There was a pause. "Does that leave you free on Friday night?"

Madeleine smiled. "Best not mix business with pleasure, Rob, but it's nice of you to ask."

"If you change your mind . . ."

Madeleine said good-bye and started up the stairs, smiling smugly. Yup, it was nice to be asked. Then her thoughts turned to poor Edmund—tied to a bed. When she'd visited him last Friday he had, in fact, looked very pale and wan. He'd seemed listless too, and had not been his hard-hitting, hawkeyed self.

However, he had noticed the absence of the brooch on her lapel and had made a point of asking why she'd not been wearing it. She'd grown fond of the brooch, and Edmund had been genuinely pleased to see it on her. She'd told him it was languishing at the bottom of a bag at home . . . she'd put it there because it had upset her mother.

The brooch . . . Turning back down the stairs yet again, she went to the kitchen, where her capacious shoulder bag sat on the counter. Rummaging in its infinite cavity, she could not lay her hand on it, yet she'd not retrieved it since that upset with Rosaria, just over a week ago now. *Damn!* She turned the bag upside down and shook out the contents. All manner of rubbish clattered over the counter, together with a shower of crumbs, gluey throat lozenges, small sticks and stones she collected for her myrmecarium. She picked through the debris. She knew the brooch should be there, but . . . it appeared it wasn't. She remembered clearly sitting beside her mother last week, in the Setton Hall living room, Mama's extraordinary outburst, and dropping the brooch into the gaping mouth of the bag. It had probably got caught up in a glove or a tissue and fallen out. So the brooch was lost. It was the only explanation.

Feeling unaccountably saddened by the loss, she faced the stairs again, vowing to allow no further distractions.

Inside her studio, a weak April sun shone through a row of roof lights. When she'd bought the house, she'd converted the attic into a work area. It was spacious enough but the ceiling was low. Peering directly down, she could just get a glimpse of her little back garden. The lane behind it backed onto an ivy-covered warehouse, home to a pine furniture factory, and the garden was flanked on one side by a sturdy stone wall. Protected from winds, it was bursting

with life. Though there was no way to rep-
licate the rampant vegetation of Key West,
she had acquired all the subtropical plants,
flowers, and trees that stood a chance of
surviving the English winters. The various
cycads and palms did well, behaving as
though they were rooted straight into Florida soil.

She looked at the blank canvas on the
easel before her. Spring often paralleled
a new beginning in her artistic phases.
She was starting a new series, a whole
new perspective to explore. She had to
put the Cave Series out of her mind. It had
not really been complete; she'd planned
another two paintings, but an ant devotee
she'd befriended through a myrmecology
forum on the Internet had phoned her from
Chicago, and after she sent him photos of
the series, he'd made her an incredible offer for all eight canvases, sight unseen.
The man was obviously ridiculously wealthy.
She knew she should be pleased; the
money amounted to several months of
hard graft in psychotherapy practice. Come
the weekend, she would pack up the paintings. Next Wednesday they would be collected by Parcelforce and shipped off to

Chicago. Neville would be pissed off, but he would have to make do with the photos. The big artist himself felt it was his right to spend a day judging each series in its entirety. He and Elizabeth came to Bath every year for this one and only visit. Neville would spend the day in Madeleine's studio, meditating on the life of her ants while gradually dulling his good judgment with a bottle of Rioja, while Elizabeth would take Madeleine out for a boozy lunch and some retail therapy. Madeleine's stepmother was only nine years her senior and very good company, and Madeleine had long ago forgiven her for stealing Neville away from her mother.

Much as she had tried to move away from ants, other subjects seemed bland. Hadn't everything already been painted? Landscapes were boring, abstract too inert. While still in Key West she'd made an attempt to become a portrait painter. Being Neville Frank's daughter, it had been easy to get commissions, and her sitters had been delighted with the results, but secretly she'd found her portraits lacking in vitality. With Neville's blessing she returned to her favorite subject. The society of ants was lively and vigorous, and her paintings reflected this energy. It came naturally to her; ever since she was a little girl ants had marched relentlessly through her psyche like a life force.

She kneeled on the hot, damp earth in the undergrowth of the giant banyan. Her dress was already filthy around the hem. Her knees were hurting and the bow in her hair had slid down and was stuck to her clammy forehead, but she didn't notice. All she cared about was that the two workers who were carrying the lump of sugar would safely reach the nest. The lump was heavy (she'd had to stomp on it with her heel to smash it up) and they'd already spent more than half an hour trying to get it up the tiled step. The steps had almost disappeared in the foliage. The aerial roots of the ancient tree were like a forest of frozen waterfalls that had descended from the sky and rooted in the ground. The main trunk was gnarled by centuries, and so wide it took ages to walk around.

Up there, way, way up in the branches,

old Angelo the gardener had built a tree house for her, a proper one with a wooden staircase circling between the trunk and the branches, ending in a platform with a fence of old ship's ropes and in the middle a little house, child-sized. It had taken him almost a year to do it, and Papa's friends all wanted to sit up there drinking and looking at the view. They kept telling her what a lucky girl she was. The problem was, she preferred to be on the ground, with her nose in the soil. The vegetation crowded underneath the massive tree, fighting for space, and in this undergrowth lived the creatures that were her playmates.

The two workers pushed the lump awkwardly between them up the vertical surface of the step, but halfway up they fell backward onto the tiles below. It was a huge drop. Madeleine pictured the fall in terms of her own size, and could feel her bones cracking and breaking, her head splitting open like an egg, but she knew their bodies were different. Such a fall would not kill them; perhaps they were bruised and mixed-up, but never beaten. They gathered themselves and began the attempt for a second time. Almost up and they fell again. Madeleine groaned in sympathy and helplessness. Why didn't they just move away from the steps? She could have coaxed them onto a leaf and lifted them to safety, but Papa had told her not to interfere. He often reminded her that everyone, even ants, had to learn that there was no such thing as a God who would sort out your problems. Mama said that the Orishas looked after all creatures on earth. Madeleine was only seven, but she suspected that perhaps Papa was right. Anyway, ants didn't need help, they knew what they were doing. They were so clever and so organized. They'd been building their nests and dragging food to them for eighty million years, far longer than people had existed on earth.

She bent over them. "You can do it," she mumbled soothingly. "You know you can."

Tension mounted in her small body. She held her breath. They fell. They regrouped. On the fourth attempt they tried to pull the lump while crawling backward. Suddenly they got a good hold and were climbing up the wall, rear end first. The lump was dragged up with unexpected ease, until a third worker came darting over to help. Madeleine gritted her teeth hard. She could see where this was leading.

"Don't butt in, you stupid," she cried, resisting the temptation to remove the interloper. He was not privy to the method they'd discovered and was a total nuisance. The two heroes ended up pulling both the sugar lump and the clueless newcomer up the vertical surface. But up they got.

Madeleine cheered and clapped her hands, but not quietly enough. Within a moment, Rosaria's head appeared over the hibiscus hedge, her face framed by the red flowers.

"Magdalena," she called, "look at you. You come in right now, honey, and sit under the fan with Mama. It's too hot outside. I don't want you on the ground, amorcete, you don't know what might come out and bite you."

Madeleine wasn't listening. She'd seen that at the first intersection above the step a large group of ants had gathered around something. She scrambled to watch. A larger red was at the center of the crowd. She didn't much like the reds, she couldn't really fathom why, perhaps because they were bigger and could be fierce, but in a situation like this one, faced with a black mob, one solitary red did not stand a chance. She stared in horrified fascination as it was set upon. Much as she didn't care for the reds, she could see how outnumbered the poor thing was. The blacks swarmed all over it and soon it crumpled and lay still. They left it alone then. Madeleine kneeled down low to examine its injuries. Papa had given her a magnifying glass for her sixth birthday, but it had disappeared. She knew Mama had taken it, it was on the little altar in her bedroom. Madeleine could really have used it now. The red was lying in an unnatural position on its side, curled up all funny. She doubted if it was dead. They often pretended, probably so they'd be left alone.

Madeleine sat up when she heard Neville's car pull up on the drive. She would have gone to him, but she wanted to see if the red would save itself, and whether the blacks would renew the attack. Perhaps just this once she could intervene, barricade them off, just long enough . . .

Her mother was calling her again. She blocked her ears with her invisible pink earmuffs. Mama's voice could not get through those, but she could hear her papa.

"For Pete's sakes, Rosaria. The kid's busy with her ants."

He came up and loomed above her, his straw hat askew and his smelly cigar between his teeth. "What's up, little girl?" he asked.

"Look at this red one, Papa. Do you think it's dead?"

His towering body bent at the knees and his face came down to her level. The smell of rum and cigar hung like a cloud around him. "It's too dark under here. I can't see the bugger without my glasses. Let's put him on a paper and bring him into my studio. You can sit at my desk and draw him." He patted her

on the head. "I never see you, little girl. I wouldn't mind some company."

Neville understood this fascination of hers—had he not fostered her interest in the dark undergrowth of life?—and it suited his vanity to tell people what a peculiar creature his daughter was.

John took a professional interest in her oddity, and his analytical opinion was that her childhood fixation with ants had been a vital displacement activity at times when her parents' stormy and unconventional life became too much for her to handle. Her escape into the predictable world of ants, John argued, was a way to shut out her fear and confusion, brought on by her mother's mystical and spiritual excesses and her father's gradual withdrawal from them both. He argued that Rosaria had probably been stark raving mad all along, and Madeleine had had the common sense to be scared of her. Ants became her "transitional object" that proved far from transitory. Madeleine had laughed at his theory, but probably it had some truth to it.

She stared at the canvas but felt overwhelmed. The new series had been brewing in her mind for a while now. It was the queen she was after, the mother ant, the fat, glossy matriarch. She was at the pinnacle of the society, supreme ruler, with thousands of man slaves in rapt attendance. Madeleine felt she knew her intimately, but when she lifted her stick of charcoal and placed it on the canvas, that moment of divine inspiration she was waiting for seemed suspended by its own disbelief. There was no tingling of the spine or hairs rising at the nape of the neck. There was nothing. In that very moment of nothingness (containing only the rapidly rising fear of nothingness) the phone rang again. Grateful, she dropped her charcoal and rushed downstairs, aware that she never answered the phone when she was in the act of painting.

"Madeleine Frank," she said with a sigh, strangely relieved to hear the sound of her own name.

"Hello, Madeleine."

"Gordon!" She tried, too late, to keep the surprise out of her voice.

"Yes, me."

"What do you want?"

"How are you?"

"Fine, yes, I'm good."

"Meet me for a drink. I want to talk to you about razor blades."

"What do you mean, razor blades?"

"You heard me. Plus, I miss you. I want to see you."

Madeleine paused, flustered. "On the same old terms?"

"Let's go for a drink and talk."

"Life is complicated enough, Gordon. Give me a break."

She hung up. There was no point in negotiating. She liked the man, but wasn't her self-respect fragile enough? Why expose it to such abuse? She looked up the stairs and felt a huge weariness overcome her. To hell with the queen ant. Turning around, she went into the kitchen and, standing by the sink, fixed herself a mango colada, heavy on the rum. Drink in hand, she was again confronted by the mess on the kitchen counter. She stopped and looked at it. Something was not right about the disappearance of the pewter brooch. In her mind's eye she saw Edmund sick with diarrhea and vomiting, agitated, and tied to a bed, twisting and groaning, his mouth frothing and his eyes rolling in his head. Then she saw her mother at her altar, in front of the seven glasses of water, seven sacred stones, and seven Cuban cigars.

Oh, no, Mama! She couldn't! *Could she?*

Chapter Six

Rachel was leaning against the railing, waiting for Sasha to come out of school. Every few minutes she glanced around. She felt relatively safe in Bath, but checking her surroundings was a habit hard to break. After London's underbelly, Bath was like a little paradise, but as she'd been told in Sunday school a million years ago, even in paradise there were snakes. Anyday now, one could be slithering into this suburban haven in the form of Anton. With a shudder she remembered the times he'd shown up at Sasha's school in London, wanting to take him away for the night or the weekend, arguing loudly with her in front of the other parents.

Rachel threw her cigarette in the gutter when she heard that first rumble of noise that preceded an avalanche of kids. The energy of their exit had increased in the last few days, since spring had reasserted itself. They were as frisky as lambs, dying to get out into the open. Suddenly the air was full of voices, laughing, shouting, yelling. Within minutes Sasha came spinning like a whirlwind around the corner, throwing himself against her legs. He was a beautiful child and stood out from the others with his dark hair, deep green eyes, and delicate face. His voice was different too. He'd picked up Anton's accent; that's how influenced he was by his dad.

They set off for the ten-minute walk home, as always doing the detour via the park. Rachel sat on the grass next to the playground, lighting a cigarette, while Sasha went for the swings. She'd known this park her whole life, and the scene had a déjà vu feeling about it, except that Dottie, her mum, had never sat on the grass. She'd sit on a bench with her knitting, keeping a beady eye on Rachel in case she fell off something. Neither Rachel nor Sasha had ever known fields, hills, beaches, where one could walk for miles and miles. In fact, Rachel knew nothing about nature. There had been the odd excursion, of course, and her parents had had a caravan for a while, in Portishead, but Dottie had been one of those anxious mothers who thought children should not explore their surroundings but be told about them via television programs. Being in front of the telly was the safest place in the world, she'd said. Rachel was conscious of the fact that she was treating Sasha the same way. But then, in Sasha's world there *was* danger, menace . . .

As she watched her boy soaring up into the air, something dropped out of his pocket. She saw him notice, and his reaction was peculiar. Dangerous too. He was trying to jump off the swing to rescue it. Rachel flew up and ran to stop him.

"Are you crazy, kid?" she shouted. "You could get killed doing that."

Rachel picked the thing up, then peered closely at it and drew a sharp breath. It was a small photo frame, wrapped lumpily with multicolored plastic strips over a base of cardboard, a small photo pressed into its center.

"What's this, Sasha?" she asked, pulling his swing to a stop.

"We did it in crafts," he said, his eyes shifting away.

"It's great. That's really clever. Did you make it yourself?" she said.

"Yep. It took ages and ages."

"Where did you get the photo."

Sasha looked at her with an odd challenge. "Daddy gave it to me."

"Oh," Rachel trilled. "When was that?"

"Can't remember."

"But we've not seen Daddy since we left London . . . right?"

Sasha leaned his back against her legs (to avoid meeting her eyes?). "Miss Bailey said they use whole cows to make sausages. Do you think they put in cows' eyeballs and bums and dinkies and fannies and everything?"

"Yeah, I think so," she said distractedly. "You go on, Sasha. Go ahead and play on the swings."

She would have liked to know more, but she hated having to interrogate him. It had been three months now, and she felt guilty about depriving him of his father, though she knew it was for the best. The boy had seen too much and he'd been snared into secrecy and lies. Anton had always tried to fasten Sasha's allegiance to him by making him think there was some very special bond between fathers and sons, a bond of loyalty in which mothers, women, could not share. He'd been teaching the kid to be furtive and must have asked him to keep the photo hidden, told him it was secret and that Mum wouldn't like it because she hated Uncle Uri.

She went back and lay on the grass, studying the photo. It showed Sasha sitting on a sofa between Anton and his brother— location unknown. Just seeing her son next to Uri alarmed her. If Anton was dangerous, his brother was lethal. While hating women, he used them mercilessly. Anton was happy to acknowledge that his brother was the brains behind the business. Though Uri was younger by nearly ten years, Anton was in awe of him.

He thought Uri was a genius, with his quick eye for an opportunity and the odd cop on his payroll. They had an icy ruthlessness in common, but otherwise it was hard to recognize them as brothers. Anton was the looker, big but wiry, with green eyes, dark hair, and pale skin. Uri, on the other hand, was stocky, shorter, fairer, blue-eyed, brooding, and silent. He liked to "break in" the girls, especially the scared and reluctant ones, the ones who hadn't quite understood what sort of work they were coming to Britain to do. He did a damned good job on the stroppy ones. He took pride in his ability to make them docile, compliant, vacant-eyed. Making them suffer gave him pleasure. But once or twice he'd gone too far in his efforts to train them.

She'd never forgiven herself. She'd just been a passive witness, too much of a coward. That was what it came down to; she was a coward, and always would be.

Having turned nine tricks, she collapsed into bed at half past three, glad that Anton had not joined her. They were staying temporarily in Uri's house in Camden, and she hated every minute of it. Anton was in the kitchen with two Russian friends. The men had arrived a week ago, bringing two girls with them. There was a lot to talk about

and they were noisy and boisterous, excited about something. They were big drinkers, these Russian guys— vodka they liked—whereas Uri drank mainly beer and Anton preferred cocaine. A lot of his money, the money Rachel earned for him, went up his nose. Still, she could hear him laughing, getting drunker on the Russian vodka, as she fell into a restless sleep.

Sometime later she awoke to a noise in the adjacent room, a sound as if a chair had fallen over. Then a soft, rhythmic whimpering. Next, a girl's voice, squeaky and shrill, pleading. She knew the voice. It was one of the Russian girls, a pathetic little creature that looked no more than sixteen. She would have been pretty had she not been so short and scrawny and her color so unhealthy. Anton had already commented on what a waste of oxygen she was. Besides, she was terrified of everything, and spoke no English. Rachel felt sorry for her, but there was nothing she could do to help her, bar trying to make her eat. The other girl had been robust and mature, a big girl with tits and ass and a hard look in her eye. She'd come to Britain quite willingly, except they'd lied to her about how long she'd have to work to buy back her passport. Once she was here, it was too late for her to change her mind. She'd already been shipped off to Birmingham to begin her years of bonded labor.

She could hear Uri's voice now, low and menacing. Whatever it was he was trying with the kid, it was proving difficult. Soon the blows started. Unlike Anton, who could get wildly angry and totally lose his grip, Uri was methodical, cold-blooded. The beating stopped every so often, and only the girl's hysterical sobbing could be heard. Perhaps Uri was getting it wrong, losing patience with her. Perhaps what she needed was gentle persuasion.

Something else fell over and crashed to the floor. The house was a Victorian end terrace and the walls were thick, but not totally impervious to sound. The Russians downstairs wouldn't care; they'd already got their money for her. The house next door was divided into a dozen tiny flats and the residents tended to be transient and kept to themselves. Still, Uri was being reckless, taking risks; it was not like him.

Why didn't the stupid girl just succumb? It was awful listening to this torture, waiting for . . . what next? But pain was relative, even Rachel knew that. It had taken quite a few beatings to keep her out on the street.

Suddenly there was an ear-splitting scream. Seconds later, someone was running up the stairs, but stopped short of entering the room. A few muffled sounds, another haunting shriek . . . and then silence.

Rachel got out of bed and put her ear to the wall. She heard nothing more. She went back to bed, but the sound of the scream would not leave her; it kept echoing in her head. Two sleepless hours later, just before dawn, she heard the kitchen door open below. She rose again and peered through the window into the shadows, trying to make out who was there and why. Anton's tall frame and Uri's bulk were unmistakable. They were hauling a large bundle

across the yard. Quickly she pulled back, her heart beating wildly. She was sure that if Uri had spotted her, she too would be dead.

"Mum, get Napoleon," Sasha shouted from the swings, breaking into her grim thoughts.

"He's too boisterous. You'll have to train him first," she called back, slipping the photo into her bag. Her memories had brought on a mounting restlessness. She was happier with four walls around her. Though a little boy needed to let off steam, needed to run and play, roll in the dirt.

"C'mon, sweetie, let's go home for tea. You know he doesn't like being on his own. He'll be standing at the door, won't he, wagging his tail, scraping and scraping, wearing down his poor claws."

That did it. It always did. Acquiring Napoleon had been a very smart strategic move. It drew Sasha back to where he belonged.

The enclave of postwar houses, set atop the steep hill overlooking Bath, was flanked to the north by nature. It had an untidy mix of neighbors. The old-timers were modest people with modest means. They had lived there for decades, bought their houses when they were built, and had long ago paid off their mortgages. Some of these houses had been sold on and divided up into flats and bedsits for young people, and those residents too were divided: lay-abouts who could afford no better and students on their way to some better place. Farther down the hill the houses were older and more charming, and in these lived the grown-up version of the students, young professionals who'd bought them for their location and their Victorian appeal. Sleek convertibles jostled for space with long-dead saloon cars on the narrow streets.

To local estate agents, Rachel's dwelling was a "town house," but in reality it was a link house, that unfortunate genre which was not old enough, not new enough, and synonymous with ugly. The only thing the houses in this aberrant enclave had in their favor was an integral garage, the imposing height of an extra floor with a view over the city, the river, and the hills beyond. Also, it was adjacent to the small, crescent-shaped park.

Mr. Bainsburrow, next door, used to try and engage Rachel in tales of when the place was built but she'd never really been that interested. He often brought up the squabble he'd had with her dad over the end link. They apparently offered for it at the same time, and Mr. Bainsburrow maintained that Alfie had slipped a tenner to the estate agent who handled the sales. As he got older, Mr. Bainsburrow often confused Rachel with Dottie, her mother. He used to waylay her on her rare visits to her dad. "You shouldn't have left your husband, Dorothy. He's drinking himself into an early grave."

"Dottie has been dead for years and years, Tom. Quit hassling me every time I come," she'd say to him. "I'm Rachel, remember? The daughter."

"Ah, yes. *The daughter.* A lot of grief," he'd say, shaking his head disapprovingly. "A lot of grief."

Mr. Bainsburrow hardly ever came out of his front door these days, but he sat in his window taking things in, waiting for the meals-on-wheels van and the district nurse to come to bathe him and change the dressings on his leg ulcers.

Sasha waved at him and the old man nodded and gave a thumbs-up sign. Sasha's cheerful presence seemed to lighten him up. There were few other children on the street, and if there had been, they would have been more likely to either goad an elderly man in a window or else not even notice he was there. Rachel gave him a perfunctory wave as she usually did, but as she turned away, she noticed his strange hand gesture. Not a wave but a chopping motion of his hand. She turned back to look at him and he shook his head. She had no idea what he was trying to tell her, but she was used to his odd behavior. She shrugged an exaggerated "What?" back at him, but he just stared at her, stony-faced.

"Do you think Napoleon is sleeping?" Sasha said to her, pulling hard at the sleeve of her jacket.

"Are you kidding?" she said, ushering her son in through the gate. "Now remember what we said: no jumping up! You tell him. We have to train him, or he'll knock over some old fart in the park, and they'll sue the socks off our feet."

Sasha tilted his head and looked at her quizzically. "Yeah, but he's not at the door."

Rachel was trying to fish the keys out of the jumble in her bag. "Of course he is," she said and then stopped. The boy was right. It was quiet. No wild barking, no scraping of sharp claws on the wood panel of the door. Had the stupid mutt already become so complacent? Could he be sick? She didn't know the first thing about dogs. She found the key and ran up the steps to the front door. As they pushed it open they were greeted with silence.

"Napoleon," Sasha shouted, bending forward and smacking his knees several times, in that way that made the dog come charging to him in delight. "Come here, doggy."

But nothing happened. The house was as still and silent as the day they had returned to live there after Alfie's heart attack. Rachel felt a rush of anxiety, wondering what they would find. The dog sick from some rotten crap he'd eaten in the park, or a door or window left open? The damned thing was agile enough.

"Stay here, sweetie, and take off your jacket," she said to Sasha. "I'll go and wake him up." She squinted her "Do as I say and I mean it" look at him, but the look she got back chilled her. She'd seen that dread in his eyes before. Last time, Anton had a grip on the back of her neck, making her whimper in pain.

"Mum," Sasha whispered, grabbing her hard by the hand, "do you think he's run away?"

She looked at his anxious little face. "I don't know, sweetie. He's probably sleeping somewhere."

Suddenly Sasha yanked his hand away and beat his fist against her midriff. "He's not here, stupid."

"Sasha," she growled, grabbing his elbow, "don't hit me, and don't *ever* call me names."

"Daddy calls you names," he countered fiercely, yanking his arm away and running through to the kitchen, shouting for the dog. His shouts reverberated from room to room, his shoes thudding hard on the bare wooden staircase. He was only seven years old, but he sensed the meaning of the silence. He knew the dog couldn't have got out of the house on his own.

Rachel just stood there. What would her son call her next? She had a vision of her darling little boy as a teenager, lashing out at her. Having seen what he'd seen, and heard what he'd heard, what could she expect? And the dog. Gone . . . What did it mean? At once she was galvanized into action. She, too, ran around checking, not under beds or in cupboards, but windows and doors, locks . . . someone had come in, somehow, and taken the dog. Everything else remained undisturbed. Someone had a key.

She'd been waiting for him all evening. In fact, she'd been waiting for three months, since the day she moved in. When the key turned in the lock, she stiffened. The time on her bedside clock said *00:15*. Quickly she got out of bed, still clad in her jeans and shirt. She slipped her boots on, somehow to appear less vulnerable, and started down the stairs to the living room. Below her the door pinged open, the pathetic chain she'd run out and bought, giving way like so much cotton thread. A screw clattered to the floor in the sudden silence.

"Hi, babes," Anton said, quietly pushing the door shut.

"What took you so long?" she muttered.

"I was busy. I'm a working man," he answered cheerily, ignoring her sarcasm.

"Where did you get the key?"

Anton held up his hand to show it to her, dangling it in the air. "Your little friend Lynne give me your dad's address long time ago, since you never." He tapped his temple with a forefinger. "Anton guessed good. You always go back to your daddy. So I copied the keys you had in your box. As your Anton does. Always thinking. Just in case. I find a good map of Bath and here I am." He grinned widely and opened his leather jacket, as if inviting her to join him inside it. The gold medallion at his neck was shining like a sun and his silk shirt shifted in dark purple and black.

So he'd found her. Anton rarely asked her anything. In all these years he'd shown no real interest in where she'd been born, where her dad lived, or what her mum had died of. When they met he didn't care about how she'd come to be waiting on tables in a backstreet café and sleeping in a seedy squat in a run-down east London council estate. Now she realized how naïve she'd been; he'd made sure he knew where she might be, and Lynne . . . some friend.

"That wreck"—he jerked his thumb in Tom Bainsburrow's direction—"tell me your daddy died. Sorry, babes."

She ignored the phony condolences. "Where's Sasha's dog?"

"Oh, the dog is alive and eating good food, meat, don't worry. Of course is Sasha's dog. He can visit the animal when he want. I explain it to him. In the morning."

Rachel had gone down the steps, hoping she could prevent him coming up into the house. The treads creaked and groaned, somehow giving her nervousness away. She stopped halfway down.

"You can't just walk in here."

"Why not?" Anton smiled.

"You might be Sasha's dad, but you are not my partner anymore. I don't want you here. I'll give you my new mobile number. Phone me and you can see Sasha at the weekend." She was aware of how shaky her voice sounded.

"Listen, Rachel." His voice had a dangerous calm to it. "I try to be patient with you, but I think you're not being very nice here."

"Not very nice?" She sneered. "Breaking into my house and stealing our dog, you think that's nice? And what you did just now—that's breaking and entering."

Anton came up the stairs toward her and she moved back, up one step, cursing herself for this show of alarm.

"You think you can keep my son away? This will never happen, babes. You know that. This is too far for me to 'pop in' to visit on the weekend."

"I'm not keeping him away from you," she almost whimpered. "It's the way you are. You give me no choice."

Anton stepped up, and she tried to glare at him, stand her ground.

"Rachel, Rachel," he said, shaking his head slowly, "I know we fight all the time, babes. If you didn't make me angry, we'd be good. You know that. But go away not telling me where you are . . . That's not right, is it?"

"Come over tomorrow and we'll make some arrangement about Sasha."

"Tomorrow? You sending me away in a hotel, are you?"

"I do want the two of you to have a relationship. Really, I do."

His eyes narrowed. *"Relationship . . . ?* With my son? Is that what is called?"

"You know what I mean."

In one agile leap he was up the stairs and had her wrists in his grasp. "You don't understand, do you? I want to be with *you* too, you stupid bitch. We are together if you want or not. You the only woman that keep me turning on, year after year. I keep trying the others. They bore me. After few days I throw them out of my bed. Is you I come back to."

"Isn't that sweet." She sneered. "I'm touched." She tried to wrench her arms away but he squeezed her wrists hard and held her arms out, away from her body. She hated her own reaction—a sudden constriction in her womb. He sensed it and smiled.

"You said it. You are sweet, I can tell, hot and sweet and wet, even after all these years . . . isn't that say something?"

He pulled her close to him and wrapped his arms around her waist. "You are mine. You hear what Anton tell you?"

She looked into his green eyes, eyes she had loved, lost herself in, so many hundreds, thousands of times. She felt herself go limp, giving in. It was always the easiest way, the safest way. *The soft option.*

He was already unbuttoning her shirt with one hand, his other still firm around her waist. "Oh God," he whispered, "I miss you." He pushed up her bra and put his mouth over her nipple. She felt it tightening, responding, the sensation shooting right down to the place between her legs, like a quivering, humming current. She looked down at the coils of his hair, glistening, smoothed meticulously into a ducktail and flecked with dandruff. It brought her back and she tensed. She used to think he was the most gorgeous male animal that ever walked the earth, but he had changed—or she had. His black leather jacket and the hairstyle were ten years out of date; he didn't know it, but now he really looked like a pimp, or a caricature of one.

He stopped, having sensed her cooling, and looked up sharply.

"Was the matter?"

"Let's quit this. I don't want it."

"You got me going now," he said, pressing his hands down the back of her jeans. "Come on. You want it. You don't think I know how you work? You just need a little convincing."

"No I don't."

"All right," he hissed breathlessly, "just do *me* then." He put his hands on her shoulders and pressed her down on the stairs. She knew she should try and fight him off, but there was always Sasha. He would wake up and hear them, or worse still, see them.

Anton stepped up between her knees, his hands worked fast, undoing his belt, unbuttoning his jeans, and bringing forth his erection. She looked at it dispassionately. It was in that state she'd liked it the best. Hefty, but not too hard, foreskin still smooth over the large head. Velvety and warm and wanting her.

He didn't mind waiting, enjoying the anticipation, looking down at her, his hands caressing her hair, feeling her cloven earlobes between thumbs and forefingers. She could just do it, and at least she'd not have fucked him. It seemed ridiculous, but she imagined confessing this to her high-on-her-horse therapist. Of course she wouldn't, but the thought made her sick.

"I'm not doing this," she said resolutely, turning her face away. "Sasha might wake up. He's really upset about the dog."

"He sleep just fine," Anton said, his breath ragged. She could hear the smile in his voice. "Anyway, what wrong is it his parents loving each other?" He turned her face back to him and guided his penis to her mouth, letting it stroke her lips back and forth, softly, waiting for them to yield and let him in.

"This isn't love," she said, leaning away. "This is a blow job and not something for a seven-year-old to see."

His fingers tightened around her hair. Wordlessly he pressed himself deep into her mouth. She held back first, then gave way, feeling that rush of desire for him. Just as suddenly she felt nauseous, sick at her own wanting. This was so vulgar, her reaction so inappropriate, yet the whole scenario so familiar. She was consenting, but still, it was a form of rape. She had said NO. *It was rape.* To test this notion she pushed at his hips with her hands, trying to remove the invasive organ from her mouth, but just as she'd thought, he wouldn't let her. Instead his hands grabbed her around the back of the neck and his movements became more urgent. That's what he really liked—a bit of resistance, not too much, just enough.

"Oh, but you *do* want it," he crooned. "Come on, you do, you do."

She thought about it, and about what was being done to her. Hadn't she enjoyed giving him this pleasure in times of love? Enjoyed every part of him and his "love-making." Even the rough bits. She'd acted resistant, to egg him on. She'd brought this on herself.

Conflict battled within her. One part of her knew that the man forcing himself down her throat was close to ejaculating, a minute away at the most, and when he'd finished he'd be satisfied, happy, gener-ous; he might even go away. The other part of her felt a growing outrage. Why must she endure this when she'd said no, wait until he emptied himself into her as if she was no more than a pail for spent sperm? She tried to twist away from him, but his hands were hard, clamping her head, his hips bucking, his breath sharp. The more determined she was to get away, the deeper and more vigorously he thrust.

"You so good at this, babes," he groaned, oblivious to her resistance, or not caring. "No one take it like you. You know that, don't you?"

So she closed her teeth on him. Slowly she bit down, but too soon into this deliberate act of vengeance he cried out and struck her hard on the temple. She saw a burst of yellow flecks on a jagged black background and fell away. Half blinded by the blow, she could hear him snarling like an animal. Another punch, another shower of stars. The edge of the stairs, one by one, scraped her neck, her back, and thighs as he pulled her by the arms up to the living room. Through a haze of pain she felt him trying to pull her boots off. It wasn't easy; they were tight. She kicked out and grazed his chin with her heel. He seemed to feel no pain but tore at her boots until she felt as if her hips were about to pop out of their sockets.

They fought hard and he laughed, as if this was a game they both enjoyed; a little pain was par for the course; he could take as good as he gave. But somewhere deep inside Rachel, *beyond* her, almost, grew a fierce resolve. Every part of her—mind, body, and soul—resisted him.

All through the act she didn't dare look up the stairs; she felt she would have died if the child had been there watching his mother slap and claw at his father's face while he, growling like a rabid dog, bucked and shoved himself into her.

With her eyes closed she kept fighting till the end, wishing she'd been braver, quicker at the outset, and had finally had a taste of his blood.

Chapter Seven

Your mother seems to think you are in some kind of mortal danger," Dr. Jenkins said. "She is totally obsessed by the idea."

Mortal danger! With an uneasy feeling in her belly, Madeleine shifted the phone to the other ear. "The last time we spoke, you told me how much better she was. Due to the ECT, remember?"

She could hear the noisy exhalation whistling through his mustache. "I said your mother was less *depressed*, Madeleine. I did *not* say her psychosis had been cured."

"Oh, you know mothers, Doctor. Aren't

their children always in mortal danger?"
Madeleine said and glanced up at the
clock. Two o'clock exactly. Eric Fyfield was
a new patient and she didn't want to keep
him waiting. Yet there had to be a good
reason for Dr. Jenkins to phone her at work
like this. "I'll try to convince her I'm fine."

"Well, listen. I was coming to that." He
paused for a moment. "I know this is hard,
but I think it would be best if you didn't visit
so frequently. For whatever reason, lately
you are the trigger for these anxiety at-
tacks in your mother. Your last few visits
have left her very agitated. It takes the
nurses quite an effort to calm her down."

*Yes, she's told me. They manacle her to
her bed and administer an injection.* "Well,
all your residents have their episodes and
crises, don't they, Dr. Jenkins? If they
didn't, they wouldn't be in your excellent
establishment. I can't see how depriving
my mother of the only person that loves
her—"

Dr. Jenkins cut in. "Mrs. Ollenbach and
her team do their best for your mother, you
know, what with the shrine and the candles and sleeping in a chair. Did you know
that some of our most exotic specimens

from the tropical fish tank often find their way to your mother's altar?"

Madeleine suppressed a giggle. Tropical fish! Well, where else was Mama going to find live creatures to sacrifice? Babalú-Ayé, her Orisha, was a deity who demanded proper blood if he was going to bestow a favor of any magnitude.

"*All* your residents are challenging, Doctor."

"Your mother is a case unto herself, Madeleine. I hate to say this to you, but I think we need to increase her medication."

"No!" Madeleine protested. "No way. She's not to be made into a zombie for the nurses' convenience." Immediately she regretted the accusation. She knew Rosaria could be a handful, but Neville had provided half a fortune for her care and it was appalling what they did to the residents, making them into barely breathing vegetables.

There was a pause and she was just about to apologize.

"Now, Madeleine," Dr. Jenkins said sternly, "you are in no position to judge your mother's condition from day to day."

"Of course not. I'm sorry. But I can't consent to you increasing her medication. I just hate what it does to her."

"Well, we'll talk about it next time you come in . . . And that's another thing. Your mother is talking obsessively about a child. She's convinced you have a child. That's not correct, is it, Madeleine? I was under the impression that you—"

"Quite right," Madeleine interrupted sharply. "It's a fantasy Mama has always had, or a hope perhaps," she lied. "See what I mean, she needs me. I'm the only child she has."

The prison was built in a star shape, a large hexagonal block from which six spurs radiated, each housing different categories of prisoners. Each spur in turn had a central corridor lined on both sides with cells, and was guarded at its source by two sets of steel doors.

The spur in which Edmund was confined had additional security, bigger cells, and more comforts for the prisoners because most of them were lifers. They were not regular lifers, however; they were segregated for the danger they posed to staff and other prisoners, as well as for their own safety.

Madeleine walked gingerly down the spur, watched by a prison officer at the door.

"Praise the Lord! A woman!" One of the prisoners was leaning his head through his hatch and shouted after her. "Get that gorgeous little ass over here."

She was used to this. What could she expect in a place full of sexually frustrated men, murderers, serial rapists, violent sex offenders, and pedophiles?

Edmund Furie was waiting for her, and he'd heard the fellow. In addition to his viciously twisted face, there was a big bulge on his forehead.

"What's happened to your head, Edmund?"

"I was taking care of people like the arsehole who just spoke to you. If you think my forehead looks bad, you should see theirs. I put one of them in hospital with fucking brain damage."

"You're forgetting your pledge not to use the F-word in my company."

Edmund seemed dangerously agitated. "Aren't we holier-than-fucking-thou today?" he snarled.

Madeleine was tired and not on her guard. You had to tread carefully around Edmund, yet at the same time he was so needy. "You were the one who insisted on the fucking pledge, remember?" she said, trying to smile.

He laughed then, exposing his multiple rows of shark's teeth.

"Right you are, Madeleine. But if that piece of shit speaks to you again, I'm going to kill him."

"Aren't you in enough trouble . . . for killing people?"

They were quiet for a moment, looking at each other. It had been a slip of the tongue. Madeleine never brought up his crimes; it was better that way. She didn't want to be in the confessional role, she had enough of that at the clinic. This was supposed to be an easy friendship, lightening the monotony and tedium of Edmund's life sentence. Yet in many ways, she was in it for herself. Nobody does anything for nothing. What she told herself was that she was serving her own sentence, yet she suspected she was attracted by the danger, some dark side of her that was nurtured between these grim prison walls. Aside from her murkier motivations, there was something overtly rigorous about her relationship with Edmund that cleansed the woolly feeling she was often left with at the end of the week. Between him and Rachel they seemed the only "real" people she was dealing with at the moment. The gritty realities of their lives was paradoxically almost a relief, certainly compared with the elitist concerns of her other patients.

"I missed our meeting last week," she said, meaning it. "I heard you were really quite ill."

"I don't believe in illness," Edmund said harshly. "It's a weakness."

"Is it?" Madeleine smiled. "We can be allowed to be weak, once in a while, can't we?"

"Speak for yourself," he snapped. "My sickness did not come from within, that I am sure of. Once I decided to fight back, it lost its grip."

Madeleine felt a sudden icy current travel the length of her spine. "Not from within?" she echoed. "Do you think some-one tried to poison you here in prison?"

"Who knows, my beauty?" he said vaguely.

In her mind's eye she imagined her mother at her altar, Edmund's brooch in a bowl before her. Her hand went involuntarily toward her left lapel. Edmund noticed it.

"You're still not wearing the brooch," he said.

"No." She looked at him. "I'm sorry. It seems to be lost. It must have slipped out of my bag."

He looked at her for a long moment, disbelief in his eyes. "A Freudian slip, was it?"

"*No*," she blurted defensively. "I have no reason to lie to you."

It was the goddamn truth . . . but where was the brooch? In whose possession was it at this very moment?

"Let's change the subject," said Edmund, seeing she was distracted. "Tell me about a patient. I just want to listen to your gorgeous multiaccented voice. I dream about your voice."

"Very well," she said, relieved. "You'll

find this interesting, Edmund, having a touch of the affliction yourself. This new patient I have spends most of his nights driving back and forth between his home and place of employment, convinced he's knocked over a child on a bike or some old lady crossing the road. Every time he makes the journey, he's sure he's caused some horrific accident, so he has to return to check, in an everlasting cycle. There can be up to twenty journeys a night. Finally the poor guy is so exhausted and confused, he has to pull into some car park or lay-by and sleep at the wheel."

"What would he do if it actually found his victim?"

"Take him or her to hospital, naturally."

"Hold on. Don't tar me with the same brush," Edmund protested. "My own obsessive-compulsive tendencies are based squarely on logic and facts. It sounds as if your patient is a bit dim. He hasn't worked out that as he never actually finds a victim, he is therefore not causing any accidents."

"The compulsion springs from his subconscious. He knows it's irrational but he still believes he is a danger to society."

"I'd say he's a hopeless idiot."

Madeleine sighed. "Now you see why I shouldn't be telling you these things. It's bordering on unethical."

"Oh, hell," Edmund protested with a dismissive wave of the hand. "How would I know who your patient was? Did you get rid of the boyfriend?" he asked, smoothly passing from one subject to another. The intensity of his gaze made her own eyes shift; she could look at him, but not really in the eye. In her line of vision was a vein on his bulging forehead. Pulsating, it looked like a worm making its way across his head.

"Well, did you?" he barked suddenly.

"Yes," she shot back angrily. "Not that it's any of your business."

"You know something, my beauty?" He leaned into the hatch. "I can do away with anybody, even from in here."

"That won't be necessary, thank you, Edmund. Now stop being creepy, or I'm not coming back."

"That sounds like blackmail."

Her anger flared. Did she really need this? "And it sounds as if you are threatening my acquaintances."

"My long arm could reach you too, if I wanted it to."

"Isn't that nice? That's just the sort of friendship I need in my life. A nice caring friend who threatens to string me up to a beam and open my veins for a long bleed to death."

Madeleine drew back, her eyes wide. It had been said in anger—what was she thinking of? She'd sworn she'd never get into the details of his crimes. It would start an aspect of their relationship that she was simply not equipped, emotionally and professionally, to handle.

Edmund could, as always, read her feelings, and he hung his head in shame. She knew that a psychopath was incapable of remorseful feelings, so his contriteness was phony. Perhaps it was fear of losing her. Fear was one emotion that no one escaped. The worm on his head had paled and stopped pulsating.

"Don't leave me, Madeleine," he said to the floor. "I need you." He looked up at her. "You might need me too. I can look out for you, and I'd never, ever do anything to hurt you. If I reach out to you from in here, it would only be to protect you. I was not implying anything else."

She saw that he meant it. How many times had he pledged his undying commitment to their friendship? He was a brutal, ruthless, sadistic murderer, but on some deeper level, she trusted him. She couldn't even explain it to herself. Suddenly she felt exhausted by his sheer need. Wasn't this part of her own screwed-up pathology, this punishing routine of doling out emotional aid, paid and unpaid? John was right, she couldn't take care of everybody forever. Her wise colleague had told her more than once that she was on some sort of codependent merry-go-round, and what she really needed was therapy for herself to sort out the guilt she carried. He thought it was Forrest's death she felt guilty about and tried to make up for. Of course it was, but that was just the half of it. If only he knew . . .

She turned back to focus her eyes on the man in the hatch. Where would this end? Was she going to visit this murderer every week for a lifetime? The brooch he'd given her said it all too clearly: *Commitment forever, till death do us part.* Perhaps she *had* lost the brooch on purpose. A Freudian slip, as he said. If that moment came when she would want to say good-bye to him, would she be afraid . . . afraid of his long arm?

"OK, Edmund." She smiled. "Tell me about this head-butting business. I'm all ears."

Chapter Eight

The phone rang. It was Sylvia's voice, a bit clipped and very low. "Damaged patient coming through."

"Thanks."

Madeleine smiled wryly. *Damaged patient!* Weren't they all damaged? Even the therapist herself, and her colleague and the receptionist.

She'd had a quick scan through Rachel Locklear's notes to remind herself of her history and the issues that had arisen in the previous session. Rachel had—to Madeleine's surprise—been faithfully attending therapy for seven weeks. Madeleine expected each of their sessions to be their last. It was a mystery why Rachel kept coming, considering her complaints about the cost, her defensiveness, and sometimes her apparent dislike for her therapist. Moreover, much as Madeleine kept attempting to hack a path through the jungle of their conflicting agendas, therapy was not really moving forward. There was no shift, no breakthrough. Rachel was not nearly ready to tackle any deeper issues, but was obviously getting something out of it, or she would not keep coming back. Madeleine's own agenda was to discover who she herself represented for Rachel, what sort of transference this woman was working out on her therapist. The anger was palpable. Perhaps her mother had not been the paragon of virtue and benevolence that Rachel claimed she had been. Perhaps guilt at being the survivor had made the adolescent Rachel elevate her mother to sainthood, suppressed the "bad mother." That way she could keep pretending to herself that her mother had been wonderful and take her rage out on a substitute mother, the therapist.

When she opened the door Madeleine

could barely hide the jolt she felt. This *was* a damaged patient. Rachel was wearing large sunglasses, but there was no disguising a swelling on her right cheek and bruising to her jaw and forehead that, though not fresh, was colored in blue and yellow.

"My God, Rachel." Madeleine closed the door and placed her hand on Rachel's shoulder. Rachel stood motionless, but as she turned toward her neither of them could avoid what it seemed they least expected. Rachel walked into her arms and Madeleine enclosed her in an earnest embrace. She was surprised and taken aback by the move on both counts. This thorny, tough, and obstinate woman was allowing herself—no, was *asking*—to beheld, and Madeleine, who rarely hugged patients, had responded instinctively to her need.

I can do this, she decided, trying not to think about the various debates on the wisdom of touching patients, of offering physical affection, consolation, or support. To hell with that. This felt real, and important.

Rachel made no move. Her arms hung limply from her shoulders and her forehead rested on Madeleine's shoulder. The moment lengthened but Rachel was still motionless, as if she'd like to stand there forever, encircled by human arms. Was there no other person in her life who could do this for her? No friends, aunts, neighbors that she could turn to? She'd never admitted to having anyone.

Finally Madeleine loosened her hold and gripped her by the shoulders. "Come and sit down. I want to know what's happened to you."

Rachel was dressed as usual in tight black jeans—though she'd exchanged leather for denim as the weather was warmer—and her trademark scuffed cowboy boots, but instead of the usual cotton shirt she wore a black roll-necked sweater bunched up under her chin. What sort of damage was it covering up? Madeleine wondered.

"Would you mind taking off your sunglasses?" she asked gently.

Rachel hesitated for a moment, then carefully removed the glasses with both hands, as if the slightest touch was painful. Madeleine sat forward in her chair and looked at the injuries, trying not to wince.

The right side of Rachel's face was yellow, the area around the eye purple, and the eye itself partially closed up. The other side had fared less brutally, but a burst blood vessel made the left eye look as if it was bathed in blood.

"Has a proper doctor looked at that?"

Rachel did not respond at first, as if the question was mere superficial pleasantry and not pertinent to real life. Madeleine waited.

Eventually she shrugged and said, "It's only bruising really. The last thing I need is some doctor putting the screws on. Mind, I think I might have to see a dentist." She half opened her mouth and pushed at a molar with her forefinger. "It's the second time this one has come loose."

"Anton?"

Rachel shrugged again. "Who else?"

"So he found you?"

"Are you implying I went looking for *him*?"

Madeleine shook her head with a sigh. "With you, Rachel, I try quite hard not to imply anything. Should I even bother to ask if you called the police?"

Rachel eyed her with weariness. "You

don't seem to get it, do you? I don't involve the fuzz in my private life, but don't worry." She leaned forward and placed both hands, bunched into fists, on her knees. "I'm not taking any more of it. Do you hear me? He broke into my house, *my house*, he beat me up, he raped me, he stole my son's dog, he took all the money out of my wallet. It wasn't much, just fifty-odd quid, but he fucking *robbed* me. *The mother of his son!*"

Madeleine gasped, trying to contain the horror she felt. "Oh, Rachel! I can't imagine what that must have been like. I hope you—"

Rachel cut her off with a dismissive wave of her hand. "I've decided that come what may, he'll never ever do any of that to me again." She stared almost threateningly at Madeleine, willing her to challenge this statement. "Do you hear me, Madeleine. *Never!*"

Madeleine nodded in silence, holding back a heartfelt "hallelujah" and noting that it was the first time Rachel had addressed her by name.

"You don't believe me?" Rachel barked after a moment.

"Yes, I do," Madeleine said evenly, "but how do you think you can enforce your decision? Grievous bodily harm, rape, and robbery is by definition not something you *choose* to be party to. It's beyond your control or it wouldn't be defined as such."

"Well, there you go," Rachel said angrily. "Always looking on the bright side. You're not going to believe me because you think it's my choice to be Anton's personal sex slave and batting ball."

"Hold on. I thought it, because that's what *you* keep saying. You *did* tell me you got off on violence and that you were addicted to the bastard."

Madeleine gritted her teeth unhappily. That impulsive embrace and brittle mutual warmth had, within mere minutes, deteriorated into a tense who-said-what. Why was it necessary to remind the poor woman of the fact that she had, consciously or not, made those choices? The appropriate thing was to genuinely validate her resolve, to be supportive and empathic.

Madeleine pulled her chair nearer, her stockinged knees almost touching Rachel's scuffed denim.

"Listen," she said, emphatically, reaching over and putting a hand lightly on Rachel's arm. "You would not believe how pleased I am to hear you say that you won't put up with it anymore. I can see you really mean it."

She saw a myriad of thin scars criss-crossing the inside of Rachel's forearm. Then she remembered the torn earlobes, which the abundant hair covered up. Her life had marked her in so many ways. "I'm with you all the way, Rachel."

Rachel's battered face softened a little, but her arm felt tense under Madeleine's hand. She looked at their point of physical contact for a moment, then slowly withdrew, crossing her arms over her chest.

"It was a sudden thing, you know. I went cold on him. It was partly that I was terrified Sasha would wake up and see us . . . having sex. Ha . . . that's a turn for the books, isn't it? I was more terrified of Sasha seeing us than I was terrified of Anton. I wanted to stop what he was doing to me. He's used to me struggling a bit, because those were the sort of fucked-up games we played. I tried to stop, really meaning it, but when I sunk my teeth into him, I got much worse than I gave." She sat back, pointing to her face. "And this is just the visible damage."

"You bit him?"

"Where it counts, but not nearly hard enough. It didn't stop him."

An unnerving picture of this scenario flashed through Madeleine's mind. She waited a moment to see if there was more. The details of Rachel's ordeal were important only if she herself thought it helpful to recount them. Madeleine hoped they could explore the promising resolve of hers, and from where it grew. Caring more about her son's reaction to seeing his parents in sexual congress than her fear of (and possible arousal by) that depraved and dangerous individual was more than positive. Rachel's sense of responsibility toward herself and her son . . . But Madeleine's *instinct* wanted her to move with practicalities. How to get Rachel to see that she was always going to be vulnerable if she tried to handle this on her own? How could she possibly protect herself if she refused to involve the police? At least a restraining order might be enough to make Anton take notice. But she knew that bringing this up, like a broken record, would only piss Rachel off, and the mood between them was delicate. It felt as if they were on some cusp . . . a leap in trust, a sense of alliance. They were in this together, and Rachel was clearly starting to feel that she could count on Madeleine's unconditional support and esteem.

"Rachel, biting a violent man . . . What you did was very dangerous. There are better ways of dealing with—"

"You're about to bring up the police again," Rachel interrupted angrily. "Well, fucking don't."

Madeleine paused before answering. She was used to all sorts of emotions being hurled at her, but Rachel's aggression was tiring. She was about to say something to that effect.

"I'm sorry," Rachel blurted out, as if she had read her thoughts. "I'm foul, right? You're surprisingly tolerant about it. I'm amazed you've not thrown me out by now. You wouldn't let your own daughter speak to you like that, would you, let alone a stranger?"

There was something in this unexpected declaration that made Madeleine ill at ease. "Whoa," she exclaimed, putting her hands up in mock defense. "It's not like you to be complimentary, Rachel. Or to apologize. What the hell would I do with you if you were to turn *nice*?"

Rachel smiled. "We *are* getting somewhere. We've established that I'm a bitch?"

"And I like you just fine as a bitch, Rachel. Don't feel you have to change anything about the way you are with me. What we're trying to do is change the way you are with Anton, and the way you treat yourself." Madeleine glanced at Rachel's scarred wrist, which had been uncovered by the sleeve of her sweater.

"How I am with Anton? I told you, I'm through with him. I'm too old to be an idiot. Enough's enough. This is *the definitive* new start. I'll be twenty-seven . . ." She stopped dead.

There was a pause. Madeleine frowned. "Twenty-seven?"

Rachel looked away, gritting her teeth angrily. "Yeah, well. I know I look like shit."

Twenty-seven. It seemed she'd given her real age away by accident, by being too relaxed, off her guard. Rachel was a striking woman, beautiful even, and sexy in a slightly sleazy way (or was that Madeleine's own prejudice, knowing what she knew about her patient?), but she looked years older than twenty-seven. It was no wonder. Drugs, fags, prostitution, and beatings don't amount to a drink from the fountain of youth.

"You told me you were thirty-three. Why did you feel you needed to lie to me?"

"Have a guess!" Rachel shrugged. "How old do I *look*?"

"Today you don't exactly look like a spring chicken," Madeleine said with a smile. "OK, fair enough. Women lie about their age."

Rachel said nothing. Suddenly she looked restless and fed up. Madeleine got a strong feeling she was on the verge of offering some excuse to leave. Perhaps this age business was a big issue for her, though she'd certainly never given the impression of being vain. Maybe it was being shown up as a liar, but again, she was always evasive and economical with the truth.

"You look unhappy, Rachel."

"I'm dying for a fag. Why the hell can't you allow smoking in here? What sort of therapy can you do with someone whose nerves are cracking up for want of a smoke?"

Madeleine looked at her for a long while, her mind churning. Something felt strange; she could not put her finger on it. The feeling grew, making her jittery.

"Take five minutes and go out into the passage."

Rachel seemed taken aback. "Hey!" she said finally and bent to get her bag. "Why didn't I think of that?"

Madeleine stopped her with a gesture. "Leave your bag here, or you might be tempted to clear off," she said. "I'll be waiting. Five minutes."

"Such trust!" Rachel smirked, taking her packet of cigarettes and her heavy silver lighter out of her bag.

Madeleine looked at the lanky figure as she left the room. She got up and put her ear to the door. She heard Rachel say something provocative to Sylvia, and Sylvia retort in turn. Those two would murder each other, given the opportunity. As soon as she heard the clinic door bang shut and the distinctive clop-clop of Rachel's cowboy boots down the wooden stairs, she picked up the phone.

"Sylvia, have a quick look at Rachel Locklear's personal details form, and give me her birth date, will you?"

Sylvia must have sensed the slight note of urgency in her voice, because just seconds later she answered, "She's left it blank, I'm afraid."

"OK, thanks."

She put the phone down and sat back in her chair. The seconds ticked by. A sudden impulse made her get up.

What the hell do you think you're doing? she asked herself as she perched on her patient's chair and carefully groped around in Rachel's bag. *This is outrageous. You'd be struck off for this, you'd lose your practice. You'd deserve it.*

A wallet! She opened it, her heart beating hard against her chest. There was a small photo in the clear plastic pocket, a photo of a boy. Sasha, no doubt. She looked at it briefly. Curly black hair and large eyes, slightly almond shaped. A cute kid, quite foreign looking.

A dog-eared NHS medical card stuck

out of a slot and she pulled it out. *Rachel Locklear.* The name was clear enough; she'd not lied about her name. Madeleine breathed out a long sigh, and lifting the tattered, half-torn medical card to the light, she scanned it for a birth date.

Oh God!

She felt the blood drain from her face. Impossible! It was a date she would never forget till the day she died.

"It's a girl, petal," said the midwife and laid the baby on her chest.

She was a big woman with a curious accent and a funny way with words that had made Madeleine smile despite the agony. The woman patted her on the cheek. "I was worried about them narrow hips of yours, but you're a joy, petal. So brave, you are. Not many girls have their babies at home. It takes courage."

"What's this stuff on her? She's all right, isn't she?"

The midwife chuckled. "I'll wash the clats off her as soon as you've popped out the rest. You just try to get her to suckle."

Mama stood beside her, big eyes brimming with tears, but Madeleine was grateful she had not interfered. Now her mother cupped her hand over the baby's head. "Magdalena, that is the most beautiful child I have ever seen."

Madeleine looked down at the little girl. My God . . . she was beautiful. This is my daughter, *she told herself.* Forrest's daughter. *Already her little mouth was puckering, blindly searching for the source of food. She remembered Forrest's lips around her breast, nine months ago, and now, his child. It was as if the wheel of her life had spun a quick cycle, too quick, and she was meeting love in the same place, yet so different.*

"Is she about the right size?" Madeleine said to the midwife. "She looks real small."

"She's a right butterball, petal. A good nine pounds. I'll get the scales from my car in a minute."

Rosaria grabbed Madeleine's hand and kissed it repeatedly. "I prayed to the Virgin of Copper to give you strength, and she heard me. You did so well. I didn't want to tell you, but there was

lightning, and one struck as the child appeared."

Madeleine grinned despite another tearing pain. "Oh come on, Mama. Lightning? I never saw that."

"Your mum is right," said the midwife. "There was lightning. Perhaps we'll have that thunderstorm yet. Look at the wee one, she knows a teat when she sees one."

Rosaria held Madeleine's hand in hers. "Your child is born to Changó, hijita. She has a strong soul."

Madeleine saw the midwife looking at her mother, no doubt wondering about this beautiful woman in colorful clothes and a strange hairstyle. 'What's that . . . Changó?' the midwife asked.

"The God of thunder and lightning," Rosaria said with passion.

"Righty-o," said the midwife, turning away to hide a smile. "My own daughter is a bit of thunder. But she sure lights up the place when she's happy. Changó! Wait till I tell her." She patted Madeleine on the shoulder. "You'll see, petal. It means the wee one will be a right handful."

"Madeleine has me—her mama—to guide her." Rosaria put her slender brown hand over her heart. "This could easily be my baby. I'm only thirty-seven."

The midwife glanced at Madeleine and a look passed between them. Mama had had three miscarriages and she was still trying. More than anything, she wanted another child.

Another pain cut through her and after it ebbed, exhaustion came over her like a thick blanket. "Call Papa quick. He's got to see this."

Rosaria bent over the tiny girl, kissing her damp head. Then she went to the door and called softly down the stairs for her husband. Neville appeared, nervously hovering in the doorway.

"I won't come in, little girl," he said. "I'm squeamish about women's stuff. But well done. When you're all cleaned up, I'll come and have a peek."

"Don't be ridiculous, Papa." Madeleine called to him. "It's your first grandchild."

His large form loomed up beside her.

"Holy Jesus!" he exclaimed, drawing back when he saw the scene of the birth. "Are you sure we don't need an ambulance here?"

He was squeamish all right, he could barely look at the mucus-covered creature in his daughter's arms. He patted Madeleine's hair. "A big fat Cuban cigar awaits," he said with a shudder. "And one hell of a tumbler of Cognac." He mopped his brow with the back of his hand. "Listen up, both of you. I'm not going through all this again."

"He's joking, Mama," Madeleine said when he'd left.

"Men!" said the midwife.

Rosaria looked crestfallen, but she went up to the little altar in the corner of the room and lit a candle. There were already flowers there, and a bowl of Florida water. She bent her head and mumbled a prayer to the effigy propped on the sacred stones. The midwife didn't know quite where to look.

"Yemaya," Mama implored, "bless this child." Then she turned to her daughter. "Magdalena, why don't you

name the child Maya, after Yemaya, the mother of all gods?"

"No," Madeleine said, looking at the baby in her arms, the miracle that was her child. "Her name is Mikaela."

She could not believe what was in front of her eyes, but the shock of seeing Rachel's birth date was almost immediately tempered by reason and logic. *Come on,* she told herself, *don't be ridiculous!* The date was just a crazy coincidence. Besides, Rachel was not adopted. And even if she had been, what were the chances of *the two of them* still living here, and more to the point, *meeting like this*? What were the odds?

Madeleine bit her lip and shook her head in amazement. Some coincidence! She put the wallet back into Rachel's bag and fell into her own chair, feeling guilty about the sneaky maneuver. Riffling through a client's private possessions . . . really, it was inexcusable. She'd never ever done anything like it in her life.

Turning her head, she looked at the clock. Almost five minutes had passed.

She tried to still the thoughts that swirled uncontrollably in her mind. Despite knowing it was impossible, she felt herself flushing, tears welling in her eyes. When would it stop, this hopeless fantasy? She could not go on all her life like this. How many times had she imagined, fantasized . . . girls in the street, in bars, pushing prams, waitresses, cashiers, TV presenters. One girl, a young painter she'd met at an art exhibition, had looked, sounded, and fitted the part, but of course, she'd been the wrong person—again. Madeleine had just barely saved herself from a thoroughly embarrassing situation. There must not be a repeat!

Closing her eyes, she breathed deeply, waiting for her patient to come back, while trying to still the pounding in her chest.

Rachel sat down and said, her voice uneasy, "So now I've made this resolve, what's there to talk about?"

Madeleine, still shaky and slightly breathless, studied her for a long moment. Who was this woman, really? Why was she here? She forced herself to collect her thoughts and put aside what she'd just done . . . and seen. Her responsibility to her patient was to be totally present and focused. Rachel had reached an important turning point and here was an opening to deepen therapy. Paradoxically, though this was a position from which she could really go forward, it was also a time when a patient feels some goal has been accomplished and the impetus for continuing therapy takes a nosedive.

"Rachel, look. You probably don't think this is a priority right now, but do you realize that I don't know very much about you? In order to understand why you've been drawn into an abusive relationship, it might help if we explore what—"

"Oh, here we go," Rachel interrupted with a mirthless chuckle. "The potty-training stuff."

"Yes, that's a good start," Madeleine asserted. Why was it that this woman always made her feel so *de-skilled*? "Tell me about your childhood. What was that like for you?"

"What was it like for me? Oh, Christ." Rachel paused, looking out the window. "So this is what you want, a great big spewing of my childhood traumas?"

"No, the agenda is always yours, but why don't you humor me for once? I'd like to move on if we can, reach a greater depth of understanding in the—"

"A greater depth of understanding?" Rachel mimicked her American accent and laughed merrily. She rarely laughed like this, with true hilarity, and her swollen lip split and bled. She pulled a tissue out of the box on the table and dabbed at it, but continued looking amused. Her strong teeth were on show and her eyes crinkled despite the swelling and the damage. They were unusual eyes, the most striking thing about her—slanted, hooded. Madeleine gazed at her.

Rachel's laugh died away. "What are you looking at? Have you never seen a case of domestic violence? No . . ." She sniggered. "I guess you wouldn't have."

She prattled on, probably buoyed by the nicotine charge and the notion that she could leave the room for a smoke (and a breather) at any time during future sessions. Looking at her, Madeleine's bewilderment returned full force. Distracted, she stopped listening. She thought of her father-in-law, Sam Serota, Forrest's dad. His mother had been Cantonese, come to San Francisco to work in her uncle's laundry. Forrest, however, was a blond, brown-eyed, all-American boy, nothing Chinese about him. But genes hopped about, skipped generations. Madeleine herself with her Yoruba ancestry could have been a black baby, though there were in her no visible traces of Negroid genes.

"Hey, Madeleine! Aren't you listening?"

"Yes, of course. Can we get back to your background?"

"My background?"

"Yes. Where did your parents come from, your grandparents?"

Madeleine gritted her teeth in self-reproach. Five minutes ago she'd decided she was not going down this road, but here she was, doing it anyway.

Rachel rolled her eyes. "My dad was an Exeter lad. His parents took early retirement and went to live in Australia because Dad's sister lives there and had a huge number of kids. I never met them. Mum was born in Bath, like me, but her dad was Scottish. He had such a strong Edinburgh accent no poor bugger could understand a word he said. He hit the bottle when my aunty Rachel died of leukemia at eighteen. Mum named me after her." She shrugged. "There you are. Background reasonably respectable, but dull as dishwater. I broke the mold, I'm afraid."

"It's just that you don't look British."

"Don't I?"

"Surely there is more you can tell me, Rachel."

Rachel kept dabbing at her lip. "No. Nothing of interest."

"I was wondering . . . you claim not to have much to say about your childhood. Could you have been adopted?" Madeleine recoiled. What the hell was she doing?

Rachel stopped dabbing. "Why would you ask a question like that?"

"Well . . . it could explain a few things about your reluctance to talk about your early life." Madeleine knew the observation was totally inappropriate. She looked at the clock. She should quit this now, before she went too far.

Rachel took a deep breath and sighed exaggeratedly. "Yeah, I've wondered. Perhaps I was."

Madeleine stared at her. "Adopted?"

"Yeah, perhaps. I can't remember a thing before the age of five."

"Really?" Madeleine felt herself go weak. Her heart started racing again, and she felt hot, the color rising to her cheeks. Should she say something? Yes, she should, she had to. But just as quickly she remembered that her judgment was probably clouded by delusion and wishful thinking. She thought of the dangers of being too impulsive, how disastrous it could turn out, especially with a vulnerable patient.

"Any other reason you might think that? Normally it's something parents tell children. That they're adopted, I mean."

Rachel cocked her head, looking at her for a moment, then sniggered.

"Madeleine, you are fishing for something that simply isn't there. I wasn't adopted. I wasn't sexually abused. I wasn't bullied at school. Potty-training was a bitch, sure, and being put on solids. I hated porridge. Boy, that was traumatic."

"You just said you don't remember anything before five."

"Oh for heaven's sake, *it was a joke.*" Rachel sighed. "Anyway, what difference does it make? I went off the rails when

Mum died, but I was a teenager. I ran away. I did drugs. I cut my arms. I nicked things from shops. And then, just to please a guy I was in love with, I fucked strangers for money. I probably would have done all that anyway. I've got a delinquent makeup, and that's it."

Madeleine didn't really hear her. She was studying her patient. Rachel was tall. She was thin. Her hands were long, slim, with square nails. There was a frown line running straight down the middle of her brow . . . all features of her own anatomy. And Rachel's birth date . . . born in Bath . . . wasn't it simply *too much* of a coincidence?

"Look at the time," Rachel said, breaking her train of thought. "I'm off."

"Hold on. We've still got ten minutes."

"What's the point? You're miles away."

Madeleine hesitated. "Yes, I'm sorry. I'm not . . . feeling that great. Look, I won't charge for this session. Can you come back tomorrow?" She picked up her diary and pretended to find her an appointment.

Rachel raised an eyebrow. "I thought you were booked solid. What's wrong with next week?"

"I can see you in my lunch hour tomorrow. All right? Why don't you come at one."

Hearing herself, she knew the suggestion sounded peculiar, but tomorrow she would know what to do, what to say. If anything. Madeleine put down her diary and looked up at Rachel, again awestruck by the enormity of this possibility (remote though it was): this antagonistic, indignant, battered-but-not-beaten woman was perhaps . . . her own flesh and blood. A sense of the miraculous suddenly came over her, swept away just as quickly by an avalanche of utter panic.

"I'll let Sylvia know," she stammered.

Rachel looked at her for a long moment, then took her sunglasses from the side table and slipped them on. "OK, if you insist." She stood up and shook her legs, pushing her skintight jeans down over her thighs. "That bloody woman had to comment on my face, she couldn't help herself. You should tell her to mind her own business."

"You're right. I'll tell her." Madeleine took herself in hand and stood too. "I'm glad you've been so open with me today" was all she could think to say.

"Yeah, well, I don't know exactly where you imagine it's going to get us. All this 'talk.'"

"You just look after yourself," she said and held the door open. "I mean, take care . . . take care of yourself, and I'll see you tomorrow."

Rachel stopped for a moment and frowned, but it was impossible to see behind the dark glasses what sort of look she gave Madeleine. Baffled, suspicious, perhaps oblivious, or indifferent? She turned away and her boots clicked sharply on the floor, a packet of cigarettes and the lighter at the ready in her hand. Madeleine watched her walk down the corridor, a gangly, slim-hipped woman with long legs and copious auburn hair, broad shoulders squared back defiantly.

Who are you? Madeleine whispered.

She sat in her chair after Rachel had left, grateful it was her coffee break. Her mind was numb, her body rigid. Yet something was happening inside her. Something that had been frozen was shifting. Her perception of everything she knew and felt was fracturing. But she was in no state to analyze this cataclysm within her.

Forrest's face appeared in her mind.

"I'm scared," she whispered. "Forrest? You hear me?"

For the whole of their marriage, it was something they'd hoped for—that they would find Mikaela one day, that when she got old enough she would put her name on the register of children seeking to know their birth parents. Their own names were on it, and as the years went by they'd checked ever more frequently to see if Mikaela had wished to make contact. The answer they got was always the same: Your daughter has not been in touch. No, nobody knows where she is. Yes, she could have moved abroad, have married, *have died* even.

And perhaps here she was now, perhaps it *was* her after all. An apparition from the past in the shape of a patient. An angry woman, damaged physically and emotionally. Rachel had no use for men, Madeleine knew that now, but had she known Forrest as a father, his influence might have averted her self-destructive impulses and prevented her seeking such dangerous company. It was Madeleine's fault. Twice she'd given her away, twice she'd robbed Forrest of his daughter. He who had wanted children so much. No number of needy patients or lonely prisoners . . . *nothing* she did for others would atone for what she'd done to the people she loved.

A door opened, and she heard John's voice in the corridor. His patient was leaving. She must talk to him. He was the one person she could confide in. She flew up from her chair and ran out to knock on his door. When she looked in he was already setting his lunch out on his desk. He looked up and smiled sheepishly.

"I've got fifteen minutes before Edna Rosen is here. I need fortification."

Fifteen minutes. She regretted her impulse. How could she blurt out her suspicion about Rachel's identity to poor old John, who didn't even know about the child she'd had? She'd have to confess to this first.

"What's the matter? Don't just stand there." John jumped up and fetched a large mug from a shelf. "Here, girl, have some."

Angus, his partner, got up early every day to make him a lunch worthy of royalty. A salad smothered by huge chunks of feta cheese, strips of sun-dried tomatoes, and glistening black olives sat in a black bowl before him. He started ladling the luxurious mixture into the mug.

"John, don't. I'm not hungry."

"You bloody well should be. Sit down, will you?" he said, pushing the mug toward her, producing another fork from a drawer. "I can't help but notice you've lost weight. Look at those trousers. They used to sit quite snugly around your arse. I used to really like looking at the way they sat on you."

"I'd be so lucky," she said with a smile, amazed that her voice sounded so normal.

A ray of sunshine fell on the table between them. They both turned to look at the thick cloud cover that had so gracefully opened, a small puncture through which the life-giving beam found its way to them.

"Hey, look at that. Daylight!" John commented superfluously, biting into a strip of pita bread. "Any date for tomorrow?"

"Edmund Furie. He's my date every Friday."

John took a swig from a bottle of Aqualibra and passed it to her. "Yes, of course, your boyfriend the murderer. And what are you doing this weekend?"

Oh God. The May Bank Holiday weekend loomed ahead like a menacing beast. "Well, I'll go and see Rosaria, as usual. I'm going to take her out for the day. She's not had any kind of outing for, well . . . weeks."

John stopped chewing and looked at her. "Yes . . . and then?"

Their eyes met briefly. Madeleine looked away. Why was she not telling him? Why did she not just blurt it out? Because it wasn't fair to him, and it wasn't fair to Edna Rosen. How could John give his patient his full attention after she dropped not one bombshell, but two? She would ask him to stay after work. Yes, that was the best thing. Just act normal and tell him later.

John pressed his glasses back onto his nose and peered at her for a long moment with a frown. "And when you've finished taking care of everybody, what'll you do?"

"I guess I'll have an ant day on Sunday,

you know, my new series. That's always exciting," she squeaked.

"People," John said. "I mean *normal* human intercourse."

"Oh, I'll probably go to a speed-dating event and pick up some guy." She shoved a large chunk of feta cheese into her mouth, though her throat had closed up and she despaired of being able to swallow it. "You know, get my sexual needs fullfilled. Then maybe go out and get drunk with the girls . . . I'll get a homeless dog from a shelter, to cuddle and talk to and stuff."

John wasn't laughing. He leaned forward, sliding his hand across the table toward her to grip her wrist. "Hey, what's wrong with you? What's going on?"

Madeleine felt as though she might explode, battling with the urge to unburden herself. She swallowed repeatedly, trying to get the cheese down. Pushing the mug away, she took a sip from the bottle.

"I'm tired. I'm not sleeping very well. I'm troubled about my mother and I'm thinking about the past." As she mouthed these excuses, she knew they were all true. Had she had a sense of something catastrophic looming? Mama's strange allusions, her own mounting unease. Had meeting her daughter been on the cards? She battled with herself, not wanting to take on board these bizarre ideas.

John pushed the bowl back toward her. "Are you being truthful now? It's not that twat of a bone digger, is it? The Gordon person. Yes, yes, don't remind me." He waved his hand to stop her interrupting. "It was your choice to dump him. I can buy that. You had a good reason."

"*No*," Madeleine barked, startling both John and herself. "It's not him. That's over."

John looked at her, alarm written all over his face. His heartfelt concern made something unknot itself in her throat. She felt a tear funnel down the side of her nose.

"But Mad . . . but heavens." John jumped up and came quickly around the table.

He bent down on one knee and wrapped his arms about her. "Listen you. You're coming down to the cottage with me and Angus for the weekend. Angus will feed you and he's got some temazepam. He's very partial to them, but I'm sure I'll be able to talk him into parting with a few and you can have a decent couple of nights' sleep."

She was sobbing quietly, feeling like an idiot.

"Is that really a good idea?" She sniffed. "Angus doesn't like me."

"He doesn't *know* you, silly. He's jealous because he knows I'm crazy about you. And he's got a stupid thing about Americans. But look here, if you gave him a chance to get to know you, he'd be smitten." He reached for the box of tissues on the side table, pulled out a handful, and dabbed at her face. "You two will get along like a house on fire, trust me."

She blew her nose noisily. "It would be awkward. Me in the bedroom next to yours. I'd cramp your style."

"We can forgo sex for one weekend."

"Why should you?"

"OK. Sleep in my camper van. It's cozy and dry. I've got a lush new mattress for it. It'll be the best sleep you're ever going to have."

"But Rosaria is—"

"*Madeleine!*" he roared. "Stop making excuses. Never mind your bloody *mama*. She'll have to wait till next week."

Yes, perhaps he was right. A weekend at the cottage might be just the thing she needed right now. She could really use the support and it was a good setting for a confession. Certainly she owed John an explanation for her many years of silence.

John's phone rang. "That'll be Edna," he said with a sigh.

Chapter Nine

Sylvia cocked her head, eyeing Madeleine with suspicion. "Why are you seeing the Locklear woman in your lunch hour? You saw her yesterday."

Sylvia was on her way out, stuffing her box of vegan sandwiches into a gargantuan rattan shoulder bag. Madeleine returned her scrutiny. Her receptionist was, unfortunately, a devotee of peculiar fashions. Her cotton dress looked as if it came from the one-pound rack in the Cancer Care shop, the leather choker around her neck from Pets R Us; her bracelet looked like dog turds on a string.

"What's with the canine theme, Sylvia?"

"Huh?"

"Off you go. Have a good lunch."

John dashed through reception, disheveled and in a hurry as always. "Taking Angus to the chiropractor," he informed her breathlessly. "You still on for the weekend?"

"Of course, Johnny. I said I was coming, so I am."

Alone in the clinic, Madeleine sat herself in Sylvia's chair to wait. Rachel was usually punctual, but the hands of the clock on the wall were creeping past one o'clock. Madeleine was anxious, having spent the whole night thinking how she should handle this situation. She'd decided to just come out with the truth. She would tell Rachel that she'd had a daughter, born on the very same day, month, and year as her, and that it was Madeleine's professional duty to check this remarkable coincidence as thoroughly as she could. Although Rachel had omitted to put her birth date on her form, Madeleine would insist she had mentioned it, and hopefully it would never occur to Rachel that Madeleine had been riffling through her bag or checking her personal details in some other underhand way. She would ask her one more time if there was any possibility she might have been adopted, perhaps without having known it. She would query whether Rachel's exotic features might not point to some other-than-English genes. *Oh God!* Now, thinking about it in the light of day, it all sounded so contrived. Well, she had to do it. She'd try to speak about it in a factual, rational way, placing emphasis on the importance of ascertaining if they were related, in which case therapy would have to stop. *Damn!* That sounded just terrible. Better say: "The importance of being able to dismiss such a possibility"—so they could lay the issue to rest and go on with therapy.

Rehearsing this spiel in her mind, Madeleine cringed. She could just picture Rachel's scornful expression. She'd probably have a good chuckle and tell her therapist to get a life, and some therapy.

Madeleine glanced at the clock. Ten past.

There was a book under Sylvia's in-tray, and she pulled it out. Surprise, surprise, it was the *I Ching.* Her meddlesome receptionist no doubt used the book of Chinese wisdom to put straight all those poor people who got nowhere in therapy. She flicked through it. Despite Forrest having a Chinese grandmother, Madeleine had never had any real interest in anything Chinese. For her own guidance she used a thick tome on the *Diloggún,* the oracle of Santeria. Like the *I Ching,* the *Diloggún* was not merely a tool for divination but the doorway to a powerful transformational process. Though her beliefs had been, in part, tainted by her mother's "malpractice" of Santeria, and in part destroyed by the way Forrest had been so pitilessly torn from her, she was often saddened by her spiritual rejection. Santeria was a faith of beauty and mystery, strengthened by a thousand years of practice, and in her youth she had trusted in its power. But coming to spiritually barren Britain had made it quite easy to dismiss Santeria as bizarre and unworkable. She thought of its wisdom now, in her need for guidance. She did not know a single practitioner of Santeria (bar Rosaria) in Britain to whom she could turn for advice, though surely there must be many.

She resolved to search for her Santeria bible when she got home and remind herself of the words of the oracle.

The minutes ticked by. At one-twenty, she realized Rachel was not coming. Why not? And why had she not phoned to cancel the appointment? It was quite possible that she'd been put off by yesterday's interrogation, Madeleine's odd behavior and intrusive questions. Might this mean that she was not coming back, *ever*? It occurred to her that Rachel might have begun to question the relationship herself and have the same suspicions. If that were the case, it was probably the last Madeleine would see of her patient. Her own daughter, Mikaela, had, after all, never wanted contact.

She locked up the clinic and went outside. People were still queuing for lunch in the trendy little restaurants in the passage. She had no appetite, but the sun was shining, so she went for a brisk walk, trying to dispel the crushing disappointment she felt. Never mind *who* Rachel was, it seemed she'd also lost a patient she had truly come to care about. If Rachel did not come back, as Madeleine suspected she wouldn't, she would miss the rigorous, heated exchanges, even her sarcasm and her mockery of Madeleine's naïveté. Rachel had shown her a side of life with which she was utterly unfamiliar. Yes, Madeleine had certainly learned a few things from their sessions.

Her route led her along the river, over Poultney Bridge, and she took a left into Henrietta Street, a graceful, curving street of Georgian houses, opposite which lay a park she used to know.

As on every morning, they took a turn around Henrietta Park. It was small, the size of a city block, but contained, some of the oldest trees in Bath, which gave cool shade in summer heat. But today the massive plane trees were like skeletons, devoid of leaves, and dew covered the grass like a cold silvery blanket.

Rosaria was pushing the buggy, Madeleine trailed behind. Though she was as thin as a bean pole, her body seemed unbearably heavy and her legs felt like lead. Her mother, on the other hand, was like a woman reborn. From behind she looked like a girl, her black hair loose to

the waist, a spring in her step, practically skipping. Her dependence on Madeleine had disappeared, replaced by the joys of vicarious motherhood.

Her voice trilled, and the child gurgled companionably.

Madeleine was numb. Her doctor had diagnosed her with postnatal depression and it showed no signs of letting up. After giving birth, nine months ago now, she'd developed an infection, the kind that used to kill women in droves before penicillin was invented. Rosaria had talked her into having the baby at home, and the doctor had not objected. But when the infection took hold, he was quick to blame the home birth and absolve himself of responsibility. Madeleine had been rushed to hospital and spent three weeks there, alone, while Mama merrily bonded with her baby. Then, as a final slap across the face, she was told she might not be able to conceive again.

She ambled along after them. In the beginning she'd been terrified of going out, of meeting her old classmates on their way to school. Who were they, these young people with their school uniforms and purposeful walk? Now she didn't give a damn about any of them. Her heart was elsewhere, she hated this place. Not that Bath wasn't a beautiful city, with its imposing golden stone façades, some covered with centuries of soot, but she'd give anything to see just one house made of sun-bleached wood, with turquoise shutters, a veranda with carved filigree and a parrot squawking at passersby, tin roof glinting in the dazzling light. Or something as mundane as a cockerel chasing a chicken across the road, or a gecko darting up a wall. The plane trees and chestnuts of Bath were majestic, but they were nothing like the gumbo-limbo trees with their red bark, the jacarandas and banyans, the green fountains of coconut and date palms.

"Wait up, you two," she called.

Her mother turned around. "Hurry up, Magdalena. You walk like an old woman." She undid the straps of the buggy and picked the baby up. "Quieto, chiauilla. We have to wait for your sister."

"Sister." This was what she was now.

She'd argued, but Mama had been insistent, her strength and her Santera powers made her formidable. Conversely, Madeleine felt sapped of strength. She was sure Mama didn't mean to do this, she loved Madeleine . . . but she loved the little one more, that was obvious.

Papa Neville was there they got home to the Georgian pile he'd bought on a whim (consulting no one). His appearances were less and less frequent.

Madeleine threw herself into his arms.

"Hey, little girl," he said, taken aback. They didn't often hug anymore. He'd grown distant over the years, more interested in his art than in his family.

"Papa, can't we go home for a holiday? It's been almost a year and a half. I hate this place."

Her father turned to Rosaria. "You see what's happening here? This kid has missed two terms of school."

"The doctor says she doesn't have to go." Rosaria shrugged. "Anyway, she refuses."

"That's ridiculous. Come Monday

she's going back, even if she has to do the year over. She's got to get some O levels, for Christ's sake."

Madeleine punched him on the arm. "I'm right here," she cried. "You can talk to me directly. We don't need a go-between."

She threw off her jacket, kicked off her shoes, and fled into the conservatory, the only place in the house she could tolerate. She spent her days there on a scuffed old sofa the former owners had left behind, her feet tucked under her, drawing ants. Ants, thousands of them, crawled across page after page; the drawings littered the floor around her.

Now she fell onto the sofa and shouted, "I'm the American slut who got knocked up and has a weird fucking family. How do you expect me to go to school and face people?"

Neville marched in. "Hold your tongue, you little shit. What's got into you? That's no way to speak to your parents."

"Really?" She sneered. "You're a fine one to give orders. You're never here.

Mama won't let me touch my own child. She calls me 'sister,' for fuck's sake. I'm like a spare fucking part around here." She burst into tears.

"Hey. Language!" her father said lamely, at a loss. She was expecting him to call for her mother to sort out the situation, but to his credit he didn't. He closed the door and came to sit beside her, waiting for her to stop crying. Meanwhile he picked up a drawing from the floor.

"My God, girl," he exclaimed. "Look at this. You sure are a chip off the old block."

She didn't answer. The last thing she yearned to be was a chip off him.

He picked up a few more. "Why so many ants?"

"You should know," she muttered through her tears. "You taught me."

He turned to look at her. It was as if he were seeing her for the first time. "What do you want, little girl? What do you want out of life?"

"Simple. I want my child, and I want to go home."

He shook his head resolutely. "You're too young, on both counts."

"Bullshit. I'm seventeen. If I want to, I can do both."

"It would crush your mother. Is that what you want?"

"Oh yeah, fine. Lay the guilt trip on me. Why the hell are you not here? You're her husband." She pointed an accusing finger at his chest. "Problem is, Papa, you've got your own life. Having a baby keeps Mama happy, and I'm here to keep her company so you can be the big artist, Neville Frank, single man about town."

He slapped her, not hard, but hard enough. The slap woke her up. It cleared her head. In fact, it seemed for the first time in ages that she was thinking properly. Her voice was icy cool.

"What the hell are you doing in London anyway, and with whom?"

She lifted her chin defiantly and turned the other cheek, but no slap was forthcoming. When she took a peek at him, Neville was staring out of the window toward Bath's skyline. He didn't face her when he spoke.

"As you speak so plainly, I'll tell you how it is. I've tried to get your mother to see that she should take you and the baby back to Key West and live in the house. She'd be far happier there. I'd provide for everything. But your mother plain refuses to leave me. Marriage is forever as far as she's concerned."

"Lucky you," she said, trying to contain the sarcasm in her voice. "Lucky you to have such a loyal and devoted wife."

"Don't think I don't love her," he said feebly.

They looked at each other. How she wished they could all go home. If they were home, all would be resolved. Papa would put on his straw hat, settle down, and paint in his studio and be crazy about Mama and show her off to his friends. They'd go back to being in love. Madeleine was sure of it. But that was not where he was heading. She knew she had to make the decision by herself.

"All right. Listen, I've thought a lot about this. In fact, it has been tearing me apart for months," she said, her heart in her throat. "We can't go on like this. Mama and I can't go on fighting over Micki. We'll end up hating each other."

Neville looked into her face. "What are you trying to say?"

"I'm capitulating, Papa. Send me home. Mama can look after Micki. I couldn't tear them apart if I tried. You can see that I'm damned if I do and I'm damned if I don't. I want Mama to be happy, and I don't want you guys to divorce."

He was quiet for a long moment, then he put his big paw on her shoulder. "So you're set on going back?"

Madeleine shook his hand off. "You have to promise me you will look after them. Mama doesn't really belong here. She shouldn't be here. She's going to need you."

"Perhaps it's for the best, little girl. We can give it a try."

"Don't call me 'little girl' anymore. And to me you're Neville."

A bell-like sound reached them. It was

Rosaria singing a Cuban milonga, *while the child shrieked with delight.*

Madeleine dropped her suitcases on the porch and put her hand to the door, tracing the grooves, circles, and curlicues. When she was a little girl of eight or nine, Neville had let her draw the pattern around the door panels and he'd used a wood-carving chisel to cut them out. She put the key in the lock and turned it. The door was stuck. It must have swelled unevenly in some recent tropical downpour. Madeleine gave it a swift kick with her boot and it flew open.

It looked as if no one had lived in the house for years, even though only eighteen months had passed since they had left Key West for England. She stood immobile for a few moments, breathing in the familiar smell of sun-dried wood. Even the pain she felt about leaving Micki and her mother receded as she rejoiced in this moment of coming home.

The place smelled of dust and the kitchen of something acrid that turned out to be a mound of fresh bird shit. By the looks of it, a family of doves must have bred several generations of offspring in the larder. Someone, a vandal probably, had punched out the insect screen, but there appeared to have been no forced entry. She'd already noticed that the outside walls were desperately in need of treatment of some kind. There were several neat piles of sawdust on the veranda, which she feared might be the product of a termite infestation. She made a mental note to tell Neville next time they spoke on the phone. He'd mentioned a budget for stuff like that.

She wandered around the sparsely furnished house, raising windows and throwing open wooden shutters. Light streamed in, together with the noise of birds and the sound of some reggae music from the garden next door. She tried to decide in which room to set up house; all of them held different memories. In her parents' room was her mother's little altar, a small table covered with a red embroidered cloth and seven sacred stones. In the middle, the small skull of a mammal sat on a stand made of conch shells. Mama had left it there to protect the house. It was such a pathetic sight, it made her want to cry. Poor Mama, no wonder she seemed such a freak in goddamned Bath. British people had no spirit, no understanding of magic. Their loss. Her mother could do amazing things for people. She could also do damage and create sickness if someone got on the wrong side of her.

Madeleine went outside to inspect the garden. It was a veritable jungle. The guy who was supposed to come and prune had obviously laughed all the way to the bank, or to the bar, more like. She checked the pond for tenants, trees for birds' nests, the palms for coconuts in danger of falling and cracking open her skull. A couple of years ago a neighbor had had one fall on his shoulder and it had dislocated his collarbone. One on the head could kill. The banyan tree was growing ever more aerial roots; a few more years and they'd take over the whole garden. She climbed the spiral staircase to the tree house. Good old Angelo, was he still alive? Ten years on, the structure looked as solid as the day he'd built it, accounting for the natural growth and movement of the tree. From the platform she could see most of Key West, a verdant landscape interspersed with polished tin roofs, like hundreds of mirrors turned to the sky and surrounded on all sides by ocean. Docked at Mallory Square was a huge cruise ship, higher than anything on the island.

She found the key to Neville's studio where it had always been, hanging under the eaves on a rusty nail. As soon as she set foot inside the shack, she knew where she was going to live. It was dilapidated and cobwebby, but it was a place where she'd spent many hours of her life, absorbed in things that her mother would rather she hadn't been. Even the ant farm Angelo had made for her sat on a shelf, its busy inhabitants long since released. Drawing back the sun-bleached curtains from the glass wall, she smiled. She'd place her bed in front of it and the garden would be hers the moment she opened her eyes every morning.

Neville's old Camaro sat grumpy and

dejected in the drive. It was covered with the sticky sap of the weeping fig that hung over the entrance. Eighteen months of inertia had flattened two tires, and the battery was dead. Madeleine shed her boots and jeans and pulled on a pair of cotton shorts and sandals. She wandered over to Bob Woods, the retired mechanic down the back lane, and asked him if he'd have a moment to come and fix the Camaro. She told him she was seventeen now and was going to get her driver's licence as soon as yesterday. His wife sat her down on the swing on her porch and gave her a glass of iced tea and a slice of Key lime pie. Would Madeleine be wanting a six-toed kitten by any chance, a genuine descendant of Hemingway's brood? God almighty, it was amazingly wonderful to be home. "Sure thing, Mrs. Woods. I'd love a six-toed kitten."

But her elation at her homecoming was soon tempered by cutting sadness. When would she see her baby again? Mikaela was thousands of miles away. In good hands, sure, but they weren't her hands. She'd learned this about life already: some things you could have, some things you couldn't. It was no good to ask too much of life. You just stood to lose it.

Still, some lost things might be around to claw back, given a modicum of feminine guile and a bit of detective work. With this in mind, two weeks later she was on U.S. 1, in a Greyhound bus headed north. A few queries around the fishing port had resulted in an address up in Key Largo: Dolphin Lodge Motel. It was a good three-hour journey, counting the stops, but she didn't even mind the heat and the kid in the back who puked up his lunch together with a fountain of undigested beer.

Joined by two parallel bridges, the derelict and the new, the Keys rolled by: Big Pine, Marathon, Layton, Islamorada, Tavernier, and all the tiny ones in between. The kid in the back was smoking a joint now and nobody complained—it's a well-known fact that cannabis stops motion sickness, and the smell covered up his previous misdemeanor. On the Seven Mile Bridge, a child started kicking the back of her seat. She wondered why she'd not waited till her driver's licence had come through. The Camaro was there for the driving, although like most people on the island she preferred a bicycle.

"Key Largo," shouted the driver and pulled off onto the service road that ran alongside the highway. Madeleine slung her knapsack onto her back and jumped out into a cloud of dust.

"You know where I can find Dolphin Lodge Motel?" she called to the driver before he shut the door.

"Back about half a mile. You shoulda said."

"No worries." She waved him off and turned to go.

She walked along the side road, her sandals filling with dust and the sun beating down on her head. Vehicles bombed past in both directions on the highway. Some boys shouted at her from a big-wheeled truck, offering her a ride. Everybody seemed to be driving those monstrous things nowadays. The Keys were changing, she could see that. The homey and congenial tackiness of

roadside cafés and shell stalls was being replaced by fast food outlets, sterile
malls, and fancy-looking resorts. But
she was happy, it was home.

The girl in reception seemed almost
too lazy to speak. "He's on the jetty,"
she drawled, "at the back."

Madeleine circumnavigated a row of
ramshackle units and to her surprise
found a beautiful seafront lawn dotted
with clumps of fishtail palms. A jetty
stretched out into the water, lined with
white wicker loungers. On one of them
sat a man looking intently at the rocks
below.

"Excuse me. Hello," called Madeleine
and approached. "Mr. Serota?"

He looked up. His torso was bare and
brown as chocolate, his face weather-
beaten, long graying hair gathered in a
ponytail. A grizzled beard hid his mouth.
He had something that Forrest did not
have: Chinese eyes. She'd forgotten
that Forrest had told her that his dad's
mother had been Cantonese. Her marriage to Antony Serota in San Francisco
had been a scandal, apparently, and

they'd moved to Florida to escape the wrath of both families. Antony Serota, his studies interrupted, had taken up shrimping as had Sam, his son, and Forrest, his gorgeous grandson.

Mr. Serota pulled on a pair of glasses to look at her. "Do I know you?"

"Madeleine Frank," she said. "Key West."

He's beard moved and split into a grin. "I'll be damned. Sure. I heard about you."

She stood there, feeling awkward. "I was told you bought a motel up here."

"Sold the boat, yeah," he said, his eyes drawn again toward the rocks below.

She couldn't resist peeking at what was holding his interest to such an extent. Under the jetty two enormous iguanas faced each other on a flat rock. They stood stock-still; one was bleeding profusely from a deep gash at the base of its tail.

"Oh God. He's really injured," she cried.

"They've been fighting since midday," he said. "But I think it's almost over."

"They're beautiful," she said, staring at the prehistoric-looking creatures, big as tomcats, as they measured each other up. In an instant the likely winner was on the injured one and they tussled and sunk their teeth into each other in a flurry of aggression, until the bleeding iguana fell into the water. Immediately it turned and started clambering back up.

"He's coming back for more!" Madeleine exclaimed. "I can't believe it."

"That's guys for you. Pride and sheer stupidity. Behavin' like they was in a barroom brawl."

He looked up suddenly. "Hey. Where's my manners? Sit down, will you?"

She sat beside him in a wicker lounger and put her feet up. She didn't really want to watch the gruesome fight. It had made her queasy. She looked out over the tiny keys dotted in the distance. Two pelicans flew overhead. A man in a canoe paddled past.

"Mr. Serota, I've come about Forrest."

He sat back then and put his feet up too. "Yup. I figgered you had, miss."

"Please call me Madeleine."

"Madeleine. You want a cold beer?"

"Yes please." She was hellishly thirsty.

He reached into a cool box and fished one out, popping off the cap with a fancy penknife.

She took a big gulp. "Mr. Serota. Did you . . . by any chance . . . get the letters I sent?"

He looked at her. "Ah, that was you, wasn't it? Letters from England."

"Did you send them on, Mr. Serota?"

"Look, sweetheart, I mentioned them to Forrest, and he told me to return them to the sender. Out of self-preservation, I guess. Besides, he was never sure where he was going to be. I'm sorry I didn't get around to sending them back. You can have them now if you want. They're in a box in the office."

She stared at him, her heart sinking. "So he never asked . . . he didn't want to know what was in them?"

"I wouldn't be opening his mail . . . No, he never asked."

"He's been gone eighteen months,"

she said, trying to sound casual, though she felt close to tears. "Is he not planning to come back?"

Sam Serota shrugged. "I honestly don't know the answer to that. I reckon he might be through with shrimping. His horizons have opened up. I'da given him the boat, but I couldn't manage it on my own. Got arthritis in the knee, see. Figgered I might as well make my plans without him, for now." He looked guilty as he said it. Hadn't Forrest told her he'd come back to shrimping for a hundred years?

"So where is he exactly?"

Mr. Serota looked out to sea. "At this precise moment, I can't tell you," he said. "Last time I had a phone call, he was teaching in a school in . . . goddamn, can't remember the name of it now. Small town in India. He said he was going to some ashram or something for a month or two, and after that he was going to try and get into Tibet, though he didn't hold out much hope of a visa."

Madeleine picked at the flaking paint on the wicker arm. The beautiful scene had lost its shine somehow. So Forrest knew nothing, nothing at all of what had happened, her pregnancy, Mikaela's birth. He knew nothing of having a daughter. Neither, obviously, did his dad. She battled with the idea of telling him. "I've been thinking about him a lot for the last year and a half," she said. "I really missed him. And there is something I need to tell him."

Mr. Serota got out another beer and drank deeply. He scratched his beard. He had big hands, like Forrest, but terribly scarred. "Oh, I wouldn't be going out there, Madeleine, if that's what you was thinking of. There is someone, I think, some Canadian girl. They've been living together for a while. She's the one keen on the ashram idea. He'd be bored to distraction, I figure, fastin' an' chantin' all day."

There was her answer. He'd moved on. Of course he had. "Will you mention me, when he gets in touch?" She hesitated. "Tell him I've left England for good and I'm back in Key West. Same house. Same phone number."

He looked at her. "Best leave him be,

don't you think? I'm sure he'll be back one day, and you can tell him yourself."

She finished her beer and stood up, peering over the side of the jetty. The iguanas were gone.

"Look, they've disappeared."

"Yeah," he said quietly, pointing with a scarred finger. "There he goes."

She looked up and what she saw made her tremble with some inexplicable emotion. One of the iguanas was belly-up, bobbing on the waves and floating quickly out to sea.

Chapter Ten

Sasha was looking out the classroom window when, as if by magic, Daddy's car pulled up outside in the street. He stared at the black roof glinting in the sunlight and saw the dark head emerge on the other side of it. Dad slammed the door shut and, with a wave of his arm, locked it with the magic clicker in his hand.

A flutter of excitement went through Sasha, excitement and alarm and dread. Although he would not have been able to name those feelings, he knew them all too well. He shut his eyes tight and brought his thumbnail up to his teeth. There was not much left of the nail, but he'd promised Mum to leave the others alone. Just punish one of your fingers, she said, and leave the others to be happy, then his thumb would be the only sad one and the other nine could cheer it up. He gnawed insistently, trying to get a purchase, but there was nothing but pain. He didn't mind the pain, it hid other things and made them seem less scary.

Sasha opened his eyes again, just catching sight of his father walking under the window toward the main door. He could only be there for a reason. He would talk to Mrs. Eastwood in the office. Mrs. Eastwood would go and get Mr. Bodell, the head, and tell him that there was a man there who wanted to take his little boy for a dentist appointment, or to meet his grandma, or something like that. He'd done that at the other school, and the head there had gone and fetched Sasha from his class and brought him to the office. Sasha had run up shouting "Daddy," and they had let him go. Somehow he doubted it would happen again, 'cause Mum made a huge fuss about the last time, especially as they didn't come back for three days. Mum had cried, her eyes had been all fuzzy, but she had been mad as hell.

One day his daddy was going to take him to Ukraine, where his whole family lived. He would get to do stuff they didn't do in England, like skating on a frozen lake and eating food he'd never tried, and they would take Napoleon with them. The other day when Miss Bailey was showing them a map of the world, he'd asked her to show him where Ukraine was. It looked big, bigger than England for sure. "So, Sasha, your dad has come here to live off the fat of the land, has he?" Miss Bailey had said, but he'd not understood what she meant.

The minutes passed, and Sasha gnawed and gnawed. His thumb started bleeding. He stuffed it in his mouth and sucked on it to stem the flow.

Miss Bailey was calling out something, and suddenly he saw that the other kids had turned toward him and were staring. Roddy was laughing.

"Sasha is sucking his thumb, settling in to go to sleep," Miss Bailey said. Her voice was soft but he heard the meanness mixed in with the softness.

"Baby!" Roddy said, sneering at him,

crossing his eyes, and sucking noisily on his own thumb.

Sasha popped his thumb out of his mouth. "Fuck you," he replied. It sounded loud in the silence. Then there was a kind of *whoosh* as the whole class drew breath. Their faces were turned toward him, their eyes wide. He glanced at Miss Bailey, who looked as if she'd seen a three-headed monster. Her mouth had fallen open so that her chin was squashed down like a sausage around her neck. He remembered, too late, that the F-word was not allowed in this school and nobody said it, not even Roddy or the older kids. It wasn't like London.

The air quivered and Sasha's skin went goose-pimply down his back. In the hush, the noise of birds sounded loud. He turned his head toward the window and looked for them, and his eyes came to rest on the car. Daddy's car.

In a burst, his limbs sprang into action. His chair went crashing to the floor. He dodged the desks, weaving back and forth like lightning. At the edge of his vision he saw Miss Bailey move toward him. Her arms went out in slow motion, her mouth beginning to form words, the shout gurgling from her throat, but before it had reached him he'd flung open the door and was already in the corridor and running. Skidding around a corner toward the main door, he ran straight into his father.

In the car, they slammed the doors and Daddy pressed a button. All the locks clonked down in unison, a sound as powerful as Sasha had ever heard. He saw Miss Bailey, Mrs. Eastwood, and Mr. Bodell spill out the door and stop. They stared but didn't come any farther. Mr. Bodell was shaking his head. Sasha kneeled on the seat, and pressing his face to the window, he stuck out his tongue. Daddy laughed and turned the key. The car hummed and the air-conditioning blew cool air over Sasha's bare legs. As the car started moving, the last thing he saw was Mr. Bodell turning angrily and marching back into the building. It was only then it occurred to him that maybe he'd have to come back.

"That's my boy," said Daddy, laughing his head off. "Living dangerously already."

The sun shone behind her. Rachel cupped her hands around her face and peered into the screen of the cash machine. She waited to see her balance flash by. There it was: *£32,282.54.*

What! Rachel blinked. That wasn't right. She waited impatiently for the machine to cough up her cash and spit out the card so she could repeat the procedure. The woman behind her was huffing and sighing, but you couldn't rush the damned contraption. Finally the balance flashed again. She stared hard at it before it was gone. *Jesus!* There was no way there could be over thirty-two thousand quid in her account. Her heart was beating hard as she walked away.

"Hiya."

Rachel turned, distracted. It was the homeless girl, Charlene, standing in her usual pitch beside the cash machine.

"Hi, kid," she said lengthening her stride.

"Big Issue?" the girl called after her. "And I babysit."

Rachel turned her head. "I haven't forgotten," she called back.

In a daze, Rachel walked around the block. Thirty-two thousand. No way. Banks made mistakes all the time, but usually not in the customer's favor. Didn't Dad always say that? She could ignore it and hope they'd never notice. How much of a mistake was it? She stopped and counted on her fingers. Something to the tune of five thousand. Five thousand pounds . . . no, they'd not let that slip by without investigating. Perhaps they'd suspect her of doing something dodgy. *Aww, shit!* The last thing she wanted was some guy in a suit knocking on her door.

The bank was imposing, with a high ceiling and fancy pillars like a church of some kind. Dad had banked there for as long as she could remember, but she'd come inside only once, to open the account for the transfer of her dad's money.

There was a queue here too and she took up her position. She'd just hand in her card and say there'd been a mistake. The queue moved ever so slowly, and she was beginning to gasp for a cigarette when somebody put a hand on her elbow. She jumped at the touch and turned. It was the manager. He'd seen her when she opened the account.

"Miss Locklear, isn't it?" he said in a quiet voice. "I wonder if I might have a word? After you've done your business."

Rachel's swore to herself. She'd known all along something was suspect about all that money. *Oh shit, Dad. What did you do?* Then again, perhaps it was only about the five thousand. A mistake they'd made.

"Let's get it over with?" she said, a little too gruffly.

The man looked at her, clearly taken aback. "Fine, fine. If you're sure now is convenient? Would you like to step into my office? I won't keep you, Miss Locklear."

Was she imagining it, or was there a sudden hush? He unlocked a heavy door and she followed him through it. They went up some steps and down a corridor. The manager was tall but not fit looking, his fancy gray suit bunched unattractively around his buttocks. He'd not been impressed with her either, when she'd opened the account. He'd thought her "banking background" incredibly lacking. Still, they had not turned down her inheritance.

In his office he motioned her to sit down across from him at a large desk. The whole scenario reminded her of a ticking off she'd once had in a headmaster's office . . . for smoking in the toilets.

"I don't need to sit," she said hurriedly. "I have no idea how the five thousand got into my account. Just take it back. I'll sign something if you need me to."

The manager looked at her for a moment and frowned. "Sit, sit, Miss Locklear."

She sat and waited while he fiddled with his computer on the desk. After a moment he spoke, without lifting his eyes from the screen. "I'm looking at your account here, Miss Locklear, and all seems to be in order. You had the quarterly deposit yesterday of five thousand pounds from Langlane Holdings."

She stared at him, but the bank manager continued studying the screen calmly. Langlane Holdings? She'd never heard of them. "That's a mistake, mate. Can you sort it out now? I don't want any hassle later."

He looked up, studying her face for a moment. "What do you mean by mistake?"

"The five thousand."

"The figure has never varied, Miss Locklear."

She frowned. "What figure?"

"You are Rachel Locklear, aren't you?"

"Yeah."

"Surely you've had a rundown of your late father's finances?"

"Well, yeah . . . sort of."

Had she? The solicitor had gone on and on, it had all been mumbo-jumbo to someone like her.

"Miss Locklear," he said primly, "It's important to be on top of your ingoings and outgoings and to keep a record of your transactions. Langlane Holdings is an offshore company that has been transferring money to your father's account for some years now. When your father passed away, we had instructions to continue the payments into your account."

She stared at him. "Instructions from whom?"

There was an imperceptible roll of the manager's eyes. "Langlane Holdings, Miss Locklear."

"But who *are* they?"

The man sighed and shook his head. "I'm not privy to that information. Perhaps you should take the trouble to find out yourself."

"Right!" she countered angrily. Standing up, she said, "OK, I'll go then."

"Hold on. I won't keep you long," he said, looking up at her.

She stiffened. "What the hell do you want now?"

The color rose in the manager's face and a frown made deep lines in his forehead. "I'd like to discuss some of our products with you."

"Products? With me? What bloody products?"

The man's face darkened further. "'Product' is the term we use these days for . . . never mind. Look, a large sum of money is sitting in your current account and not working in your favor, Miss Locklear. I'm not doing my job if I don't advise you of alternative investments. There are products with a much better rate of return."

She wandered homeward, up the hill, doubt and unease gnawing at her guts. Langlane Holdings . . . offshore. That meant abroad, didn't it? Who the hell had been giving Dad money and now her? What could the explanation for it possibly be? She could only think that her dad had been a lot more clever than she'd ever realized. She knew he had a problem with betting, there had been many arguments between her parents about money. Dottie used to chide him for wasting her housekeeping and Dad's answer to that had been to storm out and gamble some more. Could it be that he dealt in far larger sums than she'd imagined and had managed to build up a stash somewhere the tax man couldn't get it? If that was the case, he'd been a real shit for keeping his family so short. She was happy for it now, however, though she'd better not spend it, because she suspected that sooner or later there would be a more rational explanation for its appearance, like some massive mix-up on the part of the bank.

Still on a whim she went into the secondhand gadget shop on London Road. The old vacuum cleaner had bit the dust, and she needed to replace it to clean the two Oriental rugs she'd bought, which had fallen off the back of a lorry.

She sat on her leatherette sofa and studied the vacuum cleaner, trying to find a way into it. She lacked experience with gadgets and appliances; cleaning generally wasn't exactly her favorite activity. This was a bagless job with too many levers. What was wrong with bags? She fiddled with the buttons, then swore to herself as one end of the cylinder dropped open and the contents spilled out. At the same time, her mobile rang.

"Yeah?" she barked, tucking the phone under her jaw while flicking the dust off her hands.

"Mr. Bodell here," said a sharp voice. "I'm ringing to inform you that your son has just been picked up, or should I say *abducted*, by a man who appears to be his father. You did tell us categorically that no one but yourself had authority to remove Sasha from school. I wanted to notify you before I call the police."

Rachel felt the blood drain from her face.

"Miss Locklear? Were you aware this man was picking up your son, in the middle of a lesson?"

"No, of course not." To steady herself, Rachel looked at the pile of dust on the floor. "How could you let him do that?"

"I told you, Sasha was *abducted*. We couldn't stop the man. Shall I phone the police?"

"When was this?" she stammered. "When did it happen?"

"Just now, a minute ago. Miss Bailey is very upset. You must tell me what to do here, Miss Locklear. I would have liked to have been warned about this possibility. We can't take responsibility for—"

"I *did* warn you," Rachel exclaimed shrilly.

"Not explicitly."

"Look . . . perhaps they'll turn up here in a minute. I'll ring you back. Leave the police for now."

Rachel put the mobile in her shirt pocket and sank down on the sofa, her legs giving way. She'd refused when Anton had offered her his mobile number, claiming she had no reason to phone him. How stupid was that? How utterly ignorant and pigheaded and brain dead. Not that it would have helped her, once Anton had decided to take Sasha away from her. Perhaps she'd been too cocky, too determined to have her way, moving herself and Sasha from London. *Starting a new life?* More like ending her life, or at least everything that mattered in it. What had she been thinking?

Nausea welled up inside her. She rushed up the stairs to the toilet and kneeled over the bowl, but however much she retched, whatever it was stayed down. She leaned her elbows on the seat and stared into the bowl for a long while, trying to decide what to do. The phone went again and she got up and rushed downstairs, almost tripping on the steps, then realized the phone was in her pocket.

"Your humble lover," Anton said, "and your darling son."

Rachel slumped on the bottom step. "Where are you?" she cried.

"It's Bank Holiday. We go off on a little break."

"Bring him back. This minute!"

"Listen, babes. I know I was a bad asshole the other day." There was a pause. Fear made her keep quiet. "You know how I get sometimes," he continued, "but listen, I have made a promise to Sasha that I'm going to be like a normal dad, a nice English guy. No fighting with his mum." His voice faded as he turned away and said, "Haven't I, Sasha?"

Rachel heard her son in the background, over the smooth humming noise of a car engine. "Yeah, Daddy. You're not going to fight with Mum."

"Are you listening?" Anton said, his voice velvety. "I mean it, Rachel. I've done a lot of thinking. I know I hurt you terrible, and I was totally, complete out of order."

"Where are you taking Sasha?"

"Somewhere pretty. Some beach. West Wales perhaps. I never been to Wales. Or to my brother's new place in Reading to visit the animal, Napoleon. We have a little think. Probably Wales."

Did he mean Wales, she thought frantically, or was he just trying to get her off the trail? Sasha did not have a passport, she reminded herself, at least not one that she knew of, and Britain was an island. But there were ferries from Wales, to Ireland, perhaps to France.

"Bring him home," she cried, the panic escaping in her voice. "Right now, do you hear?"

"Yeah, sure. We can come back if you want . . . Can't we, Sasha?"

"No," she heard Sasha exclaim in disappointment. "We're going to the beach." A brief silence. "Can we take Napoleon too? And Mummy?"

There was a pause.

"Would you like to come with us?" Anton asked gently. "I got plenty money in my wallet. I give you a really good time, make up for . . . you know. A real family trip, nice hotel, champagne, whatever you want . . . Rachel, are you there?"

She thought frantically for a harmless response.

"Rachel?" Anton's voice was lower still, earnest. "I'm not bad person, deep down I'm not. I love you and Sasha, I just show it wrong sometimes. I'm going to get better with that. We got to throw the past away, and start again . . . respect each other. I know that, really I do."

"Bring Sasha back . . . and we'll talk," she said.

"You don't have to worry. I don't take him far. But I want you come too. It's your birthday tomorrow. See, I do remember."

"Come here, and we can . . . think about it," she said.

"Pack your bag, we pick you up," Anton purred. "Bring your bikini, just in case." There was another pause. "Don't do anything stupid now, babes. There is no need, you know what I'm saying? I bring Sasha, and there will be no trouble. I mean that. So no phone calls, yes?"

"I have to phone Sasha's school, or they'll call the police," she said, her voice cold now. "Perhaps I'll wait until you come."

"Don't be funny, now, Rachel."

"Just bring Sasha."

An hour later the car pulled up on the street outside. Rachel threw open the front door and saw them talking intently, Anton half out of the car and Sasha still with his seat belt on. It seemed Anton was telling him to wait in the car. She wanted to run out and grab him, but in the same moment Anton slammed the car door and came through the gate, looking at her attentively as he approached. He wasn't wearing his pimpy garb but a nice checkered cotton shirt, jeans, and sandals. His hair was clean and feathery, not slicked back. He looked like any family man taking his wife and son away for the weekend. Against her will, Rachel thought how beautiful a man he still was. His black hair framed his broad forehead, and he had high cheekbones, white teeth, and green eyes, his lean body hiding a potent and wiry strength.

Then he grinned at her, and he looked like himself. That smile could melt the ice caps, part boyish, part seductive, part cruel—a smile he'd sold her time and time again, and that she had kept buying. She felt the familiar dread in the pit of her being, coupled with a tingling and moistening . . . so crudely and instantly present . . . and the self-loathing that followed. It seemed that her fear and desire were interminably entwined. It was perverse that even after their last encounter (and all that expensive therapy), she could still feel something for him.

He didn't attempt to kiss or touch her, nor did he comment on the fading bruises on her face.

"Packed?"

"No," she said and turned back into the house. He followed.

"Well, get on with it," he said good-humoredly. "The kid's all fired up. We bought some playthings—a beach ball, spades, and stuff—and I got a windbreaker, just in case, but the radio say is mainly good weather, perhaps a little rain."

She knew she was taking the path of least resistance, but her fear of what he might do with Sasha narrowed her choices to this: stay, and trust that Anton would bring Sasha back after a couple of days, or go with them? Sasha probably was all fired up about going to the beach for the weekend, and Anton would not be deterred. The only safe course of action was not to let Sasha out of her sight. She had to go where her son went.

"Get moving." Anton prodded her on the arm. "We want to leave the traffic, don't we? The M4 will be a nightmare."

"I'll pack. But none of this happy families stuff. I'm not fucking you, do you understand? You're not touching me."

He put his hands up and took a step back, still smiling.

She sat in the back—she'd insisted—and read the map. The M4 was as chockablock as Anton had predicted. But Sasha's good mood would not be dampened. He chirped like a songbird, pathetically happy to be with both his parents and looking forward to his fantasy weekend on the beach. He insisted on sitting under his child-sized parasol, and the red and yellow striped beach ball was bouncing irritatingly around the car. Rachel slumped in a corner and closed her eyes, jolted only by Anton's regular eruptions of road rage. She sat up when they stopped at the toll for the Severn Bridge and looked for it on the map. Shit, they weren't even half-way to West Wales. Traffic crawled over the bridge and she peered down the estuary that divided England from Wales. She'd never been to Wales, perhaps she could find a way of switching off and enjoying some of it.

CROESO Y CWMRY, a sign said on the other side, *Welcome to Wales* underneath in smaller letters. Sure thing, she thought, wondering if Wales would be happy to see the back of them at the end of it.

"Where from here, boss?" Anton said over his shoulder, and his eyes met hers in the rearview mirror. She slipped on her sunglasses.

She studied the map, looking for places she might have heard of. "How about Tenby?" she said. "I saw it on telly once. It's cute, Sasha will like it. It's not as far as West Wales and it's on the sea."

"How we get there, boss?"

"Straight on," she said, "forever."

"Forever? I like forever, Rachel," he said,

taking his eyes off the road again and studying her intently in the mirror.

"I *mean* forever on this bloody motorway," she said, "all the way past Cardiff, Swansea, and Carmarthen, turn left by a place called Narberth. Don't try to be romantic, Anton, you're crap at it."

"Hey," he exclaimed, giving her a sharp look, "can we give a thought to the . . . little one here?"

She laughed sarcastically from the safety of the backseat. "Ho, ho. That's rich coming from you. Considering what the *little one* has seen and heard."

Sasha started crying.

"See?" Anton scowled.

Rachel reached over to stroke Sasha's hair but he slapped her hand away. He knew they were referring to him, what he'd seen and heard. She couldn't get used to how much that little head was capable of taking in. Even if he didn't catch the words, he understood everything that ran below the surface.

She fished for her cigarettes in her bag and put a fag between her lips. She lowered the window. Anton's eyes followed her every move until she brought the lighter up and put the flame to its tip.

"If you light that cigarette I will have to spank your bare bottom." He turned to Sasha and winked. Sasha was still sniveling, obviously sensing this was far from funny.

"Mum, don't light it," he said in a voice that made her heart ache.

She put the cigarette back into the packet and they fell quiet.

Though the air outside the car shimmered in the heat, inside the car it was cool. They continued along the motorway in silence, bumper to bumper with other families that had the same idea. Rachel looked at them through the window, as they went past one another in the two lanes. Happy couples, cheery youngsters, bicycles and surfboards on the roof racks, pillows and cool boxes sitting on top of bags. Families in caravans. Couples in matching leathers huddled close on motorbikes. Anton didn't notice any of them, nor did Sasha. They were both staring ahead as if the destination was all that mattered, as if Tenby would solve all their problems, the ever-present tension would dissolve, and everyone would be happy.

Everyone else seemed to be heading to Tenby too. Cars poured into the little town. Rachel shrank in dread as it became obvious that parking was near enough impossible. They drove round and round the narrow streets, barely clearing the jostle of pedestrians. Anton looked more and more tense, his jaw set. There were pearls of sweat on his forehead, even in the cold interior of the car. Was he on something? she wondered. Was he needing some kind of fix? You never knew with Anton, though he often went through periods of being clean, sharp in mind and body, giving up cocaine and his crappy Russian vodka in favor of lager and working out in the gym.

Sasha, disappointed by Tenby and sensing the mood building up to something nasty, piped up suddenly, his face lit.

"Daddy," he said, "what do you do if you see a spaceman?"

"Be quiet for just a few minutes there, boy."

Rachel leaned forward. "Tell me, sweetheart. What do you do if you see a spaceman?"

"You park your car, man," Sasha bellowed triumphantly.

It broke the ice. Rachel chuckled and then Anton. At once, all three of them were laughing, and as if by design, a blue van pulled out and Anton swerved across the road to grab the space.

"Thanks for the tip." Anton tickled Sasha in the ribs. "I got the spaceman."

"Cool, man." Sasha laughed and squirmed, his happiness restored.

They were parked just outside the old town wall. They grabbed their bags and the ball and walked toward the sea, and as if on a winning streak, they got two rooms in the first place they tried, Oceanvista Hotel on the Esplanade. The reception was a sight, with peeling wallpaper and dusty chandeliers. A fat Labrador wallowed on an Axminster carpet that had snuffed out more than its fair share of cigarettes. The plump Welsh lady behind the counter looked at them over the rim of her glasses.

"There's a bit of luck for you. I've just this minute had a cancelation. The lady had an asthma attack and had to be hospitalized. Poor dear. From Derbyshire, they are. They were so looking forward to the weekend. They come every year, with the two little ones. Sometimes twice." She drew breath.

"Fine," Anton cut her off emphatically. "*You* the lucky one."

She looked at him sharply. "Not *me*, sir. There is not a room to be had in the whole of Tenby."

Rachel tapped Anton's foot with hers. One more jibe from him and they'd have to get back in the car and go to the next town, a catastrophic prospect. He must have sensed it, because he smiled his killer smile at the woman and she looked down co-quettishly. When her eyes settled on Sasha, her face went all soft. She leaned her huge bust over the counter.

"How about this, young man?" she said. "I've got a little room, boy-sized, especially for you, just off the one from Mum and Dad."

They made their way up three floors via a formerly grandiose staircase illuminated by a tall window. Beams of sunlight lit up the dust that circled lazily in the air. Anton led the way through a darkened corridor. The main bedroom was large and smelled of bleach and stale cigarette smoke. The glass in the bay window was made cloudy by windborne sea salt, but the view of the sea was a novelty nevertheless. A door led to what might once have been a broom cupboard, containing a tiny window, a single bed, a small wardrobe, and a painting of a boy holding a duck.

"Tell you what," Rachel said to Sasha, "because it's a special occasion, you can sleep with your Dad in the double bed. I'll take the little room."

Anton gave her a sulky look. "You forget what special occasion is, Mummy babes. It's your birthday tomorrow."

"Stay out of this," she hissed at him.

She bagged the little room before Sasha had time to consider the various implications of her offer, and closed the adjoining door. She poked around in her bag. Time to get the fucking boots off for the season and put on some sandals. Her feet had not seen fresh air for eight months. She pulled her jeans off too and tried on the old denim skirt she'd thrown in at the last moment. It fitted as it always had. She knew she was lucky, her shape never seemed to change. Not that she cared. She looked at herself in the long mirror inside the wardrobe door

and immediately felt exposed, naked, piti-
fully white. Her legs seemed too long compared to her torso, but they were good legs,
she'd been told it umpteen times. Anton
liked long legs, but it was voluptuous breasts
and buttocks that got him going, and really,
she had neither, not to speak of. Why was
he so hot for her skinny shape? She brushed
her hair out and lifted it to look at her ears.
Nice as pie, he was now, but he could look
at those scarred and mangled lobes, and
the bruises on her face, and still feel perfectly good about himself. It took some
doing.

She walked up closer and studied her
face . . . pale, drawn, eyes hooded, with a
sickly yellow bruising around the right one
and part of her left eye still bloodred. Her
jaw was still swollen and her lips chapped.
She took out the lipstick she'd carried
around with her for well over a year and
smelled it. Surely they went rancid—but
better that than lips like cracked heels. From
a bottle in her wash bag she smoothed
some foundation on the discolored skin.

"Let's go, Mum," Sasha called. "Daddy's
hungry." He rattled the door. She looked at

it and noted with dismay that it had no lock.

"Coming," she called back, and slipped on her sunglasses.

"You have a nice evening now," said the lady as they walked through reception. Sasha stopped to stroke the Labrador's head, and it popped open one idle eye. She knew he missed Napoleon terribly, but he'd stopped asking, knowing that what Daddy decided you didn't question. Did he trust his father, or was he scared he'd never see the dog again? She had no way of knowing, because she tried not to probe too much. As she had nothing good to say about Anton, it wasn't fair.

The town was surrounded by a kind of fortification, a thick stone wall that looked ancient. They wandered along the Esplanade and ducked into town through an opening in the wall. The streets went this way and that, in crazy patterns, gangs of local youths and visitors of all shapes and sizes crowded them. It was like a maze; you just didn't know where you were. The sea seemed to pop up wherever you went.

Strange-shaped houses painted in pastel colors, some tall, some tiny, jostled along cliff tops overlooking a long sandy beach.

They passed a gaggle of women in matching angels' costumes, screeching some song and obviously totally pissed though it was still only eight in the evening.

"What are they, Mummy?"

"Drunk angels, sweetie."

"Yeah, but what is it for?"

"One of them is getting married, and the other ones are trying to get her to behave really badly."

"Yeah," said Sasha, as if that made perfect sense. "I'm hungry."

"Here." Anton took Rachel's arm and led them down a tiny alley through which they could see a harbor, with boats resting sideways on the wet sand. Up some steps to a rickety building was a nice-looking restaurant. It was teeming with elegant people, most of them middle-aged.

"This will do," said Anton, and they were led to a table by a spotty youth whose black trousers hung incredibly low on his hips. He gave them each a menu the size of a wall poster, and they studied it while Sasha ran off to look at a tank with live lobsters in it.

"Are you convinced?" Anton said to her.

"Convinced of what?" she snapped, not taking her eyes off the menu.

"You and me have another try. Make a family. Four of us, with the animal."

"Yeah, I'm convinced . . . just because we've had a stressful car journey and you've not punched anybody?"

Anton put down his menu, too sharply. "Didn't you fucking hear what I said when we speak on the mobile? I *said*: I am trying to be better and change. I do my best to make it up."

"You and your promises." She glared at him, then pulled back her hair and whispered angrily, "Look at my ears. Do you remember doing that? Do you remember beating me to go out and suck strangers' dirty cocks in cars? Do you remember what you did to me three weeks ago? Do you remember stealing my money?"

He grabbed her arm. "I was fucking mad at you, what you expect? You leave London with my son and don't tell me where you are. Then you try to dig your teeth into my parts."

"*Mad* at me?" she countered. "God help us. No matter what I do, you get mad at me. What would you do to Sasha if you got mad at *him*?"

She had raised her voice, and people had turned their heads toward them. The lady at the next table was staring at her ears. She dropped her hair and lowered her voice. "What's the problem? You got no girls working for you, or you like Bath as a territory? I'd be no use to you. You need young meat, Anton. I'm too fucking long in the tooth."

"So melodramatic, Rachel. Where you and I come from, business is business, not always done pretty. I was wrong making you work. Business was bad and we were broke, so you do what you have to do. Is in the past now. I've . . . changed my attitude to my life and I want something better. Like my woman and my son, for a start."

"Keep your bullshit philosophy to yourself. I'll never trust a word you say as long as I live."

He didn't press the point or get angry,

and she wondered what the hell he was up to. The nicer and more reasonable he tried to be, the more she feared what was coming next. It had always been the same.

A pretty waitress came and took their order. She didn't take her eyes off Anton even while Rachel was talking to her. She was used to it; he had that effect on women. He could have anybody—that is, anybody stupid enough to take the abuse he dished out. Of all the women he bought and sold, why the hell couldn't he find someone younger and more beautiful, more tender in the flesh, more stupid and malleable—why was he so hung up on *her*? If it was only Sasha he wanted, he probably would have snatched him by now.

When the girl reluctantly left, Anton turned to Rachel and pinched her chin.

"Tell me something. Your father's house. Was he renting it? Is it a council house, or what?"

"Yes," she lied, "and you're not moving in."

"Did he leave you anything?"

She tried to pull her head back but he held her fast. "My father was retired, on a puny pension. Yeah, he left me the furniture.

You want my furniture too? Go on, take it away. Get a van tomorrow. It's yours."

Anton looked injured and let go of her chin. "Oh, come on, babes. Relax."

She rubbed her jaw. Even when he tried to be normal, somehow he managed to hurt her. "Don't fucking touch me. No part of me, you hear? My face is damaged, can't you see that?"

He was starting to reiterate some pledge to reform when Sasha came skipping back full of questions about what was going to happen to the poor lobsters. Anton gave him some mushy story about lobster being the king of food. She was able to concentrate on her pint of beer and gradually she sagged into something akin to relaxation. God, she really was quite hungry. The food, when it finally arrived, was good and the rest of the meal reasonably unthreatening. Though the tension between them made conversation impossible, there was some small measure of mutual gratification in seeing Sasha in such high spirits. Afterward they walked down to the harbor in the twilight and sat on the sand watching the tide coming in, floating the fishing boats, one by one. She sat apart, alone, and as the night descended she lay back and tried to spot a star. When had she last looked at a star? The sand felt soothing against her arms and legs, so soft and cool, she could have stayed like that forever, alone, searching for stars in the wide expanse of the sky.

As they meandered back to the hotel through the maze of cobbled streets, Anton linked his arm with hers and she stiffened, but was too weary to be contrary. In fact, she was dead tired. Back in the hotel Anton went to bed with Sasha without protest—so far so good—and as she drifted off she heard them chatting, like a proper father and son.

In the night he came to her anyway. She woke with a start and saw him come quietly through the door. He was wearing his jeans, which surprised her, but the contours of his naked torso shone in the blue light through the curtain. Her body tensed, with fear or excitement, she wasn't sure which. It made her feel sick.

"It was a perfect day, yes?" he whispered as he sat down on her bed.

"Get out." She rolled onto her side, away from him.

"Switch the light. I've got a little envelope in my pocket. Not much, but just enough."

"You've got to be out of your fucking mind." She groaned and turned back to face him. "Don't you ever remember what you're capable of when you're coked up? Anyway, I don't do drugs anymore. You know that. Just get out of here before I scream."

"OK, OK. I just thought . . . as it's your birthday." He was quiet for a moment but didn't leave. She waited tensely for him to go. He ran his hand along her arm. "Can't I just make you feel good?"

"No. I'm still not feeling too good after the last time. You were like an animal. I'm never, ever—"

He put his hand over her mouth, gently but firmly. "Ssshh," he whispered. "Don't wake the boy."

He slowly pulled the covers from her. "Take your knickers off," he whispered. "I want to kiss your cunt."

"Fuck off," she hissed, half sitting up, trying to yank the sheet back, but he held on to it, his teeth glinting in a playful smile.

"I want to make up to you," he said. "Look . . . I leave my jeans on."

"No," she snarled, louder now, and kicked out with her leg, knocking him hard in the shoulder.

"There, there," he crooned, grabbing hold of her ankle. "Don't be silly now, babes, just relax. Let me taste you. Just for a little while." He rolled onto her, parting her legs, and with his hands clamped on her thighs, he inched his way down her body, pulling her knickers off her as he went.

She didn't have the energy to fight him or argue, or even to think about what this was. It was mild in the scale of things, she told herself, even though she'd said no. And there was Sasha next door, sleeping restlessly as he did these days. A bitter feeling in her gut reminded her that she'd reneged on her resolution, all in the space of three minutes, but it was better not to let the implications of it enter her thoughts. Addicts do that, she reminded herself. Resolutions come and go, but when faced with a fix, you say yes, give it to me, even when you don't want it and you're kicking and screaming all the way.

In another life, another world, some man could have cared about her, made her happy and secure. But what she had was this. She closed her eyes tight and suspended her thoughts. A soft whimper escaped her lips.

"See? You silly bitch, you love it!" Anton whispered from afar. "Without me you are dead!"

Chapter Eleven

The sun was shining out of a clear blue sky, but as on any British May Bank Holiday weekend worth its name, the forecast had promised the odd thunderstorm. Madeleine felt a slight lightening of her mood as, on Sunday afternoon, she drove south along the M5 toward Exeter. She desperately needed to get away. The week had passed so slowly. After Rachel's defection on Tuesday, she knew she needed distractions. She'd called up a couple of women friends she'd not seen for months and met them for dinner in a pub. She'd seen Edmund on Friday as usual, but his health seemed, again, to have taken a turn for the worse. His clothes hung loosely on him, and he kept grinning in an odd way, showing his multiple rows of shark's teeth, as if his facial muscles weren't working properly. He was clearly embarrassed about it and seemed lethargic and sullen.

Madeleine was relieved to see the back of Bath and everything in it. She'd compromised with John, arguing that one night at the cottage was probably enough of a visit for Angus, and yesterday had defied Colonel Sanders's suggestion to stay away from her mother for a while. She'd made off with Rosaria to the Pillbury-on-Avon village jumble sale. It was the only kind of outing Mama enjoyed these days because it reminded her of her neighborhood market in Havana, though this time, the useless junk offered up on rickety trestle tables by the down-at-heel had left her unmoved. She'd clung to Madeleine, ranting about some menace that loomed ever closer, in the shape of charred bodies, flesh-eating ants, sinister enemies, and blindness.

"Your papa can't see, Magdalena," she kept saying. "I look through his eyes and I can see nothing."

"Papa Neville is just fine," Madeleine tried to reassure her. In fact Neville had never been better. His retrospective London exhibition had made him a fortune.

Mama had it all wrong, bless her. If her sensitivity radar had been reactivated by the course of ECT she'd been forcibly subjected to, she was picking up wonky signals. It wasn't danger or death that loomed, but the possible reappearance of the lost child.

When she returned her mother to Setton Hall and installed her in the dining room for her lunch, Madeleine surreptitiously rummaged around Rosaria's room, looking for the pewter brooch. She noted there'd been fresh signs of worship at the altar. Rosaria had placed seven glasses of water, dedicated to the Orishas, each one next to an image of its Christian counterpart. Like the Cuban slaves before her, she hid her gods behind Catholic Saints, though the laws against the religion of the Yorubas had long been abolished. A large cigar and a cup of rum sat near Babalú-Ayé, his true features disguised as Saint Lazarus. As the father of diseases, he was the one god who might have helped Mama cast a spell on the murderer who'd given her daughter the vile brooch. While searching, Madeleine sternly reminded herself that she was no longer a practicing disciple of Santeria, she no longer believed in the power of spells. She wanted the brooch back, because she liked it. However, it was not to be found, not on the altar or anywhere else. She had to accept that it had disappeared.

She turned west on the A30. The fabulous weather was holding out so she stopped in a lay-by, folded down the roof of Neville's old Merc, wrapped a silk scarf around her head, and donned last year's big sunglasses. The verges still had their share of spring flowers and the branches of oak and beech were fresh with young green leaves. On the seat beside her was a huge bunch of tulips, still closed in sleep, a bag from the off-license with two bottles of pink Cava, a big bag of organic pistachios, a side of smoked salmon, and a box of expensive Belgian chocolates from Marks. How to impress the formidable (and jealous) Angus? Despite her ambivalent feelings about John's boyfriend, she found she was looking forward to a day in the wilderness. She urgently needed time and space to consider if there was any further move she could make in relation to Rachel, and she just hoped Angus would allow her a moment alone with John.

John had bought the ruin five years previously in an attempt to find a hobby that would take him out of town, to do something more constructive with his weekends than browsing through antique shops buying things he had no room for. Apart from a restoration project, the cottage was an overflow home for his treasures. The planners had given him plenty of aggravation, but in the end he had restored the ruin to the picturesque home it had been two hundred years ago. Thinking about it made Madeleine feel a pang of sadness. Both of them had been partnerless at the time, so John had suggested that when the builders had finally removed the last cement mixer, they spend an inaugural weekend there. During the champagne-fueled first evening they'd got maudlin, lamenting their childlessness. It had been the perfect opportunity to tell him about the daughter she'd had, but even then she could not bring herself to do it. When they'd popped the fourth cork they were already hatching this crazy plan of having a baby together. They certainly loved each other and in the haze of alcohol-induced stupidity they'd actually believed it was a fantastic idea. She'd been so drunk she'd plain forgotten that she was almost certainly infertile (several doctors and a Cuban curandera had told her so). They'd proceeded to give the project a heroic attempt, but the necessary act was never properly consummated and the following morning John told her in a flood of tears that it wouldn't work. He was not really in the vagina business, and he feared she'd end up hating him for his inability to be a proper husband. Though she conceded the idea had been dumb and almost certainly unachievable, she nevertheless felt like a walking wound for days to come. A door had been opened in her heart, then summarily shut.

She drove for a good half hour before turning left, heading south toward the interior of Dartmoor. She'd been to the cottage a dozen times since that drunken evening, so she knew her way, more or less. Anyway, she had a "sat nav" now, a Christmas present from Gordon. A deep manly voice calling itself Brad was seductively guiding her toward her destination, until the country lanes got increasingly remote and Brad admitted defeat.

The cottage was in the heart of Dartmoor, perhaps the most remote spot you could find in the whole southwest of England, up a track, six miles off a desolate country road. The track was muddy and rutted from recent rain, and more than once she heard the scrape of the Merc's already battered underbelly and she winced in sympathy. The track seemed to go on and on, once forking into two. Abandoned meadows, perhaps fields in former days, lay on either side, but as she drove higher, the scenery gradually changed, becoming bleaker and less green. In the far distance the moors looked inhospitable and forbidding. Madeleine was amazed that such a secluded and faraway place still existed in this crowded country. Growing up, she'd never known seclusion except in her own backyard. Though fertile beyond restraint, the tiny island of her birth had hardly any wilderness as such, bar a few mangrove swamps and the seas surrounding it, the Atlantic on one side and the Gulf of Mexico on the other.

As she came around a bend, she could just glimpse the roof of the little house. No driver would see it if they so much as blinked, hidden as it was in a gully obscured by several imposing chestnuts. She turned down through a cut in a crumbling stone wall and followed the faint tire marks to the gate. John's new Volvo Estate was on the graveled parking bay and she parked her car half under the hedge beside it. Strategically sited on the tiny lawn was the VW camper van (from the days before the cottage) that was to be her sleeping quarters. She smiled seeing it there, with a cast iron step by the door, surrounded by several pots of geraniums and daisies, no doubt placed there to make her feel welcome.

Angus came out to meet her, and she wondered if this was a deliberate tending of the olive branch. He seemed overly pleased to see her. Air kisses all round plus exclamations of delight and "You shouldn't have's" at her offerings. Angus's balding crown glinted in the sunlight and a the jaunty cravat made a festive red splash against his white shirt. Still, she couldn't quite see what John found sexy in the man. He was short and round and shiny, and quite a bit older. Then she scolded herself for her ungracious attitude. They were going out of their way to make things nice for her.

"Where is my man?" she asked him cheerfully, casting a glance around for the familiar sight of John.

"*My* man, you mean, surely," Angus said with a smile that was a little tight in the corners.

"Yes, of course he's your man. I meant 'my man' as in 'my partner, my friend.'" Madeleine laughed, idiotically adding, "Hell, I don't mind sharing."

That was bad to worse. She winced and resolved not to try to be funny on any account, while Angus looked away with a roll of the eyes that said, *Well, I tried.*

"I've only been here a minute and already I'm out of order," she said contritely.

"I'm sure John has told you I'm not at my sharpest at the moment."

Angus reached for her hold-all. "Let me carry your bag."

Judging by Angus's attire, even out here in the sticks dinner was quite a ceremony. To show her respect she changed out of her jeans. Nothing sexy—Angus was already on edge—but on a hunch she'd packed her deep purple raw silk trousers and matching shirt that she knew would dazzle.

"Good Lord," they exclaimed in unison, and looked her over with genuine admiration. John squeezed her hand in passing and whispered, "Good choice. You look divine."

Despite the shaky start, or because of it, Angus refused all offers of help when he disappeared to the kitchen to work his magic. So Madeleine and John drank gin and tonic, making small talk under a mushroom-shaped patio heater on the little terrace outside the living room. The evening deepened and the wild hills around the cottage that earlier had shifted in bright ochers and purples now grew ever more shadowy and misty until they lay in darkness.

Madeleine tossed back the dregs of her drink, aware she could use another one, and doubly strong. "Any ants' nests I should know about?"

"No, but there was a superhighway between the kitchen door and the pantry soon after we unloaded the food. God, they're quick! I told Angus you'd enjoy a spot of field study, but I'm afraid he put ant powder down." He reached for her hand. "But don't say anything. He wouldn't understand."

Ant powder! She struggled to contain her displeasure. It wasn't fair to judge the man on ant powder; she hardly knew him. Johnny was happy, wasn't that the main thing? She mustn't spoil a potential friendship with Angus. In the course of these quiet self-admonitions, Angus called them.

Madeleine leaned toward John, her voice low and urgent. "Any chance you and I could get away for a few moments tomorrow? There is something I need to confess, something I should have told you years ago. You're going to be really pissed off with me."

"Heavens," John said, looking startled. "That bad?"

"Yes, John. I need you and your . . . wisdom on this."

He struggled up from his rickety deck chair and nodded. "Angus's back is acting up. He won't want to come for a walk."

The dining room table had been lovingly set with a charming collection of mismatched plates, starched napkins, and fine glasses. Madeleine's uncertain mood thawed as they sat under a chandelier of five scented candles. Her smoked salmon was artistically offered up as a rose on each plate, garnished with a sprig of fresh dill, lemon wedges, and small, twirled dollops of garlic mayonnaise. Vivaldi's *Four Seasons* tinkled like a shower of crystals from hidden speakers, only slightly muffled by the noise of the generator in the shed.

"Beautiful!" she exclaimed with genuine appreciation, giving Angus a broad smile, which he acknowledged with a curt nod.

The leg of lamb that followed, baked in a crispy covering of chipped almonds, made even Madeleine ask for seconds. John was in an unusually effusive mood, drinking too fast and talking too loudly. At one point during the meal, after some particularly infantile joke, Angus and Madeleine exchanged a complicit look of *We do love him, but he really can be a pain when he's pissed,* and after that, aided by yet another bottle of wine, the conversation and laughter became progressively more relaxed. Madeleine decided that whatever she'd thought of Angus, he was impeccably gracious as a host. She probed him a little about his background and was surprised to discover he had three daughters and several grandchildren.

"Goodness, you had an early start."

"I was nineteen when Leonora was born. Two years later we had the twins."

John was working his way through the Belgian chocolates. "They're darlings, all three of them. Hey, Angus, me and my mate here are childless. Once we even thought we might—"

Madeleine shot him a warning glance and gave a slight shake of the head. Angus noticed and looked from one to the other with a frown.

"Yeah, we always used to compare notes," Madeleine said, trying to cover up.

"My husband and I couldn't have children. I was told it was my fault, but we never went so far as to do something about it, that is to say, nothing medical."

"Oh, you were married?" Angus said, a little too surprised. "I didn't know." He shot a reproachful look toward John, who was now leaning precariously into a glass-fronted dresser, making clinking noises with bottles. Angus turned back toward Madeleine. "Who was the lucky guy? Was he a Key West boy? John said you were born there."

"Yes he was," Madeleine said, drawing breath. She had her story down to a few pain-free sentences. "I lost him. Shortly after he died, I came to Bath. My father is British and my parents had come to live here in the eighties, so I kind of knew Bath already."

There was a short, awkward silence.

"So you came to Bath to brainwash people," Angus mused, choosing to ignore the fact of her widowhood. "Did you train in the States?"

"Brainwash!" Madeleine cautioned him, smiling wryly. "Be careful now. That says something about your views on our profession . . . *John*," she called over her shoulder, "did you hear that?"

John was coming back to the table, brandishing a bottle of Cognac and three enormous glasses. He stumbled slightly as the toe of his well-trodden slipper snagged on the edge of a flagstone. The top of his head barely cleared the low cottage ceiling. His glasses were askew, his shirt had detached itself from under his trousers, and he had a red wine stain at the level of his belly button. The immaculate Angus looked at him, slightly pained.

"Angus is a bit old-fashioned. Stiff-upper-lip brigade. Pay him no heed," said John.

Angus did not dispute the charge but turned to her. "No, really. Tell me. What did you do out there?"

"I made a living as a painter."

"Painting?" Angus's eyebrows went up. "What? Houses or canvases?"

"Honestly!" John frowned and leaned across the table toward his boyfriend. "Madeleine is a brilliant artist. Her father is Neville Frank. I'm sure I've told you that."

Angus looked at Madeleine, impressed. "Really? Neville Frank! And why, pray, would you leave such a glamorous occupation in order to listen to people whining and complaining?"

She knew she'd never win him over. However, though he was a condescending little prat, he had a point. She'd chosen her new profession for a variety of reasons. *Helping people,* a pathological motivation if ever there was one, and perhaps she'd hoped that understanding the human psyche would safeguard her from what had happened to her mother. Especially as her grief had made her half insane.

"I came to Bath to start anew," she said to him. "Everything in my life had changed and I was trying to put the past behind me. I ended up doing psychotherapy training, partly because Bath has an excellent program." She hesitated. "I trained with John. But you know that."

"Yeah, yeah, of course you trained with John." There was a grain of irritation in Angus's voice, and he waved his hand as if to skip the John and Madeleine happy-ever-after-in-practice story. He'd obviously had it from John more than once.

John shoved a huge measure of Cognac toward her and she had to wrap both hands around the bulbous glass to hold it. A drop of candle wax plopped onto her finger. It burned for a moment, but the feeling was pleasant. Why had she come back? She knew the logical answer: she couldn't bear to see the streets she had walked with Forrest, the marina where their houseboat had been berthed, the bars where they'd drunk and eaten, and the beaches where they'd lain and kissed. She'd come back to Bath because she missed her mother and felt bad about her being here alone. But Bath was not the place she would have chosen, left to her own devices. Or was she wrong about that—had she still been hoping to find her daughter?

"Yeah, well," she muttered, taking small, measured sips from the tumbler in her hands. "Whatever I do, I'll never make a convincing Limey."

"True," Angus agreed readily. "Nor do you seem particularly American. Have you got another ethnic background perhaps?"

There was a long moment when the only sound was John tapping a cork coaster pointedly against the table. Angus peered at Madeleine, smiling his little smile, waiting for her repartee.

"I'm gonna take that question as a compliment," she said. "And there I was, worrying you'd find me too American. John said you don't care for the nation and its people."

She shot him a challenging grimace, but Angus just laughed.

"Hey, it *was* a compliment. I think I was mainly referring to how you look. So tanned and dark-eyed and curly-haired."

Out of the corner of her eye, she could see John's jaw working tensely. He was such a softie he loathed confrontations of any kind, but even he had his limits.

"I'm probably descended from some Guatemalan domestic." She stood and stretched, trying to loosen the stiffness from sitting for hours. "It's in the genes. Watch this." She started to gather the dishes still on the table.

"Aww, come on," John protested, half rising, trying to grab her arm, "don't do that. Sit down."

"No, really. I'm beat," she said, pushing him back into his chair. "I'll load the dishwasher and then I'll turn in."

"Over my dead corpse do you load the dishwasher," John bellowed. He staggered to his feet, throwing an angry glance at Angus, and put his arm around her shoulder. "Come with me, darling. I'll show you to your rooms."

The night was calm and silent except for the intermittent call of some night bird. Madeleine tucked herself up in bed. A slight breeze blew the cool night air in through the open window. She had left the curtains undrawn to see the sky. A large oak tree loomed behind the van. The bare branches formed a tangled latticework over her head, and the moonlit clouds scudding past gave the illusion of weaving themselves through the branches. Mesmerized, she watched their seemingly never-ending progress.

She felt wide awake; it felt as if she had been awake for weeks. It had been six days since she'd last seen Rachel, and she'd hardly slept a wink since. She knew she was reading all sorts of things into her departure, such as Rachel herself discovering their connection and making a hasty exit from therapy because of it (who wouldn't?).

Mikaela's pale little face kept superimposing itself on Rachel's mature features, and the more Madeleine thought about it, the more she was convinced of the resemblance. Rationally, she was aware she was indulging in an unsubstantiated fantasy, yet part of her refused to accept that she might be wrong. Rachel *could* be the daughter she had lost. If nothing else, her birth date told her so.

Even just the possibility felt like an awakening. All her senses were sharpened. She heard and saw and felt things that were normally beyond notice, yet the impact they made seemed out of control. It was as if she was skating on ice, slipping and tumbling, drawn toward some unknown abyss. Why was that so? Where was it leading?

One thing was certain. If Rachel was her daughter, she'd never accept Madeleine as a mother. She'd be horrified by the discovery, humiliated in view of all the intimate details of her life she'd confessed, her almost deviant sexual obsession with a pimp . . . her prostitution, walking the streets of London, the drugs, the breakdown. Knowing Rachel, she'd be angry, more angry than

she already was. Furious. Livid. And unfor-
giving. Madeleine knew she would be faced
by yet another loss, a loss that seemed unbearable.

She had to still her mind. She was no
good to anyone without some sleep, least
of all to herself. Wine used to knock her
out, but these days it had the opposite effect. Then she remembered the temazepam, the promise of oblivion that had been
the carrot to get her to come for the weekend. Good old John, he'd either forgotten
or else Angus had refused to part with any;
people were funny about their drugs. Now
she desperately wished she had some.
The night would be excruciatingly long,
though she had no idea of the time and
was too lethargic to try and locate her
watch.

She must have dozed for a moment because the next time she focused on the
sky, the clouds had dispersed and the oak
branches were lit by blue light. The bird
had gone silent. She lifted her head to see
better. Dazzling moonlight illuminated the
cottage. It looked ancient and abandoned,
like the ruin it had once been. It was strange
to imagine that inside one of those rooms

slept two well-fed and happy men, lovingly entwined.

A deep sense of loneliness overcame her, but she tried to shrug it off. Well, she'd brought a book, a best-selling but tedious "urban" novel in which the characters had neither jobs nor ambition, as if these were uncool aberrations and real life revolved around trendy bars, coke dens, and sparsely furnished lofts. Then there was always the *Myraculous,* her favorite ant magazine, with a tantalizing article about a newly found species of leaf-cutter ants in the depth of the Amazon rain forest.

But the will to move did not present itself. Her command of her limbs had gone slack; they refused to gather the necessary muscular contractions to turn on the light and find the reading material. Perhaps this was a good sign. She closed her eyes.

She woke and wondered where she was. It was hot, unbearably so. She was on a narrow bed and someone was snoring somewhere else in the room. A curtain fluttered outward through an open window. She could smell a mix-

ture of diesel fumes, sea salt, and sewage and instantly remembered. She was in a youth hostel of sorts (more like a doss-house) in Vera Cruz, Mexico.

There was something lurking on the edge of her awakening, something special. Yes, now it came to her: her twenty-first birthday. Today she would embrace total adult status.

The snoring stopped, there was a long sigh and a groan, a bed squeaked, and the nasal rumbling started up again. It was her best buddy, Gina. She was a big girl with a pair of breasts that practically strangled her at night.

Madeleine reached for her watch and tried to read the time in the dim light from the street. It was six-thirty in the morning. That was the problem with "doing Mexico" with Gina. Their body clocks were totally out of sync. Gina was one of those people that could sleep and sleep, no matter what, where, or when, whereas Madeleine struggled to get any sleep, no matter how tired. Things were always tugging at her mind. How she wished she could be oblivious to everything, like Gina, as placid a person as you'd ever find. Nothing got to her; her conscience was like a tilting ice sheet, everything just slid off; she didn't know the meaning of guilt, blame, responsibility, commitment. Madeleine tried to force her to phone her parents in Key West once in a blue moon, but in the end resorted to asking her neighbor Mrs. Woods to nip over to Gina's parents' house to tell them Gina was still alive—though penniless, and could they wire more money? Here they were on the Bay of Mexico with nothing but a crappy knapsack each, two pairs of panties, one pair of jeans, one pair of shorts, a sundress, two T-shirts, and a comb. Madeleine had been moonlighting in Sloppy Joe's for the last few months and had five hundred hard-earned dollars inside a money belt worn against the skin, but Gina's money had run out. She'd taken to begging on the streets for an hour a day, something Madeleine would absolutely never resort to, absolutely never in a billion years.

Madeleine sighed loudly into the gray

room. She wished she were with someone from her own family, for this one important date. She'd not been to Bath for over a year, not seen Mama or Mikaela. It was too hard, too strange; the little kid didn't even know her anymore— her own daughter—and Mama seemed to prefer it that way. All in all, she'd been back to Bath only three times in four years, and each time she'd got incredibly depressed.

But all of them would surely have made a fuss about her birthday. Neville and Elizabeth would have splashed out on a party, Elizabeth loved stuff like that, and would have ordered some ghastly mountain of a cake with twenty-one candles, given her money and clothes. They had just got married and had moved to a fancy flat in Knightsbridge.

The sun was already baking the cobblestones, but the streets were silent except for the shrill calls of a man selling bread out of a tiny white van. Bleary-eyed women in housecoats opened their doors and handed over money for hot panes and bags of tiny sweet cupcakes. Madeleine ran after the van as it turned a corner and gave the man a handful of small change. He put two enormous flatbreads into her arms. He was good-looking in that Mexican Indian way, but unshaven, and his fingernails were dirty.

"Hoy es mi cumpleaños," *she said on a whim.*

He laughed. "Que edad tienes, niña?"

"Veinti uno," *she said proudly, wondering if perhaps twenty-one was no particular cause for celebration in this country.*

"Enhorabuena." *He bowed theatrically from the waist and held out a cupcake.*

His eyes wandered slowly down her long bare legs. For a second it looked as if he might ask her to get into the back of the van. Would she have laid herself across all that crusty, sweet-smelling bread and allowed him to make love to her? The idea, fleeting though it was, shocked her. It had been ages and ages since she'd got laid, but who else was going to mark her coming of age? No, not a stranger. That was Gina's domain.

She took the cupcake, peeled off the sticky paper, and ate it with relish as she ambled through the narrow alleys trying to remember the way to the square. When she found it and the phone box, it smelled of stale beer and cigarettes. A half-empty wine bottle sat on the floor. Only tourists would do such a thing, she thought primly. Damned gringos.

She left the door open while she dialed Mama's number. She let it ring for a long time. There was no answer. What time was it over there, anyway? Finally an answer machine clicked in. To her consternation it was Neville's voice, saying: "This is the answer phone of Rosaria Frank. She is no longer available at this number, but please call . . ."

What? Neville's own number! Had Mama moved in with Papa? He'd not long married Elizabeth, but who knew, perhaps he'd seen the light (or Elizabeth had left him) and they'd got back together? Madeleine's heart skipped a beat and a warm feeling filled her. What a birthday present that would be! Quickly she dialed his number.

The phone crackled. "Neville," she yelled. "Neville?"

"Madeleine," he bellowed. "Thank God. Thank God you called."

"You weren't worried about me, were you?" she asked, a bit perplexed.

"No, love, but you really should call more frequently. I've got bad news, I'm afraid."

She felt a sudden coldness on her back despite the morning heat. A tingling in her extremities.

"What? What bad news?"

"Look, you've got to come over. Have you got money? Where are you? I'll arrange a ticket, if you can't."

"What the hell is going on?"

There was a pause, and she called, "Are you there?"

"Yeah, yeah. I hear you loud and clear. Listen, your mother . . . has been sectioned. About five weeks ago. I didn't find out about it until the day after your last call. I couldn't get hold of you to tell you. Mikaela . . . has been placed with a foster family. Don't worry, don't worry, these . . . foster people are excellent people."

"Neville," she cried. "What's that? What does that mean, 'sectioned'?"

"You know . . . she is in a psychiatric hospital. She's had some kind of breakdown."

Oh God. Seconds passed as one frightening scenario after another played itself out in her mind. She shook her head. No, there had to be a simple explanation. Maybe Mama had been practicing and someone had reported it. They'd think she was crazy. Nobody over there understood about Santeria. Something like that must have happened.

"Christ! Poor Mama. You've got to go and get Micki."

"She's fine, she's with very nice people. It's your mother I'm concerned about."

"Yes, but get Mikaela. Don't leave her with strangers."

"She's OK. Baby, this business is your call, not mine."

"What do you mean?"

"Madeleine! You get your arse over here. I've got an exhibition in Tokyo."

"I'm coming!" she shouted. "But go

and get her. You can't leave Micki with foster people."

"Madeleine," he shouted back, "I've got to be in Tokyo the day after tomorrow. I've got a fucking opening, for Christ sakes. I'm booking you a ticket from here. Where the hell are you?"

"Mexico." Tears were clouding her vision. "Slow down, Neville. Explain it to me, tell me what's happened to Mama." There was a pause. "Neville?"

"Yeah, I'm here . . . Apparently it's been coming on for a while. It was a neighbor who alerted Social Services. She'd painted over all the windows, black, and she was taking out the furniture and burning it in the garage. She'd hung chickens and other dead animals from the trees in the garden. Talking to herself. She hadn't left the house for weeks, apparently. God knows what had been going on there."

Madeleine stood frozen. That did not sound like Mama. It frightened her.

"What about you?" she growled. "You promised me you would always be there for them. You said you'd visit every week. You don't care, do you?"

"Hold your horses, Madeleine. What about you? You've been having a ball in art college and mooching around Mexico in your spare time. How about you taking a bit of responsibility? After all, Rosaria is your mother, and you aren't a child anymore."

"No," Madeleine said darkly. "Not as of today."

"It looks that way, doesn't it?"

"That's why I rang, actually."

"What do you mean?"

"It's my twenty-first birthday."

"Oh shit," Neville blurted. "Is it really?"

"Who cares?"

"Well, Happy Birthday, what can I say? Now what about a ticket, baby? Where exactly in Mexico are you?"

It was a drab building, on the outskirts of Bath. Green walls like a hospital. Regis Forbush ushered her into a meeting room and invited her to sit down at a round table. A man of about fifty-five, Mr. Forbush had a posh accent but was incongruously tramplike in appearance. His brown trousers and a green cardie were dull and looked in need of dry cleaning. His hair was thinning badly and a greasy slab of it was plastered across his pate.

"Jetlagged, are we?" he said with a disinterested smile. "Good of you to interrupt your holiday . . . Mexico, was it?"

"I'm here to pick up my daughter, Mr. Forbush. Is she—"

"Listen, Miss Frank" he interrupted, his smile dropping off like a broken icicle. "Isn't it true that you've not been the carer of your daughter for, what . . . four years? And the last time you saw her was a year ago?"

Madeleine opened her mouth to explain, but he continued.

"In fact, according to these papers I've got in front of me"—he patted a thick manila folder on the table before him—"there was an application for formal adoption of little Mikaela. You were, in fact, already planning to give your daughter up for adoption . . . to your mother, Rosaria Frank. Isn't that so?"

"Well, sort of," Madeleine said unhappily.

Mr. Forbush raised an eyebrow. "Sort of?"

Madeleine cringed. It sounded so flaky. "My mom has always really, really wanted to adopt Mikaela. She kept telling me I wouldn't be giving her away, we're still the same family. Mikaela thinks I'm her sister, she calls my mother Mama, just like I do. I'd come to a point where I knew I wasn't being fair to my mom, she's been pressuring me about it for . . . well, five years, ever since Mikaela was born, but I had no idea she was so . . . depressed."

"It's more than just depressed, Miss Frank, Madeleine, if you don't mind me calling you that. Your mother has been diagnosed with paranoid schizophrenia. She's probably had the condition for years."

"Paranoid schizophrenia?" Madeleine said, dumbfounded. It sounded horrific. She knew it was a mental illness, but wasn't that what homicidal maniacs had? Madmen running around cutting people up with knives, or breaking into schools and shooting children.

"That's gotta be wrong, Mr. Forbush," she said flaring up. "My mom has had a nervous breakdown because of the divorce and stuff. It's nothing like paranoid whatcha-call-it. You see, my mom is an unusual woman. She's a Santera, a wise woman. People here don't understand what that means. They think it's some kind of hocus-pocus. It's prejudice, that's all."

"I'm afraid the doctors' reports are very thorough. Your father has paid top psychiatrists to help your mother . . . So you see the adoption would never have been granted in any case."

"My father!" Madeleine muttered. "What the hell does he know?" She shifted fretfully on her chair. Neville had already flown to Tokyo by the time she'd arrived in England. She'd suspected for a while now that he rarely visited Mama and Mikaela in Bath. He was totally obsessed with Elizabeth, his new wife, and their posh apartment in London, and he'd hired an old couple to be caretakers-cum-cleaners-cum-gardeners for Mama. They'd been on a caravaning holiday in Scotland when Mama's breakdown happened.

Despite Madeleine's initial resentment, Elizabeth seemed a nice enough woman, totally different from her mother, certainly a whole lot younger. She'd been decent enough to wait for Madeleine's arrival before joining Neville in Tokyo. This morning, before Madeleine left London to take the train to Bath, she'd lent her a skirt, way too big, and a pink blouse. Christ, she'd not worn a blouse since school, or tights, and never, ever shoes with kitten heels. Madeleine had done a real hack job on her own hair trying to trim the purple bits out with a pair of nail scissors, and had pulled her mass of curls back with a plain rubber band. She was trying to look demure, responsible, but it was a joke, and Regis Forbush's penetrating glare must have seen right through it.

"And Mikaela's father?" he said in an insinuating voice. "His name is not on the birth certificate. Do you know who he is?"

Madeleine was about to protest, then

thought better of it. At the time of the birth she'd refused to name the father, worried that Forrest might get into trouble. Had he not said she'd made him into a criminal? And now, five years later, wherever he was, the last thing he needed was to have the news of a kid sprung on him.

"Our only concern at this moment"— Forbush pointed his forefinger at her— "is Mikaela's well-being."

Madeleine nodded apologetically. She was shocked that she'd not noticed anything about Mama. They spoke on the phone at least twice a month, often weekly, and she'd not detected anything strange about her. Mama had always been eccentric, she was an unusual person, but what was wrong with that? Could it really be true she was mad?

Regis Forbush slipped on a pair of glasses. "The couple that are fostering Mikaela are extremely fond of her." He opened the folder and took out a sheet of paper. "Mr. and Mrs. X are forty-four and forty-two years old, respectively. They . . ."

Madeleine froze. She half stood up to

protest, but Regis Forbush continued. "They married late and have no children of their own. They own their own home, close to good schools. Mr. X is a painter-decorator, Mrs. X a housewife. They are"—he raised his eyes and looked at Madeleine over the top of his glasses—"in a very good position as regards their application to adopt Mikaela. And in view of the fact that you have never had custody of the child yourself, it is reasonable that we consider their application."

Madeleine grabbed the edge of the desk. "Adoption? You mean to say they think they can adopt her?"

Mr. Forbush smiled a little. "Madeleine, no one came forward to rescue this little girl from an untenable situation. Your father came to see me weeks ago, but he felt in no position to take on a child at his age. You live out of a backpack, it seems, and are mostly 'on the road' on the other side of the Atlantic. Your mother will not be allowed to take custody of the child again, even if she is discharged from hospital. Don't you think there is a case here for—"

"No," Madeleine blurted. "Yes, I was away traveling. I didn't know anything about what was going on. I don't think just because—"

Mr. Forbush interrupted her in turn. "It may well be that you have no recourse anyway, Madeleine. We have the authority to take the decision into our own hands, but honestly, this is a situation I think can be resolved calmly, without conflict, and above all . . . with the child's best interest firmly in mind."

Madeleine stood up. At the lower edge of her vision she saw that the top buttons of her blouse had popped open. The red bra she'd bought in Woolworth that morning clashed shockingly with the pink shirt. Forbush noticed it too and was unimpressed, but for different reasons. A vital second passed that took the wind out of her outrage.

"I don't want that. Don't forget I was only sixteen when I had her. I'm twenty-one now. I can't do what you're suggesting, it's far too . . . final. You can't push me into giving Mikaela up for adoption." She shook her head resolutely. "I'm sure you can't."

Regis Forbush gave her a perfunctory wave to sit down. "We do have a lady here you can talk to—Karen. Perhaps you'd feel happier talking to a woman. She can give you a bit of counseling, talk you through it, so you feel more reassured."

"No," Madeleine insisted. "No one is going to talk me into this. You can't make me."

Forbush shook his head.

"I want to see my little girl," Madeleine said resolutely.

"You can't. Not just now." His finger pointed directly at her chest. "Remember what I said. We all—you included—will keep the child's best interest in mind. Little Mikaela has had a very traumatic time." Forbush's voice hardened. "I don't know if you are even aware what she's been put through. She needs stability. She needs love and care and continuity. This is what she is getting now, at last, from Mr. and Mrs. X. Now and for the foreseeable future."

Madeleine felt her face whiten with both fear and anger. Could they really do this? Could they stop her from seeing her own daughter? Could they take her away . . . forever?

From the very moment she'd heard the news of her mother's hospitalization she'd felt something happen inside her, like a sprouting seed unfurling rapidly in her chest: a sense of maternal responsibility, a strong wish—no, need— to come to her child's rescue, to protect her, to shelter her and save her from harm. She could learn to be a proper mother. She could do this now, she would do this.

"I'm going to get my father onto this," she blustered. "I'm going to get a lawyer. I want my daughter back."

Forbush sat back in his chair and crossed one leg over the other. "It's not like on television, Madeleine. This is not a soap opera. This is the happiness and welfare of a real, living child we are talking about. If you love your little girl, you will do what's best for her. You will want her to be happy and stable and have a good, solid set of parents who will give her everything she needs to grow up into a fully functioning adult."

"Yeah, really," Madeleine blurted. "I've heard that in a soap. I don't buy it. I'm her mother. I'm sure that counts for something."

She paused and bit her lip. She sounded ill-mannered and immature. It was no good getting belligerent; she could see by Forbush's face that it wasn't helping her cause at all.

"Listen, Mr. Forbush. I didn't know that my mother was suffering from this . . . thing. If I'd known I would have been here like a shot. You've got to understand, I was very young and immature when Mikaela was born, and besides, I was very ill. After the birth, I developed a puerperal infection and spent three weeks in hospital. My mother simply took over, and she totally bonded with the baby. Perhaps I shouldn't have let it happen, but she was quite forceful about it. Even Neville . . . my father was all for it. You see, she'd had three miscarriages after she had me. She so wanted another child, she was desperate."

"Desperate"—how suspect that sounded now. Madeleine winced at her choice of words but rushed on. "She was a lovely mother to me, so I trusted her completely. She was young, she had plenty of time, she was lonely . . . Mr. Forbush, I haven't actually done anything wrong, and you're making me out to be a horrible, negligent person. That's not fair. I think you need to give me a chance."

Forbush, who'd been sitting back, benignly listening to her plea, suddenly leaned across the desk, his forefinger jabbing at her sternly. "You think you can look after that little girl properly, do you, Madeleine? Where are you going to settle down? Do you own a home? Do you have a job? Child care? Savings? A husband and father to the child?" He almost sneered now. "A mother to help and guide you?"

He drew back, as if knowing he was going too far. "Listen, Madeleine. I do feel for you. God only knows what your own childhood must have been like. Your father actually told me you had all sorts of problems as a result of your mother's excesses, that you could be unreachable for days on end, talking only to insects and indulging in all sorts of other displacement behavior."

"He didn't say that," Madeleine protested. "No way!"

"In fact, he said more than that. I got the distinct impression that your father agrees with me about Mikaela. He told me she desperately needs a solid, dependable family environment, and that nobody in the Frank family is in a position to offer her that."

Madeleine jumped up and glared at him.

"That's because he feels guilty," she cried. "He left her. He must have turned a blind eye to my mother's illness because it was convenient. Mama was so happy to have a child to love, it gave him the license to divorce her and go off and marry this other woman. He's the last one who should be making judgments. How dare he stick his nose in this and say such a thing?"

Mr. Forbush shrugged. "So in fact you don't have your father's support either."

"I don't believe this," she said, containing her tears. She grabbed her coat and bag from the back of the chair. "I'm going now, and I'm going to get a lawyer . . ." She marched toward the door, adding furiously, "Just like in the fucking soaps, Mr. Forbush."

Chapter Twelve

Monday morning of the May Bank Holiday dawned brightly over the sun-starved British Isles and their inhabitants. However, like millions of others, John had the mother of all hangovers. Madeleine was also battling with a headache (that last Cognac, no doubt) and Angus had had a terrible night with his back. Having slept poorly, all of them were up early.

Madeleine, being the least afflicted, offered to cook breakfast, but Angus would see no stranger presuming to take charge of his kitchen, and after much stoical huffing and puffing, he produced a mighty stack of pancakes with a bowl of sour cream and a tub of thawing raspberries.

They ate with relish, then Angus took to his bed while John and Madeleine scrubbed the kitchen. When the last dish had been put away, John shouted up the stairs. "We're off for a stroll, Angus. Don't forget your exercises. You know what the chiropractor said."

A sudden early-morning mist floated in over the bleak landscape, whitening the sun. They climbed over a stile at the corner of the garden and walked along the edge of a long-abandoned meadow. Outside John's garden, the land had long lost any connection with human touch. The grasses reached almost to their shorts, the dew soaking their bare legs and walking boots. They crashed through some nettles that stung their ankles, and down a rough stony bank toward a small stream flanked by ancient hawthorn.

"Where next?" Madeleine asked.

"I don't think I've ever ventured this far beyond my garden," John confessed with an embarrassed grin.

Not knowing where else to go, they began to follow the stream upward. The hawthorn almost closed overhead, gradually making the rough path along the little brook into a dark tunnel. The tunnel kept going upward, but the high banks and tight vegetation made it almost impossible to see where they were heading. The restlessness in Madeleine's limbs made her want to wear herself out. She walked as fast as John could tolerate, her own breath quickening and the blood pumping in her ears.

"How're you doing, buddy?" she called over her shoulder. It pained her to see him so out of breath. "Your love life is going to be the death of you."

"What love life?" he called back. "You can see for yourself the state of him."

After a while the tunnel of trees was cut sharply by a pile of large boulders. The source of the stream disappeared under it. They pushed through a wall of brambles and shrubs, coming out into the sunlight onto the naked moors. Wild country stretched far into the distance, with not a house or barn or road to be seen. Barren hillocks topped by granite tors were the only disruption in the otherwise empty, undulating landscape.

"Shouldn't we turn around?" said John, beads of sweat dampening his forehead. "We are already lost."

"Oh, come on. We're not lost. We need to work off the excesses of last night."

They wandered on, traversing spongy patches of marshland and climbing over the ruins of ancient drystone walls. The bleak moorland seemed to go on and on, not a cow or a sheep to say that people lived hereabouts. Even birds seemed scarce. It felt as if they'd entered Dartmoor in another time altogether, another century.

"We're bound to come across a group of hearty ramblers at some point," John said, scanning the horizon, shielding his eyes from the sun with his hand. "They are crazy people, they love this sort of starkness."

A fog came out of nowhere, rolling over the land, and within minutes they couldn't see five meters in front of them. Blindly they wandered on until they suddenly came upon what looked like the tail end of a dirt track. It was almost covered with moss and grasses, as if it had been months or years since a vehicle had reached this point. By this time they were indeed quite lost and decided it was best to follow it where it would take them. They felt the first stirrings of thirst, and stupidly, they'd not thought to bring a bottle of water. Madeleine knew it was nearly ten o'clock and that they'd been walking for over two hours. Rosaria had taught her about the movement of the sun; it was imperative for the right order of things, time for rituals and worship. A watch was useless for Mama's kind of timing. John looked anxious.

"Enjoy it," she said, nudging him in the side. "Civilization is bound to be nearby."

"Civilization? You obviously don't know this place. People get lost and die on the moors; sometimes years go by before they're found." He linked his arms through hers and patted her hand. "Which reminds me, we're just about out of earshot, wouldn't you say? Come on, what's this thing you've not confessed?"

"I was dreading you asking." She knew she couldn't put it off any longer. "I don't know quite how to begin, and I'm nervous about your reaction."

He glanced at her. "Heavens! It can't be *that* bad, surely?"

She laughed. "That's an amateurish intervention if ever I heard one."

"Just spit it out, Madeleine."

She braced herself. "You know the woman I'm seeing, that was hooked up with this big, bad Russian Ukrainian, the Afghanistan veteran, who forced her out on the street?"

"Yeah. The woman with the sexual obsession?"

Madeleine took a breath that stuck halfway. "There is a remote possibility she's my daughter."

John stopped. He turned to look at her. "You don't have a daughter."

"John, I do. I had a daughter when I was sixteen." She paused. "She was a love child, to me she was at any rate, but at my parents' insistence I gave my little girl to my mother to raise. Mama bonded with her to the extent that I could not bear to tear them apart. In fact, I went back to Key West to go to art college. Leaving them was the biggest mistake of my life. Five years later Rosaria was put away, and I was coerced into giving my daughter up for adoption."

John stared at her. "This is mad. You've never told me any of this."

"I know and I'm so, so sorry I haven't."

He shook his head in shocked disbelief, but seemed incapable of speech. A long moment passed and she almost wondered if he'd ever forgive her. Finally, in desperation, she grabbed him by the arm and marched him on. He didn't say a word, walking beside her in stunned silence. She kept quiet, knowing he needed time to absorb this bolt from the blue. She also knew what an enormous betrayal it was. They'd known each other for over seven years. Certainly he was the best friend she'd ever had. Many times she had asked herself why she'd not told him this fundamental thing about herself, and the answer was always shame . . . *denial.*

She knew what he must be thinking. Apart from being a shallow friend, dishonest and hypocritical, what sort of psychotherapist must she be? Those four long years in training, where participants were expected to delve deep into their own psyches, a process of self-discovery, a baring of the darkest corners of one's soul. Everyone else on the program had undertaken that difficult journey, an unquestionable requirement for someone who sought to understand and guide others in their own quest for insight and self-growth . . . but she'd held back, she had hidden the truth.

"I know what you're thinking."

"You can't begin to know, Madeleine," he said crossly.

"I need your help," she pleaded. "I don't know how to handle this. In order to establish whether my suspicions are right, I need to ask this client lots of questions. I don't know if it's ethical or utterly unethical to do so. I don't know *how* to ask her. Or *what* to ask her, or if I should ask her at all. Anyway, I think she knew something was up because she hasn't come back. Hasn't phoned to cancel or anything."

"*Oh for God's sake*," John broke in, but said no more.

They continued walking in silence through the fog. The track went on and on, curving westward.

"Let's rest for a moment," John said after a while, turning off the track and plonking himself down on the sparse heather.

She sat beside him, but he looked away and seemed lost in thought. She parted the grass at her feet and peered into the vegetation for *Lasius flavus*. They lived abundantly in the scrubby grasses of moorland but only rarely ventured aboveground. She thought them awesome, these pretty yellow ants who built such intricate nests, using live roots and shoots to reinforce their corridors and so ingeniously shitting in the crevices to encourage the growth. She'd painted an interior of their nest once, a luminous, semiabstract work, huge in size, snapped up by a Japanese collector.

John took off his glasses and mopped his forehead with his shirtsleeve. After a moment he turned to her. She stopped her pointless search for ants and raised her eyes to him. The disquiet in his face made her heart sink.

"This is beyond me, Madeleine. I wouldn't have a clue how to handle this. You need to look for someone with years and years of experience. Someone impartial."

"Oh, don't say that," she cried. "Forget you're a therapist. Help me as a friend."

"I'd do anything for you. We can talk about it, as friends, but as your 'best friend' you'd better explain why you've withheld this information from me. In fact, Madeleine, I'm angry, I'm disappointed. I'm confused, but above all, I'm *hurt*. With those feelings getting in the way, I might not be much good to you."

He took her hand and looked at it as if it was some strange object he thought he'd known, but realized he didn't. "Why the hell have you never told me?"

"Don't you remember when I met you? I told you I needed a totally fresh start. It was the only way I was going to survive. Dealing with Forrest's death was a big enough task, and we were a great support to each other . . . weren't we?" she pleaded. A moment passed. "Perhaps, subconsciously, I moved back to Bath hoping to find her. I've had my name on the Adoption Contact Register for years. Forrest and I even came to England when my daughter turned eighteen, only a year before he died. We went through the whole process of trying to make contact, but the mediator told us he couldn't find her. He assured us that if and when she was ready, the register was likely to be the first place she'd look."

She swatted at a horsefly on her ankle.

John let go of her hand. "You're obviously not sure your client is this daughter of yours."

"No," she said dejectedly. "I'm not at all sure. But listen, she was born on the same day as my daughter. In Bath. And Rachel, my client, looks quite a lot like me, I think. She has almond-shaped eyes, and Forrest's grandmother was Chinese."

John frowned. "That's it?"

"Yes, but that's a lot of things for a mere coincidence, John. Think about it."

John paused. "Rachel?" he said. "Her name is the same, presumably?"

"Ah, no, the name is not the same."

John turned and gave her a pitying look. "She at least knows she was adopted?"

Madeleine wrung her hands. "Well, actually, no. I asked her if she might have been, and she denied it." She turned to him. "But there are a lot of people, still, whose parents never told them they were adopted. It's not uncommon."

"Look here, my love." He grabbed both her hands and shook them lightly as if to get her full attention. "You just told me your daughter was five when she was adopted. It's highly unlikely she'd have no memory of her first five years. And the adoptive parents . . . would they really screw with a kid's mind to that extent? I doubt it. It's quite possible you might be wrong, Madeleine. You need to tread very carefully."

"What should I do?" she cried. "Shouldn't I tell her? Ask her?" She felt herself choking up, close to tears.

John put his arm around her shoulder. "What about Neville? Have you told him?"

"No, not yet," Madeleine said. "I'm thinking of going to London this afternoon, if we ever find our way out of this place. Unless he's away. He and Elizabeth always try to leave the country on the May Bank Holiday."

John got himself up with some difficulty. "Let's keep walking and you'd better tell me the whole tale." He offered Madeleine his hand and pulled her up.

They continued along the track, absorbed in conversation. Madeleine was grateful for the opportunity just to unburden herself. She couldn't fault John for his attention, but he was too overwhelmed by her story to offer any advice. Besides, he was not a parent and had no knowledge of the psychological implications of adoption.

Yet his strong arm around her shoulders felt like the embrace of a loving brother.

Soon the track entered a forest of conifers. The fog came and went, weaving itself among the tall trees. Neither of them wanted to admit they were becoming exhausted, chilled by the Fog and parched from the receding hangovers. An hour later they finally came upon another track. They stood there, momentarily lost, but when Madeleine looked back she recognized the big green sign: *Forestry Commission*. She'd passed the fork in the road yesterday on the way to the cottage.

"Phew! Thank God!" John leaned over and rested his hands on his knees. "A landmark. We've exactly two miles to go."

As they neared the cottage they saw Angus at a distance, standing in the middle of the road in an obvious state of agitation.

"Where the hell have you been?" he shouted as they approached. "Do you know what time it is? I've been clomping around the moors for hours shouting for you, braying like some lovesick mule."

"It's all her fault," John said, flicking a thumb at Madeleine. "She led the way."

"Don't be cheeky, you bastard," Angus ranted. "You deserve a hiding. I was shit scared."

"Oh Angus, don't be in a strop. We got lost. Honest."

"So where is your bloody mobile?"

"I'm sorry, but I can't always be at your beck and call."

Madeleine moved away from the escalating domestic exchange.

"Where are you going?" John called after her.

"I think perhaps I should pack up and get a move on. I'm off to London."

"Don't be crazy. Everyone will be going back to London now. The M4 and M5 will be dreadful, full of hungover motorists. The queues will—"

"Enough, John," Angus interrupted angrily, shoving a short, fat forefinger in Madeleine's direction. "First a cold shower and a good lunch, madam, then you'd better get the hell out."

Brutus, the Yorkie, hopped into Madeleine's lap. She'd known the little dog for years and they had a very special bond. His were the most effusive kisses she got at her father's, and his raspy wet tongue covered her hands.

"You've lost weight, Madeleine," Elizabeth said sternly, her arms crossed. "I've told you more than once: after forty a woman has to choose between her figure and her face." She pointed toward the kitchen. "Shall I make you a sandwich?"

"Stop fussing," Neville said, his voice sharp. "She doesn't *want* a sandwich."

Madeleine looked at him. It was not like him to be short with Elizabeth. "Whoa, Neville. I can speak for myself."

"Get the girl a drink," the old man commanded. "That's what she needs."

"I don't know," Madeleine protested. "I'm driving back to Bath, don't forget."

"So what! You're staying for dinner." He snapped his bulky fingers in the air as if to jog his memory. "What is it you drink these days?"

Madeleine sighed and turned to her stepmother. "A very large vodka with just a splash of tonic would be great, Elizabeth. Thanks."

Elizabeth herself was a picture of health, looking years younger than fifty-two. Her full figure was the proof of her snippet of wisdom. Her face had not a wrinkle or line on it.

They were sitting in a large, elegant living room, four floors up. The sun was shining in through the row of tall windows of Neville and Elizabeth's Pont Street flat. The spire of Saint Columba's Church graced the view at the front. The rear windows revealed the familiar sight of Harrods. After his recent retrospective exhibition Neville had enough money to buy an entire mansion in the heart of London, but they were happy in the flat they'd lived in for over twenty years. The old hypocrite liked the sound of the address more than anything. In his mind it said everything about him: venerable, famous, and very wealthy. He was too wrapped up in his own importance to understand why his address had alienated his old bohemian artist friends, and put it down to sheer envy and sour grapes.

Madeleine shifted restlessly on the sofa, smoothing the suede cushions. She was desperate to blurt out what she had come here to tell, her whole body was jumpy, but she sensed the atmosphere wasn't quite right. She turned impatiently to see if Elizabeth was coming back in. How long did it take to make a couple of drinks?

"What are you working on at the moment?" she asked, to fill in the time.

Neville's tall, bulky form spilled over every part of his Danish designer armchair; his wild gray mane glinted in the sunlight.

"I'm having a well-earned break," he said, smoothing his goatee with studied nonchalance. "I'm giving myself some time to think about where I'm going next. I was wondering about trying my hand at ceramics."

Madeleine stared at him and then burst out laughing. "Ceramics?"

A stiff silence followed. Madeleine glanced at Elizabeth, who was finally coming through with a tray of drinks. She batted her eyes at Madeleine, as if to send her some message, but Madeleine was stumped.

"Pass that by me again?"

"Why should I talk to *you* about it?" he said, flaring up. "You're not an real artist, you're a fucking shrink."

A bit on the sharp side, she mused, but surely a cue to retaliate. "The great Neville

Frank making mugs. I never thought I'd see the day."

Neville didn't bare his teeth for the combat. Instead, she saw a look pass between him and Elizabeth. Something was going on here. Neville lifted his glass of Rioja with his great paw and downed it in one pull as if it were a mere thimbleful.

Was it possible . . . She was so preoccupied with her own crisis, she just hadn't thought. The old man was seventy-nine. He'd been going strong for well over half a century, moving steadily between decades of portraits, wildlife, and landscapes, earning acclaim and respect on both sides of the Atlantic. Looking at him, she could see it now; he'd grown old. Hell, he was burnt out, tired. There had to be something akin to retirement even for artists. Maybe at was where he'd come to, but was too proud to admit it. Perhaps the quality of his work had been going downhill. In fact, the last few paintings she'd seen, some abstract flowerlike forms, were a strange deviation from his meticulous renditions, not at all up to his usual standard. Could the retrospective inadvertently have signaled the end of his career, for himself as well as the public, his buyers and collectors? Perhaps his agent had advised him to stop while he was ahead, and in doing so probably even increase the value of his work.

On a whim Madeleine jumped up and put her arms around his shoulders.

"I think ceramics is a great idea. I'm just giving you a hard time 'cos that's what you expect from me." She bent down to his level and looked him in the eyes. "We've got to keep each other on the straight and narrow, artwise. Right, old man?"

"Oh, for fuck's sake." Neville shook himself free of her hands. "Don't patronize me. Anyway, you know nothing about ceramics."

Madeleine sat down again, chastened, and took a sip from the drink Elizabeth had put on the little table beside her. In fact, she *did* know about ceramics and occasionally bought the odd piece. When she'd tried to show them to Neville, he'd huffed condescendingly and wouldn't give them more than a cursory glance. But everyone had a right to change his mind, develop new interests. Good for him.

Neville grabbed a remote control from the coffee table and turned on the television.

Madeleine frowned. She'd rarely seen him watch television, certainly *never* in company. Now he was flicking through the channels, his eyes pinned on the box, the other hand holding his glass out. Elizabeth meekly got up and filled it from the bottle on the table. Madeleine felt increasingly bewildered. Neville was an eccentric and often cantankerous old fart, but he'd always treated his wife with respectful adoration during their two decades of marriage. He'd been so chuffed to seduce such a young woman, the daughter of a proper British aristocrat, younger even than Rosaria, a woman who shared his interests, who loved booze, frivolity, fine clothes, and good food and at the same time was utterly presentable and had an accent to match his (all the things that Rosaria didn't and hadn't). It seemed inconceivable that he'd see fit to treat her with this imperious offhandedness.

Madeleine looked at Elizabeth with narrowed eyes. She looked back with a slight shake of the head, as Neville at last hit upon some soap opera. Madeleine's bafflement was gradually being replaced by annoyance. Now there would be an atmosphere, just because she'd said the wrong thing.

He'd be sulking until he'd had enough wine, and then his mood would lighten and everyone would have to be in instant party mode to please him. In that sense nothing had changed. Everything had always been about Neville, revolving around his needs and his moods. Add fame and fortune, and here was a recipe for hardboiled narcissism. How often did he phone her? Ask her how she was? Ask her anything at all about her life? How often did he ask her anything about Rosaria, bar the odd query about the financial arrangement?

They sat quietly for a moment. Madeleine and Elizabeth sipped their drinks while Neville guzzled his.

Madeleine broke the silence. "Neville, there is something I need to talk to you about."

"I'll leave you to it." Elizabeth stood up and pointedly left the room. Madeleine was perplexed. Perhaps they'd had an argument. Yes, that had to be the explanation. She turned back to him; but he didn't take his eyes off the television.

"We never talk about Mikaela, do we?"

He shrugged. "What's there to talk about? We know nothing about her."

"You might just be wrong there. Possibly I've known her for a couple of months."

Neville eyes left the screen and he looked suitably surprised. "*Possibly?* What do you mean exactly?"

"I am not absolutely sure, but it's a woman who's been my patient since March."

"Christ! What can I say? You've probably got the wrong woman."

"That's what I'm trying to establish."

"Well, if she is, you'll have to think of some way to get rid of her."

"What?"

"Listen, Madeleine," he said, looking at her with resigned forbearance, "I'll give you some fatherly advice. Don't get carried away by sentimental rubbish. It's all too easy to get slushy and dewy-eyed, but even if you were to be right about this woman, these encounters never work out very well. Don't complicate your life, girl. Your best bet is to try and think of some pretext to stop the therapy."

"That's it?" She stared at him and shook her head in dismay. "That's your fatherly advice?"

"Madeleine, for fuck's sake, you're forgetting that Mikaela doesn't want to know you. Didn't you have your name on some register, and she's not picked up on your wish to meet her? That girl is no longer your daughter, and hasn't been for over twenty years. She is water under the bridge. Accept it."

Madeleine stiffened. She should have foreseen his coldhearted, pragmatic response. But was he right?

"This is your granddaughter we're talking about. Your own flesh and blood."

Neville grimaced. "I've never believed in this consanguinity business. It's overrated, that's what I've always thought."

Madeleine felt the blood rising to her face. "What does that make *us* then, Neville? Acquaintances?"

He waved his hand dismissively. "Oh, don't be so theatrical. That's different."

"No, it isn't."

They fell into a brooding silence. His eyes flickered back toward the television. It seemed he could not be any less interested in Mikaela. Madeleine felt sick with angst and frustration. *If ever she needed a proper father . . .*

She raised her voice over the sound of the TV. "Have you any idea who adopted

Mikaela? I mean, did that slimeball adoption officer, Forbush or whatever his name was, ever confide in you? I seem to remember the two of you having some friendly little chats."

Neville sighed exaggeratedly. "Of course not. That sort of information is completely confidential."

"Does the name Locklear ring any bells?"

"None."

"So you can't tell me anything I don't already know? Please, Neville, I really need to deal with all this. This woman is my patient as well as possibly my daughter. In addition to wanting to establish the truth, my integrity as a therapist is being horribly compromised here. Can't you help me? Is there nothing . . . ?"

Neville shook his head. "Look here, I'm not being a bastard for the sake of it. I know no more than you do. I can't help you. Besides, I've got my own problems. Just put it to rest, Madeleine. Go on a holiday, or get laid, or something."

"*Get laid?* Are you serious?"

"I didn't mean . . ." He stopped and looked at her. "Oh shit." He took a deep breath that rumbled through his chest. "Listen now. I'll tell you the only thing I know, and it will prove to you that you've got the wrong person. The couple who adopted your girl were a Mr. and Mrs. Cocksworth. That grimy chap, Forbush, told me their name by accident once, when I spoke to him on the phone. The only reason the name stuck in my head is because it's so ridiculous. I remember pitying the poor little girl going to school with a surname like that. *Cocksworth*, for fuck's sakes!" He chuckled to himself. "They were not *Locklear*, my dear girl, if that's the name of your patient. Unless, of course, Locklear is her married name."

No . . . nor is she Mikaela, Madeleine thought with a sinking heart. One name change could be possible, but not two. But there was still the birth date. The date . . . *and the eyes.*

"I need to know beyond any doubt, in case she . . . comes back to therapy. I'll just have to do some more detective work."

"I don't think you need bother, Madeleine. I'm pretty sure Forbush told me the Cocksworths were moving back to Newcastle as soon as the adoption was finalized. That's where they were from." He shook his great head and took another glug from his glass. "C'mon, girl, why would Mikaela have moved to Bath of all places?"

Elizabeth appeared in the doorway with Brutus hopping at her feet.

"This hound needs exercise." She stopped and looked at her husband and his daughter, clearly sensing the tension in the room. "Why don't you come along, Madeleine? We could go for a walk in Hyde Park, take a turn around the Serpentine."

Madeleine looked at her and then at her father, who had lost interest in their conversation.

"Yes, all right. I'll come."

Madeleine waited while Elizabeth rounded up the dog, now frenzied with anticipation. Neville refused to look at them or stir from his seat.

They set off toward the park, ambling slowly and waiting as the little dog lifted his leg against bus stops, lampposts, and rubbish bins. On Sloane Street Elizabeth stopped at every shopwindow, casting her expert eye over the creations displayed there. Madeleine couldn't give a damn about overpriced designer clothes at the best of times. She just tagged along, her thoughts churning. *Cocksworth.* She'd never heard the name, and the fact that the family had moved to Newcastle should settle her doubts. If Neville was right, she might as well accept that she was mistaken.

"Look at those shoes. With your legs, they'd look stunning on you, Madeleine."

"Come on," she said, pulling Elizabeth by the arm. "It's all the emperor's new clothes."

Madeleine was, by habit, drawn toward the entrance of the park, where *Rush of Green,* Jacob Epstein's monumental sculpture, awaited them. As a young artist, Neville had known Epstein, and Madeleine could never hear enough stories about the old master. Especially the one about him hurrying to finish *Rush of Green* on the day he died. For Madeleine, the death of the artist was linked with the life of the sculpture, the long-limbed figures in flight with Pan in eerie pursuit. But as she studied it now, her heart skipped a beat. It had another meaning, an extra layer, something that Mama had brought to her attention . . . having to *run for her life.*

Elizabeth pulled on her arm in turn. It seemed she'd had enough of art and artists to make her gag. "We've looked at this monstrous thing a thousand times," she complained. "Let's walk, for goodness' sake."

They crossed the road and entered the park. The whole of London had had the same idea. The paths were full of families, toddlers, and dogs on leads, roller skaters and cyclists. Men and women on elegant horses trotted up and down the sandy bridleway alongside the Serpentine, which in itself was full of rowing boats and elderly swimmers braving the cold dark water.

Brutus took the lead and made a beeline for the trees. They picked their way between picnic blankets and lovers snogging on the grass, carrying the dog in case he thought to tinkle on someone's picnic hamper. Away from the throng, the silence between them needed addressing. Madeleine decided to be blunt.

"What's with you two and the strange behavior?"

Elizabeth hesitated but then drew nearer, putting her arm through Madeleine's and lowering her voice. "Neville is going blind."

Madeleine stopped dead. *"What?"*

"He's going blind. Nothing can be done about it. He's known it for a while now. His painting days are over."

"Oh God, no." Madeleine gasped. "Not that."

"Yes, I'm afraid so."

Madeleine shook her head in disbelief. "What is it? What sort of blindness?"

"Retinitis pigmentosa. Have you heard of it?"

Madeleine nodded impatiently. "How long has this been going on?"

Brutus pulled at the lead and they walked on, moving farther out onto the open grassland. "A couple of years."

Madeleine was shaken. Poor, poor Neville. What a devastating fate for an artist. Hence the ceramics, the mean mood, the new penchant for ordering Elizabeth around. No wonder he was bad-tempered.

Looking at her stepmother, she suddenly felt more sorry for her than for him. Neville had had a great life, and inevitably something was going to get him in his old age. Nobody was exempt from the decrepitude that went with advancing years. A wise man might see blindness as an opportunity to look inward, especially if, like

Neville, he'd lived through his eyes. But that kind of wisdom was rare. She'd seen it in a few patients, elderly men and women who, knowing the end was near, sought therapy to broaden and deepen their inner awareness. Neville was not that sort of man, however. He'd live the rest of his life resenting every moment of his handicap.

She put her arm around Elizabeth's shoulder. "I'm so, so sorry. It all makes sense now."

"He's refused to let me tell anyone, but you can see it's hard on both of us. I personally don't feel like keeping up the pretence. He's being very . . . tedious."

Madeleine looked at her. *Tedious?* It was not a word Elizabeth would ever have used in reference to Neville. They had always been "babes in the woods," a relationship model that could have been named after the two of them. No matter how good the friendship between her and her stepmother had become over the years, Elizabeth had always refrained from confiding to Madeleine the details of her marriage. Rightly so. Neville was her father, after all.

"If he could only just accept it," Elizabeth said with a faraway expression. "It's not something you can fight."

"Oh God, Elizabeth. How soon do you think . . . ?"

"It's gradual. His peripheral vision is almost gone. He says he sees everything as if through a straw."

"Of all things to happen," Madeleine said, dismayed. Rosaria's tremulous voice rang in her ear. *Your Papa can't see, Magdalena. I look through his eyes and I can see nothing.*

"How will you manage?"

Elizabeth turned and looked pointedly at her. "How do *you* feel about it?"

The question took Madeleine by surprise. "Terrible, of course. Anything I can do to help . . ." It sounded feeble, inadequate.

Elizabeth didn't answer. Madeleine studied her profile. The ski-jump nose had always made her look young and mischievous. With her rosy skin and long golden braided hair hanging down her back, she was still beautiful, but also very strong and capable. As a stepmother and friend she'd been perceptive and sensitive. Hopefully this was a time when they could really support each other. Perhaps this was the time to share her own predicament. Yes, she owed it to Elizabeth to explain the reason for her visit. Madeleine put her hand on Elizabeth's shoulder, giving it a little shake to get her attention.

Look. In case you were wondering what I came to talk to Neville about . . . it's something I could really use your thoughts—"

"You might as well know," Elizabeth cut in abruptly. Her voice was forceful—fierce almost. "This is going to sound like the most awful betrayal . . . I'm going to leave your father." She put up her hand to ward off any exclamation of surprise or protest. "The last few years have crushed me. He's become *so* difficult, Madeleine, and *nothing* is going to change that. I can't spend the rest of my life pandering to a rude and demanding invalid. I'd die of depression." Her face crumpled. "Please, Madeleine. Can you understand that? We've had many good years and I think I've made him happy, but I've always been the muse, the one he leans on, the one in his shadow. I've not minded that, but to go on . . . into this new phase, as his nurse, carer, and dogsbody. I don't want that for myself. I'm already tired, and the real difficulties have not even begun. I'm only fifty-two . . ."

She stopped and they stared at each other.

"But Elizabeth . . ."

"Please don't!" she blurted. "I know he'll be devastated, but *I can't bear it anymore.* I might as well tell you, there is nothing anyone can say or do to change my mind, so don't even try."

"You mean you haven't told him yet?"

Elizabeth looked at her pleadingly. "Will *you*?"

"Me?" Madeleine exclaimed. "No way. If that's what you've decided, you must do it yourself . . . and soon."

"I'm going to Switzerland to visit my sister on Wednesday, and I am not coming back to the flat when I return."

Madeleine shook her head, staring angrily at her. "My God, just like that? And you haven't told him anything?"

"I'm not going to ask for much," she said defensively, as if money were the main issue of concern. "He's put plenty in my name over the years."

Brutus didn't like the tone of their voices.

He kept turning around to look at them, tilting his little head in consternation. They walked on for a moment without talking. Elizabeth produced a crumpled tissue from her pocket and dabbed at a couple of tears.

"What do you imagine he will do?" Madeleine said at last.

"I don't know," Elizabeth said, her voice strangely hardened. "You need to think about it. I mean, you could consider living in London."

"You can't be serious." Madeleine pointed at her own chest, her eyes wide. "What a suggestion! I've got my practice, and I've got Rosaria to think of."

They'd turned around and were walking back the way they'd come. Elizabeth's voice broke into her thoughts. ". . . home help, a nurse perhaps. I don't know. Mind, there are lots of young women out there, artists' groupies, happy to 'do' for an old master with money and status. He'll find someone. Anyway, he's got millions, and if he works his way through those, there is always the flat."

Artists' groupies! Madeleine suddenly felt like hitting her. How could she? How could anyone turn from a loving wife into a pitiless stranger? "Listen," she said in a low voice, "you do what you have to do, but you'd better get talking to Neville about what he wants and needs. You've got to help him sort something out. *You owe him that.*"

The first thing they heard when they opened the door was a long-drawn-out rumble that almost shook the floor, followed by snorts and grunts.

"He's asleep." Elizabeth sighed. "That was not the first bottle of the day."

"Are you surprised?" Madeleine said acidly.

"To be honest, I think you should go now. The traffic will be horrendous, and he is not going to be in a good mood when he wakes up. You think about what I've told you. You *are* his daughter."

Madeleine stopped to look at her father. He was deeply asleep in his chair. His mouth had fallen open, and though large in body, he looked just as reduced, just as pitiful as the woman he'd left all those years ago. No matter how rich, how much he'd accomplished, and how brilliant a woman he'd traded her in for, he'd end up just as alone and abandoned as Rosaria. *What goes around comes around,* she thought wryly.

In a flash of darkness she saw her own self, the creation of these two, heading inexorably toward old age and a similar isolation. It seemed she could not hold on to love—it slipped from her fingers or she gave it away. Something gnawed at the edges of these grim thoughts.

For the first time she thought of the boy. Sasha.

Chapter Thirteen

Rosaria stood at her altar with her back to the door. She was wearing an emerald-colored silk dress that Neville had bought her eons ago; it still fitted her slim figure. Her legs were fairly unscathed by the ravages of illness and age, shapely and clad in black stockings, but her feet were bare of shoes. Uncharacteristically, she had let her hair down and it fell about her shoulders, still thick, reaching almost to her hips. Dyed back to its original jet-black, it was impressive, and from behind she could easily be mistaken for a young woman.

Madeleine stood immobile in the doorway, watching her quietly. Mama's offerings to her Orisha, Babalú-Ayé, were laid out on the altar before her: a glass of coconut milk, a cup of roasted maize, a chunk of bread dipped in olive oil. (Neville's guilty generosity allowed her to send for anything she needed.) The tiny flask with the ground-up bones of her Yoruba ancestor sat on a flat stone, and a small doll, devoid of hair and covered with what looked like dried blood (whose?), leaned against the effigy of the god himself.

Worshipping Babalú-Ayé during the day was rare because he hated daylight, but there was her mother evoking him at four in the afternoon. What spell was she after? It was no coincidence that Rosaria's Orisha was the father of infectious diseases, the owner of smallpox and all afflictions of the skin. The appearance of HIV in the world was attributed to the wrath of Babalú-Ayé. He could also bring cancer, paralysis, syphilis, and leprosy. But just as he could afflict, so could he heal. And his sexual powers were great, a fact that made him popular with lovers seeking a spell to reach greater heights of pleasure and passion, or with partners fearful of losing their lover to another.

Madeleine wondered if she should interrupt the ceremony. Nurses and care assistants were obviously accustomed to Mama's quirks and left her alone, or she would not be doing what she was doing, Madeleine was sure of it. She was in the midst of these thoughts when Rosaria turned around to face her. The look she gave her daughter was chilling, and Madeleine flinched. She had interrupted *something*.

"It's just as well you've arrived, Magdalena. I have to smoke this cigar." She picked up a cigar from the altar, still in its cellophane wrapper. Neville, or rather Ronald Trapp, his solicitor, had a box of Havana cigars delivered to Setton Hall every month. Neville was aware what a pleasure good cigars would give his Cuban ex-wife. What he'd probably forgotten was how integral they were to her rituals.

"Take me outside, Magdalena. *Quickly!*"

It was a lovely day, though windy, and Madeleine searched the wardrobe for a jacket and a pair of sensible shoes and helped Rosaria put them on.

"Right, let's go down and sign ourselves out," she said. "Have you got matches?"

"Don't be silly." Rosaria smirked. "Do you think they let *me* have matches? This place would have gone up in smoke a long time ago."

It wasn't often they shared a joke, and they tittered companionably.

Once signed out, they went down onto the lawns. Weather permitting, afternoon tea was served outdoors for residents with visitors. Blue wicker tables covered with starched white linen tablecloths were dotted about. Madeleine sat Rosaria at a table beneath an oak tree and went to order a pot of coffee, extra strong, and borrow a lighter.

"Have you got my drink?" Rosaria whispered when she came back.

Madeleine reached into her bag for the bottle and surreptitiously poured a good measure of rum into a plastic beaker. The cigar was finally lit, and peace descended. When she was smoking, Rosaria was in a heaven of her own. Her eyes closed and she puffed resolutely and expertly, relishing the fine cigar.

"Mama, where is the brooch?"

Rosaria stopped puffing. She was cunning, and despite the drugs she could be fast thinking. "What brooch?"

"The brooch you took from my bag."

Rosaria resumed puffing and blowing smoke. "Have you lost your marbles, *chiquitilla*?" she said, chuckling at her own sense of irony.

"It's not funny." Madeleine leaned forward. "Are you doing things you should not be doing? Or have you asked Pedrote to help you? Have you, Mama?"

Rosaria stared at her angrily. "I don't need Pedrote anymore."

That's what I figured, thought Madeleine with a shudder. She didn't like what this implied. If she believed in the magical aspects of Santeria, *which she no longer did,* she would certainly think Mama was casting spells. Add Rosaria's knowledge of Santeria to her latent psychic abilities *plus* her mental illness, and here was a dangerous mix. She could be a threat to all kinds of people. Yet there was not a person to whom Madeleine could tell such a thing. Nobody would believe what this meant, except possibly Neville. It was, after all, her talents that had mesmerized him.

"Mama," Madeleine said sternly, "do you remember years ago when you were teaching me about Santeria? You always told me that casting evil spells and making people sick was for Voodoo people, not for proper Santeras."

"Correcto, mi niña."

"Babalú-Ayé would not like you doing that. You'd be abusing the power he has given you. He could strike you down with some dreadful malady."

Rosaria's eyes were closed. "It is he who guides me," she said shrewdly.

"Don't you remember when I almost died from *mal de ojo*? You wouldn't be doing that to people . . . would you, Mama?"

"I have to protect my children, Magdalena. I will use my powers and strike down anyone who tries to do them harm . . . or take them away from me." She shrugged and studied the cigar in her hand, then gave her daughter a piercing glance. "Any mother would do the same. Wouldn't they?"

Jesus Christ! Madeleine fished the bottle out of her bag and took a large swig from it, not caring what it looked like.

"Your children?" she whispered, her throat scorching from the harsh rum. "How many children do you have, Mama?"

"Two, Magdalena. But you know that already. I have two children."

Madeleine stared at her. Rosaria suddenly stood up and threw the cigar to the ground. *"The second child,"* she cried, staring crazily at Madeleine. "You evil girl. What did you do? What became of her?"

"Now, now, Madeleine, I told you this wasn't a good idea," said Regis Forbush, patting her awkwardly on the shoulder. "Try and pull yourself together." He grabbed a wedge of tissues from the box on the table and pushed them into her hand. "Come now, you were the one who demanded this meeting. It was your choice . . . hey, hey. Listen, I'll try and find Karen. I'm sure she's somewhere in the building."

He couldn't wait to get away, she could tell. His brown cardie flapped in the draft of his exit. The door slammed shut a bit too vehemently. Madeleine

dabbed at her eyes, wishing she'd not bothered with mascara. Who was she pretending to impress? Mikaela?

She should have been late rather than early. Sitting waiting was unbearable. The couple who were adopting her daughter had apparently been understanding. There had been no obligation on their part, it was just an act of charity. She had to see Mikaela one more time, but as the minutes drew nearer to that last good-bye, she was stunned by the appalling finality of the decision she'd been coerced into making. It wasn't as if she didn't know that adoption was a permanent state of affairs, and she had tried her very best to convince Social Services that she could be a worthy mother to Mikaela, but wherever she'd turned, she'd not met any support. Even Neville had chosen to step back and keep out of it (which she swore she'd never forgive him for).

To soften the blow, in her mind there was still room for maneuver, time to reverse the verdict; surely someone would come to her rescue, offer a solution. The whole thing seemed so unreal.

She'd become, day by day, increasingly awake to the fact that Mikaela was her own daughter—not Rosaria's, not Forbush's, not the Social Services', the government's, or Mr. and Mrs. X's. Yet now that this feeling had taken hold of her, her daughter was to be separated from her forever. The decision was, of course, in Mikaela's "best interest." Though she'd never before seen herself as a proper mother, the child that was hers had been living in her somewhere, a sense that was growing and swelling within her, like a pregnancy resumed.

When Karen Enberg came through the door, Madeleine was in a state of panic. She ran up and grabbed the large, motherly social worker by the arm. "Karen, look," she sobbed. "I can't go through with this. I can't."

"All right, sweetheart. I understand," said Karen, "I'll tell them the meeting is off. I'm sure they'll be relieved. It was a lousy idea anyway."

"No!" Madeleine bellowed. "I mean the adoption. I can't go through with it. I've changed my mind."

Karen put her arm around Madeleine's shoulders. "You've signed the papers. There is no turning back, you know that. Mr. and Mrs X are doing you a favor by bringing Mikaela here. They feel for you, they really do, but they've also made it clear they want a clean start. For Mikaela's sake more than anything."

She led her back to the plastic chairs lining the wall. "You're just a wee one yourself, sweetheart. Once you're back in Florida, you'll meet some nice man and get married and have a brood of kids . . . you'll see."

Through the grief and distress, anger flared within Madeleine. "Don't patronize me, Karen. Do you really think that's what I want to hear? Haven't I already said that I might not be able to have any more children? After I had Micki I was told that I only had a twenty percent chance of conceiving again."

Karen patted her shoulder. "Don't you believe it," she crooned, settling her broad behind precariously on the chair next to Madeleine's. "Sure you can have kids."

They'd already talked it through several times. Karen had told her that her own mother had given her sister up for adoption forty years ago, and the two sisters had just made contact. It was possible and probable, more and more these days, that natural parents and children found each other through adoption support agencies.

"When Mikaela has grown up, quite probably you'll establish contact and make great friends. You can be like sisters again."

"That's no consolation. You should know that," Madeleine cried.

Karen patted her knee. "Calm down, please. It wouldn't be good for Mikaela to see you like this. It'll distress her."

After another awkward ten minutes, during which there was nothing really to say, Regis Forbush opened the door and without coming in, ushered in the little girl. Madeleine jumped up to go to her, but saw immediately that her daughter was not sure who she was. She just stood there, looking terrified, dressed in a pink puffy jacket and red trousers, with little black patent leather shoes.

"I want my mummy."

"Hi there, Micki." Madeleine bent down on one knee in front of her, trying to hold back the tears and appear normal. Mikaela had grown quite a bit and her hair had darkened. The little face was somber but she certainly looked healthy and rosy-cheeked.

"Shall we sit down?" Karen said cheerily, obviously wanting to be in charge of the meeting.

"No," Madeleine said. "I would just like to have a few moments with Mikaela, please. I'd like to say good-bye . . . privately." She saw Karen open her mouth to protest and added, "Is that too much to ask?"

"Where's my mummy?" the child said, looking tearful.

"Mummy and Daddy are waiting downstairs." Karen tried to reassure her. "There, there, let's sit down. Come now."

Neither Madeleine nor Mikaela obeyed.

"She's my sister," Mikaela piped up suddenly, pointing at Madeleine.

"There we are, there we are," Karen said, laughing a little too loudly.

Madeleine took a step toward the woman. "Listen, this is ridiculous. Please get out for a few moments. I'm not going to say or do anything stupid, now am I?"

Karen sighed, obviously keen to get this over with as quickly as possible. She gave Madeleine a stern nod and left the room.

They were alone. Madeleine had not seen her daughter for over a year, and she wondered now if she'd ever seen her alone. Mama had never allowed it. She was always keeping guard over the child in Madeleine's presence, as if she couldn't be trusted not to take her and run away.

"So you remember your big sister? That's good."

"Yeah."

She tickled Mikaela under the chin. "What's my name, then?"

The little girl squirmed and giggled.

"Lena," she said hesitatingly, then lit up and yelled, "Magdalena."

"Hey, you got it . . . So, do you have a nice house with Mummy and Daddy?"

"Yeah. I've got all new toys. I've got the teddy you gave me and one that Rose gave me."

"Oh, that one. You still have it? I had that from when I was little. Who is Rose?"

"Mummy's friend."

"That's nice. Do you have a fun time with your mummy and daddy?"

"Uhu. Yep." She reached out and took Madeleine's hand. "Are you going to come to our house?"

Madeleine felt suddenly stumped for words. What do you say to a child. Lie? "Maybe sometime. But I'm going to go and live somewhere else. It's quite far away."

"Oh."

"You'll be starting school soon."

Mikaela's little face broke into a sudden impish grin. "Why do you like ants?"

"I don't know. They're fun to look at,

and they are smarter than people, and less grumpy."

"Hmm. We've got loads in the garden. Mummy sweeps them off the path."

"Can I give you a hug?"

"Yeah," said Mikaela and allowed herself to be hugged.

Madeleine pressed her to her chest as hard as she dared, knowing she couldn't endure this final moment. With sudden insight she saw the meaning of this parting, the enormity of it, its irreversible consequences. Fear and loneliness came over her. Why, she didn't even have a parent herself. Not when it counted. Why wasn't her own father with her now—now of all times?

"You be a good girl, little darling, and I'll see you later."

"But when?" Mikaela pulled back and looked at her.

Madeleine met her eyes and looked deep into them. Would she ever look into these eyes again? Oh God, don't let this happen!

**"When are you coming to my house?"
Mikaela insisted.**

**"When we're both grown up," Made-
leine said at last, and the tears came—
there was no stopping them. She knew
she would have to walk away. Far, far
away.**

The girl on coffee service must have seen
or heard the commotion and phoned upstairs. Two male nurses were walking
briskly across the lawn. It wouldn't do to
have the dignified afternoon tea scene disturbed by the crazy cigar-smoking Cuban
witch. What would the visitors think? Madeleine knew this would be another blot in
her copybook. Perhaps Dr. Jenkins was
right about her visits making Mama more
disturbed, more agitated.

They grabbed the shrieking resident
and gently but firmly walked her back toward the house. Madeleine just stood there,
at a loss, watching her mother fighting her
captors, who were half lifting, half dragging
her across the grass.

Not caring about the stares from the
other tables, she bent down and picked up
Rosaria's still smoldering cigar from the

ground. She put it to her lips and puffed on it. A good cigar is a good cigar; she had to concede the truth of the inane saying. She sat down on the grass, leaned her back against the old oak tree, and fishing out the bottle from her bag, took another sizable swig.

Drawing on the cigar, she tilted her head and looked up into the crown of the old oak. It was a long way up and it reminded her of her childhood tree house in the old banyan tree. She wondered how the little house was faring; the last time she'd seen it the staircase was in need of repair. Suddenly she had a strong yearning to be home, home in Key West. Perhaps what she needed was a holiday, to hole herself up in the family home. The weather in the Keys would be at its best now, before the hurricane season began.

A movement beside her head caught her attention. A line of *Formica fusca* was winding its way up and down the tree trunk in a steady two-way flow. Madeleine smiled. Ants would go where no man could tread. She had a soft spot for *fusca,* a gentle, timid ant who shunned violence and would rather run than fight. She turned her head and peered closely at them, wondering how they saw her. They did, after all, have the sharpest eyesight of all ants. She put her finger on the trunk and let one of them mount it. It scurried helplessly around, trying to find its way back to work, back to the grind. She put her finger on the bark and allowed the little fellow to rejoin the neverending round he and his forefathers had made for millions upon millions of years. How many oaks had grown huge here, fallen in violent storms, or simply died of old age and rotted, to form soil within which other ants, other species, built their nests, fed their queens, and nursed their young?

Protect them with my life. Strike down anyone who tries to take them away from me . . . Her mind reeled. Everything seemed upside down. Her hard-won equilibrium was cracking, splitting open, coming apart. Why did Rosaria bring up her daughter *now*, of all times?

Madeleine knew Rachel was not her daughter, she'd been amply convinced. But somewhere in the deepest recesses of her mind, her instincts kept refuting this certainty. She had sworn she would never, ever get her hopes up like that again, and here she was indulging a fantasy that could do nothing but cause her grief. Rachel was *not* her daughter, and now she was no longer even her patient. She had left therapy of her own volition, and Madeleine had no further excuse to contact her, or any right to pursue her. That was the end of the matter.

Madeleine's knowledge of the human psyche told her she needed help herself, now more than ever, to come to terms with her losses. She had to talk to someone, preferably some experienced therapist who could help her gain a new perspective. Perhaps she should phone BACP, her professional association, and ask for the name of someone she'd never heard of, perhaps in Bristol, Reading, or Exeter.

If there is no such person, there is always the Samaritans, Madeleine thought wryly. She could always phone them. Tell some faceless stranger how she'd given her child away, killed her husband, and had never come to terms with either event.

She felt a drop on her cheek. It had started raining. Someone was quickly gathering the trays from the tables. People were getting up and moving indoors. Some of them looked over at her. She saw herself as they saw her, a foreign woman with a huge cigar in her hand, sitting under a tree in the rain, next to an ant path. How badly she fitted into this wet land, how odd she must seem.

She got up and peeled herself away from the tree. A black cloud passed overhead. With a sudden strong gust of wind, the heavens opened.

The house was as quiet as a tomb, but the rain was still batting at the windowpanes. She reminded herself that it was Wednesday, and she should paint. She'd not picked up a paintbrush for nearly three weeks. The canvas was still sitting there. A painting was brewing in her mind. It had nothing to do with the queen ant, and was a strange deviation from her planned series. It happened occasionally that she allowed something new to come in, some whim, or a fragment of a dream. But she wasn't ready for this one; it was no good even trying.

The evening stretched ahead, quiet, empty. Bar watching the news, she hated television and was too restless to read.

Studying her ants in the myrmecarium was always good for a meditation, but not for a whole damned evening. She could always mosey over to the Bath Spa, luxuriate in the spring-fed hot pool on the rooftop, or sweat it out in the steamroom, but when it came down to it, booze was more effective. She hovered by the phone for a moment, wondering whether to try and recruit some friend to go out with, but decided she had no appetite for chitchat.

She went up to her bedroom, took off her sodden clothes, and slipped into a pair of snug new jeans, fitting her slimmed-down lower half. After putting on her best bra, she hunted through her wardrobe for her most flattering top. Makeup . . . she rarely used any but now slapped a touch of pink on her cheeks, swipeed lipstick on her mouth. Her large eyes with lashes like garden brooms had always been the envy of her female friends. She gave these a good going-over with mascara. The whole procedure had taken no more than a few minutes. Her hair had curled furiously in the downpour, but the soft rainwater made it look full and glossy, framing her face strikingly. She stepped back from the mirror.

Not bad. It heartened her to see that she was still capable of a spot of effortless glamour, despite feeling like shit.

She grabbed an umbrella, stepped out of her house into Bath at night. Crossing the iron footbridge over the river, she made her way into town.

The bartender placed another vodka tonic in front of her and winked.

Madeleine frowned. "You know, I don't remember ordering this," she said, more to herself than to him. *I must be getting drunk.*

"You didn't," he said. "It's with the compliments of that man in the dark suit, back there." He nodded toward the other side of the bar.

"Really?" Madeleine glanced along the bar. It was long, and crowds of people jostled for space. Most of them were in their mid-twenties, tall, vital young men and attractive women with impossibly pared-down clothes and pushed-up breasts. She peered through the dim reddish lighting and the tangle of bronzed arms and big hairdos, made even fuzzier by the sheer volume of music, voices, and laughter. Who the hell was buying her a drink when there was all this nubile naked flesh on offer?

A tall man smelling strongly of after-shave edged close to her, holding up a beer glass in the direction of the bartender. The bartender was busy elsewhere. The man glanced at her and shrugged. They smiled at each other.

"He is incredibly slow," he commented.

"He keeps topping mine up, whether I want him to or not," she said, relieved to be talking to someone.

"You're a girl, that's why."

A minute passed. The man studied her furtively.

"Well, as I'm standing here . . . Hi," he said. "Who are *you*?"

"Old enough to be your mother, just about," she said, slurring slightly.

He smiled, revealing an orthodontic masterpiece. "Not a chance."

"I was hoping I might meet my daughter here," she said, at once grasping the irony of her throwaway comment, having just meant to put him off.

"My God. You're doing more than OK. What's your secret?"

"Not genes," she said sincerely, "nor

abstinence." She turned and gave him an appraising glance. "And yours? . . . Apart from your dentist?"

Leaning his elbow on the bar and turning to face her, he seemed to evaluate her more thoroughly. "I'm a professional sportsman."

What am I doing? she laughed to herself. He's about twelve years old.

"You don't believe me?" he said, pouting comically.

"Of course I do. You look fit as a fiddle."

He leaned closer. "Are you really waiting for your daughter?"

"Good evening, Miss Freud," someone said behind her.

She jumped, but quickly recovered. Turning around, she looked straight into Gordon's face. He looked seriously handsome in the dim light. His steely gray hair had been cut very short and he still sported designer stubble (bad choice— she remembered—for the delicate tissue of the female genitalia). He'd bought new glasses, rectangular black affairs that were both sexy and austere. As always he was beautifully dressed, in a dark green linen jacket over a black shirt.

"You?" she said with a frown. "Did you just buy me a drink?"

"Sorry to butt in. Am I interrupting something?"

"As a matter of fact . . . ," Madeleine said and turned back to say something to the young man, but he had already sized up the competition and moved aside. Some other adolescent was wedging himself into the vacant space, his hands wrapped around a bouquet of empty glasses.

"I can't believe you're sitting here alone, Madeleine," Gordon said.

"I wasn't alone. I was doing quite well as it happens."

He smirked knowingly and gestured toward the end of the bar. "Perhaps you'd like to join us."

"What?" She peered into the throng. "You and your girlfriends?"

He laughed, unperturbed. "No, just some colleagues. It gets hellishly tedious, just us dried-up blokes talking shop. We need a woman to bring us up aboveground." He touched her arm lightly. "Oh, come on, Maddy. Don't be stroppy."

She looked across the bar again. Two men were looking at them. One raised his hand and waved. What the hell! She could use some male company. What was there to lose? She slid off her bar stool.

"You look great in those jeans," Gordon said into her ear as he led her by the arm through the crowd. "So I forgive you for what you did."

"For what I did?" she shouted over the noise. "God, you're an arrogant bastard."

He laughed. "You've got one hell of a vicious side to you . . . the Cuban side, I imagine. Despite myself I find it quite exciting. Just never do it again. It scared the living daylights out of me."

She looked at him and frowned. So, she'd given him the boot. How vicious was that?

Because of the rain they moved only as far as the bar next door. Jeff, a geologist, was a very funny man in his fifties, borderline obese with a telltale ruddy face. Peter, an archaeologist like Gordon, was tall and a picture of fitness and health, with a subtle sense of humor and old-fashioned good manners, the sort of man every mother would want her daughter to marry. Madeleine soon discovered they were all part of the team excavating the Southgate site, on top of which the new bus terminal was to be built. Despite all those drinks she'd had, she was fascinated and tried to grill them on the ongoing project, but they were celebrating another discovery. Workmen attempting to dig a hole for an indoor swimming pool in the basement of a Georgian house on Rednor Street had reported encountering a Roman arch. Gordon had been called in to look at it, and he'd found remains of a Roman complex, six meters below street level.

"Can you sneak me in?" Madeleine implored. "I'd give anything to see this place."

"Anything?" asked Jeff with a leer. "Let *me* arrange it."

An hour later, when the weather finally cleared, the four of them staggered through the narrow passages above Cheap Street to find another bar. Madeleine was feeling dangerously reckless, enjoying the rare attention of three men at once. She giggled hysterically at Jeff's dumb jokes and bummed one of his cigars. They halted under an arch in the passage and all three men tried, in turn, to light it for her.

"This cigar is way too dry," she declared.

"What do you know of cigars, wench?" Jeff boomed. "You're not sucking properly. You need more practice."

"Watch your language with the lady," Peter cautioned him. "You're being a swine."

"For sure I know more than you, Jeff." Madeleine laughed, too cheery to be offended. "Only this afternoon I was smoking a Havana masterpiece. Both my parents have smoked cigars ever since I was in the cradle."

"Even your mother?" asked Peter with a raised eyebrow.

"You bet. I was born in a town where cigars are rolled in booths on every street corner. I can even roll a mean cigar myself, if I'm called upon to do so. An old Cuban cigar maker taught me how. His name was José Manuel and a shark had bitten his leg off."

"You can roll my cigar anyday," said Jeff as they assumed their unsteady walk, his hand straying slyly to stroke her back, no doubt checking the existence—or not—of a bra strap.

"Where is this place?" Peter asked. "This cigar haven? Tell us more."

"A tropical island," Madeleine said dreamily, "where palms sway in the wind, where the jacarandas drop their blossoms in swimming pools, and rainbow-colored fish swim in two oceans. Where you drink rum all day on verandas under bamboo fans . . ."

"My dear girl," Peter said, laughing, "what the hell are you doing *here*?"

They had passed and found the Volunteer Rifleman's Arms tightly closed. As they were coming round the curve of old Bond Street and heading toward a new pub on George Street, Jeff's mobile started irreverently playing the national anthem.

"Ah, that's the wife," Jeff sighed, disappointed. After a one-sided conversation during which he mumbled only, "*Yeah . . . sorry . . . yeah*," he was summarily reeled back to the homestead. As soon as he'd taken his leave and walked off with a look of misery, the other two could not wait to tell Madeleine what a cow his wife was. Though Jeff was a hairy-arsed he-man, when the cow was around he was like a cringing street dog in Calcutta. Madeleine tried ineffectually to stick up for womanhood, specially that contingent whose husbands didn't come home in the evenings.

She ended up in the middle, between the two remaining men, walking arm in arm up Milsom Street. They climbed the stairs to the raised pavement of George Street, where women in fine dresses had walked once upon a time, well above the hoi polloi and mud-splattering from horse-drawn carriages. The pub in question was lit by hideous neon tubing, but a burly doorman turned them away. Last orders had been called. It seemed their bar crawl had to be crawled somewhere else.

Peter looked at his watch and reluctantly admitted defeat. He assured Madeleine that he was single, but he had two miniature poodles that had not been out since late afternoon. Madeleine kissed him on both cheeks as if they'd known each other forever, and they promised each other another pub crawl soon. When Gordon turned his back on this smoochy scene, Peter slipped a card into her hand.

Madeleine and Gordon stood on the corner of Lansdown Road waving him off.

"Two miniature poodles?" Madeleine said, a trifle mystified. "I'm not being prejudiced or anything, but it's a curious choice of breed for a straight man."

"He's certainly not gay," said Gordon, "but he has his quirks."

"As we all do," said Madeleine, watching the long-limbed figure walking briskly up the hill. There went a man who was way taller than her.

They headed back toward the Abbey in search of another watering hole. It was getting on for midnight, but the air was sultry and the atmosphere festive with all the shopwindows lit. Milsom Street was deserted, bar one other person, whose footsteps echoed behind them. Madeleine turned around, hoping Peter had changed his mind, but the man following them was shorter, stockier. She smiled to herself. Did she perchance fancy the other archaeologist? Not really, she just felt awkward being left alone with Gordon, walking arm in arm with him. She pulled away.

"How come he's single?"

"Who?" said Gordon, turning toward her.

"Peter."

"Are you interested in him?"

"Well, why not?" she said nonchalantly. "I love tiny dogs."

"Be interested in me instead."

"I *was*," she asserted. "But not anymore. And well you know why."

He hooked his arm into hers again, pulling her close. "I'm actually madly in love with you."

She laughed and tugged her arm free. "Gordon, you're talking drunken rubbish and you know it."

"I'm not talking rubbish," he insisted peevishly. "I've been an idiot."

A young down-and-out with glassy eyes stopped them, mumbling something about a cup of coffee. Madeleine reached into her bag and fished out a fiver. "Forget coffee," she said to the young man. "Why don't you eat something?"

Gordon grabbed her by the belt and pulled her along. They tottered off, leaning on each other's shoulders. She was seeing double, a sure sign it was time to be sensible. Another drink and God only knew what she might get up to.

"I'm going home," she said. "Help me flag down a taxi."

"Can I come?" he whispered into her ear. "I've been dying to make love to you for weeks."

"Make love?" she huffed, incredulous. "Dream on."

They were walking past the darkened entrance to the Roman Baths and the spooky colonnades of Bath Street and were almost upon the Southgate site. An area the size of several city blocks, it was surrounded by steel fencing and the view was blocked by green plastic mesh. A drill with a one-meter girth gleamed in the streetlights, and two giant cranes stood like prehistoric creatures within the enclosure.

"Any chance of getting in there to have a look?" Madeleine asked.

"What would I get in return?"

"Oh forget it," she said, turning toward Pierrepont Street in search of a taxi.

"Tell you what," he said, catching up and grabbing her elbow. "There is nothing to see here, but I've got the key to the house on Rednor Street. It's a five-minute walk. Far more interesting. You'd love it."

She stopped and looked at him, trying to gauge if he was serious. He shrugged disarmingly and pointed the way. What the hell. She was fascinated by the idea of descending through the layers of the ground she walked on and exploring the ancient city that lay below. Metaphorically, it was what she attempted to do every day with her patients.

"Really, Gordon? You have the keys on you?"

"I sure do. The boys and I were there today, working till seven."

She allowed herself to be led along streets flanked by tall, imposing Georgian town houses like towering walls, so impressive by daylight, so portentously sinister by night. They entered a crescent, the edifices making an elegant sweeping curve around a central green. A mist had descended and was softening the glow of the streetlamps. Again she heard footsteps behind them, but when she turned to look, the street was empty. Muggings were rare in Bath, though there were plenty of drug addicts.

Gordon stopped her at the end of the crescent. She looked up. She'd not expected a house of this size and grandeur. He opened an iron gate at street level and led her down some stone steps to a basement.

"Don't people live in the building?" she

whispered as he fiddled with a bunch of keys.

"Don't worry." He chuckled. "The whole place is a construction site. This filthy-rich American just bought the house and is converting it from six flats back to a single-family home. That's how the Roman remains were discovered."

Once inside, he turned on the light, a single lightbulb hanging in a stark hallway. Tools for the excavation work were everywhere. The walls were stripped down to stone and he led her through a passage and down a further set of steps to a cellar. She followed him down the narrow winding staircase, barely lit by the hall light. Once there, she could see the top of a Roman arch in a deep pit the size of a large bedroom. An aluminium ladder rested against the wall of the pit. The depth of four meters was marked on the wall in chalk.

"Is there no light here?" she asked quietly, her voice echoing between the walls.

"Shit, no. The floodlight is in my car."

She approached the edge, and her eyes grew accustomed to the darkness. Looking down she saw a piece of flooring, one meter square. The earth had been brushed carefully away. An intricate mosaic pattern was clearly visible. A sense of awe overcame her, and she found herself transported back in time. She heard and smelled water gushing from the depths of the earth. Hot vapor filled her nostrils.

"There is steam here. Is there a spring or something?"

Gordon turned and looked at her for a long moment. "Yes, there *was*, as a matter of fact, but centuries ago," he said. "That's what we're using Jeff for. He's doing a geological study, investigating the past existence of another geothermal spring. Even if it's dried up, can you imagine what a find it would be? There is another pit farther in where there are remnants of a pool. The American was planning a huge swimming pool. Little did he know we'd find a Roman one already in place. Scuppered his plans rather." He clicked his tongue and imitated her American accent. "But it sure is something to tell the folks back home."

She closed her eyes. "It's incredible. You can almost touch them . . . the people who lived here . . . two thousand years ago."

He took her hand and kissed it ardently,

and though she made an attempt to resist, he pushed her gently against the wall. Despite her resolve, she was suddenly in his arms. The magic of the setting and this provocation of her senses had stirred her up. It was as if what happened underground, in complete darkness . . . in a different time . . . didn't count and didn't matter.

His hands found their way under her top and bra. With his mouth against her neck, blowing his hot familiar breath over her bare skin, he quickly undid her jeans and pulled them down. His nimble fingers found their way to her, as if he'd done nothing else with his life. An unladylike grunt escaped her lips. The overwhelming pleasure of his touch made her weak. She sank against the wall, ineffectually trying to get the button of his trousers to snap open. It was some complicated fastening system of wide metal hooks. At last she had the familiar feel of him in her hand. This mutually rewarding and utterly pleasurable pursuit did not last as long as she would have liked. Without a word he turned her around, pulled her flimsy undergarment out of the way, and pushed himself inside her.

He went about it with unusual vigor, but the loss of frontal contact made her disconnect from him. She listened for the water she'd heard, but it had gone, and so had the thrill of his seduction. Bracing herself against the rough bricks, her hands took the impact of his thrusts. Soon her legs, too, were trembling. "Gordon, slow down. Stop for a second."

He wasn't hearing her. It appeared he didn't want to stop. Three or four powerful thrusts later he suddenly went rigid, breathing out a long sigh.

"Oh shit. Sorry. Too late," he said, his breath echoing in the tomblike silence.

He pulled away, making no attempt to satisfy her by other means, though he could easily have made good his lack of etiquette. His handling of the tryst seemed uncharacteristic somehow, mechanical, and she didn't exactly feel cherished. So much for his "weeks of dying for her." They readjusted their clothing.

"What was that all about?" she said, knowing he knew what she meant.

"I guess I was nervous."

"You? Nervous?" She laughed.

He touched her cheek. "You know, I

think I might be ready for 'exclusivity.' I haven't been able to get you out of my head . . . I meant it when I said I'm in love with you."

She looked at him, smiling in the darkness. "I can see why you were nervous. Exclusivity! That must be a scary concept for you. Are you sure it's not the booze talking?"

He squirmed. "No, I think I mean it."

She felt she ought to be pleased; she knew deep down that she had missed his company, but something niggled. "Well, let's see how it goes, shall we? Why don't we meet up on the weekend and just do something fun? Go for a hike or something."

"Ah, I can't, Madeleine. Not this weekend."

Oh, God, why bother? she thought and began to look for her bag amid the rubble on the floor. "So why can't you, Gordon?"

"I'm out of town."

"Out of town . . . with whom?"

"You won't like this," he said. "I'm going to Thailand for a three-week holiday with someone . . . on Friday. I thought I'd better tell you straightaway."

"Straightaway?" She bristled. "Not straightaway, you bastard. You tell me *after* what we just did. That was a shitty thing to do. It was beneath you—yes, even you."

"Madeleine, come now. I can't cancel the holiday. It wouldn't be fair on her," he pleaded. "But when I get back, I'll drop her."

She could barely see him, but he stood there proposing this plan as if it was perfectly reasonable, indeed righteous. In her books it didn't even merit an answer. She turned on her heel and quickly climbed the cellar steps.

"Think about it," he called after her. "But skip the razor blades."

As she dashed out into the cool night air and reached street-level, Rosaria came to mind. Perhaps she'd ask Mama how to evoke the dreaded Pedrote. Or she could give Madeleine a spell to cast on Gordon, so that his self-gratifying member would start to go black, then shrivel and eventually drop off.

She was so furious she couldn't even muster a smile at the thought, and her anger canceled any fear of walking home alone. However, a small movement across the street set her heart racing. A man stood there, crouching slightly. He looked at her but did not move. As if by a miracle, a taxi came hurtling down the street, the yellow light on its roof a beacon of relief. She almost ran into the street to stop it.

Once safely inside the car, she turned to look. The apparition was still standing there, perfectly still.

Chapter Fourteen

Are we almost there, Daddy?"

"Aha, son, only about two miles more. Here, you drive."

Sasha leaned over and grabbed the steering wheel with both hands, tense with the responsibility of it. It wasn't hard. The road was quite straight, and Daddy held one finger on the wheel, just in case. Daddy always let him do stuff, whereas Mum didn't. She didn't want them to go, but Daddy was so nice that in the end she let them. They had to promise to be back before dinner, and Daddy had to leave his wallet for her to look after.

Daddy took over after a while and turned into another road. Soon there were houses on both sides. They were red, instead of yellow like the houses in Bath. The road twisted and they passed a park with swings and seesaws, but no kids. Then there were factories, and at the end of a row of car lots, Daddy stopped by a house. There were cars in the garden, two white ones, one blue van, and one car with the top off. That was Uncle Uri's car. Sasha recognized it straight off. He felt his stomach lurch, half with excitement, half with dread. Napoleon was with Uncle Uri, hadn't Daddy said so? Perhaps they were coming for Napoleon.

They got out of the car and walked up to the house. Uncle Uri opened the door. Daddy and he kissed on both cheeks.

"Hey, Sasha," Uri said and held his arms open. "My best nephew. I haven't seen you for long time. You grow into a little man."

Sasha was quite scared of Uncle Uri but he hugged him all the same.

"One day you come and live with your uncle Uri, yes, Sasha?" he teased, ruffling Sasha's hair and letting rip a booming laugh. "Uncle Uri can't make children, even trying and trying with all the pretty girls."

Sasha squirmed with unease. "No, thank you. My mum is . . ."

But they weren't listening, so it didn't matter. They went and sat in a room with big sofas. Uncle Uri had a new girlfriend, Tatyana. She was different from the last one, prettier, with very long blond hair, and younger. Sasha could see that Uncle Uri liked her a lot. He kept grabbing her bum and she giggled. She was nice too. She brought Sasha a Coke and a Mars bar. Then, when the men wanted to talk, she took him to the kitchen and they sat at a table and watched a DVD, *Pirates of the Caribbean.* For a moment he felt quite happy with Tatyana, having his Coke and finishing the Mars bar. She giggled a lot, and talked funny, a bit like Daddy. "Isn't he good-looking?" she said about the pirate.

"Are you Ukrainian?"

"No, baby. I'm from Russia."

"Oh." He had no idea where that was. She looked like a princess. Prettier than the girl in the film. "Tatyana," he said, testing out the name.

"That's right," she said. "You say it great."

Two other girls came into the kitchen. They were chattering to each other and he couldn't understand a word they said. One of them put the kettle on and was rattling and crashing with cups in a cupboard. Tatyana said something, her voice angry, and they looked at the telly and one of them covered her mouth. Tatyana waved her hand across her face, shouted something else, and the other girl stubbed out her cigarette in the sink. He thought they probably didn't like Tatyana. She was prettier than they.

"Tatyana," Sasha said after the girls had left, "is there a dog here?"

She looked at him for a moment. "What kind of dog?"

He thought about it. Napoleon wasn't any of the kinds he knew, like a Jack Russell or a rottweiler. "He is like so big." He held his arms apart, then measured up from the floor with his hand. "He's got gray fur and a tail, like so." He drew a coil in the air with his finger. "He's got really big paws."

Tatyana glanced through the door toward the front room, and then said, "Come on. We have a look."

She took him out through the kitchen door. At the back of the house there was an even bigger garden. It was full of stuff—he had no idea what it was—and some cars and motorbikes. At the end of the garden was a big wooden box. Tatyana opened the door just a little bit, as if she was scared of what was inside. Napoleon stood in the box blinking at the bright sunlight. He looked different, thin and sad. Then he burst out and flung himself at Sasha.

"Shhh, shhh," Tatyana kept saying. "Don't make him bark."

Sasha tumbled on the ground with his dog, crying silently. But it was important to be quiet. He could hear it in the girl's voice. "Shhh, shhh."

After just a few minutes, she said, "OK. We put him back."

"No, I don't want to." He clung to Napoleon's neck. "Why does he have to be in there?"

Tatyana started to prise his arms off the dog. "Please, Sasha. If you make him bark, he get a beating. We just put him back, nice and calm now."

Sasha let go. He kissed Napoleon's head a few times and cajoled him back into the box. Without a word they closed the door, wedged it with the stick, and went back through the stuff in the garden, into the kitchen, where the pirate was fighting some other guy with a sword. They sat down at the table and looked.

"You want a cup of tea?" said Tatyana gently.

"No."

"A chewing gum?"

"No thank you."

There was nothing more to say. Tatyana wasn't giggling at the film anymore. The doorbell rang, and they heard other men's voices. Uncle Uri came into the kitchen and got some beers out of the fridge. On the way back he ruffled Sasha's hair again. "You like Tatyana?"

"Yeah," he said.

"Good."

It was hot in the kitchen and Tatyana said she couldn't stand it, she just had to open the door. The outside noises blew in and Sasha fought a battle with his tears. He knew he mustn't start bawling. Tatyana looked at him and put the kettle on. Then she took a nail file and started filing her nails. She filed and filed. They were long, her nails, with a little silver star painted on each one.

"What's your mum like?" she asked without looking up.

Sasha shrugged. "Pretty."

"Is she nice to you?"

"Yeah." He bristled suddenly. "She got Napoleon for me. He's my dog, you know. My mum bought him for me specially."

Tatyana put the nail file down and looked at the telly. The film was almost finished, he could tell, but he was not interested in the endings, he never was. He didn't believe they were real.

"What food are you giving to Napoleon?" he said.

Tatyana frowned, but didn't look at him. "I didn't know is your dog. Your uncle says the dog bites. Only he give it food."

"Honest, he doesn't bite. You can give him the brown pellet things. It's for puppies. He likes those. Can't you give him some?" Sasha pleaded.

Tatyana glanced at the door. "Yeah, yeah, I will," she said, her voice hushed. "I go to buy puppy food."

"Promise."

"Yes, I promise." Tatyana looked straight at him. Her eyes were very blue.

Sasha could not hear the men talking anymore. Upstairs a woman called out twice, like a name, her voice insistent, like when Mum was calling him in for his dinner.

"Sasha," Tatyana said quietly, "maybe I phone you some time to say hi. You like that?"

He looked at her, wondering why she'd want to.

"Yeah," he said. He sort of meant it but it seemed strange, not quite right. Mum would answer. Everything about Mum and Daddy was separate. One should never mix them together.

"You know your phone number?"

He shook his head, but then he remembered. In his pocket there was a tag, attached with a safety pin. Mum always put it there. "If you're lost, or you need me, or you want to talk to me when you are somewhere with Daddy . . ."

He put his hand in his pocket and there it was. He felt quite big suddenly. He had his mum's mobile number right there in his pocket. He pulled out the tag, bent to see it, and started to read the numbers out.

"Hold on, baby. I get a pen," Tatyana whispered. "You don't tell your father, Sasha. It's our secret."

He watched her as she rummaged in a drawer. She had on purple jeans that were too tight around her bottom. The kettle had been boiling for ages, not turning itself off, getting angrier and angrier. Behind the closed door the men were talking again, in harsh bursts. He listened to their voices, to the boiling, bubbling water, trying to shut out that faint sound, the distant whimper of the starving dog.

Rachel had her feet up on the coffee table. The windows were wide open. Yesterday's rain had abated and the sun shone. Sasha was in the garden making a spaceship out of cardboard boxes he'd found in the lane.

A couple of weeks had passed since their weekend in Tenby, and relations with Anton had been easier. He kept to his word to be a nice, normal dad, even when she refused to have sex with him. He came twice a week to see Sasha, and one sunny afternoon she'd felt relaxed enough to let him take Sasha for a drive, but ever since

Sasha had been withdrawn and refused to go to school. No matter how she tried, she couldn't get out of him what the matter was. He used to love having an afternoon with his dad, but she knew something must have happened. He'd hardly said good-bye to Anton when he dropped him off, and he'd run straight up to his bedroom and refused to talk to her. Today he seemed to have recovered a little from his despondency, quietly laboring away with a staple gun, string, and Scotch tape, sometimes even humming some little song.

Charlene was on the beanbag, sipping coffee and wolfing the cheese-and-cucumber sandwich that Rachel had made her. Rachel and Sasha had seen her selling her *Big Issues* by the bank this morning when they'd come down the hill to do their shopping. The poor kid looked so dispirited, and when Rachel took pity on her she'd jumped at the chance for some grub and a bit of cash.

Charlene finished her sandwich and brushed the crumbs off her T-shirt onto the floor. She wasn't used to visiting, that was obvious. Despite the heat, she had her woolly hat on—perhaps it was a fashion thing—and her *Big Issue* bag at her feet as if she were married to it.

"What exactly was it you wanted me to do?" she asked.

Rachel gestured around her living room. "I thought we could do it together. I used to watch my dad do it when I was little. He was a painter-decorator, but it was a case of the cobbler's kids, you know, not having any shoes. He did it for everyone else, but this bloody wallpaper has been on here for twenty-odd years."

She got up, went into the hall, and dragged in the wallpaper steamer she'd found in the garage along with her dad's paint-covered stepladder. "I can't stand the sight of it anymore. My mum thought it was dead elegant. It probably was at the time. Now it's like living in a derelict Indian restaurant."

"I've never done that sort of thing," Charlene said. "How much are you going to pay me?'

"How about twenty quid for the afternoon . . . and a bite to eat after?"

"OK then."

"You steam and I'll scrape, and then we can change over. There's nothing to it."

Rachel charged up the stairs to change into a pair of shorts and an old vest, taking her bag with her as she went. She didn't quite trust Charlene, not yet anyway. It was difficult to get a handle on the girl. Getting her to help redecorate the living room would give Rachel a chance to get to know her and see if she could trust her with Sasha. Rachel was determined to get herself some little job, waitressing or cleaning or something like that. The money in the bank was still there, even the mysterious five thousand, but she knew money never lasted. Someone told her once that you were entitled to benefits if you had no work, but with all that money in the bank *and* owning a house, it surely did not apply to her. Anyway, she'd always been anxious about signing on; they asked so many questions.

Once they got down to it, got a routine going, the wallpaper came off easily. It was so old it disintegrated into a mushlike porridge and simply slid off the wall. It was hot work. Charlene even took her woolly hat off, and Rachel could see why she had it on in all weathers. Her hair was short and patchy, bald bits shining like large coins all over her skull. Poor kid. It was quite pathetic.

"What happened to your hair?"

"I don't know. Stress, I guess," she said tetchily.

Rachel thought of the woman in Madeleine's reception, Sylvia. She would have something to say about that. Some remedy.

"You could go and see a doctor about it, you know. It doesn't cost anything. Perhaps you need vitamins or something."

Charlene's face was closed. Her hair was not a subject for discussion, that was obvious. Thinking of Sylvia and the clinic had given Rachel a little start. She knew it was cowardly to drop out of therapy when things began to get hot, yet she'd lost her nerve. The day after the session she'd missed, there had been a message on her mobile from Madeleine, asking her if she wanted another appointment. Then nothing. Forgotten. What could she expect? After all, she was only a fee-paying stranger to the woman. Out of sight, out of mind.

"Are you going to paint these walls?" Charlene asked, breaking into her thoughts. "I could help you with that if you want, if you pay me. You know, magnolia or something. Something bright."

"Yeah, that's the plan. It's looking brighter already. Anything but gold and red velvet. Who the hell invented it?"

They worked in silence for a while. Rachel got down the stepladder and put the radio on. James Blunt was singing some mournful song.

"He's got a great voice, hasn't he?"

"I like Robbie Williams," Charlene said.

Rachel's mobile rang, giving her a start. Hardly anyone ever phoned her. If it wasn't bloody Anton, perhaps it was Madeleine. She sort of wished it was—but what excuse would she give for not calling her back?

"Aren't you going to answer it?" Charlene said, looking at her.

Rachel fished the phone out of her pocket, clamping it to her ear. "Yeah?"

There was a slight pause. "Is that Sasha's mum?"

"Yeah?" Rachel waited a moment. "Who is this?"

"It doesn't matter." The voice was quite low, but girlish, and there was a strong accent of some sort.

"Hold on," Rachel barked, "let me get down this bloody ladder and turn the radio off."

Charlene dashed to the radio and did it for her.

"I can hear you now."

"Listen, is not my business . . ." There was a hesitation. Rachel stood motionless on the ladder, the phone pressed to her ear. "If you know what is good for you . . . and Sasha, you forget this phone call, yes?"

Rachel's stomach lurched. "Yeah, OK. What? What is it?"

"I know someone got a passport for Sasha. I think maybe he's gonna give the passport to Anton . . . next time he come. Just for you to know."

"Are you sure?" Rachel gasped.

"Uh-huh."

"Who are you?"

"You tell to Anton—I'm dead. Do you hear what I say? Do you know Uri?"

"Yes, I know Uri."

"Well . . . use your head."

Rachel stumbled down the stepladder and ran into the kitchen, the phone clamped to her ear. "Listen. I really appreciate you ringing me, I really do. Word of honor, I'll forget this conversation the minute it's over. Trust me."

"I liked Sasha, your little boy. I was sorry for him."

Rachel was thinking feverishly. "Look. I've got money. Would you do something for me . . . if I pay you?"

"Oh, no." The girl's voice hardened. "What can *I* do about it?"

"You could get your hands on the passport and burn it . . . or better still, send it to me in an envelope." There was a pause. "You know what Anton is going to do with it, don't you? He's going to take my boy away from me. He's done it already once or twice, but with a passport . . ."

"You ask a lot."

"I know I do. I'll send you some cash, through the post. Registered mail. Anywhere you like."

"No. No money." She hesitated. "Perhaps some other time, later."

"Whenever. Word of honor. Don't say no straightaway. Think about it. Can I phone you back?" Rachel pleaded.

"No. I call you." The phone clicked off.

Rachel stayed sitting at the kitchen table for a long while. She lit a cigarette and smoked insistently. Finally Charlene popped her head through the door. "It's much harder doing it by oneself," she said. "It's boring too."

"Yeah, I'll be there in a minute," Rachel said. "I'm just having a fag." But her heart wasn't in it anymore, and her mind was churning. So that's where they had been. Anton had taken Sasha to Uri's house. Where she had feared, loved, and detested Anton in equal measures, for Uri she felt nothing but a pure hatred. He'd always teased her, saying he wanted Sasha for himself. Not that Uri would ever harm his own nephew, but knowing that some of the girls (and possibly boys) he put out to be raped and exploited were underage children made her blood run cold just to think of Sasha being near him. And if Uri had organized a passport for Sasha, there was a serious and imminent plan of kidnap. Nice, normal dad. How could she have been so naïve? Why did she fall for it time and time again?

She was shaking now, the shock of the phone call finally taking hold of her body. Her thoughts were black. She would murder Uri if the opportunity presented itself.

Before he died, she would cut off his genitals and stuff them into his mouth.

Her working the backstreets of the West End had been Uri's idea. The flat they'd been using was crowded already, and as "the looker" of the bunch, Uri thought, she should be on show. Anton knew she hated being on the street, but the money coming in made him happy. He'd been smooth as honey, taking her out for dinner at nice restaurants before her shifts and most nights picking her up in his car at the end of them. He'd bought her an expensive sheepskin coat, short and tight, but surprisingly warm. She'd sure as hell needed it. February was grim enough and temperatures had plummeted. She had chilblains on several of her toes, but even so, he wouldn't let her out of the stilettos. He had a thing about shoes. No girl of his would be walking the streets in furry boots. He had his standards.

It was a particularly cold night. She pulled her coat tightly around her, dragging on a Camel as she slowly ambled back and forth along the pavement.

She'd read that tobacco actually made you colder because it narrowed the blood vessels, which was funny because all the girls smoked to keep warm. Farther up the street there was an Indian restaurant that had heat blowing over the entrance, and each time she walked past, she stopped for a moment under the fan. The manager had asked her not to, but he was a nice guy. Once, at 2 A.M., when she was waiting for Anton, who failed to come, he brought her out a coffee laced with Tia Maria in a Styrofoam cup.

A party of smartly dressed men and women was going in there now, chatting and laughing. She slowed down a little. She hated being looked at by normal people.

"Rachel," said a voice from a car with darkened windows, and she turned to peer at the driver. She never told anyone her name. "What have you for me?" He laughed and then she knew the voice. Uri.

"Hey, Uri," she said, her voice squeaking. "Come to take me home?"

Anton was in Germany on business, and he'd made Uri promise to get her home safely. Safely! *That was a joke, considering what she was doing, what she was exposed to.*

Uri wound his window down all the way. "Come on, Rachel. What's this? Is very early for a working girl. I think perhaps I am a customer."

She stopped to look at him, to see if he was serious. He wasn't smiling. "Fuck off, Uri. Don't make me laugh."

"I am not laughing. Get in the car."

She began walking quickly, away from him, but there was little traffic and he kept pace with her. "You heard me. Get in the car."

She ignored him for a few moments, then turned abruptly to him. "If you don't fuck off this minute," she growled, "I'll tell Anton."

He leaned across the seat to see her better. "Anton told you I am your boss for the week." He smiled slyly. "Your boss say get in the car."

Rachel stepped off the curb in her stiletto-heeled sandals and leaned into the window. "Fine, be my boss, but if you want to fuck, do it with Leandra or Katrinka."

Quick as lighting he grabbed her wrist and held it in a viselike grip. "Now get in this car. I know what I want from you. I give you a big tip, and then you can go home. Have a bath, an early night. Sounds great, yes?"

She didn't argue because she knew he beat up his women for little reason. Yet he didn't have a temper like Anton, violence was a cold and calculated thing with him.

She decided at once just to go with it, though she was surprised. Somehow, she'd never have thought he'd go for his brother's woman. But it seemed he was set on it, and she wouldn't lower herself by pleading. She sensed that if she didn't comply, he'd get what he wanted anyway but the outcome would be all the more painful. Once she'd made up her mind, she calmed a little. She was good at a lot of things, but above all she was good at finishing them off quickly.

It was dangerous to challenge Uri,

yet she couldn't help herself. "I thought you and your brother were like this." She crossed the first two fingers of her right hand in the universal sign of an embrace. "From Anton's point of view you are. He's always on about the loyalty of family and the blood bond and all that."

Uri almost ran a red light and then took a sharp left. He didn't seem bothered by his duplicity, but then you never knew what was going on in his head. She looked at him, to see how he was reacting to her challenge. He seemed totally at ease, sharp in his dark gray suit. His hair was short and brushed up from his forehead. He was not a tall man like Anton, but muscular with a good layer of padding, big thighs and buttocks, powerful shoulders.

After a moment he glanced at her. "It is like cuff links," he said. "When I have no good cuff links, I go to my brother's drawer to borrow, and I know I can, because we are brothers with trust. I don't go to take my friend's cuff links or my neighbor's. When there is need, his cuff links are my cuff links. If my brother had children, and he went away, they would be my children."

That's a guilty conscience talking, she thought. She'd never heard him say more than two sentences to any woman.

"So what did you have in mind?" she said, not looking at him.

"You on your hands and knees in the backseat."

"Some things I don't do," she said, having heard of his preferences.

"No worries," he chuckled. "I do them, not you."

She shuddered involuntarily. She would do this and her degradation would be complete. Perhaps this was what she needed, the total rock-bottom humiliation. Perhaps it would make her angry enough, outraged enough, to run away. Anton had left her in the clutches of this monster. Some fucking boyfriend he was. This was it! Tomorrow she would get a taxi to Paddington and get the train to Bath. Dad would be happy to have her back. She would clean up his house and cook him bangers and mash and they'd watch videos.

Uri suddenly took a left. That wasn't the right way. So they weren't going to the lane where she usually did business. Perhaps he wanted to have her in more comfort, really relish taking his brother's woman.

"How old are you, Rachel?"

"Eighteen. Why?"

"A bit old for me, I think."

"Fine. Let me out."

"No." He rubbed his chin in phony contemplation. "I think I take you to a party. Eight guys. Nice businessmen. Have you stamina for an all-night party, Rachel?"

She froze. So this was where they were going. "I'm not doing it," she said. "No way. Anton would flip. He'd never make me do that."

"Aww," Uri commiserated. "But I think you're wrong there. Five hundred quid they pay for you. Your Anton doesn't know how to work his woman good. He's not a businessman like Uri, but he likes the money and the trip is expensive." He patted her on the thigh. "No worries. Your Anton will be happy."

He'd stopped at a red light and she

attempted to open the car door. He grabbed her by the arm and restrained her. They drove the rest of the way in silence. Uri pulled up at a large hotel. It looked as if it had once been elegant.

"You go in. You turn left to go into the lounge. A man at the bar reading a newspaper and drinking a pint of black beer. You go with him." He pinched her cheek hard. "Understood?"

"Don't make me do this . . . please," she implored him, her eyes filling with tears. "Anton would never make me do a gang bang. He'll be furious."

"No he won't. Is big money, Rachel. Is your potential." He slapped her on the thigh. "Off you go."

She opened the car door. Her hands were trembling. A smoke, she had to have a smoke. A pill would help too, but she didn't have one. She wanted her dad to rescue her. She cursed him for being weak and pathetic, yet knowing that if he saw where she was going now, what would be done to her, he would die of sorrow.

She'd get through this, take the money,

and go straight to Paddington, take the train home.

As if he'd read her thoughts, Uri said, "That man will phone me when they are finished, and I come and pick you up. I wait here and you come down with the money."

He grabbed her arm as she was getting out. "One more thing, you slanty-eyed bitch. You thought I cheat my own brother, did you? Fuck his woman?"

Meekly she shook her head, but the hatred at her core burned brightly.

"I should give you a hiding for saying that."

"Yes, you're right, Uri," she said, smiling coldly. "Aren't I the rotten, evil bitch?"

Uri's girl rang again in the evening. Sasha had gone to bed, Charlene left to go to wherever she was dossing, and Rachel had gathered all the sticky wodges of wallpaper into plastic sacks. Bits of paper were stuck everywhere. The place looked a mess. She felt drained and wondered why she'd started such an ambitious project.

At the sound she yanked the phone to her ear. "Yes!"

"It's me. I phoned before."

"I was hoping you'd ring. Thanks."

"I got the passport in my hand." The girl laughed a low mellow laugh. "It look real. It's a good one."

"If you can send it to me, I'd be eternally grateful. I might need it myself soon. I'll send you the money . . . How about three hundred?"

"No," said the girl. "I make you a favor, you make me a favor. Not now. Tomorrow maybe, next week, next month." Her voice sank to a whisper. "When I leave Uri. I have your number."

Good luck, sweetheart, Rachel thought. *No girl leaves Uri.* "OK. It's a deal. Have you got pen and paper?"

"Yes."

"My address is . . . no wait. Best not here." Rachel ground her teeth in concentration. She'd spent the whole day thinking, so how had she overlooked this? Who else did she know . . . and trust? The only other person . . .

"Send it care of Madeleine Frank, Frank & Thomas Psychotherapy Clinic . . .

North Parade Passage, Bath . . . shit, I don't know the postal code. Never mind, it'll get there."

It seemed to take the girl ages to write it down. Rachel repeated the address several times. She could hear her breathing as she labored over it.

"What is that place?" the girl asked finally.

"I don't want it coming here. For your sake as well as mine."

"Yes. I see."

They were quiet for a moment.

"Are *you* going to be OK?" Rachel asked.

"Sure. He know I never touch his stuff, and he don't know I hear them talk. He think all women are dumb shit. Well, I'm not. Anyway, they are guys coming here all the time, doing deals. They are all crap people." She laughed a little as if she was pleased with herself, getting one over on the crap people. "Uri never know who take it."

"Just be very careful. Uri is vicious."

The girl paused. "I know."

"What can I say? I owe you one, that's for sure."

"No problem."

"Well, you got my number. If you need my help . . . I'll do what I can."

There was a pause.

"Wait," said the girl. "Something else."

"What?" Rachel wished there wasn't. Christ, wasn't this bad enough?

"Uri don't like dogs . . . I'm sorry. I did my best to save the dog."

"Oh God . . ."

"Please. Don't tell the little boy."

She woke from a half slumber at 5 A.M., practically sitting up. The anxiety she felt about the phone call had ruined any chance of sleep. She got out of bed, put on a pair of shorts and a shirt, and went downstairs. The place still looked a mess, bits of wallpaper everywhere, but Charlene had promised to come back in the afternoon to help her finish the job. That'd be a test for her motivation.

She made herself a cup of tea and stood by the front window, looking over the rooftops at the view of Bath, nestled down there, all church spires and curving streets with grand houses, and the river looping around it, and practically within touching distance, lush green hills with fields of cows and sheep. It was so different from London, where the buildings and the smoke just went on and on.

What would happen now? What would happen when the passport disappeared? She tried to imagine Uri's reaction. Would he suspect the young woman, probably his current favorite, of having nicked it? She had to accept that the girl might not have the courage or the incentive to go through with her promise, but if she did . . . the consequences of Uri catching her out didn't bear thinking about.

Rachel opened the door to the garden, sat herself on the step, and lit a cigarette. She tried not to think about Uri as she drank her tea and smoked her fag. This quiet moment first thing in the morning was a time she normally enjoyed. There was plenty of time for stress and anxiety to build up over the day. Yet her thoughts went back to the inevitable.

A passport meant only one thing: going abroad. Anton sure as hell had not offered to take them on holiday. With each new thought, she inhaled a deep drag of mind-numbing nicotine until she was giddy. What was in store? What next? Perhaps nothing would happen, but that was wishful thinking. Much as she'd decided that she was never going to leave her home, run away from anything or anyone, the thought of running crept into her mind, and no matter what she did to banish the thought, fear made her want to grab Sasha and disappear.

Sasha wandered downstairs, bleary-eyed, his pajama bottoms trailing around his bare feet. He didn't say a word as they had their cornflakes and toast, sitting at the kitchen table.

"Get your act sorted now, kid. Clothes on. You'll be late for school."

Sasha sat still, holding his cup of tea tightly in both hands.

"Come on, sweetie. Get a move on."

"I hate that school. Miss Bailey is an old bag. She doesn't like me."

"Well, you stuck your tongue out at Mr. Bodell, didn't you? What did you expect? You'll have to be extra nice now, so they forget about you being such a little sod."

That bastard Anton had thought only about himself when he went and took Sasha from school; it was Sasha who had to deal with the aftermath. The kid couldn't be expected to think ahead. Perhaps he believed he was going away forever with his dad, that Daddy would fix everything.

"I don't want to be nice. I hate Miss Bailey. She says horrible things about you and about Daddy."

Rachel reached across the table and took his hand. "Like what, Sasha? What does she say?"

Sasha stared down into his cereal bowl. "It doesn't matter, Mum. I can't remember."

"Yes, you can."

He got up and ran from the table. She tried to catch his arm but failed. Poor little devil. He was obviously paying for what Anton had done, his dad's weird accent, his appearance, his car. Perhaps she was no better, smoking fag after fag outside the school gates, probably with "ex-hooker" tattooed on her forehead. Her meeting with Mr. Bodell and Miss Stuck-Up Bailey had been awkward in the extreme, and it had surprised, no, *outraged* her to realize they seemed to hold Sasha equally responsible for his abduction. What was more natural than an excited kid sticking his tongue out on a whim? What were they, walking fucking saints? Sasha was right. School was shit—hadn't she always thought so herself?

Sasha's drawings reflected his state of mind. She'd been shocked when she found some he'd hidden in his room. Bleeding dogs, crashed cars, violent scenes of fighting men and women . . . no suns or flowers or gingerbread houses for Sasha. She should show the drawings to someone . . . Madeleine would probably understand what they were about.

No, it was better to leave that idea alone.

She looked at the clock on the kitchen wall. Surely someone would be there already. Beside her on the table was her mobile and the phone number. She'd have to suffer the indignity of Mr. Bodell's scornful attitude, but the first thing she had to do was to reiterate that no one, not God himself, was allowed to take her son from school.

Chapter Fifteen

Madeleine lay propped up on her bed. A half-painted canvas on her easel sat in a corner. The face, that of a pug-nosed Kenny Carlisle Jr., age thirteen, looked accusingly at her with one good eye, the other being only sketchily painted in and missing a pupil. Unfortunately, she couldn't stand the arrogant little jerk, but his mother had already given her half the fee, so it had to be finished.

Her attention was drawn outside. The glass doors were slid open to a jungle full of greenery, sounds, smells, and movement. Titchy, the six-toed cat, sat perched, immobile, on the edge of the pond. He was hoping that any moment now, he'd be able to get at one of the baby turtles. Stoic perseverance was etched in all the tense muscles of his small body. He spent most of his days there, hoping that one of the little critters would get off the island in the middle and come within reach of his eager paw. Madeleine knew him well enough; he wouldn't know what to do with a turtle if one smacked him in the face.

She should get up, but she was too darned miserable. Thinking of those last moments with Mikaela made her insides shrink to a small screaming dot, like a black hole. Almost as bad was the image of Mama inside that hospital. She was stark raving crazy, that had been all too obvious. The dark aspects of what Madeleine had found inside the house in Bath tormented her. How long had Mama been ill? How long had Mikaela been suffering the bewilderment and chaos that had been apparent in the filth, the ripped and broken furniture, and the markings on the walls?

There had been corpses of small animals, their rotting and mutilated bodies lined up on an altar in the kitchen. Piles of ash were everywhere, evidence of small fires on the floors (thank God they were tiled). Mama could easily have burned the house down and killed them both. The shock of seeing the state of the place had been a powerful factor in her decision to go along with Forbush and his team. They had played on her guilt, fostering her shame about her family and her sense of inadequacy as a mother.

As a daughter she was no better. She'd abandoned Mama and come back home. Mama might need her but she could not cope with the responsibility, realizing that she would fall to pieces if she stayed in Bath. What could she do anyway? Mama was unreachable, drugged into stupor. Madeleine had resolved to investigate if Mama could be brought back to Key West, if there was any facility that would have someone in her condition, which she doubted. Neville could pay.

She'd been back in Key West a mere week and there was much to do. Earning money for one (Kenny Carlisle Jr.). Around her on the bed were photos of Mikaela, some of Mama, none of Neville, whom she'd cut out with nail scissors. She knew she should put the photos away, they just prolonged the agony. She would do it soon, and then she'd get up and get on with her life. In another day or two, perhaps. She dozed for a while, then became aware of a terrible racket somewhere nearby.

"Open the goddamn door," Gina shouted. Her fists beat against the wood panels in energetic bursts. "I'll be hammerin' on the goddamn thing until you open it."

Madeleine winced. She'd forgotten that they were supposed to meet at the bar on South Beach this morning. There was a Cuban bartender there who Gina had her eye on. He'd been a dancer with some famous Spanish flamenco troupe, with a body to die for, but his main claim to fame seemed to be the ultrastrong margaritas he mixed.

The racket continued. Little did Gina know that Madeleine was rarely in the house, but locked in the studio.

"Don't be a moron . . . come on, Madeleine. Open the fucking thing."

"Aww shit." Madeleine jumped out of bed and ran out. "Cut it out, Gina," she called. "Shhh, this is just the sort of thing that's gonna give me a reputation."

"Reputation as what? A nun?" Gina called back and went around the house.

"No, a troublesome party animal with foulmouthed friends."

"When did you last have a party?" Gina *looked at her disheveled appearance and frowned. "When did you last have clothes on your body?"*

"OK, OK." Madeleine trudged back toward the studio. "I'll get some clothes on."

She drew an old print dress over her bra and panties. Through the window she saw Gina plonk herself on the swing by the pond and proceed to pick at her toenails. She'd gained weight since they parted in Mexico, but she had that full-bodied sultry sensuality with the matching attitude of languorous devil-may-care that drew men to her like flies.

"You got any booze in the house?" she yelled.

Madeleine ran out. "Shut up, Gina."

Gina was kneeling by the edge of the pond. "What are these? Turtles?"

"Yeah, turtles."

Gina got up and eyed her as if she were diseased. "Oh for Christ's sake, put on something more decent. You got that dress when you were ten or eleven. I remember the day."

"Sorry about this morning. I completely forgot."

Gina shrugged diplomatically. "You'd have cramped my style. You're too skinny to take anywhere."

Madeleine went through the back porch into the kitchen. Gina followed. The fridge held little but beer, two granola bars, and a selection of rotting fruit.

Gina peeked inside and said, "You coming out or not?" She grabbed a beer and looked for an opener. "I'm thinking that new seafood bar, what's-it, Mescla Marina."

"Naw. Some other day perhaps."

Gina glugged mouthfuls of beer then looked at her. "Look here, bubba. You wanna come and stay with us for a while? Mom suggested it. She'd love to have you. I don't know what's going on with you, but I don't like it. I'd be the first one to stay in bed for a week, but you! Come on, Mad. Get a grip."

"Come back tomorrow. I'll be dressed by six and we'll go for dinner at Mescla Marina. I'll buy. To make up for this morning."

When Gina had whirled out of the house, leaving behind a strong smell of cologne and a whiff of body odor in the kitchen, Madeleine wandered through the sparsely furnished rooms. Much as she loved the place of her birth, she could not forget that it belonged to Neville. It was not even partly Mama's. He'd seen to that. Among all the other feelings that tore at her insides was a burning anger at her father. He'd shown his true colors and she was unsure whether she would ever forgive him. The idea of being beholden to him infuriated her. She'd lived here for four years now, and he'd footed the bills. It had to stop! She could see that if she was going to forget the past, put it behind her totally, and survive, she would have to live elsewhere. Suddenly she was galvanized into action. She was not going to be indebted to Neville, not in a million years.

Half an hour later she was on her bike. She'd seen a couple of For Rent signs somewhere up Watson or Grinnell, she couldn't remember quite which street, but she'd find them. After an hour of cycling up and down the wide, verdant streets, she gave up. Even the lanes held nothing in the way of offers for rent. The tourist season was approaching and she realized with dismay that it wasn't going to be all that easy.

The sun was setting and she decided to check out Mallory Square, have a drink, look at the jugglers, and listen to the musicians. Maybe she'd see someone she knew. Every Conch knew every other Conch in Key West; surely someone would know who had a shack for rent somewhere. But her head was not into crowds, that was clear when her arms steered right instead of left on Eaton Street. Shucks! Oh, well. Tomorrow maybe. She cycled lazily in the heat of the evening toward Palm Avenue, glancing out to sea. She turned down Eisenhower Drive and slowed down by Houseboat Row in Garrison Bight Marina. She had loved those dollhouse dwellings when she was a kid. Leaning her bike against the boardwalk railings, she wandered out on the jetty. If only! These were surely the quirkiest of all quirky homes on the island. Odd-shaped multicolored houses built on barges, each one more zany and eccentric than the next. Side by side, they bobbed gently on the waves. A young woman was hanging clothes out to dry on a rickety balcony, an old man was watering a sizable potted palm on his stern. Farther down, on a barge with a tiny oval-shaped two-story house made of turquoise shingles, a small dog on a chain yapped furiously at the trespasser.

"Hey, boy." She leaned toward him

with her hand outstretched. The enraged mutt would have jumped straight into the water with a view to chewing her hand off, she was sure of it. "Calm down, darling," she cooed, infuriating the dog even more.

A head popped out of a small round window to check out the commotion.

"Jesus Christ," it blurted.

She took off her sunglasses and peered at the disembodied head. Despite the passing of almost six years, there was no doubting who it belonged to.

"Forrest?" she mouthed soundlessly.

At that moment the hook that held the chain that held the dog tore out of the wall together with a spray of fine sawdust.

She opened her eyes and, as on every morning, the first thing she saw was the photo of Forrest on her bedside table. He was sitting in a deck chair on the houseboat, a dog on his lap. It was a neighbor's pet, but like most children and animals, the scruffy beast had been drawn to him and considered the houseboat its own territory, a territory that had to be fiercely guarded.

Her husband's face was turned into the wind, fair hair ruffled by a breeze, his eyes crinkled in the corners from too much sun. His near-naked body was weather-beaten and muscular, though almost too lean, yet strangely graceful. She had worshipped all of him. Her very first impression of him, young though she'd been, had never wavered in subsequent years. He had been a wonderful friend and lover, and magnificent to look at.

A sudden pain in her chest made her reach out and lay the photo facedown. How many times over the years had she not had to slap herself into shape, ruthlessly remind herself that he was dead? Every trace of him was gone, his body consumed by a myriad of creatures, his bones dissolved. Just like her irrational hope that Rachel was her daughter, her denial was part of a neurosis she should long ago have cured herself of. Any patient with a similar affliction she'd probably tell to "get a life." Perhaps it was time to put the photo away, a symbolic act to acknowledge the fact of Forrest's nonexistence once and for all. Gordon notwithstanding, how could she ever meet and love someone else? She had been judging all men through some prism in which the virtues of Forrest shone brightly like a million twinkling stars.

Gordon! Through the haze of too many drinks and too little sleep, she suddenly remembered what had happened last night, the events in the Roman dig, her ride home in the taxi, the long hot shower to rid herself of him (and her self-disgust). What had she been thinking, having unprotected intercourse with a self-confessed sex addict? Neither was it like Gordon to forget his condoms. She'd been furious about his cavalier approach to their so-called lovemaking. After his sodden declaration of love, in the end all it had been was a fuck. Well, she was no kid, she had only herself to blame. She'd wanted it as much as he had. Without discussion or promises they'd both acted out of pure lust, as sometimes happens when one is drunk and reckless.

Another image snapped clear into her mind. The figure crouching in the dark, some man who she was sure had followed them from Milsom Street to the deserted house. As she came out alone, he could have snatched her handbag and run off, with no one there to stop him. Having missed his chance, he probably would have found Gordon easy prey. *Oh God!*

She reached across the facedown photo frame and grabbed the phone from her bedside table. She dialed quickly, Gordon's number was still fresh in her memory. There was no answer. After six rings his voice mail clicked in.

"Gordon," she said, trying to sound matter-of-fact. "Just checking. There was a very suspect individual outside the dig we looked at last night. Could you just text me or send me an e-mail to say you're all right?" She hesitated. "I'm very busy over the next few days so I can't talk to you, but you have a good holiday."

She drank the dregs from her coffee cup and looked out the window over the garden. The smog that was so often trapped in the bowl of the city made the very air look dirty. Her palm trees looked out of place in this climate. She longed for her homeland, the island of her birth. She had a sudden urge to quit everything, sell up, and go back. Drug

Rosaria, put her on a plane to Miami, and find her a home for crazy Cuban people, where they worshipped Orishas, listened to samba and rumba, and spoke only in Spanish.

Thinking of home, she reached out and righted the photo of Forrest. Hell! Why deny herself the pleasure of his company?

She looked out over the myriad of tiny mangrove islands. "My God, Forrest, I hope you know your way around here. What if we run aground? It might take weeks before someone finds us. We'll be dead from dehydration and our bones picked dry by buzzards."

"Yes, ma'm," said Forrest. "They're mean bastards, them buzzards."

"No honestly . . ."

"You need to brush up on your navigational skills, honey." He steered the little boat around one of the islands. "You know the tidal bank by its color. It's brown and muddy looking, and in between you've got the azure and indigo of the channels. You stay in the channels. It's as simple as that."

"Yeah, that's logic," she said.

"And you see those long-legged wading birds?" he said with a lingering glance at her legs. "They tell you to stay away, 'cos it's bound to be shallow."

She laughed. "Yeah, OK, OK." She stood behind him and put her arms around his waist. His back was brown and muscled, his sun-bleached hair had grown long. She rubbed her face in it. She could not get enough of him.

He reached behind him and put his hand on her hip. "And if by some lapse in concentration we did end up stuck in the mud, you get to hop out and push."

"Is that right, Romeo?"

They pulled in between two islets and they did get stuck, much to Forrest's annoyance. Pushing could wait, however. It was a glorious place, the two tiny islands teeming with bright green vegetation and squawking birds. He put up a parasol and Madeleine dug out the picnic. The ate in lazy silence, lying back on the cushioned seats of the boat they'd rented at Key West harbor. Forrest was saving up to buy another shrimping boat, while his dad had put the Dolphin

Lodge Motel up for sale in order to retire. He'd pledged half of the proceeds toward the boat that was going to be Forrest's livelihood for a hundred years.

Forrest turned to her suddenly. "Will you marry me?"

Madeleine's eyebrows arched in surprise. Then she laughed. "Isn't it a bit soon? I'm only twenty-one."

She had assumed it was a reckless, throwaway proclamation of the fact that he had the hots for her in a big way, but looking at him she realized the proposal had been far from impulsive, and was something he'd planned and obviously took very seriously. She cringed with mortification at her unromantic response. She could see from his face how embarrassed he felt, and disappointed. It must have taken quite some courage to ask.

"Can I think about it?" she added quickly, then said, after a short silence, "Only if I get to live on the houseboat. And I don't have to give up my identity and my name."

He grabbed her and kissed her hard. "Is that a yes then?"

"It is a yes." She nodded, smiling from ear to ear. "On those conditions."

"I'll give you the houseboat as a wedding gift."

"Christ! You don't need to go quite that far. Is it really yours?"

"My ma left it to me. It was her dad's. It's not worth much, as you've probably gathered."

They were both quite stunned by this sudden change in their circumstances. They sat back, their arms wrapped around each other. Madeleine felt her hands start to tremble and her heart race. She should not have given him that casual acceptance. They'd been together only a month and she'd been waiting for the right moment to tell him. She had not been able to face it, and after what she'd been through, it was nice just to be loved for a while. But now there was no turning back.

"There is something I haven't told you, Forrest."

He turned his head to peer at her. "You're already married."

She disentangled herself from his arms. "Do you remember that afternoon in the garden of the house you were looking after . . . not long after we first met?"

"How could I forget?" he said seriously. "I really am sorry about the way I handled that. I was distraught when I realized that we—"

"No," she broke in. "No, not that. You were absolutely right to be pissed off, but you see . . . I got pregnant."

"Pregnant?" He stared at her.

"We had a daughter, Forrest." She felt her tears start to well.

"We had a daughter," he repeated, dumbfounded, raising himself up on an elbow and looking down into her face. "Are you kidding me?"

She shook her head, keeping her eyes closed.

"What do you mean, we had?"

She broke down sobbing. She didn't want to cry, but there was no stopping it. "I gave her away for adoption . . . only two weeks before I found you in Houseboat Row."

He grabbed her by the shoulders and forced her to look him in the face. "But darling Madeleine . . . why did you do that? Why have you never told me?" His face was ashen, his eyes wide with shock.

"I wanted to tell you. I wrote you some letters while you were in India. I went to see your dad in Key Largo three years ago. I think I would have told him about our daughter, but then he said you had a girlfriend and that you didn't want my letters. He suggested I shouldn't bother you . . . he was nice about it, but I got the gist. He told me how upset you'd been about how we parted."

A minute passed, the only sounds were the birds singing and her heaving sobs. He shook her. "Stop crying, Madeleine. We need to talk. You have to tell me why you've given our daughter away."

She tried to control her tears and told him between sobs, "My mother took control of the situation and looked after the baby from the moment she was born. I guess it was inevitable. I was sixteen and she'd been longing for another child ever since she had me. We argued a lot about the baby, and finally I could not stand living there. I had postnatal depression and I felt like a creature from outer space in England anyway, and was missing home. So I decided to come back here and try to start afresh, leaving Mikaela with my parents. Eventually, my father left for another woman and my mother had a breakdown. I was traveling in Mexico with Gina . . . I had no idea what was going on. Mikaela had been placed with foster parents. It turns out that my mother has schizophrenia and my father washed his hands of everything."

She tried to look him in the face but found she couldn't. How could she make him comprehend what she'd done, why she had done it?

"As soon as I found out, I flew back to Bath, but the Social Services people would not let me see Micki. I could understand she needed stability. God knows what she'd been through. The couple who fostered her had applied to adopt her. In the end everybody wore me down. Mikaela was really happy with these folks and I felt I had forsaken her anyway. I signed the papers because I thought I owed her that. I owed her a real family."

Forrest was speechless for a long moment, his grip on her shoulders rigid.

"Is it too late? Is it too late to get her back?"

She broke down again, and he pulled her into his arms. "If only I'd known."

"It's too late, Forrest. She's gone."

Chapter Sixteen

I cut the artery in his groin with a razor blade. It was the tiniest nick, but I got it in one," Edmund said with a hint of professional pride.

He was sitting on his bunk, leaning against the wall, his knees drawn up. He looked quite weak, having lost a lot of weight during another bout of illness, and his pallor was ghostlike.

"That was after I'd beaten him senseless and hung him up by his wrists to a beam. So, he didn't suffer unduly. I left a note for his wife on the kitchen counter, telling her not to go up into the attic because she'd find her husband there dead. In case she missed the note, I'd put a bucket under him so that blood wouldn't get through the floor, staining the ceiling below and scaring the living daylights out of her." Edmund shrugged and looked up at Madeleine, smiling slightly as if these little concessions to decency were evidence of his essential good nature.

She must have looked unconvinced because he went on hurriedly, "Their marriage was a farce anyway. The wife was in Italy with her lover, and their kids never came to the house. He always dismissed the cleaner when his wife was away and went on a bender, drinking and watching kiddie porn."

Madeleine stood by the hatch and looked down at Edmund Furie. This conversation was her own fault. She'd brought it up a few weeks previously when they'd had that unfortunate altercation. In the heat of the moment, she had alluded to this particular crime, which differed from the others—strangulation was his preferred method of killing.

As he now feared that he was dying—no diagnosis of his strange illness had been made—Edmund had convinced her to let him explain what he'd done, because, according to him, the press had made the murder sound so much more sinister and cruel than it really was. She'd tried to reassure him that she'd not even been living in the U.K. when the murder took place, and had merely been told about his convictions by the prison governor, but Edmund was on a mission to make her privy to his motivation and would not be deterred. He was adamant that if he died, at least she'd know that he was not as evil as they'd made him out to be, and she found it oddly endearing that he cared so much about her opinion of him.

Since the events of the last couple of weeks had worn down the sharp edges of her boundaries and weakened her defenses, finally, in resignation, she'd agreed to listen, as long as he sat on his bunk, well away from her. She avoided his eyes, but kept glancing at his hands. They were surprisingly innocent looking, white and slightly pudgy. Six years in prison had kept them from exposure to the elements and hard work. She imagined the soft, pale fingers carefully unwrapping an old-fashioned razor blade, then unbuttoning the victim's trousers, pulling them down, and exposing his genitals, as he hung there, half unconscious, perhaps pleading for his life.

She felt sick.

"The wanker had a conviction for pedophilia in the U.K. He and two of his friends owned a villa in Thailand. Have a guess what they did there?"

"So he deserved to die, then?" Madeleine asked, trying to sound neutral.

Edmund clearly did not like the edge of sarcasm in her words and replied in kind. "I was in it for the money, my beauty, I thought I made that clear. The client paid a fortune for the killing, but the fact that the victim was scum made it easy. I even took pleasure in his removal."

"Your victims . . . were they all scum?"

"I can't police the whole human race, now can I?" he snapped. "But yes, sure, there is a hell of a lot of scum in this business." Edmund shook his head irritably, as if the job of explaining his philosophy to the uninitiated was onerous. "Please remember, Madeleine, I've only ever killed grown men, men who screwed people. Why would they otherwise need eliminating? I'm a cleanup service. I'm the garbage man. I get rid of trash, the element that others are too squeamish to touch and the law can't get their worthless hands on. And look who is paying the price. But mark my words, if that scumbag had touched one of the judge's own little granddaughters, would the judge think ill of me for getting rid of him?" Edmund leaned forward and snarled, "Would he, Madeleine?"

Madeleine shrugged, wide-eyed with dread, but found no immediate opposition to his argument.

"I dealt only with adult males," Edmund repeated emphatically, "no young punks— no matter how obnoxious—no women, no kids. OK, so occasionally my victims suffer a bit. The clients sometimes request it. If it's for revenge, I oblige. It's the sort of service I provide."

"Provided!" Madeleine corrected.

"Provide," he shot back. His eyes hooded over as he scrutinized her. "I told you already, my arm is long."

Madeleine leaned her elbow on the edge of the hatch and put her foot on the box she'd requested. It was backbreaking to stand up straight for an hour. She'd told the governor this was why they had foot ledges in bars, to keep people there drinking for longer. He'd relented.

"Edmund, are you actually saying you can kill people from in here? You can reach out and kill people on the outside?"

"If I should wish to do so, most certainly, my beauty. There is money stashed away in a safe place. There are favors. People owe me. Some of them would go to a lot of trouble."

So it was no delusional black magic he was referring to. There were people on the outside who would do his bidding.

"I don't believe you," she said, trying to contain a shudder. "Do you think we can lay this subject to rest? The rights and wrongs of your actions you can debate in your sessions with Dr. Weatherly."

"I'm much keener for *you* to understand me than Dr. Weatherly. I don't give a shit what he thinks about me."

"You should give a shit. Dr. Weatherly is an excellent psychiatrist. He is the one who can really do something for you . . . like re-evaluating your idea that it is perfectly all right to take the life of another person, no matter how much of a scumbag he is."

Edmund stood up, but didn't approach the hatch. He put his hands in his pockets and faced her squarely. There was frustration in his expression, knowing he'd had this one chance to convince her and had failed to make her understand.

Trying to forestall another argument (or example) about his philosophy, she said, "I've told you already that our friendship might not stand up to this kind of discussion, Edmund. It would be more comfortable for me not to have to think about the reasons why you're in prison."

He seemed to mull over the concept for a while, saying nothing. She was about to change the subject when he broke the silence.

"By the way, how is your boyfriend?" His voice was silky but with an edge of menace.

"*I haven't got one,*" she cried, exasperated. But as they stood there looking at each other, something in her stirred uncomfortably.

"Have you heard from him?"

Madeleine frowned. Where was this leading?

"I didn't think so," Edmund said with a melancholy sigh.

Her eyes widened. "That long arm of yours? Edmund, *no!*"

Edmund gave her his tooth-crowded smile, bashfully modest yet triumphant. "I don't think you'll ever hear from Mr. Reddon again."

Her hand flew to her mouth. "What . . . what have done to him?" She stumbled backward from the hatch, glancing toward the exit.

"Please, don't go," Edmund blurted. "He's alive. Don't worry. He's not badly hurt."

Madeleine looked around, hoping for the presence of a guard. "Tell me what you've had done to him, Edmund. Tell me this instance, or you'll regret it."

"You can't blame me, my beauty," Edmund pleaded. "I found out he was betraying you, putting your health and happiness at risk. Already back in March he was warned to stay away from you, but he's obviously a bit dense. He didn't quite understand what a razor blade might mean, did he?"

"A razor blade?" she echoed in a hoarse

whisper. "How long has your creepy associate been spying on me? What the hell did he do to Gordon?"

"Oh, nothing drastic. He just . . . *emphasized* the warning, until it finally hit home. For men like your ex, an explicit threat of having his penis cut off at the root with a razor blade is a wonderfully effective deterrent. It works every time." He offered up the palms of his hands to show her that this was yet another scumbag purged, another job of work done well. A good example of the effectiveness of his methods.

She felt the color rise to her face. "And you claim to be a friend! You bastard. You've meddled in my life in the most repugnant way. What you did was cruel. Horrible!" Her fury escalated. "I should report it."

Strangely, Edmund was not perturbed by her anger. He seemed to think he'd won some contest between them that tied her to him rather than alienated her. He peered at her almost condescendingly.

"Oh, don't get hissy. Think about it. A real man stands by his woman. He is not cowed by threats. They only work on scum, weaklings, and cowards. Don't you see, Madeleine? He is taking no risks for you."

Yes, whichever way you turned it, Edmund was right about that. She had not heard from Gordon, and now she knew she never would.

Edmund read her thoughts and smiled. "It proves my point. He wasn't worth having."

They looked at each other for a long moment. In the distance they could hear the clanging sounds of metal doors closing. The dimly lit corridor seemed colder than usual. Shivering, she drew her jacket tightly around her shoulders.

On Sunday evening she pushed the door to the studio open. There was a resinous smell of wood baking in the heat, mixed with the lingering odor of the oils and solvents she needed. Intermittently, while trying to sort out overdue bills and clean the house, she'd been thinking about the painting all weekend, but had been too restless to actually do something about it. Now that she was finally facing the blank canvas, it was too late in the evening to start anything; it was already past midnight, and she had a full list of patients in the morning.

She decided just to look at the canvas

for a moment, before going to bed, to see if the image that had been haunting her would fit the size and shape of it. She turned on the light. The studio had an abandoned feel, but the canvas sat there, waiting for her. After a few moments looking at it she picked up a stick of charcoal and made a few lines on the primed surface, just to explore the composition. It was easy and she relaxed a little. There was no hesitation in her hand; it was as if it worked independently, yet in harmony with a subconscious part of her mind. Half an hour later the composition was established, without a single preliminary drawing. Just the reflection of the image behind her eyes.

She sprayed the drawing with a fixer and prepared to leave, but on a whim she squeezed a splodge of raw stenna onto a plastic plate, poured a little solvent into an egg cup, and picked up a two-inch flat brush . . . just for a thin wash to establish foreground and background, light and shadow. She worked quickly, aware that it was late and the hours raced by when she got absorbed. There was not a sound. Prior Park Road was silent, deserted, not even a distant rumble from Claverton Street. After a while she glanced at her watch. It was already past two, yet she was reluctant to stop when she was on a roll, and she was relieved just to be painting. There was always that underlying fear of running out of inspiration, of one day finding she had nothing more to paint. Maybe that's why she painted only ants, her "transitional objects." It was laughable, really. A psychotherapist who refused to grow up and was forever escaping, first a strange childhood, then her accountability, then the truth about herself. Who had said, *There are people who can be defined by what they escape from, and people who are defined by the fact that they are forever escaping?*

She squeezed out some vermilion and burnt ocher onto the plate, then stopped for a moment and stepped back to gaze at the emerging image. She was astonished at what she saw. It was not a man on the wooden frame but a woman. There were definite breasts and a pubic triangle. She'd had a man in mind, definitely a man. It was only men—enemy warriors—they did this to.

She'd read about it years ago, in some obscure book on ants. A native South

American tribe had an exquisite torture, almost always ending in death, for their captured enemies, sometimes even for members of their own tribe who'd committed some unspeakable crime. The victim was taken to a piece of ground in the forest, which had been cleared of vegetation, around the nest of a particular type of flesh-eating ant. There he was stripped of all clothes and tied, spread-eagled, on a wooden frame. His mouth was wedged open with a specially carved piece of wood, his anus and penis pierced and opened with a long tube of hollowed bamboo. Into the depths of these orifices, plus into his eyes and ears, the thick sweet sap of a native tree was inserted. The inside of the nose, throat, and oral cavity were carefully painted with sap so as not to choke the victim. When he'd been thus prepared, the frame was lifted up and erected vertically on top of the ants' nest.

They would leave him to his fate. Within minutes the body of the victim would be swarming with ants as they were drawn to the source of the nectar. They entered the body of the man through every orifice. He was stung and bitten, devoured alive from the inside, sometimes gradually choking to death on the insects in his nose and mouth. Mainly it was thought that it was the panic and terror that killed; the heart would just give out. But for the brave, death was invariably excruciating and very slow.

Madeleine shuddered. She looked at the dark clearing in the jungle she'd just created. Thin shafts of light illuminated the slim body on the canvas, the back was arched and tied tightly over the frame, ribs and hip bones unmistakably defined. There was something of a crucifixion in the trussed-up posture. The head was tied back so the face was not visible, but a few wisps of dark hair clearly curled around the throat. What was this? What did it mean? Was she herself the victim? Was it a form of subliminal punishment for her crimes . . . or a clear death wish?

She shook her head to free it from thought, squeezed splodges of color in a neat grid over her palette, and continued painting.

She'd been painting all night and had not slept at all. There was a temptation to cancel her patients. She was exhausted, yet felt compelled to continue painting; but when she lifted the receiver to call Sylvia, she remembered that Emilia Fredriksdottir was coming at nine. Emilia was a walk-in, a student at Bath University from Reykjavik whose brother had been arrested for allegedly pushing his girlfriend to her death over a cliff. The girlfriend had been Emilia's best friend, and she had frequently confided in Emilia about her brother's alcoholic rages. Emilia was terrified that if she went back to Iceland she would be compelled by her conscience to testify against her own brother. Madeleine could not let her down, especially as Emilia had decided to come through the trauma with her therapist's help, instead of returning home to face the horror and its consequences. Madeleine had not denied her the help, but had tried to get her to see that going back to Iceland was possibly better in the long run, a way of dealing with the trauma in a more direct way that would enable her to put it behind her sooner rather than later. But no, Emilia felt her world had been devastated. Why return to it?

Madeleine decided Emilia deserved her attention. Her situation was more than worthy of the necessary effort. She showered, got dressed, and walked to the clinic.

Sylvia was at her desk, looking chirpy and efficient.

"Good morning, Sylvia."

Sylvia appraised her with a beady eye. "You look awful."

"Thank you, Sylvia."

"I've got this 'perk-me-up' tea from the health food shop. It's got Siberian ginseng and sage and—"

"No thanks. Has Rachel Locklear phoned by any chance . . . to make another appointment?"

Sylvia frowned. "You keep asking me, but the answer is no. Why don't you call her yourself if you feel it's that important?"

Madeleine turned away and made for her consulting room.

"Wait!" Sylvia called after her. "You've got some mail."

Madeleine returned, grabbed the padded envelope Sylvia handed her, and hurried to her room. She threw her bag and jacket on the table, then glanced at the slim package. Her name was misspelled and the handwriting was odd.

The clock said ten to nine. Getting up from the chair, she started to get ready for her patient. She hung up her jacket, picked up the package, and shoved it into her bag, but a second later she retrieved it. It was small and light, but it looked personal. Ripping open the flap, she shook out the contents. She held it in her hand and blinked. A passport! New and pristine. She looked at the envelope again. It was addressed to *Madelina Frank,* but missing the postal code. She was mystified. Flipping through the pages, she came upon the photo of a boy. His hair was dark and curly. The little face was serious, but there was a glint of humor in the eyes. She looked at the name. Alexander Anatoly Ivanenko.

Alexander. Who the hell was he?

She realized she had seen that face before, on another photo. The eyes, the delicate face. It had to be! She saw it now, the resemblance was unmistakable . . . Besides, wasn't Sasha short for Alexander? Sasha, Rachel's boy.

Why on earth had Sasha's passport been sent to her, here at the office, by someone who obviously didn't know her and couldn't spell her name?

Returning to reception, she showed the envelope to Sylvia.

"Do you know anything about this? Did anyone call about a passport or something?"

"No, but I noticed the 'Madelina'! Very perky." She peered at Madeleine over the top of her glasses. "Are you applying for a name change?"

Madeleine studied the writing again, then turned to her and winked conspiratorially. "Madelina is my stage name."

"Huh?"

She leaned across the desk and whispered, "You know . . . the lap dancing." She folded the envelope and looked at her watch. "So, where is Emilia Fredriksdottir?"

Madeleine walked quickly along London Road, turning into a narrow street in the general direction of Fairfield Park. It was hellishly steep. A rusty iron banister divided the road from the pavement and there were great patches where the tarmac had been worn away, exposing cobblestones from centuries gone by. The heat was astonishing for mid-May, and though it was past six o'clock, she had to slow down and stop to rest a couple of times. The old fracture made her ankle throb; there was no doubt she'd got unfit over the last few weeks. Her runs along the canal, the odd yoga class, and bouts of skipping on her patio had dwindled to practically nothing. Yet she had a nervous energy that never allowed her to sit still. Over the last few days, when she wasn't in the clinic, she'd spent all her time in her studio. But this obsessive need to paint was more than just a distraction or a channeling of her surplus energies. It was as if something had taken hold of her, some compulsion that obliged her to finish the painting she had started. Relieved that she'd used fast-drying acrylics instead of oils since it allowed her to keep putting on wash over wash without having to wait, she'd put the last touches to the *Crucifix-ion* at three o'clock the previous morning. She conceded it was an unusually sinister painting, and she found it worrying that such an image had sprung unbidden from her subconscious. No wonder poor Mama had been fretting about flesh-eating ants. She must have seen them crawling inside Madeleine's mind or . . . had her mother *willed* the painting from her with her own tortured thoughts?

She walked along a larger road, following the horizontal curve of the hill, and passed a row of little shops. Turning left at an intersection, she went farther up the incline. Coming upon a stretch of greenery, she stopped to take her bearings. If this was Faringdon Park, she was not far off. Ten minutes later she found the house. At least Rachel had put an address and mobile number on her new-patient form. The house was the last one on the road, next to the north end of Faringdon Park. It was potentially a great spot, with panoramic views over Bath, but the house itself was unattractive, one of those utilitarian sixties link houses with a garage on the ground floor. The house was terribly run-down, with paint peeling from decaying window frames and the gate to the pavement dangling on one hinge.

Her excuse was the passport. It had been lying in a drawer at the clinic for three days now, and there had been no phone call or visit to claim it. She would present it to Rachel and ask her why Sasha's passport had arrived in an envelope addressed to Madelina Frank. She was expecting this to lead to a conversation about why Rachel had quit therapy. Really, what she wanted was a glimpse of Rachel and Sasha, hoping that seeing them would lay any lingering doubts to rest.

She went through the rusty gate, up to the front door, and rang the bell. Through a frosted glass panel she could vaguely make out a tiny hall with stairs leading up to the living quarters. The garage seemed to occupy the whole of the ground floor.

After a minute she rang the bell again and was about to give up when she heard footsteps coming down the stairs. Rachel flung the door open. The expression on her face was a mix of dread and alarm, but when she saw who it was she visibly deflated and looked as if she could have collapsed.

"Oh, it's you!" she blurted out.

Madeleine observed her discomfort, wondering what kind of visitor she had been expecting. Rachel looked disheveled with her hair unbrushed. Her face had healed but she looked pale.

"Who did you think it was?"

"Why've you come here?" Rachel asked, her voice tense.

Madeleine felt at a loss. She'd not expected quite such a brusque reception, but Rachel was clearly on edge. Perhaps every ring of her doorbell represented some kind of threat. Not least one by the boyfriend-cum-pimp who wanted to kidnap her son, a man who used any level of violence to get what he wanted.

"Oh, don't mind me," Rachel said now. "Is it the passport? Is that why you've come?"

Madeleine reached into her bag and extracted the envelope. She held it out.

"Thank God." She looked at it for a long moment, but didn't take it.

"Madeleine, please," she said at last, not looking up, "can you keep it for a while? I know it's a lot to ask, but could you not shove it in a drawer where it's not in your way?"

"I guess I can." Madeleine slipped it back into her bag. "Would you like to tell me about it?"

"It's complicated. If you don't want to keep it, that's fine. I don't blame you."

Madeleine waited, but got no further explanation. "Can I come in for a moment?"

Rachel seemed to hesitate, then moved into the little hall. She was obviously not about to invite her upstairs. Madeleine went in, but the sheer proximity between them in the confined space seemed to make things even more awkward.

"It seems you have given up on therapy, Rachel."

"I'm sorry," Rachel said. "I know I'm a coward for not telling you, but I couldn't cope. That's all."

Madeleine peered at her. "What exactly couldn't you cope with?"

"You know . . . dredging up the past." She shrugged. "Look, nothing has changed."

"Well, I don't agree. In my opinion we were getting somewhere. Anything worthwhile takes a bit of blood, sweat, and tears." She tried to smile, but her mouth would not cooperate.

Rachel forced a tired laugh. "I've got blood, sweat, and tears to last me a lifetime, Madeleine. Why would I want more of it?"

She was right. Why indeed? Much as Madeleine believed in therapy, part of her understood the reluctance to rake up old shit and then poke about, trying to fathom the reasons for it all. She'd wondered whether she was just paying lip service to something she suspected would not be right between them anymore. The therapist herself had had too many conflicting feelings, and uncertainties, about the patient she was supposed to help. Even if all of it had turned out to be fantasy and speculation, it would surely get in the way.

"All right, Rachel. I'm reluctant . . . and sad . . . to see you go. But I guess that's my own problem." She took a small step closer, putting her hand on Rachel's arm. "Are you all right?"

Rachel stepped back. "I'm surviving." She pushed open the door with one hand to indicate that the tête-à-tête was over. Madeleine had no choice but to go.

"If you want to talk, if it would help, you can always change your mind. You're carrying a lot . . . with little support. I'm there if you need me."

"OK, OK. I'll keep it in mind. Yeah, thanks." Rachel leaned out the door, again scanning the street with anxious eyes. Then she looked at Madeleine for a moment and seemed to be on the verge of asking her something.

"Yes . . . ?" Madeleine prompted.

Rachel hesitated, then shook her head. "Oh, nothing. I'll be in touch about the passport, soon. I promise."

"OK, what would you like me to—" Rachel had already closed the door.

Madeleine walked back out the gate and stood for a moment, dismayed, wondering where to go. To her right, the end of the road was joined to the park by an old kissing gate. She walked through it into the park.

Her hand went inside her bag and felt for the passport. Initially she had thought Rachel had mailed it to her for safekeeping, but it was obvious it had been sent to her by someone else, someone who didn't know her or couldn't spell her name, a foreigner most likely. She should have asked Rachel what it meant, who was this person who now knew where she worked. The idea made her suddenly uneasy. She could still go back and ask Rachel. Or she could push the damned passport through the letter box.

But she did neither.

There was a playground in the park,

currently deserted. It seemed the space was used mainly by dog walkers. Three dogs of unidentifiable breed were chasing one another while their owners shouted ineffectually for them. A woman with two Westies on leads was skirting nervously around the scuffle. Madeleine pressed her bag tightly to her body and walked across the grass.

At the far end of the park she passed two lone figures bent double, looking at something on the ground. It was a small boy and a teenager. Closer to, she saw that the teenager was a girl, wearing a wool hat with a bobble despite the heat. Madeleine smiled a little. There was something so familiar in their stance; she'd spent her whole childhood bent double, studying the inhabitants of the dirt.

"Sasha," the girl cried suddenly, "look at the time. Come on. Your mum is cooking you pasta. It'll be a mush."

Madeleine stopped. Sasha. So this was him. With a name like that it had to be. He did not respond to the girl but stood immobile. His face was hidden, his attention on the ground.

"Come on, Sasha. Don't be a pain now. They won't go away. We can come back and check it out later. Sasha . . ."

"Come in now, Magdalena," Mama **shouted through the window. "Those things are dangerous. They live only a day because they've been condemned."**

Madeleine tried not to hear. Her mother said such crazy things. She bent down and stared at the ground, watching the winged ants dying where they landed. It was their lot. She'd seen it happen before; they flew for just a few hours, free and happy through the air, and then they died. She saw them struggle against their death, and wondered if she would struggle too.

"Magdalena!"

"Sasha . . . come on. I'll have your pasta if you don't come."

The little boy finally straightened his back and raised his head, and for a second, he looked straight at Madeleine.

The doorbell was ringing insistently. She went downstairs and saw that a letter had been pushed under the door. Picking it up from the floor, she opened it. It was written on very old paper, parchment perhaps. It crackled and split when she unfolded it. It barely held together. *"Dear Madeleine Frank,"* she read. *"Finally we have news of your daughter. We regret to inform you that she is dead. She was killed in a terrible storm. Mikaela is dead, Miss Frank. That is why she has never got in touch with you. She is long gone. She is dust . . ."*

The letter crumbled in her hands and the doorbell started ringing again. She rushed to open it. It had to be Mikaela, come to tell her that it was not true. She had to be alive . . .

Madeleine reached out for the door handle, then realized it was the phone ringing. She sat up with a start and glanced at the alarm clock. It was twenty to seven. She never had phone calls at that time of the morning. She snatched the phone from its cradle and croaked, "Hello!"

"Miss Frank," said a brisk voice.

"Yes, who is this?"

"It's Mildred Ollenbach at Setton Hall."

Madeleine swung her legs out of bed.

"Is everything all right?" she asked stupidly, knowing it couldn't be.

"Well, no, it isn't quite. Mrs. Frank did not say a single word yesterday, and this morning she seems catatonic. She doesn't respond to any external stimuli whatsoever, not even pain. Dr. Jenkins has had a look at her, and he thinks perhaps we should call for an ambulance, unless you'd rather come in first."

Madeleine froze, then panic assailed her. "Could she have had a stroke?"

"He's almost certain she hasn't." Mrs. Ollenbach hesitated. "He thinks . . . he is fairly sure that this symptom is to do with a deterioration of her psychiatric condition."

A thought occurred to her. "Could this 'symptom' be in response to a sudden increase in my mother's medication?" she asked sharply.

"Most certainly not," came the clipped reply. "But Dr. Jenkins's recommendation is for electroconvulsive therapy, and fairly soon, as your mother is neither eating nor drinking. We managed to get her into bed, though I can tell you it was no mean feat to try and lay her down."

"Can you wait?" Madeleine said to the

woman at the other end. "I'll come right now. Don't do anything until I get there."

She jumped out of bed, threw on a pair of jeans and yesterday's blouse. Grabbing her bag and car keys, she left the house. The rush hour had started and as there was no wind to stir the air, it was trapped in the basin of the town and choked with fumes. The heat was stagnant between the bath-stone façades. When, ten minutes later, she'd left the city, the air began to clear. The sun shone with deceptive charm, making the opening vistas look like paradise itself. Setton Hall was bathed in light and the trees in the gardens were lush and full.

She pulled into the visitors' car park and sat for a moment, trying to clear her thoughts. Could Mama's condition be self-induced? Was she capable of bringing her life to an end? Was she so unhappy that she wanted to die rather than exist in a nursing home in Bath, forever separated from the land of her birth?

Madeleine got out of her car into the piercing light of the sun.

An attempt had been made to give the room a Hispanic flavor. Madeleine had contributed a few Cuban wall hangings made of cotton in deep reds, yellows, and purples. A screen made of Mexican beads divided the dressing room and en suite from a little sitting area. Another screen concealed Rosaria's altar and the shrine to Babalú-Ayé. *Where is he now?* Madeleine wondered, looking at Rosaria's inert figure on the bed.

She was lying as rigid as a tin soldier; her eyes were wide open. Her hands were still, not flapping aimlessly as they normally did. She seemed changed—aged and shrunken. Her birdlike form appeared no more than a scrap on the expanse of the bed. Standing at the door, Madeleine saw, superimposed on that fragile figure, a wedding picture she had of a young Rosaria, so hauntingly beautiful, black-haired, small but voluptuous, her skin dark against the snow white dress. How was it possible only this remained? Madeleine was suddenly aware that this was what awaited everyone, herself included: to be used up, dried up, until no more than a desiccated shell remained. She shuddered. When Rosaria died, she would move up that notch in the order of things, become the next in line. At the same time, there was someone behind her, a daughter, somewhere, moving up that ladder too, and perhaps other generations behind her, grandchildren and great-grandchildren.

A sudden thought came out of nowhere, sending a cold shiver up her back. Perhaps her daughter *was* dead, and there would be no one behind her, no generation to follow. It had never occurred to her. Never! She refused to entertain the possibility. For some reason Sasha's face materialized in her mind, a small boy standing in the grass, looking straight at her. As soon as she visualized his childlike form, it transmuted into a tall, handsome man in his middle years, standing in a doorway, an expression of sorrow on his face . . . and Madeleine herself the withered woman on the bed. It shocked her, this sudden vision of an unlikely future.

"It's all right," someone said. "You can come in."

It was a nurse, sitting by the window, reading a well-thumbed paperback.

Madeleine approached the bed. Rosaria's was wearing the quilted bed jacket that she had given her last Christmas. Her hair was neatly braided and coiled around her head, as she loved it, but they'd taken her dentures out. Was that really necessary? Mama was vain about her looks and she hated being toothless. Madeleine sat down beside her, kissed the crucifix and the bones of her ancestors, then bent to embrace the narrow shoulders and cover her forehead with kisses.

"Despiertate, Mama. Estoy aqui," she whispered. "I'm here, Mama."

"She's not in pain or anything," said the nurse.

Madeleine turned to the young woman. "How do you know?"

She looked blank for a moment. "I suppose I don't."

The nurse quickly got up and left, and after a few minutes Dr. Jenkins strode in.

"Shall we phone for the ambulance, Miss Frank?"

"To plug my mother into the wiring and fry her brain? No, Dr Jenkins."

He approached the bed and put his hand on her shoulder. "Come now, Madeleine, what else would you have us do?"

It was a reasonable question, and a fair one under the circumstances. Electroconvulsive therapy did actually work in these cases, but it also killed millions of brain cells. She sought frantically for a reason to keep Mama where she was, some reason to stop them doing further damage to her mind. "Can we not give it a bit of time? Could we not put her on a drip, and give it a day or two?"

"This is not a hospital, Madeleine," he said gently.

"I know, but considering how much money my father shells out each month for my mother's care, I think a few concessions are in order."

She felt close to tears and he patted her awkwardly on the shoulder.

"What about that doctor, the anthropologist who was talking to my mother? I wouldn't mind having a word with him."

"I'll see if Mrs. Ollenbach still has his phone number. Though I daresay I don't really believe in that sort of 'doctor,'" Jenkins said with slight hauteur. "I must run, Madeleine, but Mildred is in her office. Think about it. We can't leave your mother like this."

When he'd left, Madeleine bent over Rosaria, gently trying to close her eyes.

"Shut your eyes, Mama, or they will have to tape your eyelids down. You don't want that. Won't you say something, so I know you're with me? Please, *Mamacita. Dime algo, cualquier cosita.* Where is Pedrote when you need him, eh, Mama?"

At the mention of the Babalawo, her mentor, Rosaria's eyelids flickered. Her lips started to move, trying to say something.

Madeleine leaned forward. "What, Mama?"

Rosaria coughed weakly to try and clear her throat, struggling to form the words.

"Take the child and run," she whispered with panic in her voice. Her eyes closed, and she took a deep breath. *"Take the child and run."*

Madeleine's hand trembled as she stroked her mother's face. "What do you mean, Mama?"

"Take the child away," she repeated, feebly slapping the counterpane for emphasis.

"What child, Mama?"

There was no answer, just the agitated flapping of her hands.

"Mama. Listen to me. I expect you've sensed something . . . perhaps you've read my mind . . . but she is not my child." Madeleine hesitated, then whispered. "Is she, Mama? *She isn't, is she?"*

"No," Rosaria whimpered and shook her head. "The child," she repeated, exhausted. Her hands went stiffly to her neck and she pulled at the chain. "Take this now . . . put it around your neck."

"No. You need it yourself."

"No, Magdalena. Ahora es tuyo. Do as I say."

To calm her Madeleine obeyed, easing the chain from her mother's neck and hanging it around her own. In turn she pressed the ancient crucifix and the vial of ground bones to her lips. Had she not rejected her beliefs, she would be the Santera now. The talismans of generations of Santeras were against her breast, and according to what her mother had told her, would imbue her with power and protect her from evil forces.

"Do you want to bless it?" Madeleine said, and held the crucifix to her mother's lips. Rosaria mumbled her blessing and then her head fell to the side and her arms relaxed. It seemed she was asleep. At last the rigidity of her catatonic pose slackened.

Madeleine kissed her cheeks, smoothed her hair, and whispered loving words, but Rosaria was far away.

She got up and went to the altar. There was the paraphernalia of her mother's devotions: the cowrie shells, the sacred stones, and the bowls of herbs Madeleine sent for by mail order from a *botanica* in Key Largo. The gold-plated hammer lay on an embroidered doily (the sacrificial knife having been confiscated by Mrs. Ollenbach). She lifted the hammer and there, taped to its underside, was Edmund's brooch.

She removed it and held it in her hand for a moment before slipping it into her pocket. Then she took a box of matches from her bag and lit the candle before the image of Babalú-Ayé. He was a rigorous god, a man's god, really. Perhaps he didn't like all this frippery and pretty blessings. Perhaps he didn't like a brooch on his altar.

"Look after my mother, you bastard," she mumbled. "She has been your most loyal subject."

Two hours later Madeleine knocked on Mrs. Ollenbach's office door.

"Come in," the woman called. She was at her desk, looking stressed. She pushed her glasses down the bridge of her nose in order to look over the rim at Madeleine.

"Mrs Ollenbach," Madeleine said from the door, "my mother is much, much better. She has spoken to me. She is lucid. She's had a drink of grape juice and half a mashed banana. She opens and closes her eyes, and when I left her, she was sleeping soundly. I can see no good reason to subject her to a harrowing stay in hospital."

Mrs. Ollenbach did not look overly pleased, but it was not difficult to read her thoughts. Neville Frank's daughter should— despite being an interfering pain in the arse—be humored, all the way to the bank. "Well, isn't that lovely."

"I know we're not the easiest of customers," Madeleine said, returning the sugary smile. "But thank you for the wonderful care you're giving my mother."

"Oh, Miss Frank," Mrs. Ollenbach called as Madeleine was closing the door.

"Yes?"

"Dr. Jenkins mentioned you wanting to have a word with the . . . ah, with Dr. Alvarez. I gave him a ring, but according to his wife he is gravely ill and in no shape to speak to anyone."

"Ill?" Madeleine frowned. Ill from what? she wondered, but thought better of asking. Mama had said that he tried to prize the secrets from her. Oh God. . . .

"Thank you for trying. I'll be back this evening."

Madeleine hurried out the door into the sunshine, her mother's words still echoing in her mind.

Take the child and run.

Chapter Seventeen

How much are the tickets?" Rachel asked.

The woman pointed to the board, but when Rachel took too long reading the *outrageous* prices, she said: "Eleven twenty-five for an adult, six fifty for a child. Or thirteen fifty and eight, respectively, if you want to visit the Costume Museum as well." She leaned over the counter to peer skeptically at Sasha. "Children under five go free."

"OK," Rachel mumbled. "Forget the Costume Museum. One adult and one free child."

"I'm not five," Sasha piped up. "I'm seven."

Rachel rolled her eyes, and the woman stared at her crossly. "That'll be seventeen seventy-five in that case."

Rachel paid for the tickets and, grabbing Sasha by the arm, marched him toward the entrance.

"Sometimes it's best just to shut up, Sasha."

"But it was a lie, Mum."

"Yeah, yeah, kid. It was a lie."

They were given audio guides at the entrance, one for adults and one for children. She'd been meaning to take Sasha to the Roman Baths for ages; he had missed a school visit because he'd had the flu. His schoolmates had talked about it and he'd felt left out. Alfie and Dottie had done the good-parent trip too and taken her when she was twelve. Dottie had died not long after. The visit and her death were associated in Rachel's mind. Her mum had been fatally ill already. She'd been so weak that she chose to sit in the Pump Room, the fancy café from Georgian times, while Alfie took Rachel around the baths. Dottie believed the claim that Bath's springwater was curative—that's what it said in the brochure—but when they got back, her glass of sulfurous water sat untouched on the table. She looked as though she was listening to the pianist with her eyes closed, but in fact she was sleeping. It was the morphine that did that, but she was good at keeping her head upright as she floated in and out of her drugged slumber.

"You're looking out over two thousand years of history," said a suave voice when Rachel clamped the audio guide to her ear and pressed the button. Sasha was fascinated by the kids' guide and kept repeating each story, making their progress through the baths incredibly slow. She tried not to be impatient; in fact, she should try to spin this out for as long as she could. What else was she going to do with him on a Sunday? He was so restless these days, crying for no reason, wetting himself at night. He'd started talking about the dog again, asking why it was dead. He seemed to have a knack of knowing things he couldn't possibly know, and hearing things that weren't even said. She couldn't think of any gentle way of telling him the dog was gone forever, even less tell him why, or how. She'd been quite fond of the stupid thing herself. What horrors had it been subjected to? Probably kicked to death by that monster Uri, or Anton himself had killed it, to teach her a lesson.

It was late afternoon and the place was crowded with tourists, mainly Americans by the sound of them. How did they have the energy to do so much sightseeing? You heard them everywhere. And the money these people must have. But then Bath was the umpteenth wonder of the world, so it was no surprise they all came here.

"Mum, look at this," Sasha cried, pulling her.

"Yes, sweetie, that's dead cool."

They jostled with the crowds through the hall of the Great Bath. The huge pool was open to the sky and steam rose from the still, black water. Roman generals carved in stone stood above, high on the walls looking down upon them. Their people had bathed in this water and walked under these colonnades. The stone blocks on the floor were worn down by Roman feet. Sasha knelt and plunged in his hand.

"It's hot, Mum," he called to her. "Feel it. The water is boiling hot."

She bent down and trailed her hand in the water. It was unbelievable. Hot water rose out of the ground in the middle of the city. A man in a uniform tapped her on the shoulder and told her the water was not fit for touching. When she looked up, he winked and said, "I've got to say that, in case someone gets a tummy bug or something."

She allowed herself to be pulled along, a fraud among legitimate sightseers, intermittently grabbing at Sasha so as not to lose him. She stepped on someone's foot.

"Sorry," she muttered.

"You can step on the other one too if you want to," the man said, looking at her and smiling. He was handsome; blond and pale and clean looking. All she felt was shame. Her years of pulling men were well and truly over, and now, though she could sometimes still use a wink of the eye to get what she wanted, she could not look them in the face.

She moved away, following Sasha from

pool to pool, exhibit to exhibit. Her insides
felt frozen. It was best not to think abou
last week, or the last few months for tha
matter. Perhaps she shouldn't have
stopped seeing Madeleine. No, it made
her anger worse, rather than better. The
so-called therapy was a farce and she
should never have gone there. What she
needed was Valium. If only she hadn'
sworn off drugs. Now was the time she
could really have used some. She liked tc
be numb, rather than high, but she had tc
keep going. She had to keep Sasha safe
That was all that mattered.

With a throng of tourists they were dis-
gorged into the sunshine, and holding tigh
on to Sasha's hand, she wandered on tc
the Abbey Church Yard. Sasha wanted ar
ice cream and they sat on a bench in the
shade of the Abbey, their hands to thei
mouths, Sasha slurping on his ice crearr
and Rachel drawing on her Camel as if she
were drowning and it was her only source
of oxygen. It was her last cigarette anc
she'd bought the package only this morning. She looked at Sasha. So much for being a role model. Well, Anton didn't smoke

perhaps Sasha would take after him. Some ole model *he* was. It was Madeleine who had used that word. She'd said something about "nurture versus nature." She'd hinted, in that stealthy way she had, that if Rachel didn't get free of Anton, Sasha would grow up to emulate his behavior. What a bunch of bullshit. Her jaws clenched and tears of anger sprung up in her eyes.

"Now what are we gonna do, Mum?" Sasha asked.

"Anything you like, Sasha." She wiped at her eyes with the neckline of her T-shirt. "It's your day."

"Can't *you* think of something?"

"My mind is blank, sweetie."

"Let's go on that boat. On the river."

"Hey, good idea." It was the last thing she felt like doing, but why not?

They caught the last boat trip of the day. It was nice on the boat, after all. She could just sit back as it puttered along. Huge trees grew on the riverbank and one almost had to duck to avoid the branches hanging over the boat. The boatman had a running commentary going, making everyone laugh, even Rachel. He seemed such a nice person, and Sasha had abandoned her to sit next to him, up front. They were getting along ever so well.

She watched as they chatted and laughed, Sasha bombarding the poor man with questions and jokes of his own. He wasn't like that with Anton. He looked up to his dad like some superhero, but at the same time he tended to be anxious and was constantly sucking up to him, which made Rachel cringe with unease. Thankfully they hadn't seen Anton since he'd taken Sasha for that outing that had so upset him. She hoped it would be a long respite, and as she did every time Anton went away, she hoped he'd never come back.

But there was the passport. It spoke for itself.

The boat turned around by the weir in Bathampton and made its way back, a little faster now. Sasha chatted undeterred to his new mate. The guy had taken off his captain's cap and put it on Sasha's head. He looked so cute, holding on to it anxiously as if it might fall into the water. She wished the boat tour could have been longer, all day. It soothed her to be able to sit still, without any thoughts, and just watch her boy being happy, framed by greenery, water, and blue skies, like a picture in some soppy book. But soon enough they drew under Poultney Bridge and docked on the left bank. Sasha looked as if he might not care to hand back the captain's cap, but when the man asked for it, he did. He looked tearful, not wanting to leave the boat, and she had to coax him off it.

From habit she felt anxious about wandering outside. It went back as far as she could remember. Dear old Mum had been ridiculously overprotective, and the years living with Anton hadn't helped; being out on the street had a meaning all of its own. Yet, edgy though she was, for some reason she felt equally uneasy about going home.

She should have trusted her sixth sense, developed over the years that she'd been with Anton. As soon as she put the key in the door, she knew something was up. She could have grabbed Sasha, turned around, and run, but she didn't. This was *their home,* hers and Sasha's, and she was not going to be made to run from it.

He was coming to make good his threat, with or without Sasha's passport. He must know it was gone or, worse, knew who had stolen it or, worst of all, knew it had been stolen at Rachel's request. If Uri put the screws on, that girl would sing, of course she would. These Eastern European girls looked and talked tough, but they were cowed and helpless. She'd known enough of them.

She saw the shambles as soon as she opened the door. The floor was littered with the contents of her drawers: jackets and clothes lay in heaps. She didn't own much, but the place had been turned over as if a gang of professional burglars had ransacked it. Anton had obviously been at it for a while. He was sitting on the sofa watching a film, a can of strong lager in his hand. There were half a dozen cans strewn on the coffee table. It was not a good sign; booze made him vicious.

"Hi, Daddy," Sasha called out. His voice was shrill; he knew the devastation meant trouble. "We've been on a boat, Daddy. I got to be the captain."

"That's nice, son," said Anton, looking steadfastly at Rachel.

She swept her arm around the room. "What have I done to deserve this?"

"Oh, I was just looking for something," said Anton, his eyes glued on her.

"Yeah, like what? Money? I don't keep cash in the house. Not since last time." She sneered at him. "I'm a single mother on benefits, doing my best to support my son. Why would an *international businessman* like you need to raid—"

"That's enough, Rachel."

"Haven't you had enough money off me over the years?" She turned away to go into the kitchen. It was best if he couldn't look her in the eyes. He was good at reading her face. If he mentioned the passport, would she be able to keep this up, be convincing enough?

He turned the television off, got up, and followed her. He picked up her bag from where she had flung it and in the kitchen he emptied the contents onto the table and fingered through them. When he didn't find what he was looking for, he grabbed her by the arm. "Who is Madelina?"

"Madelina?" For a moment she was genuinely confused. "I haven't got a clue."

"You should know. It was the name you

gave to Tatyana. You know what I'm talking about now, don't you?"

She shook her head even though she knew the game was up. Once questioned that poor girl had not been able to fudge the truth.

He grabbed her by the hair. "You stolen something that belongs to me."

She laughed at that, and he slapped her.

The fury that swelled within her hid her fear. "You bastard. Are you going to beat me up in front of my son? He's getting too old to watch this, Anton."

Anton's hand was raised, but at the sound of a deafening noise, they both stopped dead. It was the television turned up to peak volume. Suddenly Sasha started singing in a loud, high-pitched voice. It was no song she recognized, but the sound was shattering. Even Anton looked stricken.

"What the hell, just forget it." He took her by the shoulders, raising his voice over the racket. "This is what we do. You and me and Sasha going to Warsaw for a while. I got a really nice place for us. Just a few months, just to let things cool in London." He bent toward her and brushed the hair away from her ear. While feeling the scarred lobe between his fingers, he spoke softly into it. "I don't want to be months and months without my son. He's not a baby and he should be close to his father. If you don't like to come"—Anton shrugged exaggeratedly—"that's fine, but Sasha come with me. Like I said to you in Tenby, I want my family. You keep telling me we are finished, but I know you will come because you want to be with your son, yes?"

Rachel drew back. Her fury had deflated; fear rolled in like a tidal wave.

"*Sasha,*" Anton bellowed, "turn it down, now. Your mum and I are talking. We're not fighting. Just talking, Sasha . . . Come on, boy."

They stood there for a few seconds looking at each other, then Rachel broke free from his grip and ran to the living room. Sasha was on the sofa with his eyes tight shut, singing and singing, his hands pressed hard against his ears. She took the remote control and turned off the television.

"It's OK, Sasha sweetie," she said, falling to her knees and taking him into her arms. "We're not fighting. Don't you remember

Daddy saying he wasn't going to fight anymore? He means it . . . Don't you, Anton?" she called.

Anton joined them and sat down on the sofa. After a few moments' silence, he said, "Sasha, is your bedtime, yes? You've been out all day. You must be so tired."

Rachel glared at him. "He's not had his dinner yet."

Sasha scrambled to his feet. "I'm not hungry," he cried and ran from them, out of the living room, up the stairs, and into his room. The door slammed.

"So you think you're a good, caring father to that boy, do you?" Rachel hissed, moving away from him toward the stairs. "He's scared shitless of you."

"Where's the fucking passport?" Anton got up and followed her. "Come here, Rachel. Don't go away when I talk to you." He grabbed her by the wrist and dragged her back to the sofa, pushing her down. He stood over her, clasping her thighs between his knees. "Now talk quiet and tell me who this Madelina is. Uri's silly bitch send the passport and then throw out the paper with the address, like you must have told her to do. Before I leave here, you will call this woman to bring the passport, or we take the car—with Sasha—to pick it up. Unless you hide it elsewhere. You get it, Rachel?"

"What did you and your monster of a brother do to that girl?"

"Don't you worry."

She glared at him. "She's still alive then?"

Anton laughed cruelly. "Uri is not stupid. That girl is making a fortune for my brother. She work shit hard now to pay off the trouble."

"God help her," she said, her insides turning at the thought of what the poor young woman would be subjected to. "And who murdered the dog?"

Anton clamped her legs harder between his knees. She winced in pain. "I buy the kid a whole fucking zoo when we get to there. Now *where is the passport?*"

"OK, Anton, I'll tell you," she said, calling forth the best of the many alternative strategies she'd concocted. "Madelina is a friend of mine. When she got the passport in the post, she freaked on me. She was pissed off as hell and told me to take the passport and never show my face at her place again. She wanted no part in it. You see, she knows what guys like you are like. She's got one herself—a right mean bastard, the same as you and your brother. The first thing I did was take the passport to the park next door and burn the bloody thing in a bin. I'll show you where, if you want. It's two minutes' walk from here."

Anton's knees tightened further and he grabbed a fistful of her hair. "That is crap talk, Rachel. I can stand here till your legs drop off."

She could see the conspicuous swelling at his groin. He liked this sort of game, but she'd been no better. In times past, seeing him aroused used to turn her on too, and she hadn't minded a bit of grief for the plea-sure it gave her. Now, all she felt was a burning hatred.

He smiled at her. "No way," he chuckled. "There is no way I get between those teeth of yours. Sorry, babes."

"Fuck you."

His face hardened. "Listen, Rachel, what-ever way, I take Sasha with me this eve-ning, and if you do anything to try and stop me, you have Uri and his whole crew come here to make you regret. Passport or no passport, you will not see Sasha again . . . unless . . . you go upstairs now and pack a bag; two bags, one for you and one for Sasha. I *want* you to come, Rachel. Really. Sasha need you." He let go of her hair, reached into his back pocket, and held up her own passport; she'd used it only once on a trip to Amsterdam.

"You and I have our passports, babes. Now we must get a new one for Sasha. Too bad, Rachel. Don't you think?"

It seemed he believed the story about the passport. Without it, it would make it difficult to leave the country. Where the hell was Warsaw, anyway? She couldn't think straight. He'd mentioned the place more than once in relation to his business, but she'd not paid attention.

"Let me go, Anton," she pleaded. "Let's talk about it."

"No, you talk," he said. "Are you coming or are you staying?"

He meant it this time. He wanted Sasha, and he was going to have him. Her only option was the one he offered her.

"You got me where you want me. I'm going where Sasha is going . . . you couldn't keep me away even if you wanted to."

Anton smiled and released the pressure on her legs a little. "That's my girl. We go to Uri's house to stay for now. Uri can get another passport for Sasha, but it is expensive and it takes a little time. So we go there and we wait for new passport. But I warn you, Uri is very angry with you. He think I should teach you a lesson." He shook his head and laughed. "My little brother tells me how to teach my woman a lesson. It's funny, yes?"

An icy jolt went through her. "I refuse to go anywhere near your brother's. And you're not taking Sasha there. You hear me?"

"We have to go there, Rachel. Unless you have Sasha's passport, you have left no choice."

"Listen. We don't have to go anywhere. We can get a perfectly legal passport for Sasha. It shouldn't take long."

"No way, babes. We go to Uri's." He looked at her, but there was something vague about his eyes. She couldn't fathom what it was, but it was different from anything she'd seen. It petrified her.

She nodded. "We go to Uri's."

A look passed between them, and for once he glanced away. It confirmed her chilling conviction. He released her suddenly and she watched him turn toward the kitchen. Terror churned her insides, mixed with fury, revulsion, and hatred.

"You pack and I have a drink, yes?" he said over his shoulder. "I saw a nice bottle of scotch in your shelf."

As her thoughts reeled, her eyes rested on the mess on her dad's old coffee table, all the scrunched-up cans he'd drunk and the hideous cut-glass ashtray she'd bought in a charity shop, full to the brim with her own stinking butts. She remembered it was so heavy she had cursed, carrying it all the way up the hill in a plastic carrier bag that had practically cut her hand in half.

She stared at the ashtray for an instant, then she flew up from the sofa and grabbed it with both hands. He'd half turned by the time she caught up with him, and grasping the rim she slammed it into the side of his head. Despite her speed, part of her mind was in slow motion, and she was surprised at the strength she had.

A spray of ash and cigarette butts seemed suspended in the air, while Anton's eyes were on hers, frozen in astonishment. He seemed dazed by the blow but he lashed out at her with a closed fist. She twisted her body sideways and his knuckles just grazed her upper arm.

He shook his head a couple of times as if to clear his mind, and his right hand moved instinctively to his temple, where blood poured freely from the wound. It gave her an instant in which to lift the ashtray over her head and dart forward. Steely determination had taken hold of her and she moved with a swiftness she'd never known. In that split second he stared at her, stunned and unbelieving. One blow he could have understood—she'd attacked him more than once—but this was different. He must have seen the rapt intent in her eyes. She was not frightened of him, she was not backing down. She was coming for him again.

His arm flew up to shield his face, the other reached out to stop her, but the sharp edge of the heavy glass came down, slicing a deep gash in his forehead and crushing his nose as it went. He let out an unearthly shriek and his eyes rolled back. He hit the floor a second after the ashtray did. His face was awash with blood. Before he could recover, she grabbed the ashtray and straddled him, smashing the edge of it into his mouth. The rim crushed his teeth as if they were bone china.

For a few seconds his hands grasped at her arms, trying to hold her back. She shook him off and again smashed the ashtray into his forehead. The noise of the impact was peculiar, like that of a wet log split by an axe. His body arched under her, then began to jerk.

Perhaps it meant he was dying, she wasn't sure. Only one thing was certain: it was too late to turn back. She looked away while her hands kept lifting the object of her deliverance and letting it come down by its own weight, the edge of the glass crushing his face, again and again.

Throughout the commotion, there had not been a sound from Sasha. She didn't dare go up and check on him in the state she was, covered in blood and tissue, disheveled, gasping, all but out-and-out hysterical. She couldn't think clearly beyond knowing that she had to get rid of the body somehow, before there was any chance that her son might come down the stairs.

She was trembling uncontrollably, but her strength seemed undiminished. She'd heard this somewhere, people finding superhuman strength when faced with a sudden crisis—women lifting cars off children or carrying unconscious people out of burning buildings.

She had to do it soon, now, before the strength ebbed out of her, before the whole horror hit her. She looked at the body. It was big, but the hardness had gone out of it; it looked spongy as it lay on the floor. Averting her eyes, she searched through Anton's pockets, finding the two passports and his wallet. His car keys she'd seen on the coffee table. He was wearing expensive Italian shoes, he always did. She took them off and hooked his feet under her arms, dragging him backward. Down the stairs was easy. His head bounced on each step like a ball on a string, the way hers had a few weeks ago, when he pulled her up the stairs by the arms to rape her. The image of that evening recharged her hate-fueled energy. It was better than thinking about what she was doing, pulling a dead man down the stairs, a man she had once loved, the father of her son. One moment he'd been alive, his heart beating, his body coursing with blood, the next he was dead, cooling, stiffening. How simple it had been, how quick and mindless. She had thought about killing him often enough, but never imagined she would finally snap, pick up the nearest weapon, and actually murder him.

On the tiny downstairs landing, she had to let his legs go and one of his heels crashed against the frosted glass panel on the front door. A crack shot across it, but the glass didn't break. Breathlessly, she fumbled with the door to the garage. It was locked and the key was troublesome; it always had been. She managed to turn it and gave the door a swift shove with her shoulder, then grabbed Anton's body by the wrists and pulled. Her strength was failing now and she felt sick. She heaved him down the three steps onto the concrete floor. There she left him, locked the door, and rushed back upstairs to the kitchen sink, leaning over it and spewing out what little there was in her gut.

Her clothes had to go and everything that had blood on it; the floor was awash. But

she didn't know what to do first. She
stripped off her shorts and T-shirt and
stuffed them with her sandals into a bin
bag. In her underwear she got a bucket
and mop from the cupboard. Swabbing
the floor manically, she slopped up the
pool of blood and the streaks it had left
along the floor and down the stairs. Sasha
was apparently sleeping, thank God; he
must have been tired after a long day in
the sun.

She tiptoed up the stairs. In the tub,
having no shower, she used a cleaning
bucket to rinse herself off. There was no
time to scrub her skin raw, but she knelt
and put her whole head under the tap.
When she touched the sore patch on her
head, righteous fury rose again in her. Yes,
she was livid—not repentant, not sorry.
He had hurt her onc too many times. He'd
brought it on himself. Years of abuse and
exploitation had made her do it. She wondered if the judge might see it that way
too. Hardly! Not if he saw the state of the
corpse.

She dressed in jeans and a warm top.
Despite the heat still lingering in the house,
she was shivering. Opening the door to

Sasha's room, she saw he was fast asleep, fully dressed on top of his bed. Carefully she removed his sandals, and opened the window a little. He was hot, his face red and moist, his eyes under the lids moving restlessly.

She lingered upstairs, wandering to and fro in her bedroom, fearful of facing the scene down below. But soon she could not stand being there either; there was much to do and she had to deal with it. She went downstairs to the front door and looked out on the street, scanning both sides up and down, but Anton's car didn't seem to be there. Of course, he was too clever for that. Had his car been outside the house when she and Sasha got back, she might have turned and run. Well, she'd run for the last time. It was probably parked a few blocks away, and she decided there was enough to worry about for now. She glanced at Tom Bainsburrow's house. The old man tended to watch television till way past midnight, and looking side-on into his window, she saw the reassuring flickers of violet light in an otherwise darkened living room.

She stopped for a moment before she

closed the door. Was there some other way? She could still phone the cops. There was still time. It was now or not at all. She knew that her aversion to the police was based on her own experiences and that normal people were actually sometimes helped by the fuzz. Then the picture of the carnage flashed in her mind: the crushed head, the blood-filled crater that had once been a face. What normal woman would perpetrate such butchery? Self-defense seemed a laughable justification. No doubt she'd be hauled into custody; Sasha would be taken away somewhere. No, not that. It was not an option. Not at the moment. Yet no one got away with murder; it was only a matter of time. Anton was gone but she was not free; on the contrary, her freedom would be short-lived. Unless there was some way . . .

With the mop and boiling water mixed with bleach she resumed cleaning the living room floor, a cheap imitation wood laminate that Alfie had laid at Dottie's request. She searched everywhere for stray blood-soaked cigarette butts. There was precious little furniture but she looked it over, piece by piece, and scrubbed at imagined spots of blood. The sofa had been closest to the scene of the crime, a nasty brown leatherette thing she wiped over and over with a bleach-soaked cloth. For hours she scoured and sluiced; it seemed as good a way as any to spend the night. She tackled the walls, the fireplace, the door frames, the skirting boards, and the stairs. She'd seen it often enough on TV. Forensic people could find blood anywhere.

It was almost morning when she thought of the body again. She would have to hide it better, until she could think of some way to get him out of there. She almost laughed at the childish notion of dumping it. How the hell would she do that? Still, as the hours ticked by, the possibility of reporting the killing receded, the threat of what such an action might mean grew. The body would be detected in her garage soon enough, why and how she didn't dare contemplate. Something to do with the heat—"putrefaction" was the word she was looking for—and the smell that it generated. Or perhaps Anton would have told Uri where she lived—had he not said she'd have Uri and his crew to answer to? She could take Sasha and run, but where to? She'd said only hours ago she'd never run from here. This was Sasha's home.

She steeled herself and went down to the garage. Turning her head, she stepped over the body. There was such a mess here, she could cover him with something and hide him away among a lifetime of junk, boxes, ladders, wallpapering tables, tins of paint, trays, buckets, and blankets, the tools of her dad's trade. Strange that Anton had not thought to search the garage for the passport, he who had been so single-minded when he wanted something. Perhaps he'd not realized there was a garage, or that it was hers.

Flung in a corner was the large sheet of plastic off a new mattress she'd bought for Sasha's bed. She'd kept it to cover the sofa in case she and Charlene ever got around to painting the living room. She looked at it, and at the same time remembered the huge roll of industrial packing tape she'd come across in one of boxes. It had stuck in her mind, having *Richie's and Rosie's Right-On Removals* stamped along it in Day-Glo orange. She stood still for a moment, pondering her options. Everything was silent but for her ragged breath and the drip-drip of a leaking pipe.

"Now, Richie and Rosie," she muttered out loud, "where the hell did I see you?"

Chapter Eighteen

Madeleine had an uncomfortable feeling that she was using her patients, but during the last week, hard work had become an escape. However, much as she needed the distraction of other people's problems, she was tired of them too. She knew some kind of burnout was happening to her, and really she should have a break, or quit. The idea had been brewing in some hidden corner of her mind. The pull of her homeland was getting stronger, but she tried to dismiss these thoughts. God almighty, the sheer enormity of such a move was a hurdle she'd be unlikely to undertake. And what about Rosaria?

Peter, Gordon's colleague, had phoned her at the clinic to invite her for a weekend walk and lunch in the country. In a bid to get her life back to some kind of normality, she'd accepted the invitation. They'd had a lovely time; he was a very appealing man, sincere, caring, modest . . . and trustworthy. There was certainly room in her life for a new relationship, someone positive and ordinary to take her mind off everything that had just happened, but was that really fair to the poor man? As she'd looked at his kindly face, her thoughts had strayed to Edmund Furie and his shadowy agents. A new boyfriend would have no idea what he'd be letting himself in for. A murderer's henchmen might stalk him with the aim of cutting off his penis, while a crazy Cuban witch would slaughter tropical fish to a pagan god in order to make him ill with syphilis. And she herself was no picnic, with her nasty torture paintings and love affair with ants. When he'd asked her for another date, she'd put him off with a regretful "I'll call you."

Her shrinking gaggle of female acquaintances phoned less regularly to suggest a night out. She felt no sense of loss over it, though she missed her runs along the canal with Patricia, who was now encumbered by a first grandchild. Neville, who normally contacted her rarely, now rang her almost daily to grumble, whine, or rage about his wife's desertion. Elizabeth, in turn, had phoned on Sunday morning to say she was coming to Bath to take her to lunch. Her stepmother—now ex—took her to the Pump Room and spent a fortune on wine, but it had soon been apparent that what she was really after was some free counseling, plus a handy go-between. Could Madeleine try and soften her father a little, get him to part with a bit more than she'd asked for? Her aims had hardened now that she'd tasted independence, and perhaps some lawyer had encouraged her to fight for half of everything. Astonishingly, she wanted Madeleine's support. Incredible gall, really, and anyway, Madeleine had no support to give. All her emotional energy was reserved for her patients. If she was going to use them, she owed them that.

* * *

Between patients there was a timid knock on the door. John's face, spectacles askew, peered in.

"Can I?"

"Of course, John. Come in."

He slumped down in the patient's chair. Madeleine studied him, concerned. His hair was on end and his glasses smudged. He'd seen only the occasional patient for the last few weeks and she'd hardly laid eyes on him.

"You look as though you've been through the wringer, Johnny. How is poor Angus?"

"He can hardly move. They're talking about an operation."

"An *operation*?" She'd never seen him looking so pale and tired, and reproached herself for not being more alert to his difficulties. "What's the prognosis?"

"It's not good, Madeleine. Would you believe it, they had this guy coming to talk to us about wheelchairs, and I mean long-term. Mind you, what these things can do these days is amazing. They can practically wipe your arse and read you a bedtime story."

"Oh God, John. I'm so sorry."

John flopped further into the chair. "It's the disc. It's practically ground to dust."

She looked at him searchingly. "Wha does it mean for you . . . I mean, in the future?"

He met her eye and shrugged. "I love the pompous old fart," he said simply.

She smiled. "That's truly heartening." She meant it genuinely, in fact she was awed that such a sincere and selfless sentiment actually existed. "Lucky Angus."

John spread his hand in a gesture o helplessness. "I wish! How are *you* doing Madeleine, with the 'daughtergate' affair."

"Oh, that's a nonstarter. You were right of course. I jumped the gun . . . as I have so many times before."

"Oh, darling. What a bummer." John leaned forward and took her hand. "Are you seeing someone about it yet? I do hope so If you aren't, *I'm* going to find someone for you."

"I'm sure you're right. I should deal with all these ghosts from my past, once and for all."

John took off his glasses and rubbed his eyes. "I've been meaning to apologize I didn't handle that bolt from the blue very well. I felt injured. I thought the trust between us was absolute. And I know I've not been supportive."

"Don't worry, your troubles are far worse than mine." She hesitated. Perhaps this was a good time to tell him. "Listen, John . . . I'm toying with the idea of quitting psychotherapy."

He looked up sharply. "Oh no, don't do that." He seemed genuinely horrified. "I can understand you needing a break. For heaven's sake, take a holiday."

"This is not about a holiday. I'm not as good at this job as I thought I was."

John let go of her hand and slapped it. "Rubbish, Madeleine. You can't judge yourself on something like this. Anyone would—"

"Yes, I can," she cut in emphatically, "and how I handled this ridiculous fantasy was inappropriate."

"Oh, come on. How else could you have handled it? You can't stop! You're one of the best there is. You just need a bit of your own medicine: a good therapist and a sabbatical, that's all."

"I'm talking about a gut feeling. I suspect I'm in the wrong job."

"What about me?" John implored. "Can't I keep you here?"

"You and I will always be friends, we'd just have to find you another partner. The practice is going so well, the location is great. It ought to be a cinch."

"I don't *want* another partner," he exclaimed. "For heaven's sake, Madeleine, don't do anything rash now. Give yourself time. You're acting on a—"

The phone interrupted him. "There's my next patient," said Madeleine.

"We've not finished this conversation." He got up and gave her a lingering hug. At the door, he turned. "Tell you what. Why don't you have a week at the cottage? Have a good, long meditate, away from the source of all this stuff . . . While you are at it, air the place and soak the flower beds. Angus can't hack the car journey."

"Yes, it's a thought. Perhaps. Thanks for offering," Madeleine said with a wan smile, watching his ample girth go through the door.

Her hand hovered above the telephone, but she did not pick it up. Somehow the very idea of Mrs. Hartley-Wood and her tedious complaints exhausted her. Finally she lifted the receiver.

"Send her through, Sylvia."

"Mrs. Hartley-Wood just phoned to say she'll be a few minutes late. She's driving round and round, trying to park her car."

"Okey dokey. Thanks."

She slumped back in her chair. She accepted John's suggestion that she needed therapy. She smiled suddenly. A woman named Esperanza had popped before her inner eye—in all her largesse and glory. Esperanza's sort of rigorous treatment was what she really needed to slap her out of her idiocy.

She was hugely fat and her head was covered with rows of tight braids. The pure African blood that flowed in her veins was evidence of her slave ancestry. By all accounts she was quite old, but strangely beautiful, clothed in a long purple dress that clung to her massive but shapely curves. She was covered with gold jewelry, and had a gold front tooth. Her nails were long and bloodred. Despite her size, her waist was well

defined and she moved like most Cubans, as if she were hearing the strains of some rumba in her mind.

Esperanza was a curandera, a Santera who specialized in the knowledge of herbs and healing. She was known among Cubans from top to bottom of the Keys for her ability to diagnose and cure illnesses, especially those caused by malefactors and enemies. Madeleine remembered her from the time when, at age thirteen, she was afflicted by mal de ojo, *received from the old man who preyed on the energy of children. Rosaria had called Esperanza to the house to cure her of the effects of his evil eye.*

She'd not changed at all, though fifteen years had passed, and the curandera remembered the occasion well, having been a good friend of Rosaria's.

"We almost lost you, chiquilla," *she cackled, and gave Madeleine a crushing hug.*

Madeleine laughed, turning to Forrest. "This lady saved my life once."

Forrest looked quite overwhelmed, by the lady herself, her parlor, and by the fact that the woman he loved was still on this earth because of her.

"**Esperanza, this is Forrest, my husband.**"

Esperanza's jolly face beamed and a huge gilded smile crossed her lips as she gripped his hand and shook it with vigor.

"*Sit, sit,*" *she said.* "*Let me get you a* cafecito." *She shouted for a young mulatta woman and gave her instructions for coffee and* bollos. *The room was full of birds in cages, all of them chattering and squawking in a shrill cacophony. Herbs, feathers, trinkets, and flasks hung from the beams, and effigies of saints and Orishas adorned the walls, each surrounded by frames of colorful garlands and plastic flowers. In between hung paintings, naïve in style and composition, of her forefathers, staring stiffly from years gone past. Candles burned on every surface and the moisture from potted ferns steamed up the windows. The furniture, too, was a mix of old Spanish, driftwood, homemade and broken wicker apparently salvaged from refurbished bars. The lady's bulk could be supported only by a two-seater sofa of former elegance, now terribly scuffed around the edges.*

While they waited for the merienda to

be served, Esperanza asked Madeleine about her mother.

"Mama has been sick for the last eight years," Madeleine murmured, her guilt about leaving her mother in England impossible to hide. "She is in a nice place and very well looked after."

"Caramba!" Esperanza exclaimed, sitting back and folding her massive arms over her bust. "I thought something like that might have passed. Rosaria spent her powers most unwisely. I told her so, many times. She could make sickness, whereas I can only make health." Esperanza shook her head in regret. "She started too young. Ay, ay. She left Cuba and did not have her mother's guidance. When I saw her in that booth on Duval Street, calling herself a fully fledged Santera and offering to make spells for all and sundry, I was very alarmed. I sent word to her mother." She shrugged. "Her mother is still angry, to this day. But what could she do? She was stuck in Cuba with no desire to escape."

"I had no idea about all that," Madeleine said, taken aback. "So you know my grandmother? What's she like?"

"Your grandmother is a very powerful Santera, Magdalena. She has been initiated into the Pinaldo, the fifth rank. It is as high as a woman can go in Santeria. She was given the sacrificial knife, an enormous honor and achievement." Esperanza *paused and looked at the ceiling, her face grim. "She claimed that Rosaria stole the knife from her when she escaped from Cuba, taking it with her to impress the Cubans she met in her new life in Florida. It was a dangerous move . . . and that is no doubt why she is ill, put out of harm's way in some land of the beyond."*

Madeleine stared at Esperanza, shocked. So the sacrificial knife had been stolen. Mama had not got it by her own merit, as she had so often claimed. She glanced at Forrest, whose eyes were wide, fascinated by this larger than life colossus of a woman and what she had to say about his terrifying mother-in-law.

"Are you saying that my mama is not a proper Santera?" Madeleine asked.

Esperanza swayed in her seat, as if finding the question difficult to answer. "Your mother has a special gift and she got by on it. But marrying a big fat gringo with plenty money can take the humility out of a woman, if you know what I mean. She ran many risks, always slightly out of her depth and relying too much on her sixth sense. A treacherous mix."

Madeleine realized how much of all this she had already suspected. She was embarrassed that Forrest should hear it. "Tell me more about my grandmother, Esperanza. Will I ever meet her, do you think?"

Esperanza shrugged. "She is old now, and will certainly never leave Cuba. She hates America with a vengeance. As a woman she was a real tyrant, and probably still is. It was thought that she put a spell on her husband when, once, he developed a passion for a singer and disappeared somewhere with her. Your grandmother found some of his hairs in a comb and wove them into a bracelet with hairs of her own. She wore it on her right wrist for nine days and pulled him back through the sheer strength of her will, but so fierce was her jealousy that the spell made him ill. Your grandfather died with great lumps growing in his groin. Nobody could do a thing for him, not even his wife, who was thought to have caused the sickness."

The mulatta servant appeared with the coffee and bollos and they ate to the accompaniment of the deafening racket of the birds. Madeleine could not force down the dry bollo. She drank her coffee in silence, too shaken by what she'd heard to make small talk.

Esperanza suddenly fixed her beady eyes on the young couple. "What ails?" she said.

Madeleine and Forrest looked at each other. They'd had a series of tests and investigations and been told that a pregnancy was unlikely to occur because of scarring due to the postnatal infection she'd suffered. But as the doctor had said: You never know, keep trying. Forrest had laughed when she'd suggested Esperanza, but he was willing to try anything.

"Forrest and I have been married seven years." Madeleine paused meaningfully. "Seven years, Esperanza."

The old lady studied them thoughtfully for a while. Madeleine found her silent scrutiny almost physically uncomfortable and focused her eyes on a large ant scurrying the length of a fern leaf. It annoyed her that she could not remember the name of this big placid fellow, whose nest she'd only recently studied in a friend's garden.

"Let's see what can be done." Esperanza got up and shook the crumbs off her dress. Tiny birds appeared from nowhere to pick at them on the floor. "Not you, Mr. Forrest," she said putting a hand up to stop him coming along. "I suspect the trouble is not with you." She cackled heartily and gave his physique a saucy appraisal.

In a tiny room, Madeleine was told to lie down on a bed. The mulatta brought in three trays with hierbas and put them on a small altar. Esperanza sat down on a stool in front of the altar and the mulatta sat next to her. They spoke in Yoruba, which Madeleine could not understand, and it ap-

peared that the curandera was passing on her knowledge to the girl. Occasionally they glanced at Madeleine, then continued mumbling between themselves. Madeleine could see the girl handling the bunches of herbs, dividing them, gathering a large bunch by the stalks. Then she got up, and leaning over Madeleine with her eyes closed, gently whipping the herbs over her abdomen. It seemed to go on for a long time, and Madeleine was starting to feel dizzy and nauseated, as if she'd drunk a pitcher of Cuba libres on an empty stomach. Finally Esperanza heaved her bulk off the stool and approached her. She'd taken a large cigar from the altar, and after lighting it she blew small puffs of smoke over Madeleine's body. Suddenly she stopped. "What is this?" she said, passing her hand over Madeleine. "You have already had a child in your womb."

"Yes," Madeleine whispered, frightened by the anger in Esperanza's voice. "I should have told you. There was a child once, but I desperately want another."

"It's not possible," Esperanza said. "There is a blockage."

The mulatta stopped her lashings with the herbs and disappeared from the room.

"What do you mean, a blockage?"

Esperanza threw her hands up in annoyance. "A blockage, nothing more, nothing less. Don't expect me to have fancy-ass words for it, like in a hospital. You are unlikely to conceive again, chiquilla. *It simply wasn't meant to be."*

Esperanza had no words of consolation. Perhaps she sensed how the first child had been forsaken and was a bit annoyed they'd been so cagey with the truth, but still, she slapped Forrest on the butt and told him to think on the positive; from now on they could make love for pleasure only. Then she charged them ten dollars and advised them to go out and get drunk.

They left Esperanza's house, Madeleine fighting her tears.

"We've got each other, honey," said Forrest, his arms around her as they walked down the street in the blazing late afternoon heat. "You are all I need. Let's get cats and dogs and parrots and chickens and ants, anything you like. Or let's adopt!"

But she found it hard to be brave. She would never be given a second chance, and the curandera had finally convinced her of it.

"One day we'll find Mikaela, even if we're old," said Forrest, smoothing the tears away from her cheeks. "Let's keep looking and hoping."

"She's only twelve. It's too soon to look or hope."

Mikaela was twelve! They'd celebrated her birthday, rigging up balloons around the houseboat and eating a mountain of ice cream. They'd put a present in the box they kept, one for every year, hoping one day to give them to her in one huge celebratory bonanza. Twelve was a difficult age in a girl's life, she was neither child nor woman. Madeleine did not much credit a sixth sense, but if she possessed one at all, she sensed her daughter was troubled. For several weeks Madeleine had been anxious and sleepless, waking in the night, thinking of her and hoping she was all right.

"Well, let's live for the moment, then,"

Forrest said, clearly relieved to be out of the curandera's creepy den. "Let's do what the wise woman said." He kissed her neck and tickled her waist, trying to cheer her. "Let's go out and get totally drunk."

Madeleine was jerked out of her thoughts by the phone ringing insistently.

She picked it up. "OK, send her through."

"It's not Mrs. Hartley-Wood," Sylvia said, her voice strangely stifled.

"Thanks. Whenever!" Madeleine said and was about to hang up.

"No, wait. It's Rachel Locklear. She's . . . here. She does *not* have an appointment today but she insists on seeing you. She says its urgent." There was a pause and a muffled exchange of words. "In fact, she says she's not taking no for an answer."

Madeleine sat up straight. "It's all right, send her in. Tell Hartley-Wood . . . tell her just that a patient showed up with an emergency. Tell her I'll be with her shortly."

Seconds later Rachel burst through the door, slammed it shut behind her, and without ceremony sat down in the chair she had occupied when she'd been Madeleine's patient. She was dressed in black sweatpants, black trainers, and a gray T-shirt that showed a thin line of white skin at her waist. She had lost weight. Her thick auburn hair had grown, but was uncombed; she looked tired and had a hunted look in her eyes. Madeleine studied her, concerned.

"I'm not here because I want to be," Rachel blurted.

"Hello to you too, Rachel."

Rachel's demeanor changed. Her eyes shifted away and she suddenly looked close to tears, something Madeleine had never seen. "I need your help. You have to help me."

Madeleine waited, feeling an unpleasant coldness wash through her body. Whatever the problem was, it had to be pretty serious for Rachel to come back. But Rachel was quiet, offering no immediate explanation for her return.

"I'll do my best, but you'll have to book an appointment." She motioned to the clock on the wall. "Right now I'm waiting for someone."

Rachel did not seem to hear a word she'd said.

"Don't think I'm going to be beholden to you," she said in a flash of anger. "If you can help me, which I doubt you can, that's it! We are quits, you and I. *Quits*, you understand? You can go about your life, and you can rest happy that you've done your bit and don't feel you have to be laden with guilt forever and a day."

Madeleine frowned. "What on earth are you talking about?"

"I'm talking about what you owe me, Madeleine."

Madeleine stared at her in confusion. "What do I owe you?"

Rachel was quiet for a moment, her face a picture of suspicion and hostility. "You know exactly what you owe me."

Madeleine was stumped. "I'm afraid I don't."

"You figured it out weeks ago. I know you did."

Madeleine could not answer. Her thoughts were swirling.

Rachel crossed her arms over her chest. "Oh, let's cut the crap, *Mother!*" she snorted. "You figured it out in that last session we had, when you sent me out so you could go through my bag. You probably already guessed it when I accidentally confessed my age."

Madeleine was too stunned to speak. So it was true . . . She shook her head in an attempt to realign its mechanisms of reason. "Hold on," she whispered. "What you're saying is . . . you are my daughter? You're Mikaela?"

"I'm Rachel now. *Rachel*. And don't pretend you don't know me."

A moment passed while they just looked at each other, Madeleine in shock, Rachel in defiance.

"So we can make a deal," Rachel continued. "You help me and we are quits. Wouldn't you like that?"

"Quits? How?"

"Surely you feel bad about dumping your innocent baby on a crazy woman who killed neighbors' pets for kicks. Off to la-di-dah art college in Florida, weren't you? Couldn't be fagged with a sniveling brat. And when that didn't get me off your hands, surely you remember having to interrupt some holiday, rolling in to sign adoption papers, giving your five-year-old daughter away to some strangers." Rachel's voice hardened. "Any guilt or remorse you might feel about that, here is your chance to make good."

Madeleine suddenly understood. The anger . . . the fury that had been there from the start. "You knew me, didn't you? You knew who I was when you came."

"Of course I did."

Madeleine shook her head in incomprehension. "You came to therapy, knowing I was your mother?"

"*Yes*, for fuck's sake."

"But why? Why did you feel the need to do it this way? You must know I've been wanting to meet you. Why did you play this charade for all those weeks? What were you hoping to achieve?"

The phone rang. She paused, waiting for Rachel's answer, then had no choice but to pick it up. "Yes?"

"Mrs. Hartley-Wood is here."

"Give me five."

"I'll tell her. Five minutes."

Turning back to Rachel, she said, "We can't talk about this right now. A patient is waiting out there and she won't go away. I'm going to have to deal with her."

Rachel didn't seem to hear. She just stared out the window, looking suddenly deflated. Her face was pale, her cheeks sunken, the faint acne scars shone blue as if she'd been deprived of oxygen, dark circles under her eyes.

"I'm in deep shit, Madeleine," she said in a quiet monotone. "Unfortunately for you, I have no one else to turn to."

Madeleine was almost paralyzed by the shock of her discovery. It was too much to learn the truth finally, only to find that her child was in some kind of terrible trouble. She felt a sudden impulse to go and put her arms around this woman who was her daughter, but knew better than to act on it. The sheer unhappiness, the fear and the self-loathing that Rachel had manifested all those weeks in therapy, now had another meaning altogether.

"Listen. Whatever the trouble is, I'm very glad you came to me for help. But I don't want to be quits. That's not what I've spent the last twenty-two years hoping for."

"Oh, you'll *want* to be quits when you find out what I've done, believe me," Rachel said vacantly.

"We'll see about that. Where can we

talk? Not in this room, not after what we've done here."

"Can you come to my house?" Rachel raised her eyes and looked at her. "It's very urgent. I mean it. It can't wait."

Madeleine stood up and took Rachel resolutely by the arm, leading her to the door. "Go home, Rachel," she said with as much authority and calm as she could muster. "I'll try and cancel my appointments and come to you as soon as I can."

"Tell no one about this, or about me. Promise."

"I won't." Just as she was closing the door, Rachel suddenly put her hand out to stop her.

"*Sasha's passport!*" she cried. "Have you got it here? If all else fails, I might need it."

"Yes, it's here. I'll bring it. We'll talk later. Just go."

She took the car though she would rather have walked. If only she had a little time to compose her thoughts. The adrenaline surged through her bloodstream, allowing her to sprint to her car on Pierrepont Street without the slightest exertion. She could easily have sprinted all the way up to Fairfield. Her reactions were sharp as she drove purposefully through the traffic to Rachel's house. Though she remained outwardly cool, she was frightened of what she would find, and her feelings were in a flurry of confusion. Coming to terms with Rachel's true identity was hard enough. Now she sensed danger. Anton either had stepped up his plans to abscond with the boy or was threatening them in some other way. There was much to fear from a man like him: cruelty, beatings, rape, and robbery. Then there was Anton's evil brother, who Rachel so hated. Perhaps there was more, horrors that Rachel had kept from her, things from the past, threats, crimes she'd witnessed, or committed . . . Perhaps she was back on drugs . . . *No!* Madeleine bit her lip, trying to push away her thoughts. There was no point in speculating.

Part of her felt angry. Why had Rachel played that idiotic cat-and-mouse game? Madeleine understood the human psyche well enough to know there could have been any number of reasons why Rachel would want to observe the person her mother was, without having to compromise herself. And then there was the anger . . . all that anger which needed an objective, a focus. Yet had she not known the truth ever since she saw Rachel's birth date written starkly on her medical card? In her heart she had been convinced Rachel was her daughter, despite evidence to the contrary—Neville's certainty, John's cool perspective, Rachel's own feigned denials about being adopted.

She turned on the radio. Some infantile weather girl chirped about a severe storm, with flood warnings. Madeleine shuddered. She hated storms, she hated floods. The river Avon sometimes rose menacingly in Bath. The city was shaped to welcome floods, though they were rare. Madeleine turned off the radio, parked her car near Rachel's house, and got out. An elderly man in the house next door stood in the window and observed her approach. Had she not seen him standing there when she came the other day? Poor old boy, probably a widower with nothing better to do than to watch the comings and goings in the street while he ticked off the days.

She rang the doorbell. Looking up, she saw the skies were heavy with dark clouds. She shivered with apprehension; a hot, humid wind tugged at her blouse.

Rachel opened the door. Without any kind of greeting she scanned the street in both directions before pulling Madeleine into the entrance by her sleeve. She had changed into a pair of shorts and Madeleine glanced at her long legs and bare feet. How familiar they looked, how similar to her own.

"We haven't got much time," Rachel said and motioned Madeleine up the stairs into a sparsely furnished lounge. Tufts of fluffy scarlet wallpaper stuck to bare plaster walls, blackened by dampness and age. With a furtive study of her daughter's bleak living environment, Madeleine allowed herself to be planted on a dated brown leatherette sofa, sporting both rips and cigarette burns. A big picture window in front of her gave a sweeping view over Bath and the green hills beyond, but apart from that the room was grim. It had an ugly fireplace made of green tiles, and the curtains were a dingy faded floral pattern.

Rachel plonked herself down on a beanbag and immediately lit a cigarette, dragging deeply with an air of desperation. "I've got rid of Sasha so we can talk, but he'll be back soon."

Madeleine paused, looking around. "Where is he?"

Rachel almost jumped out of her skin at the question. "In . . . the garage."

"What is he doing?"

"Who?" Rachel frowned. "Did you mean Sasha?"

"Yes, Sasha."

Rachel laughed a loud, almost aggressive laugh. The fractious sound triggered something in Madeleine and she felt tears spring to her eyes. "Look, Rachel, perhaps it's not the time to talk about us, but I know you're angry with me . . . You've had a whole lifetime of not knowing—"

Rachel cut her off with an exasperated, "*Oh, fuck that.* Don't start. Not now."

"We'll leave that for now. So just tell me what is going on."

Rachel was silent for a moment. "I'm sorry, Madeleine," she said in a voice betraying fear rather than anger. "I can be a real bitch, I know it. I'm freaked out, that's all."

"Well, *talk* to me."

Rachel looked at her, eyes filled with sudden anguish. "First, I want you to swear an oath. I want you to swear on someone's life, someone you love. When you find out what's happened here, you might not want to help me, and I'd understand, but either way you have to swear you'll not go to the police or tell anyone about this. The safety and security of your grandson depends on it."

Madeleine was taken aback, both by the somber declaration and by the vehemence of the request. "All right, Rachel, I swear on my mother's life," she said.

"Anton is in my garage—dead," Rachel said, her face expressionless. "I've killed him."

Madeleine gasped. It was an instinctual reaction, and for a moment she was incapable of speech. "Oh God, no."

"I did it on an impulse, but really, deep down I knew what I was doing. I had no choice. Anton and Uri had run out of patience. I thought getting my hands on the passport would stop them taking Sasha, but silly me, it was only a matter of time. Anton tried to lure me along, saying he wanted me, but I knew what was in store for me. I saw it in his eyes. I'm sure they planned to kill me."

"Oh, Rachel . . ."

Rachel shrugged impatiently. "Can we shortcut all that? I've already been through it. I've torn my hair out, and cried and vomited and shat and all the rest. I expect I'll go down for murder, and Sasha will end up in some ghastly foster home, but I'm hanging on to a shred of hope that there is some way out of this. So, please, Madeleine," she begged, "use that cool head of yours."

Madeleine closed her eyes for a moment and breathed deeply. Shock, like icy water, enveloped her. Despite the heat, her skin had risen into goose bumps and she shivered. She'd always thought there'd be some joy in finding her daughter, but what she'd just heard was nothing short of a nightmare. It was not Sasha kidnapped, or Rachel raped and beaten, or blackmail or vile threats. It was *murder.*

Or was it?

"What were the circumstances, Rachel? Tell me how it happened."

"He came for us. If I'd let him take Sasha, I might have been spared, but I couldn't do that. So I attacked him," she said matter-of-factly. "He turned his back to me for a second and I smashed his head to a pulp with a glass ashtray. There is almost nothing left of his face."

Oh God. It wasn't even self-defense. Madeleine hid her face in her hands for a moment, trying to overcome the shock of it all. Rachel brought her back.

"I've thought about turning myself in, but I can't, because of what it would mean for Sasha. Perhaps if I'd done it immediately, but I was in some state of shock. Now it's too late."

"When did this happen?"

"Last night."

"Rachel, come on," Madeleine exclaimed. "You can still phone the police."

"*What did I tell you?*" She snarled. "Don't go there. Do not even mention the fuzz."

"All right, all right. Forget that for the moment."

Rachel jumped up. Madeleine watched her pacing back and forth, her long fingers clamped around her forehead. "We've got to get rid of the body. If we did that, if we got rid of it, and if Anton has not given his brother my address, I might possibly get away with it." She stopped and faced her. "Do you hear me, Madeleine? You've got a car, haven't you? We've got to take the body somewhere and dump it. His brother will know something has happened, but he may not think it had anything to do with me. And as they're not officially in this country, he is not likely to report Anton missing."

"Rachel, where *is* Sasha?"

"Why?" Rachel frowned and looked straight at her. "With Charlene. They've gone to see a film."

"Who's Charlene?"

"Just this homeless kid who helps me out now and then."

"What about them? Have they seen anything?"

Rachel put her hands over her face and groaned. "I don't think so. I don't know. I've got to try and think of some way to get rid of them for a few hours."

Madeleine stared out the window while trying to listen to Rachel's garbled strategies. The reality of a murder was growing on her. The sky darkened, and in the distance there was a rumble of thunder. The clouds were so low, they enclosed the city like a dome, heating the moistened air and adding to the feeling of oppression.

She stopped Rachel's rambling monologue and suggested she would go home and change out of her work clothes and come back after dark, late in the evening. Meanwhile Rachel would have to devise some plan to get Sasha out of the way.

Rachel looked ghostly in the darkening afternoon, her skin almost translucent, her catlike eyes glistening in the twilight. Madeleine wanted to hold the frightened woman and tell her everything would be all right, but she knew that nothing would ever be all right again.

Chapter Nineteen

Huge drops of rain burst on her windscreen as she drove toward the city center. It was as if someone up there were hurling balloons full of water over Bath. The splashes jolted her and she slowed down and parked by the roadside. Since the hurricane she had never lost her fear and hatred of storms. She reminded herself that Rachel had been born to Changó, the Orisha of thunder and lighting. Perhaps Changó was coming to Rachel now, in her hour of need.

She sat there for a moment, looking over the rooftops and at the clouds pressing ever lower over the city. Reaching for he bag, she fished out her mobile phone. She scrolled down her directory until she hit on *HMPR,* and pressed the dial button.

The rain held off as she drove—faster than she should have—up the A46 toward Rookwood. It was madness, but she could not think what else to do. She leaned her head back against the headrest and drove on automatic pilot, trying to ignore the images, yet willing her subconscious to present a solution to this horror.

A man had been killed, and her daughter had killed him. *Murdered* him. Wasn't life sacred? Of course it was . . . but much as her instincts told her to involve the police, she could not take it upon herself to do so. However the death had happened, she knew she could never go back on her oath. She'd forsaken Rachel twice in her life already, she would not break her trust or turn her back on her again.

Instead, she considered the obvious second option: talking *Rachel* into calling the police. She would have to try and convince her it was the only logical step. Madeleine could testify it was a clear case of diminished responsibility. She had her patient's notes to back this up. Rachel had been under the worst form of duress, coupled with physical violence and the imminent threat of her child being kidnapped by a ruthless thug. What mother would not react instinctively to protect her child against such a threat? A desperate act, committed under unbearable pressure: Rachel was terrified of the man, and Madeleine had seen firsthand what he was capable of doing to her.

She tried to imagine convincing Rachel to call the police. She would throw a fit. God knows, she might use the ashtray on her too. She would have to play it by ear when she went back to her house and spoke to her again.

As she flipped the possibilities around in her mind, her imagination took another turn: taking the blame for the killing herself. It would not be hard for her to feign. What mother would not want to do away with a monster who had so abused and tormented her daughter? She herself could have been his killer, his executioner, and could pay the price; what better way to atone for abandoning her child? A sacrifice of that magnitude had an appealing aspect to it, but when she tried to imagine how to go about it, she knew it was ridiculous. Forensic science was so advanced these days, as was the understanding of the psychological aspects of crime, the truth would emerge anyway. If only Rachel had come to her last night, right after the deed. Then there would have been a better chance of convincing her to phone the police. Self-defense would surely have been a plausible reason. But now she'd have to try to persuade her.

But Rachel was right about Sasha. What would the little boy be put through? What would they tell him about his mother . . . about his father? Where would he end up until such time that Rachel was free (if she was set free)? Sasha fostered, oh God . . . this was history repeating itself. Then it occurred to her that if Rachel was found guilty of murder, Madeleine, as Sasha's grandmother and his closest relative, might well be the child's natural guardian. It was a startling thought, but Rachel would never accept it. However, the other natural guardian was

Sasha's evil uncle, this Uri Rachel talked about with such unbridled hatred.

Then, there was the final option: to get rid of the body and hope for the best. It seemed unimaginable, disposing of a human body.

All life is sacred, she whispered, testing the truth of it. She believed it deeply, she had never even stepped on an insect, not knowingly, but the life of a ruthless criminal, a trader in sex slaves, a rapist, and quite possibly a murderer himself—how sacred was his life? He had lived by violence and died by it. Now his body was in a garage, rotting in the heat of a thunderstorm. At this stage it was just a matter of disposal. Wasn't it?

Why else was she driving toward H.M. Prison Rookwood?

She walked down a corridor with an officer she'd never met. He glanced at her sideways several times, seemingly taking all of her in.

"Do you want to ask me something?" she inquired angrily.

He shook his head and stepped back from her a little, letting her walk ahead. Thei footsteps echoed, bouncing against the walls of the corridor.

After a moment the man said from behind her, "Miss? Yeah, in fact I would like to ask you something." He quickened his steps to catch up.

"Go ahead," she snapped. "Just be damned sure it's relevant to what we're doing here."

"It is actually," he said brightly. "Are you one of those women who hopes to find true love with a prisoner? You see, my girlfriend is doing a psychology degree and she's fascinated . . . I mean, you're American, right? She was telling me about these women who want to get to know guys on Death Row over there and—"

Madeleine stopped dead and turned to him. "Do tell me you're not serious."

He shrugged disarmingly. "Well, nah, you're too good-looking to need to . . . I guess I was just wondering why a woman wants to spend her time with a strangler. Whether there was some particular fascination with his crimes, or—"

"Listen, between you and me . . ." Madeleine marched on, making the young man almost run to keep up. "It's not the strangling that turns me on, but the other bit, you know, the bleeding. Does that satisfy? Now open the door and stay away from me, or I'll report you for harassment."

He unlocked the large metal door that led to the spur where the perpetrators of monstrous crimes were kept. Most of the prisoners were in their cells but Madeleine was relieved to see that the catcaller had his hatch closed.

"I've got to stay by this door, miss. Orders from the governor. Sorry," the prison officer said haughtily.

"Then stay on the other side of it. I don't want to see your face." She gave him an icy smile. "All right, sunshine?"

Madeleine walked down the length of the spur. Stopping at Edmund's door, she took a deep breath. She'd got hold of Rob Reese for permission to visit Edmund out of her normal time slot, citing as an excuse an impulsively conceived two-week holiday, so hopefully he'd been told she was coming. He'd have hated not being primed for her arrival with his ritual preparations, but when she knocked lightly on the hatch, she realized he'd been standing there, waiting. His responding knock was instant and she opened the little hatch, only to be met by a glacial stare.

"To what do I owe this untimely visit?" he sneered. "It appeared you were too busy to get yourself here last week. Who is he?"

"Would I dare?" she answered, rolling her eyes. "I did leave you a message, my friend. If you must know, I had a hell of a time on Friday. My mother collapsed into a catatonic state and they threatened to fry her brain with electric shock treatment. Edmund, I'm sure you know what that's like. Didn't you say you'd had it once yourself?"

He seemed to soften a little. "I've been terribly restless without you. If ever I were to string someone up for pure pleasure, the last few days would have been it." He paused, looking intently at her, then his gray eyes lit up. "The brooch, Madeleine. You found it." He smiled broadly, revealing his two rows of teeth.

"Yes, I found it." *And you look so much better,* she noted.

"It means you belong to me, after all."

"I belong to no one, Edmund, and sadly this might be the last time I see you."

Edmund's smile died and his face stiffened into a cold mask, but looking at her, he clearly began to grasp the serious nature of her visit. She moved closer to the hatch; she didn't want anyone to hear what she had to say. She'd been told that prison visiting was confidential and there were never any bugs, but the glassy eye of a closed-circuit camera monitored everything that happened in the corridor. She half turned her back to it.

"Do you recall a few months ago, you said that I could tell you anything? That we were friends forever and you would never let me down?"

"Of course I recall it. I've got a photographic memory." He tapped his forehead. "It was your birthday. Fourteenth of March."

"Edmund, listen. I'm taking a huge leap of faith here. I need your help. Only you can tell me what to do. You must swear first that you meant what you said."

"I never, *ever* go back on my word," he said icily.

"Would that hold if I could not come back and see you again?"

They looked fiercely at each other. The grief he felt about losing her was gradually etching itself on his face. After a long while he nodded. "You heard me."

Her hour was almost up. The young screw poked his head around the door at regular intervals. Madeleine was as close to Edmund as she'd ever been, their heads almost touching in the hatch.

"Are you sure he can't be identified?" Madeleine asked.

"Madeleine, my beauty, if he's an illegal alien and has nothing on him, it'll certainly be difficult to trace who he is. If his identity was discovered, which I very much doubt it will be, it'll look like a gangland killing." Edmund paused. "As I said, I can easily have him disposed of, but it would take a day or two to arrange."

"No, forget that. My daughter would not be able to stand the wait . . . and there is the heat."

"Just remember the first rule. *Location, location, location.* You sure you've got somewhere good?"

Madeleine nodded. "Yes, trust me, that I do have."

"With or without the car?"

"Yes."

"Repeat to me what you need."

"A torch, a knife, newspapers, lighter and backup matches, plastic gloves, a plastic container or glass jar, rubbish bags, two cans of petrol."

"Aren't you forgetting something?"

She shuddered. "Yes . . . the pruning shears." Suddenly tears sprang to her eyes and she shook her head. "Edmund, not that! Please. It's too much. I can't go through with it."

Her tears upset him. He reached forward as if touch her face. "OK, OK, my beauty. Don't start crying on me. Forget it. It was just an added precaution. That's all. You don't have to do it."

"Time's up," shouted the screw from down the spur. They looked at each other.

"Just be calm," Edmund said. He smiled sadly. "Treat it like a job."

"All right."

"I'll be thinking of you, my love."

"Thank you for this. Keep well, buddy. I won't forget you . . . ever."

She stuck her hand through the hatch. Edmund took it in his and brought it to his lips. She didn't pull away or care if the screw saw them.

The assassin's kiss was the least of her worries.

As she drove back to Bath the rain started in earnest. A strong wind lashed water across the windscreen. There was hardly any traffic. Anyone with any sense would not be driving on a night like this.

She stopped off at her house and changed out of her skirt and blouse and put on a pair of well-worn jeans, a T-shirt, and trainers. She stuffed a flashlight and a waterproof jacket into a carrier bag, in another she threw two boxes of matches, her Marigold gloves, a cheap lighter, and all the newspapers she could find.

For a long moment she stood in the hall, hesitating. She knew she had to leave; time was of the essence. She could bring the damned things, even if she had no intention of using them. Dashing out to her garden shed, she extracted the pruning shears, stopping only for a moment to look at them in her hand. They were new, acquired to tackle the fibrous fronds of the Washingtonia she had in the garden. If, on that sunny March Sunday in the garden center when she'd tried them out on a twig, she'd seen herself using them for the first time . . .

Shielding herself with an umbrella, she hurried back to her car. The streets were empty and the raindrops burst in a myriad of small explosions on the shimmering tarmac. She took a detour and stopped at a petrol station, filling the Merc to the brim . . . and the two petrol cans in her boot.

Setting off for Rachel's house, she thought about Forrest. *Forrest!* Where was he? What sphere did he occupy, what dimension? What would he think of this journey to hell?

Chapter Twenty

Charlene and Sasha were playing tiddly-winks. Rachel could hear them giggling and chattering as she came through the front door.

"Hey, kids," she said when she came up into the living room. "Who's winning then?"

Trying to look normal, she threw herself down on the sofa. Had they looked closely at her they would surely have noticed her frightened eyes and her incessant puffing on her cigarette, but they were absorbed in their game and barely noticed her return. Sasha was obviously winning. He was popping in the chips as if he'd been doing it in the womb, his face flushed with both excitement and heat.

She prayed that Charlene would agree to the plan. She probably would. In fact, the girl was trying so hard, being useful and making herself indispensable as a babysitter, and it was increasingly difficult to get rid of her. She'd been sleeping rough for some time and obviously relished the comforts of a home. Rachel felt sorry, knowing she must dismiss her but the less people knew about her life, the better.

"Charlene," Rachel said, "I need to talk to you in the kitchen."

Charlene looked puzzled but she got up and followed her.

"Sasha, you put the TV on," Rachel called. "I'll bring you some juice and biscuits in a minute, sweetie."

"Mum! We're in the middle of a game," he protested, but he pressed the remote and the noise of the television came on.

In the kitchen, she made Charlene sit down at the table. "Listen, you're old enough to understand," she said. "There's this man I've met. He's coming here this evening. I want him to stay the night . . . you know what I mean?"

Charlene cocked her head and smirked. "Yeah, I get it."

"I want you to do me a *gi-normous* favor. I don't feel good about Sasha being here. Not the first time. Just in case he wakes up and finds us in a, you know . . . compromising position. And anyway, I'd rather this guy didn't know I had a kid, like, right away. It might scare him off."

Charlene's teasing smirk faded. "Really? What's wrong with having a kid? You can't hide that fact . . . Well, that's *your* business."

She was right of course, but Rachel had to ignore the scornful look. "There's this little B and B on Faringdon Road. Just down from the park. I popped in there just now. Would you mind? Just for one night? You kids will probably love it . . . watching TV in bed, full English breakfast, and all that."

Charlene's smirk returned. "Yeah I guess . . . It's your money."

"You mind if we all walk down there now? He could be here anytime."

Charlene got up and adjusted the cap on her head. Rachel had given her an old baseball cap to replace the ridiculous bobble hat, and though her hair was beginning to grow back, she never removed it.

"Yeah, Ok," she said, but when she got to the door, she turned, still with that cheeky grin on her face. "I can say this now that I know I'm safe. For some reason I thought you were into girls." She made a sign of the cross with her two forefingers and held it up in mock defense.

"Oh fuck off, Charlene."

Low, dark clouds had gathered. On the news they had said heavy rains were on the way, and how great that was, considering the water shortage. Rachel couldn't decide whether it was bad or good. It would be darker, and there would be fewer people on the streets.

It was half past nine and it had already begun to rain very heavily when Madeleine came to the door. She looked different. Pale beneath her golden tan, her eyes blacker, larger, more deep-set, her nose sharp, her lips white. The rain had made her hair corkscrew around her cheekbones, and her jeans and T-shirt were already wet. In her bedraggled state, stripped of her business-like façade, she looked younger, almost beautiful. There was something raw yet innocent about her.

Rachel opened the door and peered into the street. There seemed to be no one about. "Where's your car?"

"Down the road."

"Is it big enough?"

"We need to talk."

"Oh, no." Rachel shook her head and her fists curled at her sides. "You can forget it."

"Let me in, Rachel."

Rachel took a deep breath. It wouldn't do to be ranting and raving and losing one's cool. She led the way upstairs and into the living room.

"Look," she said, turning abruptly at the top of the stairs, "if you were about to mention the police, you can go right back where you came from."

"Cool it," Madeleine said firmly. "I've got a plan."

"No shit?" she muttered skeptically. "I'm going to get us a tot of whiskey. We're going to need it before we . . . survey the lay of the land. Besides, I think we should wait a couple of hours, until after midnight. The old fart next door is always looking out the window. And you . . . you look as if you couldn't even remove a dead mouse from anywhere."

Madeleine didn't answer and seemed too restless to sit down. She went up to the mantelpiece and looked at the photo of Sasha, taken on his second birthday.

"Oh, for fuck's sake," Rachel barked. "Sit down."

"I know what Sasha looks like," Madeleine said curtly. "I've seen him."

"What! You've been spying on us?"

"I saw him in the park when I left here the other day." Madeleine turned to her and looked her straight in the eye. "No matter what you say, however much anger and resentment you carry, you cannot deny me my feelings. I've made some dreadful mistakes where you're concerned, but I'm never going to apologize for my feelings. You're a mother yourself, you should understand that."

Rachel stared angrily at her for a moment, then turned on her heel and went out to the kitchen for her Camels and the whiskey bottle. A part of her reluctantly understood the sentiment. To any normal person, a grandchild was precious, but this woman was far from normal. Her own child, she'd been happy to dump.

She shrugged off these thoughts. This was not the time or the place. They'd have to concentrate on a plan and stick to that subject, because if they just sat there waiting for the clock to move, God only knew what turns the conversation would take. They couldn't afford to have any kind of showdown. Not when there was a body to dispose of.

When she returned to the living room Madeleine was sitting immobile on the sofa, her eyes focused on the window and the lights of the city behind a curtain of rain. Rachel poured her a drink, then sat down on the beanbag and lit a cigarette. "The main thing we need to decide is where to dump him," she said. "As far away from Bath as possible."

"I know where." Madeleine's eyes turned on her face.

"You do?"

"Has he got anything on him, identification or anything?"

"Of course not. I've gone through his pockets. I took the whole lot and burnt it. Everything with blood on it went in there."

She flicked her thumb in the direction of the fireplace. It was clean, she'd scraped it out thoroughly and bleached it too. "His mobile phone I tossed in the river on my way to your clinic, and the . . . murder weapon."

For a while they sipped the whiskey in concentrated silence, avoiding each other's eye.

Madeleine broke the silence. "How many people know of your relationship with Anton?"

"Nobody here, except perhaps for the old codger next door, who saw him go in and steal Sasha's dog."

"What about in London?"

Rachel thought about this for a moment. She and Anton had not been in a proper relationship for a couple of years. In her last year there she'd been embarrassed about the convoluted relationship they had. She could not remember confiding in anyone, and his comings and goings had not been all that frequent.

"No one really. But there *is* Sasha." Rachel felt a sudden contraction of her gut. And *there is Uri.* If they found Anton's body, the police might not give a shit about some dodgy foreign guy without papers, but Uri would. He would soon know something had happened. He would certainly give a shit. In fact, he would never let it go. Uri was like a rottweiler with a bone, and his loyalty to Anton would make him root out the truth. He'd come looking for *her* in the first instance. Already he was on the alert; he knew about the passport and her part in its theft. He'd come with a couple of his brutes and make her talk, sure he would. He would make Sasha talk. And without a doubt he'd take Sasha. He'd told her once that his brother's children were his children. Since she'd given birth to Sasha, that comment had often come back to haunt her. Now it flooded her with panic. It was all she could do not to scream. There was no way out for her, she knew that now. Whichever way she turned, she and Sasha would be torn apart.

"What are you thinking about?" Madeleine asked gently.

"Nothing."

"Where is Sasha?"

"In a B and B with Charlene."

"What did you tell them?"

Rachel looked at her coldly. "What difference does it make? I told Charlene I needed privacy to shag some bloke. I didn't bother telling her I'd killed a man and my mother and I were just off to dump him in a ditch."

"Why don't you drop the sarcasm, Rachel?" Madeleine said with a frown. "I could really do without it."

Madeleine was right. She was being a right arsehole, and Madeleine was trying to help her, after all. "You can see why you don't want me for a daughter," she said grimly.

"What about a passport? Did he have one on him?"

"Yeah. He had a Swiss passport with a fake name. That's burnt too. But for all I know, there might be other passports. Somewhere he'll have a Russian or Ukrainian one, I'm sure of it."

Madeleine took a dainty sip from her glass and said, "Problem is, there is always DNA and dental records."

Rachel flared. "Well, what the fuck do you want me to do about it? There is nothing left of his teeth, I can assure you."

Madeleine visibly recoiled. Rachel found it gave her a perverse satisfaction. So the woman wanted to find her daughter? *Ha!*

The cute little toddler she merrily gave away turns out to be a scar-faced prostitute-turned-murderer, a loose cannon, unpredictable, dangerous, capable of just about anything if provoked.

"Let's go and look at him," she said brusquely. "I want you to see him. We need to think about how to get him into the boot of your car."

Madeleine took a big gulp of whiskey, draining her glass. It almost made Rachel laugh, and something in her softened against her will.

They made their way downstairs.

"Look, I've not been down there since last night, so I have no idea what we'll find," she said, cursing herself for the obvious tremor that had crept into her voice. "It's quite warm. The hot-water tank is there, you see."

"But it's only been a day . . ." Madeleine grabbed her arm and looked her searchingly in the face. "It did happen last night, right, Rachel? It didn't happen earlier, like the day before, or the day before that?"

Rachel stared at her. How had she guessed? "Perhaps. Perhaps it was the day before." She turned away abruptly. "What do you expect? I spent a whole night cleaning the place up. I wasn't in any state to make decisions yesterday."

Madeleine uttered a quiet curse, and Rachel hurriedly described how she'd dragged Anton's body across the floor and down the staircase. She struggled a moment with the lock to the garage door. She got it open and they went down the three steps and she pushed it shut behind them. It was dark but for the strip of evening light seeping in through a space at the top of the roll-up door. She'd used Richie's and Rosie's Right-On duct tape to secure sheets of cardboard over the side window. Flicking the switch flooded the cluttered space with light from a glaring fluorescent tube.

They stood still a moment, getting used to the light. There was an imperceptible smell, probably just damp and dirt; she'd done a good job of the taping, using almost the whole roll. She went forward and lifted Sasha's old mattress where it leaned against the wall. There it was—the large, sluglike shape. A couple of blowflies buzzed around it.

"Come here," she commanded, and Madeleine moved forward. For a second there was complete silence but for the leak that still dripped. She hoped the water was the cause of the wet patch under the body.

"Oh, God," Madeleine gasped, and backed off.

"We can back the car in," Rachel said quietly, her voice shaking. "Then haul it into the boot. It's not going to be easy."

"That will never fit into the boot of my car. It's too . . . long."

In three steps Rachel was up against her, grabbing her T-shirt at the neck and growling in her face. "Then it's going to have to fucking bend, Madeleine. Unless you want to cut him up into little pieces and take him away in bags. We can do that if you prefer. My dad left me a sharp saw . . . I don't care. I'm up for it."

In a flash Madeleine had struck her across the face. It didn't really hurt, but Rachel was stunned by the gesture and felt her cheek turn red.

"You listen here," Madeleine said evenly, "do you think I need this? I can change my mind anytime. If you prefer, I'll leave now and you can deal with this on your own."

For a long moment they looked at each other. Rachel dropped her grip on the T-shirt. "I'm sorry," she said. "I didn't mean to lose my cool like that. I'm a nervous wreck."

Madeleine put her hand lightly to the reddening cheek. "I'm not surprised. This is too much for anyone. Are you sure . . ."

"Yes, I'm sure," Rachel said, her voice firm.

"Let's go back upstairs. We can't talk here," Madeleine said. "Anyway, it's still too early."

The thunderstorm was intensifying. Every few minutes the distant rumble jolted them. They went back and sat in the living room, looking out the window. The black clouds were intermittently lit up by lightning. The air felt so thick it was hardly breathable. It made it impossible to think. Rachel was about to pour them another whiskey, but Madeleine stopped her. "No more. We've got to drive, remember. We don't want to be stopped and Breathalyzed, do we?"

"We? You mean *you,* don't you?"

"How did Anton come to your house?"

"By car."

"And where is his car?"

Anton's car! How had she not even thought of it? "Hey," she exclaimed. "It must be parked somewhere around here. It's absolutely massive."

Madeleine leaned forward. "You've got the keys?"

"Yes. I've still got the keys. I was going to throw them away with the mobile, but I didn't. They're still in my bag." She could see that Madeleine had found a way around having a leaking corpse in her car. Rachel almost smiled.

"Who is it registered to?" Madeleine asked.

"French license plates. Nicked, I'm sure. I remember him coming back in it on the ferry from one of his 'business trips.' He had two girls with him. Nice crossing it would have been for him, the three of them in a cabin."

Madeleine was quiet for a moment, her eyebrows bunched in a frown. "Do you drive?" she asked.

"I don't have a license, if that's what you mean. My dad used to take me driving but I've not driven for years." She fixed her eyes on Madeleine. "You're so much better at it. You don't want me behind the wheel."

"Let's go for a walk." Madeleine stood up. "Let's look for it."

It was well past midnight before Tom's television lights went off, then fifteen minutes later his bedroom light went out too.

Madeleine was watching from the window. "It's time. Let's get this over with."

She went down the street to get Anton's car while Rachel prepared the garage. When she heard the car in the drive she tackled the roll-up door. It slid open surprisingly easily and Madeleine backed the car halfway in. They listened for sounds of cars or people, but the rain poured relentlessly and it seemed the neighborhood had shut down for the night.

They kept the light off but could hardly see in the darkness, and approached the body hesitantly, dreading having to touch it. Gripping the plastic, they tried to drag it toward the car, but the sweat on their hands made it nearly impossible to get a good enough grip. It kept slipping from their hands, the duct tape ripping open and the body almost rolling out. A swollen, bluish hand flopped onto the floor and they both looked at it, horror-struck. It was all too human, too lifelike, as though still able to reach out, grasp them, and pull them into some hell beyond.

Madeleine suddenly straightened up and touched her shoulder. "His fingers," she said quietly. "Do you think . . . ?"

"What?"

"The fingers . . . gone. It would look so much better."

Rachel felt the goose bumps tighten on her arms. "What do you mean, *gone*?"

"I've got some pruning shears in my car."

"*Oh shit,* Madeleine. *No!* That's monstrous."

"It would give it that underworld touch, don't you think?" Madeleine stood stock-still, peering at her in the dark. "Besides, a woman, *the mother of his son,* wouldn't have the resources, physical or emotional, to sadistically torture a man by mutilating him, or, for that matter, to cut off his fingers after smashing his head to a pulp."

"You'd be surprised," Rachel murmured. She mopped her forehead with the back of her hand. "I appreciate the thought, though it's pretty sick. I didn't think you had something like that in you." She studied Madeleine for a long moment. "I'm sure it would be convincing, at least where the fuzz is concerned."

"And Uri? Might it not convince *him* it was a gangland killing? We could mail the fingers to him."

Revolting idea though it was, Rachel could see she had a point, were it not for . . .

"No, Madeleine. If Uri finds out Anton is dead, he'll come for Sasha. I know how he thinks. He will never leave me to bring up his brother's son. Don't you see? My only hope is that he believes Anton has taken off somewhere, and is coming back." Her voice broke in a sob. "This nightmare has barely begun."

Madeleine nodded and in silence they returned to the job at hand.

The corpse was bloated and soft, and there was already a stench coming from it. Flies buzzed around them as they worked, sweat dripping into their eyes. They'd only managed to drag it a couple of meters, the horror of the job unspoken between them, when finally Madeleine fell to her knees and with a low gasp wrapped her arms right around Anton's chest.

"Grab the other end," she snarled.

Despite her revulsion, Rachel obeyed, warily grabbing hold of the legs and half lifting the body off the ground. This way, bit by bit, they hauled it to the car. Madeleine had been right. It was not easy to bend.

The heavens opened. Rachel grasped the steering wheel hard and peered through the rain into the distance. She was so tired she could cry; she was not used to driving, and trying to follow Madeleine's car in front of her took all her concentration. Taking both cars was mad, it was more than mad. Several times she'd wondered what Madeleine was up to. She'd let Madeleine take charge of the operation without giving her a clear idea of what she'd had in mind. If Rachel lost sight of her, she'd be left here with the body in the boot, driving around in the fucking boonies, in the dark, in the howling wind, and the rain, with not a clue where she was, what she was doing, or where she was going. She was already in a state of severe anxiety, in part through nicotine withdrawal—in the haste and apprehension of setting off, she'd forgotten to bring her fags—in part through feeling constantly on the verge of being sick as her thoughts went obsessively back to the loading of Anton's body. For some reason it had been more gruesome than the murder itself, the smell, the blowflies, the soft feel of her lover's rotting flesh. It would be a deed difficult to forget, the sort that would wake her in the night, gagging, probably until the day she died.

She had been following Madeleine for over two hours. First through Bristol and down the M5 for an hour, then turning off on some other road, God knew to where. He eyes were glued to the bumper of Madeleine's car and she'd missed all the signs It was getting more and more remote. There was not a light anywhere, and it had to be approaching three o'clock in the morning The rain was lashing at the windscreen with incredible force. Madeleine turned into another road, a country lane at best. After a while her car slowed down a little, then turned right onto yet another narrow lane

Why the fuck didn't the woman stop? Why not right here? They could drag the body into any one of these fields, there were plenty of farm gates; roll him under a hedge and make a run for it. But no, Madeleine just drove on and on. Had she lost the plot? She'd said she knew a place, but had refused to say where it was. Couldn't describe it, she'd claimed. Rachel had no choice but to follow in this mindless hunt for a dumping place. What had made her think Madeleine knew best?

The track went upward and got worse and worse, narrower and narrower. Water gushed down it in a flood, branches scraped the side of the car. She was about to stop and phone Madeleine on the mobile number she'd given her at the last minute, when Madeleine's car turned left by a big sign. Rachel peered at it through the rain, *Forestry Commission* something-or-other, *Private Road*. On they went, through a big wood, dark and gloomy. After a few miles the trees stopped abruptly and they came out into an open rocky landscape with not a tree or shrub on it. The track became overgrown and in places barely visible. Still it went upward. The rain had eased temporarily but a thick mist rolled in, making it difficult to see Madeleine's car. When it cleared a little she realized they were driving up onto bare moors. Bolts of distant lightning lit up the desolate landscape. After another couple of miles Madeleine's brake lights came on and her car rolled to a halt.

She hopped out and in the beam of the headlights Rachel saw her waving, signaling her to drive up into a flat space and turn off the engine. Rachel got out of the car. She saw they were at the end of the road. If you could call this a road.

"Where the hell are we?" she demanded, her voice cracking. "We've been driving for hours! Was it really necessary to come this far?"

Madeleine didn't answer. Her hair was getting drenched, but her stance was determined. For a brief moment Rachel felt something. There was something in the assurance, the calm authority, something indefinable. She didn't care to think the word "Mother," but it came into her head anyway. Someone who took care of things, someone who would do anything . . . and not let one down. It was sentimental nonsense, and angrily she shrugged it off.

"Stay here and don't move, no matter how long I take over this," Madeleine said. "Sit in my car."

"We're in this together," Rachel protested feebly.

Madeleine glanced at her. "Perhaps. But in a roundabout way I'm responsible for what's happened. Let me do this. There is no need for both of us."

She opened her boot and took out two large plastic containers and two plastic bags. She hauled them into the backseat of Anton's car, jumped in, and turned on the engine.

"What the hell are you doing?" Rachel shouted through the rain. She got no answer. Bewildered, she watched as Madeleine revved the engine and tore off. The big black car cleared a stream and hurtled across the moorland. It vanished from view, but she could hear its engine roar and then die down. Rachel was soaking wet and she got into the passenger seat of Madeleine's car, her eyes glued to the place where Madeleine had disappeared.

Minutes passed. What the hell was the

woman doing? She calmed herself and thought of the obvious. She was dumping the car with the body, whereas Rachel had imagined they would leave the car, minus corpse and license plates and so forth, at the back of some Safeway car park somewhere. She could not think if this was a good idea or a bad one. It was too late to argue it anyway. She had no choice but to trust. Madeleine must trust her too. She could easily get into the driver's seat and drive off. But they were in this together, and though she had every possible conflict about it, it was something that bound them. The minutes passed, ten, fifteen, twenty. The rain started up again with renewed force. What had happened? Where was she?

Rachel was starting to wonder about getting out of the car and walking over the moors in the direction of Madeleine's disappearance when suddenly there was an almighty roar and the sky was lit by a raging fire. The car was burning. *The plastic containers.* Of course. Petrol or some other inflammable liquid. A few minutes later Madeleine came running. Breathlessly she jumped into the car and threw the bags into the backseat.

"Thank God it's raining so heavily," she said. "We'd burn down half of Devon."

"*Christ*, Madeleine!" Rachel said with a suppressed chuckle.

Still the flames reached high into the sky.

They sat quite still watching the distant fire. It was lower now, almost hidden by some ravine, but the mist spread an orange glow to the land around it.

Rachel turned to the wet, disheveled woman beside her. "What exactly did you do?"

"I rolled the car down into a gully," Madeleine said. "I was hoping the fire wouldn't be so visible. Let's trust no one is sitting in a window somewhere miles away watching the rain and the lightning and phones the fire department."

"Where are we anyway? How do you know this place?"

"Dartmoor. My colleague has a cottage a few miles from away. We got lost up here not so long ago. This is in the middle of nowhere. I wouldn't be surprised if the car isn't spotted for weeks or months. Anyway, burnt-out cars are a common feature in today's landscape."

"But the body?" said Rachel grimly. "Not many of those in today's landscape."

The car exploded. Flames shot in every direction and the sound it made was fearful, but the rain and thunder muffled the noise.

"I opened the plastic and soaked him thoroughly, his hands, and especially what was left of his face," Madeleine said matter-of-factly, switching on the engine. "I doubt there'd be much of him left, so don't worry about him being identified. He's a gangster from a world in which gangsters murder each other regularly. He ripped someone off or muscled in on someone else's territory, and he got wasted. Right, Rachel? Simple as that."

"Uri might not believe it."

"We'll have to think what to do about Uri." She put the car into gear and switched on the headlights. "One down, one to go," she added, as if to herself.

Drained of thoughts and words, they drove back to Bath. Madeleine took a cross-country route, and they wound their way between the undulating fields of Somerset. How she knew the way through the tangle of country roads was a mystery to Rachel; besides, visibility was poor. Heavy showers came and went. Dawn showed a thin strip of crimson on the horizon, between the land and the black clouds.

Rachel glanced at Madeleine a few times, thinking she might be nodding off. She looked dead tired but her eyes were fixed on the wet road ahead, her expression blank, her hands clamped on the steering wheel. They'd better get talking about something, if only to keep her awake.

"Not that I have much enthusiasm for the subject," Rachel said into the silence, "but I assume you know who my father is."

Madeleine did not answer for a few moments. "My husband? His name was Forrest Serota," she said at last.

Rachel let out a surprised laugh. "You guys were married? I thought you were sixteen when you had me."

"We married later," she said, then added so quietly that Rachel barely heard her, "when it was already too late."

"Tell me something else."

"He was simply . . . a very decent human being. Funny. Sharp . . . but gentle."

"So if he was that great, why aren't the two of you together?"

"If you'd seen the letters I left for you, you'd know he was dead. He died when you'd just turned nineteen. He would have given anything to have known you, Rachel. He was driven by the need to find you." She turned and gave her a sharp look. "We did everything that was humanly possible to find you."

Her father was dead. Rachel was not quite sure how she felt about this. He had been *a man*, a father, someone who had been looking for her . . . not the pimple-infested adolescent she'd imagined having fumbling intercourse with an equally inadequate teenaged Madeleine.

Madeleine reached into a pocket in the door and handed over a laminated photograph. Rachel held it gingerly and looked at the man in the picture. He was good-looking, there was no doubt about it, and smiling as if he had not a care in the world so much for being driven by the loss of his daughter. His face was too open. It unset tled her. People with faces like that had to be hiding something.

She handed it back and they drove in silence for a while. A sign told them they had twelve miles to go when she felt Madeleine's eyes on her.

"Why did you do it this way, Rachel?"

"You mean with the ashtray?"

Madeleine turned her attention back to the road ahead, a small smile on her lips.

"No. I meant, why did you come to me for therapy? If you wanted to get to know me, you could have. Surely you knew about the Adoption Contact Agency. You rejected the idea of knowing me."

"Rejected?" Rachel said sharply. "You're a fine one to use that word." She paused for a moment, knowing she owed Madeleine some kind of explanation.

"I suppose I just wanted to check you out without having to go through all the stomach-turning melodrama of a mother-daughter reunion. The problem was, you're too good a therapist. You kind of got under my skin for a while. I thought as I was paying half a fortune for the farce anyway, I might as well see if you could help me get cured of Anton."

"I think it was quite a perverse thing to do to me."

Rachel let rip a shrill laugh. "There you go. Yep! I'm good at *perverse*." She turned and looked coldly at the woman who was her mother. "Perhaps I had in mind some perverse kind of revenge. I do remember, you see. I remember everything."

"So tell me," said Madeleine, slowing the car to a stop in a lay-by and turning off the ignition. "Tell me what you remember."

"I remember being *shit scared*, that's what I remember," she snarled. "You left me with an insane old witch. Your mother, I suppose."

"Yes, my mother. She was young actually, younger than I am now, but I completely understand what a frightening and bewildering experience it must have been for you, watching her go mad. For what it's worth, I had no idea she'd got ill. She loved you so much, and you loved her." Madeleine reached out and touched her on the arm. "Did she hurt you?"

Rachel yanked her arm away. "Hurt me? You must be kidding? Look at how my life has turned out." She stared out into the rain. Then her thoughts went to Sasha. He too had been hurt by the madness of his parents. Who was she to cast stones?

"And how did you get so well informed about me and my motivations, Rachel?"

"My parents. They knew all about you."

Madeleine frowned. "No, they certainly did not." She was quiet for a moment and Rachel hoped she would leave the matter alone; she didn't want to talk about it. Sure, what she'd done was perverse. Nevertheless, after finding Madeleine Frank in the telephone directory and learning that she was a psychotherapist, it had been all too easy to fall for the temptation. She'd watched Madeleine leave the clinic a few times, followed her to her house. Next, she'd walked into the clinic on a whim and made an appointment. She hadn't meant to keep it, but she did.

"I don't believe you wanted revenge," Madeleine said into the silence. "I think you wanted to have a mother. I think you need me."

"Bullshit!"

"I think you did it this way because you're a coward. You didn't have the guts for a proper confrontation. You came and told me all about your scandalous past to test

me, to see if I could ever accept you as th
person you are. And you found that I di
accept you. I liked you and cared about yo
and respected you, despite your constar
attempts to shock me and piss me off. Ther
you backed out of therapy when you knev
we were getting close to the truth." She
turned and looked at Rachel. "I would have
welcomed your anger, your *honest* anger
I know I'm guilty of atrocious mistakes, bu
I'm still your mother. In my heart I've alway:
been your mother. It has never left me, nc
for as much as one day."

"Oh, *please*," Rachel groaned. "Haven
we had enough excitement for one night?'

Again silence descended between them
Madeleine started the car and drove or
They entered Bath from the south. It wa:
coming up for seven in the morning and the
traffic had begun in earnest. The rain hac
eased off a little, but the sky was still blacl
with clouds.

As they drove up the hill toward Fair
field, Rachel said, "Drop me at the end c
my road."

"No," Madeleine said. "You should see
yourself. You'd be arrested for vagrancy
I'm taking you to your door. And listen, the

first thing you must do is to get rid of those clothes. They'll have Anton's DNA on them. And clean the garage thoroughly."

Rachel chuckled wryly. "Yes, *Mother.*"

Five minutes later they pulled up at the house. Old Tom was sitting by the window watching them park the car.

"OK then," Rachel said, putting her hand on the door handle. "We've done the deal. Haven't we, Madeleine? We're quits."

Madeleine frowned. "No. As far as I'm concerned, that was *not* the deal."

"After this? After what we've just done?" Rachel shook her head vehemently. "It's no good. I'm sorry."

She opened the door.

"Hold on," Madeleine said. "I know that now is not the place or the time, but I want to talk to you. I want to explain. *You owe me that.*"

Rachel pulled the door shut again. "It's not a good idea. Think about it. There is a dead body between us."

Madeleine looked suddenly anguished, but said nothing. She rummaged in her bag and handed over a scuffed padded envelope. "Sasha's passport," she said.

Rachel took it from her hand.

"Don't come back here," she warned, her voice hard. "I don't want to see you again. And I don't want you following Sasha or any shit like that." She opened the car door once again, but hesitated, regretting her harsh words. "Look, Madeleine, seeing you is dangerous for me and Sasha. And probably for you too."

Madeleine detained her with a hand on her arm. "Perhaps you're right about that. For now. But listen, I've been thinking of leaving Bath and I think you and Sasha should come with me. You'd be safe where I'm going."

Rachel shook her head. "Forget that idea. Leaving Bath would give Uri all the more reason to suspect the truth. He'd come after us, I know he would. And if the police found Anton's remains, they might come after me too. So you see, I must stay here and pretend I know nothing about Anton . . . and you leaving Bath is a good idea, under the circumstances."

Madeleine's face was somber. "Well, I don't think I could bear living here anymore, knowing that you and Sasha were so close and yet so far. If you are certain beyond any doubt that you don't want me in your life, my leaving is the best solution, isn't it? We both need to put this behind us and get on with our lives."

Rachel snorted angrily. *Get on with our lives.* What a cliché that was! Well, good old Madeleine could just swan off and leave Bath and the troubles behind.

"Where are you going?" she said, cursing herself for asking.

"Back to Florida. Back to where I come from. Look, I'm going to leave you my address, both here and over there, with John, my partner at the clinic. You might need my help. You might decide to come after all."

"No!"

Madeleine turned on her, saying heatedly, "Think of Sasha. Why close off *his* choices, especially as my help could make a big difference to his future? When my father dies I'm likely to inherit a lot of money. *You* might not want anything from me, but you should remember it with Sasha in mind."

Rachel shrugged, but a part of her was astonished. It had not occurred to her that there were more people attached to Madeleine, more people with the same bloodprint. If she wasn't so frazzled and exhausted she might have been tempted to ask who they were. "Money is never going to solve my problems, Madeleine, besides, I've got plenty in the bank." A sudden thought came to her. "Have you been putting money into my bank account? Are you Langlane Holdings?"

"Langlane Holdings?" Madeleine shook her head, her face blank. "No. Who are they?"

"Never mind." Rachel pushed the door open and got out. Before closing it she leaned in. "I could never have done it without you . . . and I'm grateful." She lowered her voice and said gently, "Try and forget me, Madeleine. Had it not been for tonight, things might have been different. If it helps, you're forgiven. I mean that. But this has to be good-bye." She hesitated for a moment. "Now, *please*, drive off and don't look back."

She hurried through the gate and up to the door. She didn't want to turn around, but in the end she did. Madeleine was still there, looking at her, her beautiful face somber, etched with grief. That face had sparked her fury once, now it only hurt her to see it.

She put the key in the door, and her thoughts turned away from the woman in the car. There were other, more sinister people to worry about. She would change the locks today. It was the first thing she was going to do.

Chapter Twenty-one

Madeleine woke with a start. The night was pitch-black but a fearsome crack split through her senses and the room was lit by a cold blue light. Thunder followed. The rainstorm had returned. It seemed that every cataclysmic event in her life was accompanied by an upheaval of the forces of nature: her own birth, her daughter's birth, the death of her husband, the burning of her daughter's lover.

She glanced at her bedside clock. It was just past four in the morning. Twenty-four hours ago, she'd been setting off from the bleak fells of Dartmoor for the long drive back to Bath. High on the moors she'd burned a human body as if it were no more than a bag of inconvenient rubbish. Only evil people did things like that—individuals without a conscience who destroyed the dignity of humanity. She'd done it without blinking, just like Edmund . . . disposing of scum. After the initial shock of looking at the bloodied crater that had once been a face, she had not even felt particularly sick. As Edmund had advised, she'd treated it like a job and had done it mechanically, to the best of her ability.

She got out of bed. Barefoot, dressed only in panties and a paint-stained shirt, she went to the kitchen to make coffee. She sat in the living room with her mug in front of the *Crucifixion*. The painting dominated the room. A woman (herself?) eaten alive, tortured to death. It was a chilling image, but she liked it. In some terrible way it was purging . . . especially now.

There was a lull in the storm and the sudden silence was pierced by a shriek. Then another. The sound had an unearthly quality, as if ripped from the throat of the devil himself. Perhaps it was the cry of a fox. There was a lair on the scrubland up the road. Yes, of course, it had to be a fox. Madeleine shuddered. It would be all too easy to lose one's grip on sanity. How would the deeds of yesterday ever be laid to rest in her mind? She could rationalize them, she had done so, but the images would come back to her. If only she could talk to someone, unburden herself.

She knew who she could talk to, she knew what would help, but she'd sworn she never would again. Why?

She buried her face in her hands, trying to reach for the true answer. Why had she denied her legacy, her true beliefs? That ridiculous mantra she intoned—*I am a British psychotherapist*—to deprive herself of the wisdom and guidance that was always within her grasp was no longer valid. The certainty grew. As of now she was no longer a psychotherapist, so she could believe what she wanted. Madeleine smiled. Her ancestors called to her, reminding her that Yoruba blood flowed freely in her veins.

She got up and went into the hall. In the closet under the stairs she pulled the string for the light switch and half on her knees crawled to its deepest recess. There, in a cardboard box, was her shrine to Oya. She pulled out the box and took it to the living room. Lifting the shrine out, she placed it on the coffee table. The shrine consisted of a small mahogany cabinet with two doors, and with her heart skipping a beat, Madeleine opened them. Inside were an image of Saint Teresa and, nailed to it, a small black doll, representing the two faces of Oya, blackened by the soot of former rituals.

She'd brought the shrine with her when she left Key West, but had sworn it would never be opened again. Since hurricane Angelina had taken her husband's life, Madeleine had hated her Orisha and blamed her for the disaster, but now, seeing her beloved image, she felt strengthened. Oya was the bearer of women's power, and she favored the use of magic . . . She was fearless, the only goddess who fought in wars, as well as sharing the power of hurricanes, of wind, thunder, and fire, with her lover, Changó. She alone was the guardian of graves. Looking at her, Madeleine realized that Oya had come to her aid and led her. Perhaps her Orisha had sought atonement. She'd brought this storm, provided her with a grave, and given her the fire.

When dawn brought light through the clouds, she put away the shrine and tidied up her living room, finally able to sweep from her thoughts what had happened in the last forty-eight hours. She would not brood on what she'd done, she would not brood on the daughter who had rejected her. If it was meant to be this way, she would accept it. She felt strengthened, her mind sharp, her plans focused.

She made another pot of coffee and started a to-do list in her mind. She'd get an estate agent over as soon as possible to get the house on the market, put her car in the *Auto Trader* or give it back to Neville. In the next week she'd try and see all her clients and explain that she was no longer able to continue their therapy. It was a horribly abrupt way to dismiss them, but she was in no mood to draw it out. She ticked off minor things like canceling subscriptions, meetings, and services. The major tribulation would be to tell Rosaria and Neville that she was leaving. It was awful to abandon them, and the first thing to do in Key West would be to try and find a place that could accomodate Rosaria. Mama would refuse, of course, claim that she was waiting for her husband (now that he was free of that woman). And it would be hard to match Setton Hall. But Rosaria had to come to her, and would have to lower her standards.

The doorbell rang. It startled her. She looked at her watch. It was just gone seven o'clock. Despite her state of undress, she went to the door.

On the doorstep stood Rachel, her shoulders slumped and her hair and clothes totally drenched.

"Rachel," she blurted. "What on earth?" She took a step forward and grabbed Rachel's arm, pulling her in and closing the door. "I'll get you a towel. Go in there." She motioned toward the living room.

She ran up the stairs, her thoughts churning. What had happened? Something very bad, or Rachel would not be here. Not after their parting yesterday morning, not after the night before. She pulled on a pair of jeans, grabbed a towel and an old sweatshirt, and with trepidation went back down.

Rachel was standing in front of the *Crucifixion.*

"Is this your work by any chance?"

"Yes."

"I can see where he gets it from."

Madeleine stopped beside her and peered at the painting. "Who? What do you mean?"

"Gruesome pictures," Rachel muttered. "Sasha. He's very good at art, but sometimes he draws the most horrific things."

"An expression of his fears, no doubt," Madeleine said curtly. "How did you find my house?"

"I followed you here once," Rachel said, her eyes turned away. "I wanted to see . . . Oh, never mind."

"What's happened? What's brought you here?"

Rachel turned sharply and looked her in the eye. Her face looked wild. Madeleine felt a sharp stab of fear and she shivered involuntarily. She draped the towel over Rachel's shoulders and handed her the sweatshirt. "Dry yourself off and sit down. I've just made some coffee." They sat at each end of the sofa, half turned toward each other. Madeleine waited, wide-eyed with dread.

"I've thought about it all night," Rachel said finally. "I want you to take Sasha with you to wherever you are going. You're the only person I know who can take him to safety. Uri is going to come. He will want to know where Anton is. He will torture me or kill me and take Sasha. If I call the police, even if I managed to have him arrested, he will have others come after me. If he suspects I've killed Anton, he'll never let me have Sasha and live in peace."

Madeleine moved to sit beside her and grabbed her hard by the arm. "Then you must come too. You both come with me and we disappear from here. If you are in such danger, I'm not leaving without you."

Rachel tore her arm from Madeleine's grasp. "No," she cried. "Can't you see? If Sasha and I disappear, Uri will know. The business with the passport, Anton vanished, us moved out of the house—it will give him a clear idea of what's happened. All the more reason to come after us. You don't know these people. They'll find us. He'll stop at nothing."

Madeleine jumped up and walked agitatedly about the room. "So, you're just going to sit there and wait for him. You must be mad. You don't have to have yourself killed to save Sasha." She felt like grabbing Rachel and shaking her. It was a convoluted and highly dangerous plan.

Rachel flew up too and stood in front of her. "Madeleine," she cried, her voice fighting for control, "it's the only way." She seized her by the wrist and led her back to the sofa. "Listen to me. Hear me out. This morning at dawn I saw the solution and there is only one way to go with this. There is no doubt that Anton was in some kind of trouble, like you suggested yourself. He was a gangster who had pissed someone off. He was getting out of the country and Uri knew that he was planning to take Sasha with him. Uri himself organized the passport. *I must make him believe Anton has taken Sasha and got the hell out—just as he had planned.* Uri must think Anton was in so much shit, he's had to disappear and is maintaining silence in order to protect Uri and their whole operation. Perhaps Uri will even suspect that Anton has betrayed *him* in some way. If he comes to me—which he will—and Sasha is gone and there I am hysterical, crazed with worry and anger and grief . . . if I pull this off, he might believe it happened that way. I mean, where else would Sasha be? Uri knows I can't bear to let my son out of my sight."

Madeleine stared at her. It sounded plausible enough. Perhaps she was right.

"Is he not still going to hurt you . . . to see if he can make you tell him some other truth?"

"It's a risk I'll have to take."

Their eyes locked for a long moment as one frightening scenario after another reflected on each of their faces.

"And when will you come for Sasha, Rachel?"

"When enough time has passed and I feel it's safe. I'll have to sell the house and move away. It might be a while. A few months, a year . . . maybe more."

"That's a long time to trust me with your son."

"I have to, don't I?" After a second Rachel lowered her gaze. "I do trust you. You're not the coldhearted bitch I made you out to be. I know that now. Hell, I can't judge you. I knew how much you longed to meet me, and playing that game was a rotten thing to do." She looked up again, her eyes searching Madeleine's. "I know you'll be good to Sasha. I trust you. Please take him."

Madeleine nodded. "If you think it's the only way . . . I will."

"How soon can you leave?"

"As soon as it's humanly possible. A week, two perhaps. I wonder if there'll be a problem for me to get him out of the country."

"Shit!" Rachel exclaimed. "How can we check that out?"

Madeleine got up, restlessly walking about. "I'll phone emigration. If we need some kind of certificate or consent form, I know a lawyer who'd oblige." She hoped Ronald Trapp could help. As Neville's long-standing lawyer he was surely a person she could trust with an awkward query like this.

"When can I bring Sasha?" Rachel pleaded. "I don't want him in the house. Soon Uri will start wondering . . ."

"Bring him here." Madeleine went back to sit beside her. "Listen, Rachel, what about the passport being sent to me? Who did you give my address to?"

"The girl I gave it to had no idea who

you were and according to Anton she'd got rid of the address as soon as she sent it. God knows she must have suffered for her actions. I feel very bad about that. All she was able to tell them was your first name, and looking at the envelope, even that was wrong."

"Have you told anyone you've been having therapy? Can anyone make any connection between us?"

Rachel sneered. "Hell no. It wasn't something I was running around telling people." She got up. "I'll go home now. I can't leave Sasha with Charlene any longer. I have to get rid of her too somehow. Chase her away. It's too bad. She's a nice kid, and Sasha loves her company."

By the door they faced each other again.

"You'd better start preparing Sasha. He doesn't know me. Think about what you're going to tell him."

"Yes, of course . . . Oh God, I almost forgot," Rachel cried. She drew the passport out of her back pocket and handed it to Madeleine. For a moment their hands touched as they both clasped it. "Look after my boy," said Rachel, her face grave. "I'll bring him tomorrow! Please get ready to leave the country as soon as you can."

Madeleine put the passport on the hall table.

"Hold on, Rachel, wait."

She lifted the chain from her neck and pulled it off. Removing the vial with her ancestral bones and slipping it into the pocket of her jeans, she held up the chain with the crucifix. "I want to you to have this. It has been passed down through generations of women, most of them very wise. It's imbued with a special strength, which one day I want to tell you about. In the meantime it will protect you from evil. You will need it, so please take it. Wear it, Rachel, and don't take it off."

The walk to Harrods took ages. Neville had decided that he was now elderly and infirm and he embraced this new status with a vengeance. He clung to Madeleine's arm, hanging the weight of his bulk on her. Elizabeth had recruited a sturdy Finnish matron to see to his needs. To Madeleine's surprise, Neville seemed to like the woman. She was servile enough with that touch o no-nonsense dedication that appealed to Neville's childlike neediness. His daily phone calls to Madeleine had begun to abate, which was surely a good sign, and she listened to his occasional tirades with all the sympathy she could muster. Now she had just an hour or two to try and make *him* listen to *her*.

The sun was hot and the air smelled faintly of city sewers. Neville refused to walk via Beauchamp Place, because he now resented not being able to stare at the people in the cafés or stop to criticize the paintings in the gallery windows. Harrods was different, he told her; it was the smells that drew him, the ground coffee, the perfumes, the flowers, the lush aromas of the food halls, spices, herbs, and chocolate, freshly baked bread. As his sight went, other senses had sharpened. Madeleine was glad that there was at least one positive aspect to his misery.

They circled the gardens of Hans Place and up Hans Road, slowly, one step at a time.

"Is there something wrong with your legs?" Madeleine asked.

Neville stopped in his tracks, staring

ahead. "I'm fucking blind, right? I beg you to remember it."

"Just wondering." Madeleine sighed to herself. She was about to suggest that perhaps a white stick would be useful, if nothing else for the sake of safety, but then realized what outrage such a suggestion would bring on.

They went in through the bakery and sweet shop, following their noses; Neville knew his way and had no problems with his image here. He let go of her arm and walked straight, his impressive bulk like a ship sailing between the counters. They passed through the flowers, fruit, and veg into the meat and fish hall.

"Forget the coffeeshop. I fancy some oysters, don't you?" said Neville. He didn't wait for an answer but directed Madeleine with sure steps toward the oyster bar.

They sat themselves down and without looking at the wine list Neville ordered a bottle of Laurent-Perrier champagne; he'd obviously done this before. Madeleine didn't dare question the price of this nectar, but she would certainly partake—why not?—of a last drink with her father.

"This would normally be my painting day, you know," Madeleine said, infusing her voice with a smile, "and here I am in London about to get pissed with my old man."

"I'd rather not hear about your painting day, if you don't mind," he said.

She watched the barman case the cork from the bottle. He poured the frothing pink champagne into very tall thin glasses.

"Don't be so sensitive, Neville," she said. "You've had sixty years of painting. I'd hate it if I couldn't talk to you about art. You've always been my mentor, for God's sake."

He laughed, grabbing his glass off the counter—he could see the glass perfectly well—and took a hefty swallow without waiting for Madeleine. "We don't see eye to eye on art anyway, Madeleine, though I admit I like your subject. You know I do. And you've got talent, you're a chip off the old block. You don't need me to tell you anything."

"Perhaps I *do* need you to tell me. I'm quitting psychotherapy and I'm planning to paint full-time."

She was curious to see how this piece of news would go down, but he seemed only marginally surprised, or interested.

"Good thinking, girl. You're good, there is no doubt about it. Keep the Frank fame going."

"Neville," she said, impatiently, "I can't help but notice that you never ask me anything."

"What are *you* complaining about?" he said tetchily. "You haven't got a clue what this is like . . . I'll never paint again and my wife has just up and left me now that I'm a blind old fart. Well, she won't get a fucking penny, not if I can help it."

"I can't help noticing you never ask me anything," Madeleine repeated pointedly.

Neville turned to her with an exaggerated sigh. "What the hell is it you want me to ask you?"

Here was a choice. She could have a predictable couple of hours, gobbling oysters and champagne with her famous and formidable father, having exalted but meaningless conversation, laughing too loudly at his tired old jokes and, lastly, commiserating when he was drunk and maudlin. It would be one way to remember him. Or she could tell him that she was leaving the country, and was probably never coming back.

She took a sip of the bubbly. It was delicious. "Listen, I've got a few things to ask you . . . and to tell you."

"Go on, then," he said, glancing at a dish of oysters that another customer had ordered. "Shoot."

"I take it you're leaving me the house in Key West, am I right?"

His head swung toward her. "Hold on! I'm not dead yet."

She had neither energy nor patience for the necessary placating bullshit. "But you will leave me the house, won't you?"

He took his time to answer. "Eventually, I guess I will."

"Neville! I'm your only child, at least that I know of."

"Have the fucking house," he said, his voice quite loud. Madeleine avoided looking around. This was bad enough.

"Good. I'm moving to Key West shortly, and the house needs major work."

"I suppose you want me to pay for that too," he said acidly, not seeming to hear that his daughter was about to up sticks and move to the other side of the globe.

"No, I don't, but it's quite an investment, so I want to clarify my position."

"What *is* this? A fucking business meeting? You just said you came to London to get pissed with your old man." In one move he turned to the barman, snapping his fingers and ordering a plate of oysters.

She ignored his displeasure and bashed on. "The next thing I want to tell you is that Rachel Locklear, the patient I was telling you about, *is* my daughter after all."

He paused for a second, then raised an eyebrow. "Ah well, I guess that's what you wanted. Cheers to that."

Reluctantly she lifted her glass and touched the rim to his. A dish of oysters appeared before them. Neville's fingers wandered searchingly over it like a hungry crab.

"That's it?" she said. "You have no comments to make?"

His lips pursed as he grasped a shell containing one of the slimy creatures. "Well now, isn't that some coincidence!" He slipped the oyster down his gullet.

"No, as it happens, it was no coincidence. She sought me out and engaged me as her therapist, knowing I was her mother."

Neville just shook his head and she said no more for the moment. It was best to le him finish his oysters; he was no good at multitasking, especially where food was concerned. Two young men in sharp suits sat down beside them. They dropped their sleek briefcases on the floor, put their mobile phones on the counter, and began talking in overly loud voices. Neville's eyebrows narrowed dangerously. *Here we go,* thought Madeleine, waiting for some scathing remark.

"Have the last one," he said to her, ignoring their neighbors.

"Don't like oysters," she said, taking a large gulp of the champagne. "Do listen, Neville."

"Go on, go on."

"Did you hear me when I said I'm moving permanently to Key West?"

"Shit . . . *You are?*" His blood-sugar levels restored, he seemed finally to hear her. "Well, that's just fucking great, Madeleine! First Elizabeth abandons me, and now you . . . and I thought I'd move back to Bath. I've actually put Pont Street on the market, and my agent tells me I can get one hell of a pad in Bath." He pouted truculently. "I thought you'd look after me in my old age."

"We'd kill each other," Madeleine said, laughing. "But moving back to Bath seems a great idea. You can have *my* house."

"Good God! What a ghastly thought."

"Yeah, well. The offer is there. A house for a house."

"What about your mother, Madeleine? You're going to abandon Rosaria as well?"

Madeleine peered at him. On the tip of her tongue was a scathing reminder of his own desertion. But one of the mobiles on the counter started shrieking. The sleeker of the two businessmen picked it up. His voice rose as he barked out instructions and figures, peppered with clichés. Neville's florid face rose another notch in color.

"No, of course I'm not abandoning her. I saw her last night and told her we were returning to Key West. I'll be looking for a place for her, hopefully one in the Keys, but it might take a few weeks to arrange." She paused. "In the meantime, perhaps you could take a little interest in Mama. You could visit her sometime. You two have a lot to reminisce about. It would do you both a whole lot of good if you went to see her."

Neville eased the champagne bottle out of its ice bucket and managed to pour him self another glass without spilling a drop. He was polishing off nearly the entire bottle on his own.

"What's interesting is that Mama seems to have gained back 'the sight,'" Madeleine continued pointedly. "For instance, she told me that you were going blind, well before I knew. She sensed it."

This seemed to interest the old narcissist. "She did? I'll be damned. What did she say?"

"She said she couldn't see through your eyes."

"Did she really?"

"Yep. She knew."

They were quiet for a moment. Neville snapped his fingers for another bottle.

"And she also told me, way back in April, that your marriage was over."

Neville chuckled. "Yeah, I bet she bit the head off a live bat to put a curse on it. I'm surprised she hadn't done it earlier." He waited impatiently for the champagne to be poured, and then gulped the glass down.

"Well," he said at last, "I suppose it wouldn't hurt to go and see the barmy old witch."

"She's not *that* barmy. She could still tell

you things that would surprise you. She talks about you all the time. She knows you better than anyone. Remember, she's a very skillful Santera. You're one of the few people in this damned country who understands what that means."

It was no good overplaying the strategy, so she stopped there, but she could see that something had been set in motion in the old man's mind. He was visibly mulling over this information. There had been a time when Rosaria's powers had fascinated him. It would be so good for her to be able to say good-bye to him. Madeleine suspected it was just the closure her mother needed.

"What else can we eat?" he said after a while. "Fancy some lobster?"

Suddenly she found she was quite hungry. It seemed days since she'd eaten anything substantial. "Yeah, I could handle that."

They gave their order to the bartender and soon they were chomping their way through two lobsters as if they'd ordered a couple of doughnuts. *The trappings of wealth,* thought Madeleine. *Better start scaling down my standards.*

"I want to ask you something else," she said when they'd finished.

"Ohhh, no, forget it. I'm not having her living with me."

"This is about my daughter."

Neville looked suspicious. "What about her?"

"If she was ever in dire straits, would you help her?"

Neville was inelegantly mopping food off his goatee with a linen napkin. He was getting drunk and she wondered if the direction of the conversation was wise.

"You mean money?" he grumbled. "I've already sunk half a fortune into that family."

Madeleine turned to him and frowned. "What did you say?"

Neville bit his lip. "Oh, shit!" he said with a sigh. "Well, it's all in the open now, isn't it? You know who she is. Alf Locklear kept claiming they were hard-up. He blackmailed me, the groveling bastard."

A moment went by in stunned silence.

"Neville." She grabbed him by the arm. "What the hell are you talking about?"

He sipped, paused, and burped. "That fellow Locklear. The couple who looked after Rosaria. I hired them myself. Mrs. Dottie, apt name, dotty bird she was, she took a shine to Mikaela. They had no children, not surprising, I couldn't see him getting it up."

Madeleine could barely comprehend what he was saying. She snatched the glass from his paw and put it down on the counter with a bang. "Christ, Neville . . . what are you telling me?"

He focused his failing eyes on her. "Now you're going to be pissed off with me, aren't you?" He took a deep breath. "The Locklears were good to her, Madeleine dear. You should be happy about it. And to keep them sweet, I paid them a bit of money, five thousand a quarter I think it was. I left the whole business to Trapp, better let these things go through the proper channels, just in case . . . you know."

"What are you saying?" Madeleine closed her eyes for a moment, her head spinning. "All this time . . . you knew where she was?"

"I couldn't very well tell you, now could I? That slimy little Locklear fellow kept making veiled threats. He knew I was famous God knows how, 'cos he didn't know shi about the art world."

Madeleine felt her face go scarlet. He

heart was pounding. "That couple, Rosaria's caretakers . . ."

"Yeah. I didn't want any trouble, any scandal. The Locklears had been away on a holiday. They were the ones who found your mother in that dreadful state. You can just see the headlines, can't you? Neville Frank's wife killing small mammals and feeding the blood to a child in a baby bottle. My God, imagine the uproar. The gutter press would have gone berserk with excitement. Satanism and all that. That would have been my career and reputation down the pan." He patted her awkwardly on the shoulder. "I did the right thing, Madeleine. The Locklears wanted Mikaela, and the whole business was silenced, all in one transaction."

"But *Cocksworth*, you said their name was."

"I lied." He threw his hands in the air. "There you have it."

Madeleine felt dizzy. She swayed slightly on her bar stool, and she took hold of the edge of the counter. The bartender was observing them with covert interest. He approached, taking the bottle from the bucket and filling her glass. Something stronger would have been more appropriate. She was close to murdering her own father.

"You've had more than one chance to tell me, you old bastard," she growled. "How could you keep something like this from me all these years, knowing how much I yearned to find her? Even after Forrest's death . . . you kept it quiet."

Neville put his hand on her shoulder. "I had lots of reasons, Madeleine. I bet your worthy daughter didn't tell you that she's a two-bit hooker, or was. I couldn't take any risks. Trapp told me to stay well away. Never mind Alf Locklear, a woman with her morals would be even more likely to go for black-mail. It would have ruined me." He shook her by the shoulder. "Are you hearing me, Madeleine? I was giving them money, for fuck's sake. Even after the old man died, I told Trapp to keep putting money into her account. *I am helping her.* Doesn't that count for something?"

Madeleine felt numb with shock, hardly able to take on board what her father had done.

"You cooked this up with Forbush, didn' you? How much did you pay him to cal me an unfit mother?" she cried, not caring about the bartender or the businessmen. "And later . . . you've had every opportunity to put me out of my misery. You knew Forrest and I were desperate to find her. What you did was despicable. All this unhappiness, just to save your goddamned image, your stupid reputation."

For once Neville looked worried. "You're forgetting that she chose not to have any contact with you."

Madeleine slammed her fist into the counter. "You sold her. *You sold my daughter.*"

Neville scrabbled about in his pockets for money and threw a wad of cash on the counter.

"Let's go," he said in a low voice.

They made their way through Harrods and out into the sunshine. Whatever else he could have told her, Madeleine was not interested in hearing it. The picture was all too clear. She led the way through the streets, Neville hanging on to her arm for guidance.

"Just a question, my dear," Neville panted. 'Why are you off to Florida to live when after all this shit, you've found your daughter? Just float that by me, will you?"

She stopped and turned to him, speaking through clenched teeth. "The reason I asked if you would help her is because she's in deep trouble, and me leaving has everything to do with keeping her safe."

Neville contemplated her answer for a few seconds. "A person with her sort of lifestyle will always attract trouble, Madeleine."

She glared at him and said fiercely, "My daughter's life is in danger, Neville. She has a seven-year-old son who is also in grave danger. Do you understand what I'm telling you? I asked you if you would help her, if you would give her shelter if she needed it, but I can see I was wrong in asking."

Neville looked shocked. "You didn't mention a son," he said. His eyes flickered back and forth, as if some goal posts of his own had been moved. "So there is finally another male in this cursed family. What's he like?"

"The little boy is coming with me to Florida."

"He is?" Neville's failing eyes focused on her for a long moment. "Listen, if your daughter needs shelter, I'll do what I can."

She looked at him searchingly. "Can I give Rachel your phone number?"

"Yes, Madeleine. Give her my number." He reached out and clumsily stroked her hair. "Do you think you can forgive me, little girl?"

The traffic rumbled past as they stood on the street corner, facing each other. Neville suddenly looked very old. She had to forgive him. Whatever he'd done, Madeleine knew she was equally to blame. She'd not fought hard enough. She'd let her daughter go. She had signed her name on that cursed piece of paper.

She put her arms around her father's expansive middle and her tears began to flow. *Perhaps,* she thought, as Neville folded her into a tight embrace, *perhaps in the end, all can be forgiven.*

Chapter Twenty-two

Rachel stood by the door in the little hallway on the ground floor, waiting for a taxi. She glanced at herself in the mirror. She sure as hell looked the part: pale, hollow-eyed, anxious, exhausted. She felt the part too, being perilously close to a nervous collapse, like the one she'd suffered in London after having been worked half to death by Anton at the height of his cocaine consumption.

She'd delivered Sasha to Madeleine that morning, packing only a few bits of clothing, his sketch books and crayons and his CDs. It had been a terrible ordeal to leave him, especially as she had to keep a smile on her face and tell him he was going to stay a few days with his new grandmother. To her credit, Madeleine had handled it very well, not gushy or even solicitous, but cool, calm, and friendly, leading Sasha by the hand to look at a huge Perspex box with tubes and bridges leading to smaller boxes, all full of earth, through which ants tunneled all over the place. The creepy painting of the trussed-up woman was turned, facing the wall. Sasha had been so fascinated by the ant box he'd barely noticed his mother leaving. Rachel had promised to drop by every day until they flew off into the wild blue yonder, but she knew that going to Madeleine's house was unsafe, putting Sasha at risk. It was best not to.

Tears began to roll down her face and she fumbled in her shirt pocket for a tissue. A car honked the horn; surely the taxi she'd called for. The driver was a man in his late thirties, jolly and talkative. He couldn't understand why she'd not thought to take the train to Reading, she'd have saved a fortune. He even rattled off the train times, the dumb git, but he was a good driver.

As she was about to say something to

shut him up, her mobile rang. She jumped with fright. Who and why and what? Uri? Madeleine? Sasha had never been away from her for long and perhaps he'd thrown a wobbly. Madeleine was not used to children after all.

"What?"

"It's Madeleine, don't panic. I just wanted to tell you that Sasha is fine. He is fully occupied." She lowered her voice. "Rachel, are you sure you know what you're doing?"

"Yes, I am sure."

"Please be careful, be very careful. I'll be thinking of you."

Rachel closed her eyes trying to calm herself, a long sigh escaping her lips. "I'll phone you when its over," she mumbled, half covering her mouth with her hand.

Madeleine was quiet, and Rachel was about to say good-bye when she spoke again.

"Listen, Rachel. If you spot any hairs on Uri's shirt or jacket, could you try and get them for me? Try to pick them off . . . you know, casually. I'm sure you're good at that sort of thing. Or if he manhandles you, perhaps there might be a way of snatching at his hair. If you can come back with a few, even just one or two . . . Shove them in your pocket or something."

"*What?* Whatever for?"

"I've not gone mad or anything, but don't bother asking why I want them."

Hairs! As if this mission weren't bizarre enough—and dangerous! Perhaps the episode on the moors had driven Madeleine over the edge. Her mother had been insane, after all. And here she was, in charge of a vulnerable little boy.

"Madeleine, really—"

Madeleine cut her off. "Do it *only* if you find a way. Be careful and take no risks."

So this was where he lived now. This was where he held his slaves, bought them, sold them, worked them too perhaps; on the edge of a bleak industrial estate, east of Reading, just ten minutes off the M4. It had cost her quite a number of devious phone calls to get the location, and now, half a fortune for the taxi.

Before getting out of the car, Rachel paid the driver—he was happy enough—then told him to wait.

"How long?" he said, glancing uneasily down the road, then up at the building.

"I'm not sure. It could be up to, say, half an hour."

"I don't know, lady." He shook his head. "That'll cost . . . You want to go back to Bath?"

"Didn't I just give you a huge wad of cash, man? Here!" She took out her silver lighter and shoved it between the seats. "I didn't know you'd be so bloody expensive. We've got to stop at a cash point on the way back, but for now, hang on to this. It's my one worldly possession of any worth."

"OK, I'll wait," he said, refusing to take it. "As long as I know you're coming."

She stood on the road for a moment and gathered her courage, but she felt numb. What she had to do felt so unreal, even her terror had shrunk to a dull ache in her gut.

She raised her eyes and looked up at the building. It was set back from the road on a large scrubby plot, its brick-faced façade grim and characterless, the sort of place they built in the sixties or seventies to house the administrative offices of some import-export outfit (which, in a way, it was). It was well placed between London and Reading and all those motorways, plus Heathrow and Gatwick at a stone's throw.

Any evidence of occupancy was concealed by window blinds in battleship gray. She could just imagine the sort of dark deeds that happened behind them. But currently, there were no signs of life. It was midmorning and people who worked mainly at night were still sleeping. It seemed no one had noticed the taxi pulling up. She went through the gate and walked up a concrete path covered with cracks. Weeds sprouted in them, and the spindly remnants of flowering shrubs lined the edges. This neglect was at odds with the workaday austerity of the building. Alfie had once been keen on gardening, and she could see that the shrubs should have been pruned years ago. All the vegetation around the building was scorched as if some hellfire had swept over it.

A small camera was trained on the entrance and there was a doorbell and an intercom, but she ignored them. Taking a deep breath, she battered at the door with both fists.

After a couple of minutes Uri himself opened the door. They had not seen each other for two years, but in that fraction of a moment—before she pushed past him—

she noticed he looked well, tanned and toned, a man pleased with himself.

With the element of surprise on her side, it took him a moment to react. He'd seen the taxi, shut the door behind her, and just managed to grab her arm as she ran toward the interior of the building.

"Are they here?" she shrieked, wrenching herself free. Without waiting for an answer, she made a dash for a staircase on her left, but he caught her by her shirt and yanked her back, turning her to face him.

"Crazy bitch. What fuck you doing?" His English had not improved, the accent just as heavy as when she'd last heard his voice.

"You know damned well what I'm doing," she wailed, genuine tears stinging her eyes. "Where are they? Where is my son? You're going to tell me. You'll never get rid of me, do you hear me?"

He studied her for a long moment, his dark eyes at half-mast. "*You* tell *me*, bitch. You tell me where they gone."

So Uri knew Anton had disappeared. She curled her fists and glared at him. "Don't try and fob me off. Your fucking brother came and took Sasha away for the day, and they never came back. But you know that, don't you? You arranged Sasha's passport. I know what a passport means."

"When did he take Sasha?" Uri asked evenly, betraying no emotion.

She shook her head in disbelief. "Last week. I've spent a whole fucking week try-ing to find out where you live." She leaned forward and spoke in a low voice. "If you don't tell me where my son is, I'm going straight to the police to report them miss-ing."

He drew back his hand and slapped her. Her head snapped to the side, but in the next second she lunged at him, grabbing his hair with one hand, punching wildly at his face with the other. With a look of sur-prise he took her forearms, digging his thumbs into the soft inside of her wrists, compressing the artery.

"Say again," he growled. "You are going to police?"

The mention of police was dangerous. Once she'd voiced the threat, her fear had returned full force.

He looked probingly into her face for a long moment, her wrists still clamped be-tween his thumbs and forefingers. The pain was almost unbearable but she kept her right fist tightly closed. Then he shrugged and let her go. "Ukraina is big place, huge country. You think English cops go there?"

"Ukraine?" she whispered, returning his stare with shocked disbelief.

"They come back soon," he said slowly. "You just go home and wait like good bitch. You make shit, you call cops, I kill you." He shrugged again. "Simple."

"No you won't," she snarled. "I've written it all down: a list of names, addresses, contacts, deeds, routes, everything I know— and that's *everything*. I've left several copies with someone, all sealed up in envelopes with stamps on them. If something happens to me, *pop*, off they go in the mailbox. You understand?"

A shadow of rage passed over his face, perhaps just at the concept that Anton, his own blood brother, might have exposed him to a threat like this, but he obviously didn't want her to notice.

"Go home, Rachel," he said, pushing her toward the door. "I find out."

"Find out?" she cried. "So you don't know? You have no idea where they are?"

"Fuck off now." He opened the door and

shoved her roughly through it, but she kept her foot on the threshold.

"Hold on. Wait!" she cried. "How can you get hold of me? Do you know where I live? Do you have my phone number?"

He glared at her. It was obvious he didn't. The last thing she wanted was to tell him how to find her, but she had to play the part and see this through. She rummaged inside her bag for a scrap of paper, shaking her hand to release the hairs stuck between her fingers. Pulling out a used napkin and a pen, she scribbled her mobile number. He took it from her and pushed the door closed in her face.

She was shaking from head to foot as she walked away. The taxi was still there, thank God. The driver smirked when she got in.

"Lovers' tiff, eh?" He glanced at her through the rearview mirror. "He'll be back. He'd be crazy not to."

"I'm going to have a smoke and don't try to stop me," she said.

"All right, sweetheart, I can see you need one. But just the one."

"And I don't feel like talking."

The driver pulled out from the curb. She

fumbled in her bag for the cigarette packet, wishing she had something stronger to calm her nerves. Casting a last glance at the house, she saw it had closed up again, mute and hostile.

That was not the end of it. Soon enough he'd come looking for her. She was prepared for that. Death was a clear possibility, and not just any death. She would be made to talk first. And the consequences of talking were too frightening to contemplate.

Either way, her little Sasha would soon be on his way to the other side of the world. Her eyes prickled with tears as she dragged deeply on her cigarette. The driver turned the radio on.

Sasha was leaning over the railing, peering through the green plastic mesh down into a large hole in the ground. The woman called Madeleine was holding him by the hand, pointing down into the hole with the other.

"See there, see that stone circle? That's the top of a wall. That's where the Romans kept their goats or sheep."

"How d'you know?" Sasha asked warily. "The Romans were rich and swam in hot baths. I know that for a fact. I've seen it."

"Yes, but they had to eat, didn't they? Besides, not every Roman was rich. Did you know there is a whole other city under Bath?"

"'Course I did." He looked at her. She had black curly hair, and sparkly eyes, and she was wearing jeans. "Are you really my grandmother?" he asked suspiciously. "You don't look like one."

"What do grandmothers look like?" she asked, laughing.

"Old," he said. "White hair. A dress with flowers on."

"Oh yeah?"

"You talk funny."

"I'm American."

"Why have I never seen you before?"

"Your mother and I . . . well, we just kind of found each other."

"Were you cross with each other?"

Madeleine squeezed his hand. "Maybe a little." She looked around, her hand tight on his. "Let's go home, shall we? Keep the hat and the sunglasses on, Sasha. You look really cool in them."

Madeleine's house was different from his own. It had really thick walls and one felt safe inside. She had no husband. No one came visiting or rang the doorbell. In the ants' house in the living room, ants were busy all day and all night making tunnels and nests, and dashing through the tubes to see their neighbors. Madeleine promised him that soon they would build another ant city, much much bigger, just for him.

And there were paintings everywhere. Almost all of them were of ants, zillions of them. Madeleine had taken them down off the walls and put them on the floor so he could look at them properly. There was just one painting she didn't let him see. It was big and she'd turned it around so it faced the wall. He'd tried to sneak a peek at it, wanting to know what it was, but Madeleine told him not to even try. The painting could fall on top of his head, she said.

He knew they were waiting for something important and in the meantime he looked at the ants, the live ones and the painted ones, and he sat on her sofa and made drawings. Madeleine sat beside him and made her own drawings.

"What are we waiting for?" he asked for the thousandth time.

Madeleine took a deep breath, then

turned to him. "OK, Sasha, here is the deal. The day after tomorrow, you and I have a ticket to go to an island. By plane. You'll like it there. We've got a great old house to live in. In the garden there is a tree house up in a massive tree. It used to be mine when I was a little girl, and if you want, it can be yours, your special place. How does that sound?"

"But what about my mum? Does she know about it?"

"Yes, she knows."

"She's coming too, right?"

Madeleine was quiet for a moment. "Of course she is. But later. She has to get everything sorted out here, and it could take a little time. If you don't like it over there, we could come back."

"So she won't be there for my birthday?"

"When is your birthday?"

Sasha rubbed out one of his ants with a rubber. It was a crap ant—nothing like Madeleine's. Hers were perfect. "In three weeks. On Sunday."

Madeleine stopped drawing. After a moment she touched his arm. "In three weeks, on Sunday?"

"Yeah."

Madeleine started to laugh. "My God, child, I should have guessed," she said. "You're born to Angelina."

Sasha frowned. "No," he protested. "My mum's name is Rachel."

Madeleine, still laughing softly, had tears running down her face. She turned to him and took his hand. "Angelina was a hurricane. That's what I meant. You were born on the day of a hurricane."

He couldn't fall asleep. The bed was strange—softer than his own—and huge. He would have his own bed when they got where they were going, to that island where the sun shone almost every day. He longed to be there, far away from harsh voices and cries in the night, but he missed Mum.

He lifted his head from the pillow and cocked his ear. Not a sound. Madeleine must be asleep in her own bedroom. He wondered if ants slept during the night. Did they lie down on their sides and nod off, alone or all cozy together, or did they keep working nonstop?

He got up and tiptoed to the door, opening it. The night-light that Madeleine had put in the hall for him glowed yellow, but there was a light on downstairs too. He walked to the top of the stairs. One by one he padded softly down them. He peeked into the living room, and there sat Madeleine on her knees in front of the ant farm, with her back to the door. He observed her quietly for a moment. She had a dressing gown on and was doing something with the ant house. She dipped something in a jar, then dropped it into the opening at the top. She did it slowly, one at a time, staring into the hole.

"What you doing?"

She was startled by his voice, turning to look at him as he approached.

"I'm having a chat with my little friends," she said with a smile.

"You're feeding them, aren't you?"

"Yes, sort of."

He stood there watching, and she resumed what she was doing. She had a pair of tweezers to pick up the food and dip it in the jar. When she dropped it into the ant farm, dozens of ants came swarming around it and carried it off into their tunnels. He bent forward to examine the ant food in the black bowl she had in her hand. He could not see it. The food was invisible.

"There is nothing there," he said, looking at her, mystified. "You're just pretending."

"Yes, in a way you are right," she said, and continued picking up the invisible food.

He leaned closer and stared into the bowl. There *was* something there, a tiny pile of something on the bottom that looked like cut-up hairs.

"Are you giving them hair?" he said, staring at her.

"Yes. They seem to like it, don't you think? They'll probably use them for building their nest."

"And what's that? The stuff you're dipping them in?"

"It's a kind of honey . . . from a tree. The little guys go crazy over it." She dipped another one. It looked like hard work, picking up the hairs, one by one.

"Why are you doing it like that?"

She smiled at him and she was pretty in the soft light. "I'm experimenting," she said. "I don't know if it will work. I'm not sure I know what I'm doing, but I'm having a go."

"Do you like your ants?"

"Yes, I really do," she said.

"I had a dog before. I really liked him, but he's dead now."

Madeleine stopped and looked at him. Then she took the bowl and tipped the rest of the hairs into the ant farm. She put the jar on the table, sat down on the floor, and opened her arms. "Come on, Sasha. Tell me all about the dog you really liked."

He went to her and she hugged him close. He didn't normally much like to be hugged, but for some reason her arms around him made him feel good.

Chapter Twenty-three

It was a fine June Saturday. The sun shone over Bath, and the air had been washed clean of city fumes from two days of rain. Visitors and locals alike wandered around town in the skimpiest of clothes, eating ice cream or sitting in cafés drinking cool drinks. Tables came out on pavements in front of pubs, and pints of beer were poured down gullets in a boozy free-for-all. People smiled at one another and gave money to down-and-outs.

Rachel saw nothing of this summer elation. Glancing over her shoulder, she'd slunk into an Internet café, where she sa hunched over a keyboard, painstakingly sending and receiving the weekly e-mail that kept her in touch with Madeleine. Reading Sasha's little message to her—*Having fun time mum love you*—she had a vision of him skipping around on a sandy beach in some American resort, playing with nice kids, and then sitting under a palm tree, eating a picnic of peanut butter sandwiches and watermelon, and drinking juice right out of a coconut shell. His body was brown and his hair stood on end, his excited little face flushed with pleasure. Madeleine was reassuring: her boy was absolutely fine, but missed his mother.

She wandered back through town and on the way bought a bottle of whiskey and a carton of two hundred cigarettes, a bag of dried figs, half a pint of milk, and some instant coffee. It was hard work carrying food up the hill and she had her priorities. In fact, she was already tired as she started walking up toward Fairfield. How long would she be climbing this damned hill? It exhausted her just thinking about it. Was there any point to it, really, walking up and down between two locations, liking neither? She threw her fag in the gutter, not able to smoke and climb at the same time, but she knew that as soon as she got to the top, she'd light another. She was trying to cut down, because the cost of it, both physical and financial, was more than noticeable. Every few steps she had to stop to regain her breath.

As she stood there panting, her mobile rang in her pocket and it took her a moment to realize what the noise was. Not one person had phoned her in the three weeks since Madeleine and Sasha had left. She stiffened, then fumbled to get the phone out in time.

"Who is it?"

"Uri."

So, here it was. Finally! Despite a wrenching pain in her gut, she welcomed the end of the torment of waiting.

"Uri!" she cried. Her terror sounded genuine enough. "Why haven't you called me? Any news?"

"We must talk."

"Why? What, Uri? What's happened?"

"I tell you in person. Where is your place?"

"Oh, my God! What's happened to Sasha? Tell me now!"

"Your address?"

"Sasha?" she whispered. "Has something happened?"

Uri was quiet for a moment. She could almost hear his mind churning.

"I bring Sasha to your house. Tonight."

This threw her. He was lying, of course, he had to be. "You have Sasha?" she said, sounding suspicious. "Anton has brought him back? You're lying, aren't you?"

"I find you so easy, Rachel, but is better you give me your address."

"I'll give you my address," she said. "But let me talk to Sasha first. Just a couple of words."

A short pause, then Uri's phone clicked off. Her knees went from under her and she sank onto a low stone wall flanking a row of front gardens. She dropped her mobile into her bag and fumbled for a cigarette. With shaking hands she lit up and inhaled deeply. A woman at a window next door was frowning angrily at her. Rachel didn't care; they could come and knock her off the wall, she'd sit on the pavement.

Think! Think! she told herself. *What to do?* A month had gone by since she'd seen Uri and with the passage of each day, she'd feared more what was going to happen. He must still be in the dark or she'd be dead by now. Unless he had just discovered something, or had begun to suspect that his brother had not absconded but been murdered, murdered by someone other than an enemy. No doubt an interrogation was imminent. He would be merciless—an accomplished sadist with a will to match. After extracting the truth, he'd kill her, then he'd go looking for Sasha. Even if she had the stamina to keep Sasha's whereabouts to herself, he'd leave no stone unturned until he found his little nephew. If he lacked every other normal human quality, blood loyalty was an exception.

"Get the hell off that wall," the woman shouted through the open window.

"What's it to you? It's not your house," Rachel said wearily, but didn't move. She was going to finish this cigarette, she could not afford to waste them.

"It's private property, and my neighbors are pissed off with the likes of you, throwing butts and cans into the garden."

"Is that a fact?" Rachel mumbled, her voice too hoarse and too tired to raise.

The woman slammed the window shut so hard the glass rattled in the frame.

After a few more concentrated inhalations of nicotine Rachel stubbed out the cigarette on the pavement and set off again, pausing and walking, pausing and walking, like an old woman. Perhaps she was hungry, she'd not eaten all day. She'd lost her appetite, what little she'd had. She'd love nothing better than to numb herself with pills of one kind or another, but she had to remain sharp every moment of her day. The thought of numbing herself gave her an idea. She could go back down into town and score a huge bag of heroin. Shoot the whole lot up and in this simple, pain-free way, eliminate a whole assortment of problems. Her life was shit. Her son was gone, and soon the monster from hell was going to come through her door and beat her up or torture her, probably worse. Instead, he would find her dead from an overdose, and conclude that she was nothing but a loser, a drug addict who Anton had had the sense to rescue Sasha from. At least he would not be able to get anything out of her and if he asked the neighbors, they'd tell him the story she'd foisted on them: Sasha had gone to live with his father in the Ukraine. That's what she'd told everyone, old Tom Bainsburrow, the young couple who'd moved in opposite, the kid in the news agent's. Sasha would probably have a wonderful life with Madeleine, who was his grandmother after all, and because of the guilt and remorse she evidently felt, she would do everything to make him happy and keep him safe. In fact, an overdose was a brilliant solution. Besides, she was tired and there was nothing left.

She walked back through the park, and by the swings sat herself down on a bench. She lit another cigarette and took out the bottle of whiskey. Unscrewing the cap, she tipped the bottle to her lips and took a swig. She tried to imagine the process, how she would go about it. First she'd have to get her hands on a syringe and needle, new or used, it wouldn't matter. There were plenty of drug addicts in Bath, she'd have to get talking to one and find a dealer. The rest was easy, she'd seen it done many times. Heat the gear with a drop or two of lemon juice and some water, draw it into the syringe through a bit of cigarette filter, and shoot it all up.

But after all she'd gone through at the hands of the two brothers, and having lived through the nightmare of eliminating one, should she really let the other have command of her life—and death? They'd have won after all, they'd have taken everything from her. *No, she could not let that happen.* She had to be there for Sasha. Even if he was better off, safer, happier in that far-away place, he might still need her and she had to be alive.

From the back of her thoughts came the recollection of something Madeleine had said in one of their therapy sessions. It was not just Sasha who needed protection, it was not just her son who was precious and important. *She mattered too.* As an idea it made sense. She was a human being after all.

She was sprawled on the sofa, reading *Zen in Self-Defense,* a martial arts manual written by some ditsy airhead who'd clearly never been attacked, when the doorbell rang. At the sound, all the muscles in her body contracted into a spasm as if she'd been hit by a bolt of lightning. She flew up, instinctively looking around for a place to hide. She sank her teeth into her knuckle to steady herself, feverishly rehearsing the plan. What was she going to do, to say? She hid the book under the sofa and made her way downstairs, her thoughts quickening, realigning, the features of her face reorganizing themselves into an expression: at once frightened and hopeful. She'd been through it in her mind enough times: "Have you found them?" "Have you heard from them?" "When are they coming back?"

She flung open the front door, and her thoughts scrambled. Openmouthed, she just stood there. It was not Uri or his henchmen. It was Charlene.

For several seconds neither of them said anything. Charlene looked baffled by her wild-eyed lunge at the door, her agitation and trembling hands. Rachel herself could not take on board that here was, not the monster from hell, but her onetime babysitter.

"Hiya, Rachel," Charlene said after a moment. "Can I come in?"

"Christ, Charlene. Sure, OK, but I've gotta go out in a moment."

This would have to be quick. She couldn't risk having Charlene in the house. She ushered her upstairs and into the kitchen. Charlene settled herself at the kitchen table, while Rachel put the kettle on and got two mugs from the draining board.

"I know you said to give you a break," the girl murmured. "But I've not seen you guys for weeks, and I thought perhaps you needed—"

"Sasha has gone to live with his dad in the Ukraine," Rachel interrupted without looking up.

Charlene peered at her.

"Really?" she said, her face a picture of disbelief. "What? Do you feel OK about that?"

"Sasha's crazy about his dad. He wanted to go and live with him."

Charlene smirked. "Are you sure it's not because of the guy?"

Rachel looked at her, mystified. "What guy?"

"The one you spent the night with, when you dumped me and Sasha in that grotty B and B."

Rachel clenched her jaws in self-reproach. She would have to be a lot more on the ball.

She had to be sharp, clear, quick thinking. One wrong move, one lapse of concentration, and the whole web of lies could come crumbling down. "Oh, *that* guy! Christ no, I just see him once in a while. It wasn't really serious."

Charlene looked troubled. "And you are OK with it? Sasha going away?"

"Not deliriously OK, no." Rachel said, waiting impatiently by the kettle, willing it to boil. "But Sasha was really keen to go and live with his dad."

"Really?"

"Yes, *really*," she snapped, her edginess mounting. She got two tea bags from the packet on the shelf and dropped them into the mugs.

"I'd never have thought in a million years you'd agree to let Sasha out of your sight. I think little kids should be with their mother," Charlene said bluntly, getting up and fetching a pint of milk from the fridge.

Rachel poured the boiling water. "Well, that's how it is, I'm afraid, Charlene. Maybe you're just too young to understand how complicated these things can be. Basically you've got to go with what's good for the kid. Sasha has all sorts of relatives over there, aunts and uncles and grandparents and stuff, a big house, lots of cousins, you see what I mean." She knew she should stop babbling. She'd not been prepared for this. Charlene's appearance had upset her carefully set-up constructs.

Charlene was looking at her intently, a series of expressions playing themselves out on her face, disbelief being the main one. She was a sharp little cookie. How easy it would be to tell her the truth, blurt out all the horrors, the murder, the funeral by fire, Sasha's escape, but Charlene was too young and too innocent. She had to get the girl out of here as quickly as possible. Uri turning up now would be nothing short of catastrophic.

They sipped their tea. The morning sun shone on the table, making the absurd scene feel even more unreal. Her stomach ached and she needed to go to the loo, but didn't dare leave Charlene alone. After a few minutes she drained her mug and looked at her watch, exclaiming, "Oh, hell! I've got a dentist appointment, *now*, at eleven. I'm sorry, I better get a move on." She jumped up and snatched the mugs away.

Charlene stood up too. "I'll walk with you."

"No!" Rachel blurted. "It's just round the corner." She paused and put her hand on Charlene's arm. "Listen, kid. I'm really, really sorry to seem so dismissive. I hope everything goes OK with you. You look really thin, Charlene . . . should you not go back home, to your parents? Surely they are worried about you, living rough and hanging out with all sorts of weird people?"

Charlene gave her a cynical sneer. "I know where I'm not wanted."

"But perhaps if you tried phoning them—"

"Not them," Charlene interrupted. "*You.* You're telling me good luck, and fuck off . . . right?"

Rachel closed her eyes for a moment; a sense of wretchedness overwhelmed her. "I'm so sorry, Charlene. I can't help you and I've nothing to offer, not even friendship," she said. *And coming around here is dangerous, so yes . . . please go away,* she thought with regret. She could have used a little company, and Charlene was a nice person, someone she might have called a friend.

On an impulse she grabbed the mobile from her shirt pocket and held it out. "Here. Phone them. Phone them now. You were just giving me heck for letting Sasha go away. You said that kids should be with their mothers. Phone them, or I'm not letting you out of my house."

"Hey!" Charlene laughed mockingly. "Be careful. That would suit me just fine."

"I mean it. You can't go on living on the street. There must be someone who misses you."

Charlene sank down into the chair again, hiding her face in her hands. Rachel patted her shoulder awkwardly. "Is there *no one* you can phone?"

After a moment Charlene looked up at her. "Perhaps I can phone my sister. She lives in Stoke."

"Tell me her number."

Charlene gave the number from memory, and Rachel dialed, praying that this sister would pick up the phone. When a woman's voice said, "Hello," she handed the mobile to Charlene and left the kitchen.

Ten minutes later Charlene came into the living room, looking pale. "They've been worried sick about me," she said in a flat voice. "My dad has practically had a breakdown and had to go off work."

Rachel grabbed her bag from the coffee table and took out all the money she had in her wallet, cramming it into Charlene's hand. "Go home, kid. Go straight to the station and get on the next train. Don't think about it. Don't stop anywhere. Just go, Charlene."

As soon as she closed the door behind the girl, Rachel broke down and cried—cried harder than in the days after taking Sasha to Madeleine's house. With Charlene having promised to leave immediately, her loneliness suddenly felt crushing. She missed Sasha so much, her heart was at breaking point. Why had she not taken Sasha herself and run? They could have found somewhere safe, *somewhere* in the world. An igloo in Greenland or a hut in Borneo or a cave in Brazil or New Zealand. She still had money and Madeleine had offered her more.

Why hadn't she? She wasn't sure if she

felt she had to pay for Anton's death, or if she was a bad-luck factor that would destroy her son's life, or if as a murderess she had no right to bring up an innocent little boy. No, none of those, or all of them. Her main aim had been to make herself into a wall against the tide of Uri's wrath. A wall behind which Sasha would be safe. But the wall could not endure forever and would soon crumble.

She lay back down on the sofa. All she could do was wait. It would probably take him some time to track her down and she'd have to try to get through each day with her sanity intact. With both hands she clasped the crucifix around her neck. What had Madeleine said about it? It was imbued with special power that would protect her from evil. Generations of wise women had worn it and they'd shield her from harm. She tried to believe this.

At first she had no idea who they were, the men standing at her door. One was an ugly giant with a mustache like Saddam, skeletally thin. The other man looked familiar. He was considerably shorter, less emaciated than his companion, but with a shrunken slope to his shoulders. He had a ruddy complexion, a crazed look in his eye, and was entirely bald.

Without a word the two men pushed themselves into the house, and it was only the manner of his walk that made Rachel realize the shorter man was Uri. The change in him was astonishing. He had lost a lot of weight in the few weeks since she had gone to see him at his place in Reading. His thick mop of ash blond hair had vanished, though at a closer look she could see he'd shaved it off. The hair follicles were clearly visible. Despite her terror she almost smiled. The lengths a man would go to, in order to appear more of a thug than he already was.

He hardly spoke a word in response to her ridiculous pleas for information, but pushed her down on the sofa while both of them searched the place. Rachel followed him with her eyes and could see that something was wrong. Not just his frantic ransacking of her house, but the strange way in which he tore at his clothes and rubbed the skin around his neck and throat with a grimy handkerchief. He seemed anxious, manic. There was nothing of the unhurried, deliberate way he normally had of conducting himself.

She'd been in the bath when they called and now she shivered with cold and fear, sitting there in her dressing gown, her hair sopping wet. Part of her felt a sense of destiny, almost relief. Fate was finally having its day. It could go either way. He'd believe her or he wouldn't.

After twenty minutes of turning over her meager possessions, Uri came and stood in front of her. He was wearing a smart beige suit that had grease stains on the jacket. It had probably once looked good on his bulky form, but now hung sacklike on him. His face was blotchy and marked by red streaks, as if he'd cornered a tomcat or had had a run-in with a woman who'd given as good as she got.

"You lie," he said.

She crossed her arms in protest. "What the hell do you mean by that?" she said, trying to look incredulous.

"My brother has not left this country."

"Excuse me, Uri. You were the one who said they'd gone to the Ukraine. Not me. You said I should sit here and wait, because they were soon coming back."

"I think Anton is dead." He tapped her shin with his foot, just a nudge, but it made her wince in pain.

"Dead? Oh God, no!" Her alarm was easy to fake. *"And Sasha?"* she cried.

Uri said nothing, just took all of her in with his eyes.

"What about Sasha?" she screamed, trying to get up. But he pushed her back easily.

"Anton come here to get Sasha, right?"

"Yeah, that's right. Just as I told you," she countered, eyes blazing. "But where did they go?"

He laughed excitedly. "Yes, but *did* they go somewhere? Did they?"

"Of course they fucking did," she wailed. "Where the hell would my son be? Did you think I'd let him out of my sight voluntarily?"

Uri's face turned somber. "You are a sly woman," he pointed out, his voice low. He moved his shoulders in apparent discomfort and scratched at his chest. "Anton always tell me what a handful you are. I tried to teach my big brother how to keep a woman in control, but he was soft for you, he let you do anything you want. That's not our way, is it, Rachel?"

"Your swine of a brother and I were finished long ago. His only connection with me was Sasha."

"You say *was*, Rachel? Not *is*?" Uri observed shrewdly, thrusting his hand into his pocket for the handkerchief and rubbing it over his head and neck.

"I'm not playing fucking word games with you, Uri. If you can't tell me where my son is, get out of my house."

Uri leapt forward and punched her square on her left breast. It knocked the wind out of her. Her heart skipped several beats.

"Stupid bitch," he snarled, grabbing her by the upper arm and yanking her to her feet. "While Anton is away, you come and stay with me. Is my job to look after my brother's woman, keep her out of trouble. You want to see your son again?" Twisting her right nipple through her dressing gown, he breathed in her ear. "Remember, Rachel, Anton and I are blood brothers. What is Anton's is mine. I said to my brother, when you fed up of the slanty-eyed bitch, I buy her. We keep her in the family. Joking, of course. Anton and I have a laugh." He let go of her and, stepping back, eyed her appraisingly. "But you're still pretty good meat. I put you to work and we make him a little money for when he and Sasha come home. I think Anton would like that. Is a great idea, yes?"

She could hardly catch her breath, but she heard him.

"You dress and Ruben and I wait for you here. Bring some clothes." He winked, then tore at his cheek with a gnawed fingernail. "Nice clothes, you know what I mean."

She was in too much pain to answer. Her whole chest ached; he'd punched her straight in the heart.

They let her go upstairs by herself. At least that was something. A small measure of dignity in her humiliation. Slowly she made her way up while the two men stood in the living room watching her progress. She locked herself in the bathroom. It was a good lock, she'd had it put in by a proper locksmith. There had to be one safe refuge in a house, she'd learned that long ago.

The bathroom had a sash window, and she'd sprayed it with silicon to make it slide more easily. She opened it. She could scream or she could jump. Jumping was best. It would surely kill her. She leaned out to look. Three stories with a concrete drive below. What if she just broke her legs, or her back? They could still drag her to their car and take her away.

Her hesitation was her undoing. An explosion stopped her momentarily. Someone had kicked in the door. She didn't turn to see which one of them it was. She threw one leg over the sill but realized that her head should go first. After all that planning, it seemed she'd not planned very well for this. Hands grabbed her around the waist and she was dragged backward away from the window. The man called Ruben slammed it shut. Uri held a tiny bottle to her mouth and tried to made her drink.

"Come on, swallow this, Rachel. It will make a good girl. You will feel so nice and you will tell everything to Uri. Everything."

Rachel screamed and kicked and clawed with all the strength she had in her possession. She was not going to let them drug her. Her dressing gown was practically torn off and her nakedness pitched her into further frenzy. It wasn't as if she'd never defended herself, and the two men failed, time and time again, to get the liquid down her throat. In the midst of this struggle, she remembered an important piece of her strategy.

"You forget the letters," she screamed, kicking out at Uri while Ruben held her arms behind her back. "Anything happens to me . . . if I leave this house, alive or dead, the letters go off in the post."

Uri stopped dead, so she went on. "Your brother was not as loyal as you think. When he was sweet in bed, he told me everything about you and your operation. I could make him talk. I'm not just good meat, Uri. I'm sly. Just as you say. I could make anyone talk, and I did. You should see what's in those letters, Uri, the information they contain."

He stepped back and stared at her, his eyes wide with some undecipherable emotion. His teeth ground audibly and small specks of white froth foamed at the corners of his mouth. Rachel was sure he was about to kill her. She knew it was probably the best thing that could happen, the most humane at least. Better than an interrogation at his house, a process that could last for days and would probably end in death anyway, by accident if not by design. Instead of fighting, she waited quite calmly for the fatal blow.

But it did not happen like that. Uri suddenly bent double as if punched in the gut and, grabbing his head in both hands, let out an anguished grunt. The man called Ruben let go of her and ran forward, taking hold of his arm as if certain he might fall. "OK, boss. OK. No worries."

There was silence for a long moment, Ruben standing, flustered and at a loss, propping up the groaning Uri.

"What? No worries? Oh, that is *sooo* wrong, Uri," Rachel taunted him. "You've got every reason to be scared shitless, man."

Uri's response was to turn to Ruben, his eyes pleading. "Take me out of here."

Without letting go of Uri's arm, the skeletal Ruben took a step toward her.

"You better tell me where is Anton, bitch."

Rachel stepped back, pulling her dressing gown tight around her. The sudden pressure on her chest made her breast throb with pain. She looked down, noting that it was turning black. The sight of the ugly bruise enraged her. "Not you too," she snarled. "Doesn't any fucking moron around here listen to what I'm saying? I have no idea where he's gone. But I want to know, because he has my son, and I want my son back. And then I want to kill him."

The man called Ruben suddenly looked fed up, almost embarrassed. His bony shoulders drooped. He did not think this visit had been worth his while, that was clear.

"Well . . . if he get in touch, tell him we need him urgent. Tell him his brother is . . . ill." He turned his attention to Uri and his mouth thinned with contempt. "Enough now. I take you home," he growled. With rather rough manhandling, he managed to drag Uri down the stairs.

Miraculously, it seemed that Uri and Ruben were leaving. Rachel watched their retreat in stupefied silence. She heard the wheels of a car tear at the tarmac as it drove away. After a minute of standing rooted to the floor, she took a deep breath. Filling her lungs with air, she breathed out slowly. Tears came to her eyes and strangled coughs began to escape from her throat. She thought she was crying, but it was laughter. She was laughing. It sounded so strange, she could not believe the noise came from herself.

Snorting and chuckling and wiping tears from her eyes, she tiptoed down to the living room. From there she peeked down the stairs. The front door had been left ajar, but the men were gone. It was fear she'd seen in Uri's eyes—pure unbridled fear. Whatever had happened to change him so? It seemed he was nothing but human after all, a beaten man, weak, pathetic, and easily frightened. She closed the door, slid on the chain, and took her cigarettes out of her pocket.

As she turned to go back up the stairs, something gray caught her eye. At her feet was Uri's grubby handkerchief. Seeing it there set her off again, and half hysterical with suppressed laughter, she bent down and gingerly picked it up with the tips of her thumb and forefinger. She'd have a tumbler of whiskey, burn the nasty item in the fireplace, and exorcise its owner from her house.

Her eyes were caught by a movement. Microscopic dots darted aimlessly within the soiled creases of the cloth. Rachel held the handkerchief up to the light and peered at it.

They were ants—tiny red ants.

Epilogue

Sasha sweated and swore as he hauled planks, in bundles of four, onto his shoulder and up the staircase, all the way to the platform. When the stack on the ground had dwindled to nothing, he reckoned he'd dragged up at least one ton of timber. Lastly he came down for his new cordless screwdriver, a saw, claw hammer, tape measure, and stuffed the bag of stainless steel screws in his back pocket. He'd been putting off the job for over a year, and there were no excuses left. As the trunk and the branches had grown, the wood of the structure was splitting everywhere, making it unsound.

He began by prising up some of the old planks, bleached and cracked by the years. The nails were so rusty they literally sheared off. He'd decided to work from the top downward, the job seemed less daunting that way. Sweat was pouring off his back even though he was laboring under the thick canopy of the tree.

For over ten years he'd been sitting up on the platform looking at the view, the shrimping fleet coming and going, the sailboats, the cruise ships. He even imagined he could see the faint coastline of Cuba on a clear day. He'd made love to a girl there, slept, worked, and studied there, he'd even sat through a minor tropical storm once, with the idea of overcoming his fear of hurricanes, and then got hell for it. The chimney of the houseboat was just visible, if you knew where to look and what to look for. He had suggested to his mother that she should hoist an English flag when she was at home, and he'd know when to come and visit (and when not to).

There were two deck chairs on the platform, and often he invited Madeleine to come up with a drink to watch the sunset.

She'd bring her *mojito*, and for him, a Coke. Lately she'd begun to bring him a *mojito* too, and it made their conversations about art and life and spiritual mysteries all the more lively.

He had half finished the deck of the upper platform when he heard the gate creak. There she was, arriving on her old bicycle, her salt-and-pepper hair fastened in an untidy spray of curls at the back of her head. She leaned the bike against the veranda and disappeared into her studio. Her movements looked businesslike so he didn't bother to call out. They had an unspoken pact about that. During the day they worked and rarely talked. Life was different since he had finished college. To paint alone you had to be incredibly disciplined.

"Sasha, dammit, you are being careful, aren't you?"

He stopped hammering and perched on the edge, looking down at her. Madeleine was standing among the root pillars below, gazing up, Napoleon dancing at her feet.

"Timber!" he yelled at the top of his lungs.

"All stand back. Dogs. Turtles. You too, Madeleine." He hurled a rotten plank onto a heap in the garden.

Madeleine tried to look stern but she was smiling. Shaking her head, she strode back into the studio. Her walk always reminded him of Rachel. As they were mother and daughter it was no wonder, both long-legged like storks, slim, and broad of shoulders, but there the similarities ended.

He put down the hammer and fingered the tiny glass vial hanging on a chain around his neck. The position of the sun told him it was time to go. His twice-weekly dinner on the houseboat was a treat he looked forward to, the only English food he was likely to eat in his lifetime. England! He would never set foot in that dreary wet country again. His memories of the place were a dark color, murky brown. He'd been frightened as a child, and he'd rather forget why. He now lived his life in bright orange, indigo, and pure white, and thought it better not to sully these bright colors of his life . . . until he was old enough to handle darkness.

After a quick shower and change of clothes, he pilfered a bottle of rosé wine from the shelf in the kitchen and dropped it into the pannier of his bike. "See you later, Granny baby," he shouted impertinently, rattling the bell on his bike.

Madeleine's face appeared in the studio window. "Have fun," she called back. "Say hi."

As he pedaled briskly through the lanes, the atmosphere felt particularly humid and heavy. Even though the air was still, he knew a storm was gathering—he could feel it. A shiver of anxiety went through him. Every year he tried to persuade his mother to spend the hurricane season at the house, but the very thought of trying to get her to abandon the houseboat, even for a night, made him tired. That was the problem, she was ridiculously self-sufficient, fiercely private, and above all stubborn—like a goddam mule.

Veering across Roosevelt Boulevard, Sasha slowed his bike and rattled along the boardwalk of Houseboat Row. He came to a stop. His mother's modest dwelling—by far the oldest and quirkiest—bopped precariously on choppy waves. Leaning the bike against a post, he extracted the bottle.

"*Oi,* Rachel," he shouted.

She was on the back deck, cleaning fish.

"Kid, peel the potatoes and light the gas under frying pan," she yelled back, holding up a fat blackfin snapper by the tail.

Momentarily he was stunned by the beauty and brilliance of the image. Rachel was radiant in the fierce sunlight, her long auburn hair and the fish in her hand lit up like liquid gold. Then a shadow fell over it. He looked up and saw a band of dark clouds on the horizon. The wind whipped fiercely against his face.

About the Author

Kitty Sewell was born in Sweden and has lived in Spain, Canada, England, and Wales. After running an estate agency in the frozen north of Canada, she trained as a psychotherapist and then as a sculptor. She now divides her time between Wales and Spain, where she owns and runs a fruit plantation.

Ice Trap, her first novel, was shortlisted for both the Crime Writers' Association's New Blood Award and the Wales Book of the Year 2006, and won the BBC Wales Readers' Prize. An international bestseller, it has now been translated into thirteen languages and sold in more than twenty countries.

DATE DUE			
AUG 0 1 2009			
AT SEP			
FB OCT			
WC NOV			
SC FEB			

	DATE DUE		